D0548382

PASSENGER 23

SEBASTIAN
FITZEK

PASSENGER
23

translated from the German by
Jamie Bulloch

HEAD
ZEUS

First published in Germany as *Passagier 23* in 2014 by Droemer Knaur
First published in the UK in 2021 by Head of Zeus Ltd

9 7 5 3 1 2 4 6 8

A catalogue record for this book is available from
the British Library.

ISBN (HB): 9781838935795
ISBN (XTPB): 9781838935801
ISBN (E): 9781838934521

Typeset by Divaddict Publishing Solutions Ltd

Printed and bound in Great Britain by
CPI Group (UK) Ltd, Croydon CR0 4YY

Head of Zeus Ltd
5–8 Hardwick Street
London EC1R 4RG

WWW.HEADOFZEUS.COM

In memory of my mother, Christa Fitzek
Coffee later!

Since 2000 at least 200 passengers and crew members have gone overboard on cruise ships and ferries worldwide.

'Vanished without trace',
Tagesspiegel, 25/8/2013

Cruise ships are like small cities. But [...] no one falls off a city never to be heard of again.

US Senator Christopher Shays,
Guardian, 2007

Record passenger numbers: the cruise ship industry has broken the 20 million barrier. [...] The sector is celebrating a growth of ten per cent and believes that much untapped potential still exists.

Spiegel Online, 11/9/2012

Prologue

Human blood:

- 44 per cent haematocrit
- 55 per cent plasma
- And a one hundred per cent mess when it spurts un-controllably around the room from a punctured artery.

The *doctor*, as he liked to call himself, even though he'd never completed a PhD, wiped his brow with the back of his hand. This only smeared the spatters of blood, which must have looked pretty revolting. But at least the stuff wasn't dripping into his eye any more, like last year when for six weeks after treating the prostitute, he'd been terrified that he'd contracted HIV, hepatitis C or some other horrific disease.

He hated it when things didn't go according to plan. When there was the wrong dose of anaesthetic. Or the chosen ones offered resistance at the last moment and ripped the cannula from their arm.

'Please don't… no,' his client slurred. The doctor preferred this term. Chosen one was too pretentious, while patient sounded wrong to him, because only very few of the people he treated were properly ill. Like most of them, the man lying there now was as fit as a fiddle, even though at this moment he looked as if he'd been wired up to the mains. The black athlete rolled his eyes, frothed at the mouth and arched his back as he struggled in desperation to escape the shackles pinning him to the surgical bed. He was a well-toned sportsman and, at twenty-four years old, at the height of his physical prowess. But what use were all those years of hard training when an anaesthetic was coursing through his veins? Not enough to knock him out completely, for the cannula had been wrenched off, but enough at any rate that the doctor was easily able to push him back down onto the bed once the worst of the fit had passed. And since he'd managed to apply a tourniquet, the blood had stopped spraying out.

'Shh, shh, shh, shh, shh.'

He placed his hand on the man's forehead to comfort him. It felt feverish and the sweat glistened under the halogen lamp.

'What on earth is wrong with you?'

The client opened his mouth. Fear sprung from his pupils like a jackknife. It was hard to make out what he was saying. 'I... don't... want... to... d...'

'But we agreed,' the doctor said with a reassuring smile. 'Everything has been arranged. Don't go backing out now, just before the perfect death.'

He looked to the side, peering through the open door at the instrument table in the neighbouring room. He saw the scalpels as well as the electric bone cutter, plugged in and ready for use.

'Didn't I explain it to you clearly enough?' He sighed. Of

course he had. For hours on end. Again and again, but this ungrateful fool simply hadn't grasped it.

'Of course it's going to get rather unpleasant. But I can only let you die in this way. It won't work otherwise.'

The athlete whimpered and yanked at the straps around his wrists, albeit with far less force than before.

The doctor noted with satisfaction that the anaesthetic was now having its desired effect. Not long now and the treatment could begin.

'You see, I could break it off here,' he said, one hand still on the sportsman's forehead, the other adjusting his face mask. 'But what would your life be after that? Nothing but fear and pain. Indescribable pain.'

The black man blinked. His breathing became calmer.

'I showed you the photos. And the video. The one with the corkscrew and the half eye. Surely you don't want anything like that, do you?'

'Hmhmhmhmhmmm,' the client groaned, as if his mouth were gagged. Then his facial muscles slackened and his breathing grew shallower.

'I'll take that as a "No",' the doctor said, unlocking the brake of the bed with his foot, to roll his client into the neighbouring room.

Into the operating theatre.

Forty-five minutes later the first and most important part of the treatment was finished. The doctor wasn't wearing latex gloves any more or a face mask, and he'd thrown the green disposable apron, which had to be tied behind the back like a straitjacket, into the rubbish chute. But now, in his dinner jacket and dark patent leather shoes, he felt far more dressed up than in his operating outfit.

Dressed up and tipsy.

He couldn't remember when he'd started allowing himself a snifter after every successful treatment. Or ten, as now. Christ, he had to stop, even though he never touched a drop beforehand, only after. Still. The hooch made him reckless.

Gave him silly thoughts.

Such as taking the leg with him.

Giggling, he looked at his watch.

It was 20.33; he had to hurry if he was going to make the main course in time. He'd already missed the starter. But before he could devote himself to the guinea fowl that was on today's menu, he had to get rid of the organic waste – the blood he didn't need and the right lower leg, which he'd sawn off directly below the knee with a splendidly clean cut.

He'd wrapped the leg in a compostable plastic bag, which was so heavy he had to carry it with both hands as he made his way across the stairwell.

The doctor felt woozy, but he was still sufficiently in control to realise that, had he been sober, he'd never have entertained the idea of carrying around body parts in public rather than just tossing them into the incinerator. But he'd been so infuriated by his client that this bit of fun was worth the risk. And it was a low risk. Very low.

A gale warning had been issued. Once he'd negotiated the intricate route – the narrow shaft you had to crouch in, the corridor with the yellow ventilation pipes that led to the goods lift – he wouldn't come across a soul.

4

And the place he'd chosen to dispose of the leg wouldn't be caught on any camera either.

I may be drunk, but I'm not stupid.

Having reached the final section, the level at the top of the steps which were only ever used by maintenance, and once a month at most, he pulled open a heavy door with a porthole window.

A strong wind whipped into his face and it felt as if he were having to push against a wall to get outside.

The fresh air made his blood pressure drop. He felt sick at first, but soon recovered, and the salty tang of the wind began to revive him.

Now it was no longer the alcohol making him sway, but the powerful sea swell, which thanks to the stabilisers hadn't been so palpable inside the *Sultan of the Seas.*

With his legs apart he staggered across the planks. He was on deck 8½, an intermediate level that only existed for aesthetic reasons. Viewed from a distance it made the rear of the cruise ship appear more streamlined, like a spoiler on a sports car.

Arriving at the furthest tip of the stern on the port side, the doctor leaned over the railings. Beneath him raged the Indian Ocean. The headlights pointing backwards illuminated the white foamy peaks formed in the wake of the liner.

He'd actually wanted to say some last words, something like 'Hasta la vista, baby' or 'Ready when you are', but nothing amusing came to mind so he silently threw the bag with the leg overboard in a high arc.

I somehow imagined that was going to feel more exhilarating, he thought, slowly regaining his sobriety.

The wind tore so loudly at his ears that he couldn't hear the leg slapping against the waves fifty metres below him. But he did hear the voice that came from behind.

'What are you doing?'

He spun around.

The person who'd given him the fright of his life wasn't an adult employee, *thank God* – someone from security, for example – but a young girl, no older than the little one whose family he'd treated a couple of years ago on the west coast of Africa. She was sitting cross-legged beside the box of an air conditioning system, or some other kind of unit. The doctor was less of an expert in technology than he was in knives.

As the girl was so small and the surroundings so dark he'd failed to notice her. Even now, staring into the darkness, he could only make out her silhouette.

'I'm feeding the fish,' he said, pleased that he sounded considerably calmer than he felt. Although the girl wasn't a physical threat, he could do without her as a witness.

'Are you feeling unwell?' she asked. She was wearing a light-coloured dress with dark tights and an anorak on top. For safety she'd put on the red life jacket that was in the cupboard in every cabin.

Good girl.

'No,' he replied with a smile. 'I'm fine. What's your name?'

His eyes gradually became accustomed to the gloom.

The girl had shoulder-length hair and ears that stuck out slightly, although this didn't mar her appearance. On the contrary. He bet that if you saw her in the light, you'd be able to appreciate the striking woman she would be one day.

'I'm called Anouk Lamar.'

'Anouk? That's the French diminutive of Anna, isn't it?'

The girl smiled. 'Wow, you knew that?'

'I know a lot of things.'

'Really? So do you know why I'm sitting here?' she said boldly.

Because she had to speak loudly against the wind her voice rose to a high pitch.

'You're drawing the sea,' the doctor said.

She hugged the pad of paper to her chest and grinned. 'That was easy. What else do you know?'

'That you've no business being here and ought to have been in bed long ago. Where are your parents?'

She sighed. 'My father's dead. And I don't know where my mum is. She often leaves me alone at night in the cabin.'

'And you find that boring?'

She nodded. 'She never gets back till late and then she stinks.' Her voice went quiet. 'Of smoke. And drink. And she snores.'

The doctor couldn't help laughing. 'Grown-ups do that sometimes.'

You ought to hear me. He pointed to her pad. 'Have you been able to draw anything at all today?'

'No,' she said, shaking her head. 'There were beautiful stars out yesterday, but it's all dark tonight.'

'And cold,' the doctor said in agreement. 'How about we take a look for your mummy?'

Anouk shrugged. She didn't appear particularly enamoured of the idea, but said, 'Okay, why not?'

She managed to stand from the cross-legged position without using her hands. 'Sometimes she's in the casino,' she said.

7

'Oh, that's handy.'

'Why?'

'Because I know a short cut there,' the doctor said, smiling.

He cast a final glance over the railings at the sea, which at this point was so deep that the athlete's leg probably hadn't yet reached the ocean floor, then he took the girl's hand and led her back to the staircase he'd just come from.

1

Berlin

The house that was the venue for the deadly party looked like the kind of place they'd once dreamed of. Detached, with a red-tiled roof and a large front garden behind the white picket fence. Here they would have had barbecues at weekends and in summer put an inflatable pool on the lawn. He'd have invited friends and they'd have chatted to each other about their jobs, their partners' quirks or just lain on loungers beneath the umbrella, watching the children play.

Nadja and he had looked at just such a house at the time when Timmy was starting school. Four rooms, two bathrooms, a fireplace. With cream-coloured plasterwork and green shutters. Not far from here, on the boundary between Westend and Spandau, and a mere five-minute bike ride to the primary school where Nadja was teaching at the time. A stone's throw from the sports ground where his son could have played football. Or tennis. Or whatever.

They hadn't been able to afford it.

Now there was nobody to move house with. Nadja and Timmy were both dead.

And the twelve-year-old boy in the house they were

monitoring, which belonged to a man called Detlev Pryga, would be dead soon too if they wasted any more time out here in the black van.

'I'm going in,' Martin Schwartz announced. He was sitting inside the windowless rear of the panel van. Having injected himself with a milky fluid, he tossed the used syringe into a plastic bin. Then he stood up from the monitoring console, on its screen the external view of the building. His face was reflected in the vehicle's tinted panes. *I look like a junkie in withdrawal*, Martin thought. That was an insult. To every junkie.

He'd lost weight in the past few years, more than you could call healthy. Only his nose was as plump as it had ever been. The Schwartz conk, which for generations all male descendants of the family had been endowed with, and which his late wife had found sexy – the ultimate proof, he thought, that love does make you blind. If anything, his hooter gave him a kindly, trustworthy look. From time to time strangers would nod at him in the street; babies smiled when he bent over a pram (probably because they mistook him for a clown) and women flirted with him quite openly, sometimes even in the presence of their partners.

Well, they certainly wouldn't be doing that today, not while he was in these clothes. The tight-fitting leather jacket he'd squeezed himself into made unpleasant creaking noises even when he breathed. As he moved to get out it sounded as if he was trying to tie up a huge balloon.

'Stop, wait!' said Armin Kramer, who was in charge of the operation and had been sitting opposite him at the computer table for hours.

'What for?'

'For—'

Kramer's mobile rang, preventing him from finishing his sentence.

The rather overweight inspector greeted the caller with an eloquent, 'Hmm?' and during the course of the conversation said little more than 'What?', 'No!', 'You're bullshitting me!' and 'Tell the arsehole who fucked up to get dressed nice and warm. Why? Because in October it might get fucking cold if he's lying unconscious outside the station for a few hours once I'm finished with him.' Kramer hung up.

'Fuck.'

He loved sounding like an American drug cop. And looking like one too. He wore tatty cowboy boots, jeans with holes in them and a shirt whose red-and-white diamond pattern was reminiscent of dishcloths.

'What's the problem?' Schwartz said.

'Jensen.'

'What's he up to?'

And how can the guy make any trouble? He's in one of our isolation cells.

'Don't ask me how, but that bastard's managed to send Pryga a text.'

Schwartz nodded. Emotional outbursts like those exhibited by his superior, now tearing his hair out, were alien to him. Apart from an injection of adrenalin right into the chambers of his heart, there was barely anything that could set his pulse racing. Certainly not the news that a con had once again managed to get his hands on drugs, weapons or, like Jensen, a mobile. Prison was better organised than a supermarket, with a larger selection of items and more customer-friendly opening hours. Including Sundays and public holidays.

'Did he warn Pryga?' he asked Kramer.

'No. The fucker allowed himself a little joke that amounts to the same thing. He was going to let you get caught in the trap.' The inspector massaged the bags under his eyes, which got larger with every operation. '*If I wanted to post them they'd have to be sent as a parcel*,' Kramer had recently quipped.

'How so?' Schwartz asked.

'He texted him that Pryga shouldn't be shocked if he turned up at the party.'

'Why shocked?'

'Because he's tripped and broken an incisor. Top left.'

With his sausage fingers Kramer tapped on the corresponding spot in his mouth.

Schwartz nodded. He hadn't credited the pervert with that much creativity.

He looked at his watch. Just after five p.m.

Just after 'too late'.

'Fuck!' Kramer slapped the computer table in anger. 'All that preparation – a complete waste of fucking time. We've got to call it off.'

He started clambering into the front seat.

Schwartz opened his mouth to protest, but knew that Kramer was right. They'd been working towards this day for six months. It had started with a rumour in the community that was so unbelievable they thought for ages it was an urban legend. And yet, as it turned out, 'bug parties' weren't a made-up horror story, but actually existed. They consisted of HIV-infected men having unprotected sex with healthy individuals. For the most part this was consensual – the kick was provided by the risk of infection, and this made such events more of a case for a psychiatrist than the public prosecutor.

As far as Schwartz was concerned, adults could behave exactly as they wished, so long as everything happened consensually. All that angered him about this was that the insane behaviour of a minority was unnecessarily aggravating the dumb prejudices against AIDS sufferers. For of course bug parties were the absolute exception, whereas the overwhelming majority of infected individuals lived a responsible life, many of them involved in an active battle against the disease and the stigmatisation of its victims.

A battle to foil the suicidal bug parties.

Not to mention the psychopathic variants.

The newest trend in the perverted scene were 'events' at which innocents were raped and infected with the virus. Mostly under-aged victims. In front of a paying public. A new attraction at the Berlin funfair of filth which kept its tents open around the clock. Often in elegant houses in middle-class areas where you'd never suspect anything like that might occur.

Detlev Pryga, a man who in normal life sold plumbing equipment, was popular with the youth welfare office, as he regularly took in the most difficult foster children. Drug addicts, victims of abuse and other problem cases, who'd spent more time inside children's homes than classrooms. Troubled souls who were perfectly used to exchanging sex in return for somewhere to spend the night. Nobody noticed if they soon vanished again, to be picked up again some time later, dishevelled and ill. The perfect victims, troublemakers who shunned the law and who were rarely believed if they ever sought help.

Liam, the twelve-year-old boy from the streets, who'd been living in Pryga's house for a month, would also be thrown back into the gutter very soon after this evening. Before that, however, he was going to be forced to have sex with Kurt Jensen, a forty-three-year-old HIV-infected paedophile, in front of an audience of guests.

Pryga had met Jensen via relevant chatrooms on the internet, thereby falling into the police's net.

The child abuser had now been in custody for two weeks, during which Schwartz had been making preparations to assume Jensen's identity. This was a relatively simple matter, as there hadn't been any exchange of photos between him and Pryga. He just had to wear the leather outfit that Pryga had requested for the filming and shave his head, because Jensen had described himself as tall and slim, with green eyes and a bald head. Features which, thanks to the shave and contact lenses, now applied to Martin Schwartz too.

The most difficult aspect of his disguise was the positive AIDS test that Pryga demanded. Not in advance, but at the party itself. He'd explained that he'd be equipped with a rapid test from an online Dutch pharmacy. All it needed was a drop of blood and the result would be visible on the test strip within three minutes.

Schwartz knew that this fundamentally insurmountable problem was the reason he'd been the one chosen for this operation. Since the death of his family he'd been regarded in police circles as a ticking time bomb. A thirty-eight-year-old undercover investigator, marching briskly towards retirement age in his profession, and lacking the key thing that kept him and his team alive in emergencies: a sense of fear.

He'd been examined four times by police psychologists. And four times they'd come to the conclusion that he hadn't got over his wife's suicide – let alone the fact that she'd killed their son beforehand. Four times they recommended early retirement, because a man who no longer saw any point in his life would take irresponsible risks in the line of duty.

They'd been right four times.

And yet here he was again in the police vehicle, not only because he was the best for the job, but chiefly because no one else would voluntarily have HIV antibodies injected into their bloodstream to manipulate the instant test. Although a special sterilisation process purified the blood serum of pathogens that triggered AIDS, the team doctor refused to declare it one hundred per cent safe, which is why as soon as this was over Schwartz had to start a four-week course of drug therapy, known as post-exposure prophylaxis, or PEP for short. Something he'd already been through once before when a junkie in Hasenheide Park jammed a bloody needle into his neck. The instruction leaflet that came with the 'after pills', which had to be taken two hours at the latest after the danger of infection, noted that the possible side effects were headache, diarrhoea and vomiting. Schwartz seemed to be more sensitive than other subjects. He may not have been sick or spent longer on the loo than normal, but terrible migraines had driven him to the verge of passing out, even beyond sometimes.

'I've got to get cracking,' he said to Kramer while eyeing the monitor. Nobody had entered the house for ten minutes.

They'd counted seven guests: five men, two women. All had come by taxi. Handy, if you wanted to avoid your registration number being taken down.

'What if Pryga has made contingency plans and found a replacement for me, just in case I pull out?' Schwartz asked. In all likelihood the guests were healthy. Certainly not mentally, but physically so. But of course they couldn't know for certain.

Kramer shook his head. 'There aren't so many infected paedophiles prepared to do such a thing. You know how long Pryga had to look for Jensen?'

Yes, he did.

All the same. The risk was too great.

They couldn't just storm the house either. They wouldn't be able to provide a valid reason for doing so. The rape was scheduled to take place in the basement. Pryga had dogs that announced the arrival of every visitor. Even if they went at lightning speed they wouldn't manage to break down the doors and catch the perpetrators in flagrante. And on what suspicion would they arrest those present? It wasn't a crime to lock oneself into a boiler room and set up a camera beside a mattress. Not even if there was a young boy lying on it with a bare torso.

'We can't risk a twelve-year-old boy being raped and infected with HIV,' Schwartz protested.

'I don't know if I spoke too quickly back then,' Kramer said, stressing each word very deliberately, as if talking to an imbecile. 'You're not going in there. You've. Got. All. Your. Teeth.'

Schwartz rubbed his three-day or seven-day beard. He couldn't say for sure when he'd last slept at home.

'What about Doctor Malchow?'

'The team doctor?' Kramer looked at him as if he'd just asked for an adult nappy. 'Listen, I know you're a sandwich short of a picnic, but even you can't be so crazy as to have your teeth sliced off. And even if...' Kramer broke off, checking his watch. 'It would take Malchow at least twenty minutes to get here. You'd need another three for the anaesthetic, and five for the operation.' He pointed to the monitor that showed the front of the house. 'Who's to say the party won't be over in half an hour?'

'You're right,' Schwartz said, sitting down exhausted on an upholstered bench that ran along the side of the van.

'We'll abort then?' Kramer said.

Rather than answering, Schwartz felt under his seat. He pulled out his army-green duffle bag that accompanied him on every operation.

'What's going on?' the chief asked.

Schwartz threw the clothes he'd exchanged earlier for his leather gear onto the floor and rummaged around at the bottom of the bag.

It took him no more than a few seconds to find what he was looking for amongst the cables, rolls of sticky tape, batteries and tools.

'Tell me this is a joke,' Kramer said when Schwartz asked him for a mirror.

'Forget it,' Schwartz replied with a shrug. 'I can manage without one.'

Then he put the pliers to his upper left incisor.

2

Six hours later

'You're completely insane.'

'Thanks for putting it so gently.'

'No, you really are.'

The suntanned dentist looked like she wanted to give him a slap. Now she was going to ask him if he thought he was Rambo, just as Kramer, the head of special forces, the two paramedics and half a dozen others had done since the operation finished.

The dentist, Dr Marlies Fendrich according to the nametag on her hospital coat, sounded under stress as she breathed through her sky-blue, disposable face mask.

'Who do you think you are? Rambo?'

He smiled, which was a mistake, because it allowed cold air to get to the open nerve. He'd snapped the tooth off just above the jawbone; pain shot through his body each time he touched the stump with his tongue.

The chair he was on sank back. A wide arc lamp appeared above his head and blinded him.

'Open up!' the dentist commanded, and he obeyed.

'Do you know how much work it is to reconstruct that

tooth?' he heard her say. She was so close to his face that
he could see her pores. Unlike him she set great store by
grooming. His last exfoliation had been a year ago, when
the two Slovenes dragged him by his face across the service
station car park.

It was never good when your cover was busted.

'You've left me with barely a millimetre of tooth to
work with, far too little to put a crown on,' Marlies kept
grumbling. 'We could try an extrusion, that's to say pull out
the root that's still in the jaw. But better would be a surgical
crown-lengthening, then we might get away without an
implant. But first the root canal needs to be thoroughly
cleansed. After what you did, I imagine you don't need any
anaesthetic if I grind the bone a little...'

'Twelve!' Martin said, interrupting her verbal torrent.

'What do you mean twelve?'

'That's how old the boy was they'd chained into a swing.
He was wearing a clamp to keep his mouth open so he
couldn't refuse oral sex. I was supposed to infect him with
HIV.'

'Jesus Christ!' The dentist's face lost several shades of its
holiday tan. Schwartz wondered where she'd been. In the
middle of October you needed to go a fair distance to lie in
the sun. Or you were just lucky. As he and Nadja once had
been, six years ago. Their last trip to Mallorca. They'd been
able to celebrate Timmy's tenth birthday on the beach, and
he'd got sunburn. A year later his wife and son were dead
and he hadn't gone on holiday since.

'The perpetrator was expecting a bald man with a
missing incisor. What can I say...?' He rubbed his hairless
scalp. 'My barber is in just as bad a mood as you.'

The dentist forced a nervous smile. Schwartz could tell that she didn't know if he was joking.

'Did he, the boy, I mean, was he...?'

'He's fine,' he replied. Or at least as fine as a foster child could possibly be, back in a home right after having been freed from the clutches of perverted lunatics. Schwartz had waited until he'd recorded Pryga's order to *give it to the boy in every hole*. The camera in the studs of his leather jacket captured the expectant grins of all the guests, to whom he'd turned before saying 'toaster', the agreed signal for the SWAT team to attack. Together with the seemingly positive HIV test and the video from Pryga's tripod camera, they had enough evidence to put the bastards away for a very, very long time.

'Maybe even two and a half years, with a bit of luck,' Kramer had said gloomily as he drove Schwartz to the hospital where they gave him his PEP medicine: three pills a day for five weeks. Kramer had to sort out all the paperwork, which is why Martin was obliged to make his own way to the dental clinic, where now, after another two hours' waiting, he was finally being seen.

'I'm sorry,' the dentist apologised. She had a small face with ears that were slightly too big, and cute freckles on her nose. In another life Schwartz might have considered asking for her telephone number, only to think twice because he was married. The timing was never right. Either you met a pretty woman and had a ring on your finger. Or the ring was off and every pretty woman reminded you of what you'd lost.

'All they told me was that you'd injured yourself in service. That you were just a...'

'A madman?' Schwartz finished the part of the sentence the dentist hadn't dared complete.

'Yes. I didn't know that—'

'It's alright. Just get the rest of it out and sew it all back together.'

Dr Fendrich shook her head. 'It's not as simple as all that. You must want it reconstructed…'

'No,' Schwartz said with a dismissive wave of his hand.

'But surely you care about being disfigured like—'

'If you knew how few things I care about,' he said flatly. His mobile vibrated in his trouser pocket. 'Hold on a sec, please.'

He had to turn to the side slightly to fish it from his back pocket. Whoever it was calling him, they were withholding their number.

'Listen, there are other patients waiting outside—' the dentist began another incomplete sentence, turning away in irritation when Schwartz ignored her protest.

'Hello?'

No answer. Just a loud rustling that reminded him of old modems and the AOL advertisement from the 1990s.

'Hello?'

He heard the echo of his own voice and was just about to hang up when there was a clatter on the line, as if someone were playing with dice on a glass table. Then the rustling grew quieter, there were two loud crackles, and all of a sudden he could understand every word. 'Hello? My name is Gerlinde Dobkowitz. Am I speaking to a Herr Martin Schwartz?'

He blinked in alarm. People who rang this number had no reason to ask his name. He'd given his private number to a select few, all of whom knew who he was.

The unfamiliar voice on the phone had a Viennese accent and belonged either to an old woman or a young lady with a serious alcohol problem. Schwartz thought the first more likely, because of her antiquated first name and old-fashioned way of speaking.

'Where did you get my number?' he asked.

Even if the woman was from the telephone company, which he didn't believe, she wouldn't have addressed him with his real name but with 'Peter Pax', the pseudonym he'd registered the number under years ago. It was his favourite alias as it reminded him of Peter Pan.

'Let's just say I'm a dab hand at research,' the caller said.

'What do you want from me?'

'I'll tell you that as soon as we meet.' Gerlinde Dobkowitz gave a hoarse cough. 'You must come aboard as quickly as you can.'

'Aboard? What are you talking about?'

Schwartz noticed the dentist give him a searching look as she arranged her instruments on a side table.

'The *Sultan of the Seas*,' he heard the old woman say. 'At the moment we're sailing somewhere in the English Channel, on our way from Hamburg to Southampton. You have to join us as soon as you can.'

Schwartz went cold. Earlier, when he'd been standing opposite Pryga, he wasn't nervous. Not even when he'd given blood for the HIV test in Pryga's hallway and it had taken more than the three projected minutes for the second line in the window of test strip to appear. Not even when he saw the naked boy in the swing and the fire doors had closed behind him. But now his pulse was racing. And the wound in his mouth throbbed to the rhythm of his heartbeat.

'Hello? Herr Schwartz? You know the ship, don't you?'
Gerlinde asked.

'Yes.'

Certainly.

Of course he did.

It was the cruise liner on which, five years ago, during
the third night of the transatlantic crossing, his wife
had climbed over the railings of her balcony cabin, and
leaped fifty metres into the depths. Just after she'd held a
chloroform-soaked cloth over Timmy's sleepy face and then
tossed him overboard.

3

Southampton
Seventeen hours later

Naomi loved thrillers. The bloodthirstier the better. For the cruise on the luxury liner she'd hauled a whole wagonload on board the *Sultan of the Seas* (she hadn't been able to get used to this newfangled e-reader), and on a good day she could get through almost an entire book, depending on how thick it was.

Or how bloody.

Sometimes she wasn't sure who was nuttier: the author who thought up all this sick nonsense, or she who actually paid money to get cosy around the pool with axe murderers and psychopaths, within range of the sexy waiters who, between chapters, would supply her with coffee, soft drinks or cocktails, depending on the time of day.

In the seven years of her marriage, before God decided that an urn on the mantelpiece suited her better than a ring on her finger, her husband had once said he wondered why there were age limits for films and computer games, but not for books.

How right he'd been.

There were scenes she'd read years ago that she was still unable to get out of her head, no matter how hard she tried. For example that one from *The Cleaner*, where Joe's looking forward to a wild sex adventure with his conquest in the park, but instead the crazed bitch rips off one of his balls with a pair of pliers.

She shuddered.

After a description like that you have to think the author's a pervert, yet the book was a huge success, and its writer, Paul Cleave, who she saw at a crime festival reading was charming, good-looking and amusing. Funny, like large sections of the book itself.

Very different from *Hannibal* by Thomas Harris. It made her sick when Dr Lecter ate the brain of his adversary from the man's open skull while he was still alive. The book got almost seven hundred five-star ratings!

Sick.

Almost as sick as the story of the thirty-seven-year-old woman who is kept in a well by her abductor until one day a pail is lowered down with a bowl of rice in it. On the bowl are two words, which the woman, a PhD in biology, can barely make out in the darkness: *Spirometra mansoni*.

The Latin name of a parasite which exists predominantly in south-east Asia, as wide as a shoelace and up to thirty centimetres long, and which grows into a semi-transparent, ribbed tapeworm. This migrates beneath the human skin to the brain. Or behind the eye, as with the woman in the book, whose hunger is so unbearable that in the end she is forced to eat the contaminated rice to avoid dying a miserable death.

For Christ's sake, what's that book called again?

She thought of her shelves in the conservatory back home, of the authors sorted alphabetically, but she couldn't remember it.

Hold on, is that a possibility? It's not so long ago that... oh, yes, now I remember!

At the moment when the pain wrenched her back to reality from her momentary doze, Naomi remembered.

It wasn't a book.

It was her life.

Somewhere on the *Sultan of the Seas*.

And much to her displeasure it was long from over.

4

With a duffle bag over his shoulder, Martin Schwartz climbed the steps of the *Sultan of the Seas* amidships, and felt terrible.

He hated this ship, the subtle pastel-coloured panelling, the mahogany and teak furniture, and the soft carpets you walked along as if in a meadow. He hated the ridiculous staff uniforms, worn even by the lowliest porters, as if they were in the navy rather than at a funfair of mass tourism. He hated the discreet vanilla aroma mixed into the air conditioning system; hated the euphoria in the eyes of the passengers he'd boarded with. Women, men, children, families. Looking forward to seven nights of luxury, twenty-four-hour, all-inclusive buffets, restorative days on deck or in the two-thousand-square-metre spa with its 'above-ocean' fitness centre. They were planning to see the shows in the most modern musical theatre on the seven seas and enjoy cocktails in one of the eleven bars dotted around the seventeen decks. They were going to drop their children off at Pirate Club, clamber up the longest water slide ever built on a liner, fritter away their money in the casino or spend it in the shopping mall, which had been designed in the style of an Italian piazza. Maybe they boarded the ship with the same mixed feelings as when getting on a plane, a respectful concern as to whether the technology they were surrendering themselves to would get them unharmed from A to B. Martin was certain, however, that none of the almost three thousand passengers would have given the slightest thought to the fact that they'd be spending the next few days living in a small city, in which thousands of people belonging to the most diverse cultures and classes would collide, starting with the two-dollar-per-hour workers down in the laundry to the millionaires on the wind-protected loungers on the upper deck. A city where *everything* existed, apart from law enforcers. Where if you dialled 110 you got room service rather than the police. A city where the moment you stepped aboard you submitted to the legal system of some backwards banana republic, under whose flag the ship had been launched.

Martin hated the *Sultan*, its passengers and the crew.

But most of all he hated himself.

He'd sworn he'd never set foot on a cruise ship again. Especially not on this one. Yet a single call from a pensioner he didn't even know had made him toss all his resolutions overboard.

How true!

As he laughed cynically to himself, an elderly, overweight couple coming towards him on the steps gave him a suspicious look.

Toss overboard.

It would be difficult to put more aptly.

Having reached deck 12 he studied the sign with the

cabin numbers. To get to suite 1211 he had to go to the port side.

Martin yawned. Although – or perhaps because – yesterday the dentist had convinced him to have a temporary implant, the toothache had given him no respite all night; he hadn't slept a wink apart from a ten-minute doze on the plane to London.

Then, in the taxi from Heathrow to Southampton, the calls on his mobile were the last straw. First Kramer tried to phone him, then the boss personally, to bellow what the hell did he think he was doing missing the operational meeting without an excuse. If he didn't come to the station immediately he needn't come back ever again.

'What's more, you fucking well promised to pay regular visits to the doctor. The shit you'd better be swallowing every day can cause cerebral failure, though I doubt in your case there'd be any noticeable difference.'

At some point Martin had let the insults go into voicemail. He doubted that they could get by without him. The moment the next kamikaze mission came around, this entry in his personal file would be forgotten again. Or this time had he actually overstepped the mark simply by booking his passage on the *Sultan* without consulting his superiors or requesting time off? In a 150-square-metre suite on deck 11 for two thousand euros per night, including a business-class flight from New York back to Berlin.

And yet Martin didn't have any intention of making the crossing. He just wanted to talk to Gerlinde Dobkowitz, take a look at her supposed 'proof' and then get off again as quickly as possible. But the cranky old woman had refused to leave the ship for him. As Martin had learned yesterday evening from some online research, in cruise forums the seventy-eight-year-old Gerlinde Dobkowitz was something of a legend. From her pension she'd rented one of the few permanent cabins on the *Sultan* for the rest of her life. And since the ship had been launched eight years ago, she only ever left it when maintenance work required she do so.

So Martin had to go aboard to her, and as nobody was permitted aboard the *Sultan* without proof of passage he'd been forced to book himself a cabin. The veranda suite at the stern of the liner had been the only one that could be booked online at such short notice, which was why he was now paying twelve thousand euros for a twenty-minute conversation. The sailing schedule ought to have given him more than two hours for their meeting, but on the drive to Southampton the taxi driver had made a point of showing him every traffic jam in southern England.

Oh, well, the cost wouldn't bankrupt him.

Although his police salary wasn't huge, he had hardly spent any of it for years, which meant that his account had swelled to such a size that a couple of months ago the bank had even sent him a card on his thirty-eighth birthday.

At that moment, however, with his finger on the bell to cabin 1211, he felt more like someone on the wrong side of fifty.

He pressed the polished brass button and heard a subtle chiming inside. The door was opened a few seconds later and he found himself facing a young man wearing a tailcoat, patent leather shoes and an obsequious smile. Martin recalled that the *Sultan* prided itself on providing a butler for every guest who booked an overpriced suite.

The specimen standing before him was in his early

twenties, with short, black hair that, with its middle parting, stuck to his rather narrow skull as if ironed on. He had watery eyes and a receding chin. *Courage* and *determination* were not the first words that came to mind when looking at such an individual.

'Show the gentleman in,' Martin heard Gerlinde Dobkowitz call out from inside her suite. The butler stood to one side.

Martin's brain had great difficulty in processing all the sights that assailed him once he entered.

As an investigator he knew that often you needed a very sharp pencil to draw the line between an eccentric lifestyle and madness requiring therapy. At first glance he could see that Gerlinde Dobkowitz straddled both sides of this line.

'Finally!' she greeted him from her bed. She was enthroned in a sea of pillows, newspapers and computer printouts. Her overladen bed stood in the middle of a space which the shipyard's interior designers had originally specified as a living room. But they had not reckoned with Gerlinde Dobkowitz. At least Martin couldn't imagine that flowery wallpaper the colour of raspberry mousse, a zebra fur rug or fake antlers above the air vents were part of the basic design of every three-room suite aboard the *Sultan*.

'You need to recalibrate your tachometer,' the old woman said, her eyes fixed on a wooden grandfather clock at the entrance to the suite. 'It's almost six o'clock!'

With a grumpy gesture she shooed her butler away to an antique, felt-covered bureau, which stood at right angles to the partition wall, beneath an oil painting that presumably once depicted Rembrandt's *Man with the Golden Helmet*, but was now covered in notes attached to the canvas by drawing pins.

The old woman gave Martin the evil eye. 'I thought I'd have to wait until New York to bring my brownies to the White House.'

Gerlinde reached for a huge pair of glasses on her bedside table. He was amazed she didn't need both hands to put them on her nose. The lenses were tinted pale pink and as thick as the bottom of a whisky tumbler, which made the alert eyes behind them assume owl-like proportions. Indeed it required little imagination to see Gerlinde's overall resemblance to a bird. She had claw-like fingers, and her long, crooked nose stuck out like a beak from the old woman's narrow, corvid face that was nothing but skin and bones.

'I hope it's not that sandpaper stuff again. Just put it beside the organic waste bin and then nighty night.'

She waved in Martin's direction as if trying to swat away a bothersome fly.

'I fear you've got me mixed up with someone else,' he said, putting down his duffle bag.

Gerlinde raised her eyebrows in bewilderment.

'Aren't you the man with the loo paper?' she asked, astonished.

Martin, who'd gradually realised what *organic waste bin*, *brownies*, *sandpaper* and *White House* meant, wondered how he could have been so foolish as to come here. What madness had induced him to rub salt into those wounds of his that would never heal? It must have been the hope of finally bringing closure to the tragedy. And hope, that treacherous serpent, had lead him down a blind alley, at the end of which a grandmother in bed was waiting for him.

Martin followed Gerlinde's puzzled look to her butler.

'Who the devil is this, Gregor?'

Gregor, who'd sat at the bureau in front of a typewriter which would have drawn in the crowds to the Berlin Museum of Technology, peered cluelessly over the top of a sheet of paper he'd inserted. 'I regret to say I'm at as much of a loss as—'

'Who are you?' Gerlinde interrupted the genteel stammering.

'My name is Martin Schwartz, we spoke yesterday on the phone.'

She hit her forehead with a loud slap of the hand.

'Oh, yes, of course, goodness me!'

Gerlinde pushed a pile of papers to one side and threw back the duvet, beneath which she'd been lying in her snow-white trainers.

'I'm delighted you've come. I know how difficult it must be for you...'

She swung her legs over the side of the bed. Gerlinde was wearing a pink tracksuit she could have fitted into twice.

'... seeing as how it was here on the *Sultan* that your wife and son—'

'Excuse my impatience,' Martin interrupted. He had neither the time nor energy for pleasantries. He wasn't even bothered by the presence of the butler. 'You said on the phone you had proof that my wife didn't jump to her death of her own accord.'

Gerlinde nodded, not in the least annoyed that he'd interrupted her. Pulling herself to her feet with the assistance of a wheelchair parked beside her bed, she yanked open the drawer of her bedside table.

'Not just that, young man, not just that.'

She cast him a conspiratorial look, before adding, 'I may even have proof that your family is still alive.'

As she uttered these words she tossed Martin a small, tatty teddy bear, which once upon a time had been white, but whose coat had now taken on the hue of dirty sand.

A hand opened in Martin's stomach and a long finger tickled his oesophagus from within. He felt sick. He wouldn't be getting off this ship again so quickly.

The old toy, reeking of sweat and oil, was missing an eye and its right paw, but the initials were still in the same place.

T.S.

Exactly where some years ago Nadja had sewn them with the machine, just before Timmy had gone on his first school trip to the field centre.

5

The same time, deck 5,
cabin 5326

Loss. Grief. Fear.

Just as often as her path had been lined with trapdoors over the past few years, Julia Stiller had hoped that by now she was well trained in avoiding the dark entrances to the cellar that life held open for her. Or that next time she wouldn't fall into them so deeply. Only so far that, with her own strength, she could haul herself up again from the edges of her psychological chute.

But far from it.

This time it was a telephone call that had scared her to death, proving that you could never prepare yourself for the guillotine of destiny. It had descended just at the moment when she finally felt happy again after a long, long time, here in the port of Southampton aboard the *Sultan of the Seas*.

It had now been three joyless years since her husband had been unfaithful, her group of friends had broken up, and her daughter had blamed her for the fact that they no longer lived in the villa in Köpenick, but in a two-room apartment in Hermesdorf. Small and cramped, but still so expensive that she had to work every night shift she could get as a nurse in the premature baby unit at the clinic, so as to make ends meet somehow.

Even her parents told her she'd overreacted. As if she'd deliberately been looking in the recycling for the bill – two plane tickets, but just one double room. To Capri, though Max had told her something about a training course in Dresden. One ticket was in his name, the other in that of his assistant. The one with the cheap hair extensions and boobs laced up ridiculously high. Julia hadn't thought twice about it. She'd gone straight into the basement, grabbed the full laundry basket, driven it to Max's office, where he worked as a lawyer, and tipped out the washing onto his dumbfounded lover's desk with the words, 'If you're screwing my husband you can wash his dirty underwear too.'

That had felt good. For about twenty seconds.

'Where are you?' she heard Tom Schiwy ask, and was already annoyed that she'd answered the phone in the first place. She'd made a pact with her daughter to switch off their mobiles at the start of the holiday, but in the excitement of the trip she must have forgotten. And now Julia had one of the indiscretions of her life as a single woman in her ear.

Albeit one of the more pleasant ones.

'I told you what we were doing for the half-term holidays,' she replied, smiling to Lisa who was just going into her own cabin through the connecting door.

'I'm just going to have a quick look around the ship,' her fifteen-year-old daughter whispered. Julia nodded.

To Tom she said, 'We've just come on board.'

'Oh, shit!'

Her daughter's liaison teacher sounded unusually agitated, almost worried.

'What's wrong?' Julia asked, surprised, as she fell back onto the unbelievably comfortable box-spring bed that occupied almost the entire cabin.

Why are you calling? Didn't we agree that we'd only contact each other in an emergency?

'We have to see each other. Immediately!'

'Yeah, sure.' Julia tapped her head. She wasn't going to leave the *Sultan of the Seas* all of a sudden, not for any man in the world. Lisa exhibited the full range of problems you could develop during puberty. She refused meals together, kept getting thinner, she'd had her nose pierced, undermined her position as top of the class with bad marks, and now only hung around with friends who dressed in the same vampire-like way that she did. Since her fifteenth birthday she had been cultivating a Goth phase, whereby only black, second-hand clothes were permitted. They should be as ripped as possible and so full of holes that even moths would starve feeding off them. It must be an unwritten rule of her clique that you couldn't laugh or ever give your mother a kiss. A rule that, ten minutes ago, Lisa had broken for the first time in weeks.

'This is so great, Mum,' she'd cried for joy as they stepped out onto the balcony of their cabin. The tears in Lisa's eyes may have been stirred by the wind blowing up to deck 5 from the port, but Julia preferred to believe that it was Lisa's delight at the gigantic cruise ship and the luxurious outside cabin which would be home for the next seven days. And they had one each.

In her current circumstances, with her income as a nurse and living as a single mum, Julia couldn't have even afforded an inside cabin on the *Sultan of the Seas*. But Daniel Bonhoeffer, the captain of the *Sultan*, had invited her personally. She'd known him for years, almost decades, but she had great difficulty explaining their relationship to outsiders. They weren't close enough to be considered friends, and yet the ties between their families were too great for them to be called casual acquaintances. Besides, Daniel was Lisa's godfather. Without this connection she would have lost contact with him long ago, but Daniel had been a kindergarten friend of her husband's. Julia had never fully understood why her ex had sustained a friendship for so many years with a man who basically was interested in one person only: Daniel Bonhoeffer. Within five minutes he never failed to steer the topic of conversation around to himself. This could occasionally be entertaining when he regaled his listeners with tales about the exotic destinations he sailed to. But, as far as Julia was concerned, it certainly wasn't enough to constitute a reciprocal friendship. In any case he always gave her the impression that his politeness was put on, and that he simply told other people what they wanted to hear. Each time she met him she felt as if she'd been to a fast food joint. Everything was okay, basically, but a strange feeling lingered in your stomach.

Now that she was on his ship for the first time, however, she wondered whether she hadn't been judging Daniel too harshly. After all, once again he'd proven how highly he worshipped his goddaughter. Every year Lisa got a huge birthday present; this time it had been the transatlantic crossing to New York. 'Thank your godfather,' Julia had said when Lisa fell into her arms on the balcony. Her daughter had smelled of tobacco and her pale make-up had rubbed off on Julia's cheek, but she'd been as little bothered by this as by the studded collar pressing into her face. The only thing that mattered to Julia at that moment was the fact that she was finally holding her daughter in her arms again. She couldn't recall the last time she'd felt so close to her little girl.

'It's an absolute dream here,' she told Tom.

They'd become friends after she'd been summoned to the school because of her daughter's deteriorating marks and lack of contribution in class. When, a month later, she learned that Lisa was a regular visitor at Tom's pupil consultation hour, Julia ended the affair. She didn't feel comfortable with the idea of a relationship with the one person her daughter currently trusted and confided in. In any case, he wasn't really right for her, not just because of the age difference – at twenty-nine Tom was a good ten years younger – but more importantly because he was so demanding. He'd wanted to see her almost every day and sleep with her all the time. Even though she felt flattered by the interest of such a young and attractive man, this telephone call was further proof that she'd made the right decision.

Did Tom really think that all he had to do was call and she'd abandon her autumn holiday with her daughter?

'Wild horses wouldn't get me back off this ship.'

'Maybe wild horses wouldn't, but a video might!'

Julia sat up straight.

'What sort of video?' she asked, sensing that the elation of the past half hour was soon going to dissipate.

'I don't think a mother ought ever have to see something like it,' she heard Tom say. 'But you've got to. I've sent you the link.'

6

It took Julia Stiller less than a minute to retrieve the small tablet from her handbag and log in to the ship's free Wi-Fi. Beforehand she closed the balcony doors of her cabin and drew the curtains so the setting sun didn't reflect in her screen.

'You're scaring me,' she said to Tom, and sat down at the dressing table beside the television.

The email he'd sent her just a few minutes earlier had no subject or accompanying comments. She tapped her finger on the blue underlined text, immediately opening a website with a simple design. It looked amateurish, like the privately run forum on which Julia occasionally exchanged information with others who suffered mood swings due to an underactive thyroid.

'What's that?' she asked.

'Isharerumours,' Tom replied. 'The plebs' version of Facebook. Lots of schoolkids use this portal to bitch about teachers or fellow pupils. It's hugely popular because you can log in anonymously and there are no controls whatsoever.'

From the breathiness in his voice Julia could tell how uncomfortable Tom was finding this conversation.

And she could imagine the expression on his face as he sat at home in front of his computer, while she was focusing on the imitation iPad she'd bought from a food discounter.

Tom Schiwy had the knack of earning affection and sympathy from those in his presence just by looking at them. Not a bad qualification for a liaison teacher, although when she was a girl Julia would never have disclosed to such a good-looking man that in PE the class sneered at her for being a roly-poly. These days her weight was still north of the German average, but the years had been good to her. The podgy teenager had turned into a round, but well-proportioned woman who'd learned not to get exasperated by her powerful upper arms and thighs, big bottom or chubby cheeks, but to accept the compliments that plenty of men gave her: for her eyes that sparkled with life, her pout and her dark, slightly curly hair that framed her oval face like an expensive painting when not tied up as it was now, emphasising her high forehead with the little beauty spot above her right eyebrow.

'What now?'

A postcard-sized video window had opened up before Julia's eyes.

'What's that?'

'That... that...' Tom stammered. 'It's hard to... Please just watch it.'

'You're really scaring me,' she repeated, but tapped on the large arrow in the centre of the video file.

The recording that now began was typical of the quality of those hidden cameras familiar to reality TV shows, where amateur detectives try to catch out unfaithful husbands. A time code in the bottom corner of the screen revealed that the video had been taken five months earlier, in the spring of this year.

To begin with neither the lighting nor zoom were right, assuming that the gadget responsible for these shaky pictures had such a function. It took a while for Julia to see that someone was filming from a moving car. It was dark, and drizzle was falling onto the windscreen, which was why the tail lights of the car in front blurred the picture for the viewer. The camera panned across a black dashboard to the passenger seat and captured the front of a sombre tenement block, a grey concrete eyesore of the sort you see on every second corner in old West Berlin.

'Why do I need to watch this?' Julia asked as the car slowed down and now passed at walking pace by the forecourt of a second-hand car dealer.

'Because of this,' Tom replied at the moment when the car stopped at a driveway and the electric window on the passenger side disappeared into the door.

To begin with Julia couldn't see anything apart from a dense row of trees which virtually concealed the playground behind them. If there was a streetlamp here it was either faulty or far away; at any rate there wasn't even enough light to make out what the poster was advertising on the huge billboard by the side of the road. Likewise, the woman who suddenly emerged from the dim twilight, wiggling her hips as she approached the car, was little more than a shadow at first. Even when she bent down to the passenger window, thereby entering the light of the camera, Julia couldn't recognise the face because it was pixelated. In a pretend wicked voice, the woman whispered into the camera, 'You can do anything you like with me, sweetheart, but filming costs extra.'

'Christ Almighty!' Julia panted, inching herself away from the dressing table. She turned around, but Lisa had closed the connecting door. She was alone in the cabin and, besides, her daughter had said she wanted to take a look around the ship.

Is that...?

The woman in the video was the same height, had the same black hair and the same slim build. And worst of all: she had *her* voice.

'Is that...?' Julia gasped, but couldn't utter her daughter's name.

No, it can't be. It's impossible.

The girl, who'd now taken a step backwards and turned around to show off some flesh, was wearing clothes that could easily be in Lisa's wardrobe: a petticoat dress, fishnet tights and spotted peep toes. It was the sort of thing she'd worn before switching from her rockabilly phase to her Goth one without any transition.

But the voices weren't that similar, Julia tried to convince herself.

'Please tell me that's not my daughter,' she begged Tom as the film cut to a radically different camera angle.

'No...' Julia groaned softly when she saw the steering wheel. The dark dashboard. And the back of the girl's head, moving back and forth rhythmically, accompanied by squelching noises, while the faceless man in whose lap her head was buried moaned with pleasure.

'Is that Lisa?' Julia rasped.

She heard Tom exhale. 'Hard to tell. Possibly.'

'*Possibly* is not *definitely*. It could be someone else, couldn't it? A fake?'

'Yes, maybe. I mean, you don't see any faces.'

'My God,' Julia sighed. She closed her eyes, unwilling to face up to the significance of what she'd just seen.

'Okay… Okay…' It took her three attempts to complete her sentence. 'That's not her!'

*It **mustn't** be her.*

'I'm not really sure either,' Tom agreed. 'But I'm afraid that what *we* think is irrelevant.'

He asked her to open up the comments column below the video. Julia felt ill. The screen was flooded with vile contributions from users hiding behind pseudonyms, while her daughter was referred to by her full name:

easyeast: Sick! Lisa Stiller?

Habbybln85: Yup. I've had her too.

Tao I: She'll do anything for cash.

sventhebam30: Quality's shit. Just a blowjob, no fucking? Boooooring.

JoeGeothe: Fuck me, what a slapper. Bi@tєh!

GuestI: Yes, filthy whore. Hate sluts like that.

'Can this be deleted?' Julia asked. She felt numbed.

'Hardly. The server's in Togo. And even if we locate the

provider, which I doubt, it can be found on half a dozen other portals. This shit stays on the web forever.'

'It's nonsense. It's got to go. My daughter doesn't do things like this. I mean, she's not a prostitute! It's... You—'

Tom interrupted her. 'I'll say it again: it's completely irrelevant whether she does these sorts of things or not. Your daughter lives in a world where rumours are stronger than the truth.'

'How long has this filth been on the internet?' Julia's voice was quavering.

'About six or seven weeks, if the date when the file was uploaded is right. I only discovered it today in the playground when the kids were handing round their mobiles to watch it.'

'This explains everything!' Julia said in a fluster.

Her bad marks, why she's barely eating anything, her ghastly clothes.

She slapped her forehead in anger. 'And I thought these were the perfectly normal excesses of puberty!'

*Or the after-effects of our separation. Or both. But surely not **that**!*

'You mustn't blame yourself,' Tom said, but this wasn't any comfort. What Max had said when she was awarded custody was right.

I'm not up to it.

Once again she felt helpless. The world around her was teetering; she felt dizzy. No wonder – the carpet had just been pulled out from beneath her feet. Never before had she been so painfully aware that she'd failed as a mother. In every respect.

'Now do you understand why the two of you have got to get off that boat immediately?' she heard Tom say.

Yes. Of course. That means…

She was unable to order the thoughts in her head.

'I'm not sure. I mean, Lisa seems to be happy here, perhaps—'

'Of course she's happy!' Tom protested.

'—this holiday's good for her!'

'No. No way!'

'Why not? Surely a bit of distraction is exactly the right—'

'No!' Tom was almost screaming. At that moment she heard the first bang.

A shot?

Julia jumped and looked at the balcony door. The explosions in the port grew ever more frequent. Behind the curtains the light had changed. Outside there were flickers and flashes.

'Because I know teenagers who've done things to themselves after far less cyberbullying,' Tom said imploringly.

Suicide?

Julia got up laboriously from the table, yanked open the glass doors to the balcony and stared at the blue-and-gold sea of light in the evening sky from the fireworks shooting into the air to mark their departure.

'I can't take her off the ship,' she heard herself say.

'But you have to. If Lisa's planning to take her own life, there's no better place to do it than on a cruise ship sailing the high seas! All you've got to do is jump. It's the perfect place to die!'

For heaven's sake. No.

Tears streamed into Julia's eyes and, in her case, it was certainly not down to the wind.

It's too late.

She felt the vibrations that were now far stronger than when they'd boarded the ship. She gazed at the people waving on the jetty. Looked down, searching in vain for the gangway they'd used to embark.

On deck music rang out from the loudspeakers, an orchestral theme that could have been from a Hollywood film.

And as the cruise liner slowly pulled away from the jetty, Tom's ominous voice mingled with the whooshing of the water, the departure music and the bass drone of the foghorn that sounded a further six times before falling silent for the duration of the transatlantic crossing.

Just like Julia's hope of a carefree holiday with her daughter, of whose whereabouts on this gigantic ship she didn't have the faintest idea.

7

Martin stood on the veranda of Gerlinde Dobkowitz's suite, barely registering that the distance between the ship and the quay wall was steadily increasing.

The *Sultan* had moved about one hundred metres from the harbour basin and was now turning sideways. A huge crane slowly disappeared from view.

The liner was flanked by an unusual number of motor boats. The music from the upper deck, the fireworks, drowned out by the foghorn, all this bypassed his consciousness.

His thoughts were focused exclusively on the barely comprehensible fact that in his hands he held his son's favourite cuddly toy.

Timmy had called him Luke, maybe because he'd just seen his first *Star Wars* film and was a big fan of Luke Skywalker. But maybe there'd been no particular reason for it either.

Not everything in life had a point to it.

Once upon a time Timmy and Luke had been inseparable. Timmy had taken him to bed, to school and even to swimming lessons, where he put Luke in the locker only under great protest after having been caught with him in the shower. His interest in the furball may have waned a little in the time before his disappearance, but not so much so that Luke was denied a place in the luggage for their cruise. The commission that investigated the tragedy on the *Sultan* hadn't attached much significance to the fact that they hadn't found Luke in the cabin. Nor to the fact that one of Nadja's cases had been missing. They'd suspected that the mother had given the unwitting boy his teddy bear before throwing him overboard. But that was as strange as the lack of a suicide note.

Nadja had always made a point of letting him know where she was. Whenever he came home he'd find a note, either on the kitchen table or his pillow, depending on whether she'd just popped out (usually to go shopping) or had gone for longer (usually after a row). Would she really have embarked on what was, after all, her final trip without a single word of farewell?

Nadja wasn't the type to commit suicide. Of course this was the line peddled by all those left behind who didn't want to face the truth. But all her life Nadja truly had been the opposite of suicidal. A fighter. Martin had sensed this the very moment he met her at the casualty department where he was waiting for a colleague who'd been stabbed. Nadja hat sat next to him in the waiting room with a swollen eye, and talked quite openly about how her boyfriend had beaten her. Out of jealousy. Not on account of another man, but because his son from his first marriage preferred cuddling the new girlfriend in bed in the mornings more than his papa. '*He loves his boy; he'd never lay a finger on him. Luckily he let his anger out on me,*' Nadja had confided in Martin, but when he tried to express his sympathy she dismissed it with a grin. *'You ought to see the state that bastard's in!'*

That very same night she moved out of her ex-boyfriend's place and a year later they married. She hadn't been depressed a single day. He'd never got any sense that she might run away from problems or do anything to herself. And she'd certainly never harm Timmy, her little prince who she'd idolised and hugged whenever he'd let her.

Martin pressed the teddy bear to his face in an attempt to find a smell amongst the musty stench that would remind him of his son. In vain.

He turned to face the sound of the sliding door opening behind him.

'Ah, here you are,' Gerlinde Dobkowitz said. With the words, 'I'm just going to squeeze some filth from my hindquarters,' she'd left him alone with the slightly mortified-looking butler and had shuffled into the bathroom with a loo roll. Now that she was back Martin could ask her the most important question of all: 'Where did you get this?'

He held Luke in both hands as if fearful that the *Sultan*'s airflow might snatch the teddy from his fingers and whisk it into the harbour.

'Found it,' Gerlinde replied tersely, fishing a packet of cigarettes and lighter from her tracksuit pocket.

'Where?'

'In the hands of a young girl.'

She put a filterless cigarette between her lips. 'Come with me. I'll show her to you.'

8

Captain's cabin, deck 14A

'What? Stop the ship?'

Daniel Bonhoeffer freed himself from her embrace and gave a resounding laugh.

Julia felt like an idiot and just wanted to leave again.

It had been a mistake to immediately go running to him.

But she was desperate. Lisa hadn't come back; in all likelihood she was still exploring the ship, which on a luxury liner of this size could take days. It was irrational; everything was probably fine. But after having watched that awful video, Julia's entire body seemed to be quivering with worry, like the ship beneath her feet, which had been under tension since they'd left port. She felt little of the gentle undulations of the English Channel; now there was droning, whirring and hissing everywhere; the diesel generators lent a slight vibration to the walls and floors, while from outside the noises of the waves drifted into the cabin, albeit muffled by the large floor-to-ceiling windows.

'Come on, don't look so miserable. Let's have a coffee,' Daniel said with a wink. 'I really ought to be on the bridge, but fortunately I've got superb watch officers.'

He led Julia into the living room of his captain's cabin which, if she wasn't mistaken, was on the starboard side below the bridge. On the way here she'd lost her bearings somewhat. Not really a surprise on an ocean liner that had to be photographed from a kilometre away to fit the whole thing in the picture. From one end to the other it was the length of three football pitches, and if you stood on the top deck when arriving in New York you could look the Statue of Liberty in the eye.

'So, how do you like my little realm?' Daniel asked.

'It's beautiful,' Julia said, without looking properly.

Like her cabin, this one was dominated by bright rugs and dark leather furniture, although it was much bigger. The décor was luxurious, but completely impersonal. Perfect for ten days' holiday, but if Julia were living here permanently she'd have exchanged the bland prints on the wall for more individual pictures long ago.

'When did we last see each other?' Daniel asked, placing two cups under a coffee machine in the wall unit.

As the machine vibrated into life, he ran his other hand through his blond hair, shaved at the back of the neck, where it seemed a little lighter than his eyebrows, causing Julia to wonder whether the colour was now coming from a bottle. Lisa's godfather had always been hopelessly vain. She knew no other man who went so regularly to the hairdresser's, for manicures and even to the waxing studio to have bothersome hair removed from his chest, legs and other parts of his body she'd rather not think about.

'The last time I spent leave in Berlin was two Christmases ago, wasn't it?' he thought aloud. Daniel smiled nervously and suddenly Julia sensed she wasn't the only one who had something on her mind.

The captain was pale, almost grey around the corners of his mouth, like someone in urgent need of fresh air after a long illness. Standing lost in the room beside a wall unit of heavy mahogany, he looked, in spite of his impressive stature, like a man whose white uniform with the four golden stripes on the epaulettes had become too big. Fine blood vessels showed on his cheeks, making the skin beneath his tired eyes look like marble. At least those eyes weren't swollen, a sign that he was still on the wagon.

It was a miracle that he was still wearing the captain's hat at all. Five years ago there had been an incident on the *Sultan* that Daniel had never wanted to talk about, partly because his contract apparently included a non-disclosure clause. All Julia knew was that the episode had hit him so badly that he drank himself stupid over it and was suspended from his job for a year. After coming off the booze he would most likely have turned up on some clapped-out freighter if his boss, the ship owner Yegor Kalinin, hadn't also been a recovering alcoholic who preached the principle of a second chance.

'Right then, say it all again, but this time nice and calmly,' Daniel said. He put the china cups on a table by some chairs. The aroma of freshly ground coffee beans mingled pleasantly with the air freshener that was ubiquitous on board.

'What did you mean when you said I had to stop the *Sultan* and turn back? Are you bored already?'

He smiled uncertainly as he sat down on a chair with curved armrests. Julia huddled in her seat and wondered just how much she needed to tell Daniel for him to take her concerns seriously. She opted for the whole truth and thus spoke succinctly and soberly about her affair with Tom and Lisa's problems. And about the video.

'So now you're worried that your daughter might commit suicide on my ship?' Daniel asked when she'd finished. She'd hoped he'd laugh at what she said, as when he greeted her earlier. Tell her she was seeing ghosts or something else to dispel her fear. But Daniel had gone unusually quiet.

He blew on the steaming cup in front of him and rubbed his finger over the cruise line's logo, a bear surrounded by golden laurels with a stylised crown on his head.

'Don't you worry,' he said finally, sounding strangely sombre.

'But—'

'I know where Lisa is,' he said, interrupting Julia's feeble attempt to protest.

'You know…?'

He nodded. 'She's already come to say hello; she wanted to be on the bridge as we pulled out of port.'

'You mean, she's…'

'Safe and in good hands, yes. I left her in the care of my hotel manager. As we speak she's personally giving Lisa a tour of the ship.'

'Phew!' Julia exhaled audibly, momentarily closing her eyes in relief. Her pulse was still fast, but only because a huge weight had been taken off her mind. She thanked Daniel, who looked weary.

'Lisa and suicide…' he said, shaking his head and with a faint smile, as if repeating the punchline of an absurd joke. At once his smile froze. Wearing an expression that now looked as sad as that of a little boy who's just heard that his favourite pet has died, he said, 'Maybe it would be for the best if *I* jumped.'

Julia blinked. She suddenly had the bizarre feeling that she was sitting opposite a complete stranger.

'What are you talking about?' she said.

Daniel breathed heavily. 'I'm in trouble. *Big* trouble.'

Julia suppressed the urge to look at her watch. Had five minutes passed already, or had Daniel succeeded more quickly this time in steering the conversation around to his own problems?

The captain sighed, pushed the cup away and said, exhausted, 'Damn it, I really shouldn't say this to anyone. But at the moment you're virtually the only person on the ship I can trust.'

'What's wrong?' Julia asked, mystified.

'You mustn't tell anybody else, but we've got a Passenger 23 on board.'

9

Martin followed Gerlinde Dobkowitz from the balcony back into the suite.

'If you'd please excuse us,' the old lady said to the butler, pointing to her bed and winking. 'Herr Schwartz wants to show me a new Kama Sutra position.'

'Of course,' Gregor answered, without batting an eyelid, and got up from the desk.

Gerlinde shot Martin a look as if it were the butler whose mental state ought to be a matter of concern.

'He's completely humourless,' she apologised with a whisper, yet loud enough that Gregor could hear. 'But he's helping me achieve my life's work, aren't you Gregor?'

'I'm delighted to be of assistance, Frau Dobkowitz.'

'Yes, yes. And chickens die of tooth decay.'

She rolled her eyes and waddled, stooped, over to a globe screwed to the floor. Opening the lid she took out a bottle of advocaat. She put her cigarettes back in her pocket.

'I know what people say about me,' she said, after Martin declined the drink she'd offered him.

He wanted answers, not alcohol.

Gerlinde poured herself half a tumbler and took appreciative sips. 'People think I'm frittering away my husband's inheritance on the seven seas. But *I* was the one with money in the family. It was *my* construction firm. I only signed it over to the poor fool for tax reasons. Do you know what slogan we used for roadbuilding?' She was already giggling at the punchline: 'Dobkowitz – we put stones in your way!'

Martin kept a straight face. 'Very interesting, but you were going to…'

'And do you know why I'm aboard this ship?' Gerlinde took another sip of the viscous liquid that Martin had never been able to even contemplate drinking due to its pus-like colour.

'Not to have a holiday. Not to squander my last days before they stick me in wooden pyjamas. But to toil away.'

She fluttered her right hand in the air. 'Tell him, Gregor, what I'm working on.'

'I have the honour of assisting you in writing a book,' the butler said obediently, seemingly uncertain as to whether he should go now or answer further questions.

'And not just any old book!' In triumph Gerlinde clapped her hands, which were adorned with thick rings. 'But a thriller about crimes on the high seas that are hushed up. I'm so well informed because of my research. I have ears everywhere and every night I walk my patrols. Or should I say "ride" my patrols?' She pointed at her wheelchair. 'Whatever… I wouldn't have seen it otherwise.'

'Seen *what*?' Martin asked. By now his patience had run so thin that he felt like grabbing the old woman's wrinkled neck with both hands and shaking the truth out of her about how she'd found the teddy.

'The girl. To begin with they wanted to deceive me into believing that it was just a laundry bag. But since when have laundry bags been weeping on deck 3 after midnight, looking as pale as Jesus on Good Friday?' She put her glass of advocaat down on a chest of drawers and pushed past Martin into the neighbouring room, through a lilac-coloured string curtain that divided the two parts of the suite.

Martin followed her and found himself in another room that reminded him of the opening credits of a psychological thriller where the killer pins newspaper reports of his crimes to the walls and uses a carpet cutter to scratch out the eyes from the face of his next victim.

'This is my research centre,' Gerlinde explained succinctly. The room was dominated by a black filing cabinet that stood in the middle of the cabin like a modern kitchen island. Shelves stuffed with books and files filled three of the four walls. The external wall was coated with a green paint you could write on like a blackboard, interrupted only by a window. On it were photos, outlines of the ship, cabin floorplans, newspaper articles, Post-its and handwritten notes that Gerlinde had scribbled in white Sharpie between the documents.

Martin saw arrows and lines. 'Killer' was inside a fat circle, as was 'Bermuda Deck', which he read three times.

Opening one of the upper drawers, Gerlinde took out a thin hanging file, from which she plucked a newspaper article.

'Missing at sea,' read the headline from the *Annapolis Sentinel*, a local American paper.

'One of the shareholders of this cruise line is a media mogul. He did all he could to prevent the story from being published everywhere. Apart from a few internet blogs, this is pretty much the only rag that reported on the case.'

Gerlinde tapped her index finger on the photo of a mother with her daughter just before embarkation, at the bottom of the gangway where all the *Sultan*'s passengers had their picture taken so that they could later acquire an expensive photograph of themselves.

'Didn't your wife and Timmy disappear on the *Sultan*'s transatlantic crossing five years ago?' Gerlinde asked.

She tapped the photo in the article again. 'Barely eight weeks ago Naomi and Anouk Lamar vanished into thin air, four days' sail from the Australian coast.'

Martin grabbed the article from her hand.

'It's happened again?'

Another mother and child? On the Sultan *again?*

The eccentric old lady shook her head.

'Not again. It's happening still.'

10

Julia put down the cup without having taken a sip and looked askance at Daniel. 'A passenger *what*?'

The captain gave a bleak laugh. 'Of course. You don't know what I'm talking about, do you? But believe me, that'll soon change. The phrase will be on everyone's lips.'

Passenger 23?

'I hope it's not catching,' she said, essaying a tired joke she didn't even want to laugh at herself.

'I need to fill in some detail for you to understand.'

Daniel reached for a pilot case that he'd put under the bench. Julia heard the catches snap open, and soon afterwards a thin, black paper file lay on the table before her.

He removed the rubber band that kept the cover shut and opened it up.

'It happened two months ago on the leg of our world trip between Fremantle and Port Louis,' he said, turning the file to allow Julia to see the postcard-sized colour copy that showed two faces. One was a laughing, suntanned woman with a pageboy haircut, who obviously spent a large proportion of her free time in the gym and never entered a supermarket without a calorie chart. She had her arm around a young, equally thin girl who reminded Julia of Lisa when she was ten: a serious but open face, with reddened cheeks and silky, shiny, windswept hair, each strand shimmering in a different, natural tone of brown, although none as dark as the eyes that captured the viewer's gaze. The girl had slightly sticking-out ears, which she would 'grow into with time', to use a phrase she tried to comfort Lisa with whenever her daughter discovered something new about her body she didn't like. And yet the defiant look the girl gave the camera suggested this flaw didn't cause her to suffer.

'That's Naomi and Anouk Lamar,' Daniel explained. 'Mother and daughter. Thirty-seven and eleven, from America. Both of them disappeared from their balcony cabin during the night of the seventeenth to eighteenth of August.'

Julia looked at the photo. 'They disappeared?'

Daniel nodded. 'Like all the others.'

The others?

'Just hold on a sec.' Julia gave him a sceptical look. 'Are you trying to tell me that people vanish on the *Sultan*?'

'Not just on the *Sultan*,' Daniel replied, tapping his finger on the table top. 'On *all* cruise ships. It's a massive problem, but you won't find a single word about it in any of the catalogues. Of course there aren't any official statistics – this sort of thing mustn't ever be made public – but at the last US Congress hearing the industry was forced to come clean. After much debate we admitted to the figure of 177 passengers disappeared without trace over the past ten years.'

One hundred and seventy-seven?

'So many? What happened to them all?'

'Suicide,' Daniel said.

Her heart started beating faster and she felt her breathing getting more difficult.

'That's the official explanation, at least. And in most cases it's true. Lisa's liaison teacher is right. There's no better place to commit suicide than a cruise ship. You don't need razor blades, rope or tablets.'

Julia's throat grew tighter.

Now do you understand why the two of you have got to get off that boat immediately?

'Jump over the railings and it's all done. No body. No witnesses. The perfect place to take your own life. Unnoticed on the high seas, preferably in the middle of the night; nothing can go wrong. At a little more than sixty metres, the impact alone is enough to kill you, and if not...' Daniel said, assuming a pained expression, 'then have fun with the propeller. The best thing of all is that your nearest and dearest don't have to be shocked at the sight of your dead body.'

Julia glanced at the photo of Naomi and Anouk. Something in Daniel's little performance didn't quite fit.

'Are you telling me that mother and daughter threw themselves overboard together?' she asked him.

'Obviously not hand in hand. In their cabin we recovered a cloth soaked in chloroform. Presumably Mrs Lamar put her daughter to sleep first and jumped once she'd thrown her overboard. It wouldn't be the first time something like that has happened.'

Julia nodded. She remembered a television programme

about cases where parents first killed their children before killing themselves, which was ostensibly such a frequent occurrence that in forensic medicine they'd come up with a specific term for it: murder-suicide. She tried to imagine what must go through a mother's head who chose to murder her own daughter, but found she couldn't. 'One hundred and seventy-seven suicides?' she thought out loud, still astonished by this unbelievably high figure.

Daniel nodded. 'And those are just the ones we couldn't keep quiet. Believe you me, the number of unknown cases is higher. Much higher.'

'How high?'

'If you take all cruise ships currently sailing across the globe, we estimate that each year an average of twenty-three people go overboard.'

Passenger 23!

Now she understood what Daniel was getting at.

'Have you lost another one, then?'

We've got a Passenger 23!

'No.' Daniel shook his head. 'That wouldn't be a problem. We're well used to covering up that sort of thing.'

Covering up?

'Let me guess. It was something similar that almost cost you your job and your health back then.'

'Yes,' Daniel conceded frankly. 'But this time the mess is far more complicated.'

The captain pointed at the photo of the sweet girl with the slightly sticking-out ears. 'Anouk Lamar disappeared eight weeks ago. We stopped the ship, informed the coastal stations, spent $800,000 on a completely pointless search with boats and aircraft, declared her dead, organised the funeral with an empty coffin and put our hands deep into our pockets for hush money so that the media would report the story as a suicide, until we could finally shelve the case.'

Daniel took out a second photo from the black paper folder. Julia barely recognised the girl because she'd aged so much. Not physically, but emotionally. The confident expression in her dark eyes had given way to an uncanny emptiness. Anouk's gaze was as lustreless as her hair. Her skin exhibited an unhealthy pallor, as if she hadn't seen the sun in ages.

'When was this photo taken?' Julia asked anxiously.

'The day before yesterday.' A smile of desperation played on Daniel's lips. 'You heard me correctly. The girl cropped up again two nights ago.'

11

She was missing for eight weeks?

Martin still couldn't believe what he'd heard.

Obviously he knew that it wasn't rare for people to go missing at sea.

In the period after Nadja's and Timmy's death he'd made a detailed study of every case over the past few years. They ran into dozens.

He'd frequented self-help groups, founded by relatives of 'cruise victims', spoken to lawyers who specialised in compensation cases against those responsible, and had tried to make the captain personally liable for the fact that the search operation had been as inadequate as the preservation of evidence in his wife's cabin.

Until the unsuccessful action against the captain Daniel Bonhoeffer and the cruise line, some years after Nadja and Timmy's disappearance, he'd kept up with every report about crimes on cruise ships. He then realised that his campaign against cruise lines was merely an attempt to anaesthetise the pain. Whatever he did, nothing was going to bring back his family. Once he'd accepted this fact he stopped following news reports about missing persons at sea. They'd lost all meaning for him, as had life itself. Which is why this was the first time he'd heard the name Anouk Lamar.

'And now she's reappeared out of the blue?' he said, parroting back the words with which Gerlinde Dobkowitz had just finished a long monologue.

'Yes. I saw it with my own eyes. It was at the end of my daily patrol, amidships in between decks 2 and 3. I was just turning a corner when I saw the scrawny creature running straight towards me, her head turned back as if fleeing from someone. I heard rapid footsteps, muffled by this metre-high carpet my wheelchair always sinks into like quicksand. Well, anyway, what's important is that I saw Anouk stop to throw something into a brass bin affixed to the wall.' As she spoke she went red in the face; the memory of the episode seemed to animate her.

'After this she stayed exactly where she was, while I wheeled myself as fast as possible behind one of those elephantine flowerpots they use for planting on this boat. I managed to get out of the way just in time before the captain could see me.'

'The captain.'

'No idea what he was up to at that time of night, but he practically ran into the young girl. Here, take a look for yourself!'

Gerlinde took a mobile phone from her tracksuit trouser pocket and showed him a photo. It was dark and blurred. 'Yes, I know. I'm no Helmut Newton with the lens.' Gerlinde pursed her lips. 'It needed a flash, but I didn't want to be discovered. I really had to strain to get anything at all on camera through the foliage.'

'Who else is that in the picture?' Martin asked. Besides a girl and a tall man, the photo showed a third person standing between the two of them. She was barely bigger than Anouk and almost as thin.

'That's Shahla, such a kind soul. She cleans my cabin sometimes too. Shahla bumped into the other two after fetching a pile of vomit-soaked towels from the infirmary. It was a rough night.'

With her right hand Gerlinde simulated the movements of a rocking ship.

'I'll admit that when I took the photo I wasn't sure exactly who the girl was. I only worked it out when I'd gone through my research files and came across Anouk's missing-person photo. I knew at once that the girl needed urgent help. I mean, it was half past midnight, she was wearing nothing but a T-shirt and panties, and her eyes were puffy from sobbing. When the captain asked if she was lost she didn't reply. Nor when he asked her where her parents were.'

'You heard all of this?'

'Do you think I'm in a wheelchair because I'm deaf? The plants may have blocked my sight, but not my ears. I also heard the captain warning Shahla pointedly not to tell anyone about this. Then they took the poor thing to Dr Beck in the infirmary. When they'd all gone I found this in the bin.'

Gerlinde pointed to the cuddly toy that Martin still held tightly in his left hand.

'She threw it in there?' Martin stared at the teddy, which weirdly looked both familiar and strange.

'I swear it on the sweat of my compression stockings,'

Gerlinde declared, raising her right hand. 'You recognise it, don't you?' Gerlinde didn't say any more until he looked her in the eye. 'That's the teddy your son, Timmy, was clutching in the photos that appeared in the media, isn't it?'

Martin nodded. Strictly speaking, only one magazine had reported on his family's fate and printed Timmy's photo, and not until a year after the tragedy under the headline 'Lost – why are more and more people disappearing without trace on cruise ships?'

Gerlinde was astonishingly well informed.

'And that was two days ago?'

'Yes, on the Oslo–Hamburg leg.'

'Does anyone know where Anouk has been hiding all these weeks?'

Gerlinde waggled her bony hand from side to side.

'I don't imagine so, given how agitated the captain was when I paid him a visit the following morning.' She smiled mischievously.

'He denied everything to begin with and tried to tell me that my beta blockers had been making me hallucinate. But when he saw the photo, the captain started sweating his arse off and ran straight to Yegor.'

'Yegor Kalinin? The ship owner? Is he on board?'

'He moved into the Maisonette Suite a fortnight ago in Funchal. Do you know him?'

Martin nodded. He'd come across him in court. Most people expect former members of the Foreign Legion of German–Russian descent to be total hulks, whereas in fact the fifty-seven-year-old, self-made millionaire who owned the second-largest fleet of cruise ships in the world looked more like an academic schoolmaster. Stooped, rimless glasses on a pointed nose, and hair receding behind the ears.

What's he doing here on board?

'In fact that's how I got your mobile number,' Gerlinde explained.

'What?'

'Yegor came to see me personally and told me some cock-and-bull story about how damaging a false rumour could be about passengers who vanish and then turn up again. He was trying to intimidate me. He handed me the file from the case you took out against him, with the comment that surely I didn't want to let false accusations ruin me like they had like you, Herr Schwartz.' Gerlinde gave a crooked smile. 'He must have overlooked the fact that your private number was in the case notes. Because of this, it was he and that imbecile Bonhoeffer who first gave me the idea of contact—'

'Bonhoeffer?' Martin interrupted her in horror. 'Daniel Bonhoeffer?'

The crook who hadn't even thought it necessary to turn around?

'Yes. Why have you turned as white as a sheet?' It was impossible. Martin may have lost the case, but Bonhoeffer had been suspended after the incidents.

'Yes, Daniel Bonhoeffer. The captain.'

A bolt shot through Martin's skull, as if someone were stabbing his brain with a hot needle.

'Oh, goodness me. Didn't you know that he'd been reinstated?' Gerlinde asked in dismay.

Martin didn't say goodbye. Not to her, nor to the butler

in the neighbouring room. He packed his duffle bag, stuffing the teddy into one of the outside pockets, and stormed out of the cabin with the same speed that the pain was spreading through his head.

12

'We haven't the faintest idea where Anouk was,' Daniel said, answering the question Julia had just put to him. 'The little one's not saying a word. She's completely silent.'

'That's unbelievable!' she said.

So unbelievable that she wondered why she hadn't heard anything of this sensational case in the news. She'd leafed through all the papers on the flight from Berlin to London. Not a single one had reported about this Jesus girl who'd come back from the dead on a cruise ship.

'The sea was rough that night and at the end of my shift I was on my way to the infirmary to check that everything was okay, when the girl ran into me. At first I thought she'd got lost in the dark, but she looked strangely familiar. What was also odd was that she wasn't wearing the bracelet that all children have around their wrists here on board – a rose-coloured plastic band with a tiny microchip. This allows them access to the area reserved for children and they can use it to buy soft drinks, sweets and ice creams at the bars.'

'And personal data is stored on the chip?' Julia asked, without averting her gaze from the picture of Anouk that

Daniel had handed her. It had been taken in a room flooded with artificial light; in the background she saw a white cupboard with a red cross.

'Precisely. But once we'd got to the infirmary we were soon able to establish her identity, even without the bracelet. When I took her to Dr Beck her first thought was that it could be Anouk Lamar, and then we got confirmation by comparing her to a passenger photo taken two months ago.'

'Unbelievable.' Julia rounded her lips as she breathed out. 'What about the mother?' she asked.

'She's still missing.'

'And the girl's father?'

'Died of cancer three years ago. There's just a grandfather left near Washington.'

'How did he react to the news that his granddaughter's still alive?'

'The granddad? He didn't. We haven't told him.'

Julia frowned in disbelief. 'Why ever not?'

'For the same reason we haven't spoken to the authorities yet.'

'What, you mean the police *haven't* been informed?'

'No. Not in Germany, nor in the UK or the US. If we'd done that, we wouldn't be on our way to New York now.'

'Hang on,' Julia said, stretching out the 'a' for an unbelievably long time. 'A young girl, first declared missing some weeks ago, then dead, suddenly turns up again as if from nowhere – and it's all swept under the carpet? Just like that?'

That's why there weren't any reports in the newspapers.

'Not just like that,' Daniel objected. 'It's very complicated. You don't understand.' Tears welled in the captain's eyes.

'Shit, you don't even understand why I'm telling you all of this.'

That was true. She'd come to see him to discuss her concerns about Lisa and now the conversation had turned into a confession by her godfather.

'Enlighten me then,' Julia said softly.

If they'd been standing closer Julia would have reached for his hand.

'I'm sorry, I'm at my wits' end. I'm being blackmailed and I don't know what to do.'

'Blackmailed? How? And by whom?'

'By my boss, Yegor Kalinin. I'm supposed to find out where Anouk was and what happened to her. I've got six days. Until we get to New York.'

'On your own?'

'At least without the authorities, without official help.'

'But why, for goodness' sake?'

'Because we can't afford any publicity in this matter. It would be the end of us.'

Daniel stood up and went over to the desk with its polished mahogany top and two cabinets beneath, in which files or other documents could be stored behind lockable doors. In the right-hand cabinet was a hotel safe, bigger inside than it looked at first glance, for Daniel took from it a black lever arch file once he'd tapped in the code to open it.

'Do you remember me saying that in most cases the cause of a Passenger 23 was suicide?'

'Yes.'

'That was a lie.'

Sitting back in the chair with armrests, he opened the file at random somewhere in the first third.

He tapped his finger on the page before him, which looked like the cover sheet for a police file. 'This is just an example. 2011, the *Princess Pride* sailing down the Mexican Riviera. Marla Key, thirty-three, American. Vanishes on the night of 4 December. According to the crew, the young mother fell drunkenly over the railings. But why is her beaded purse damaged? And why was a cardboard box put over the one security camera that could have proved she fell?'

Daniel turned a few pages.

'And here, a year later, again in December, this time on our sister ship, the *Poseidon of the Seas*. Cabin 5167. A twenty-five-year-old woman from Munich went to take a quick dip in the pool on the morning of her wedding anniversary. She was never seen again. After a rudimentary search the crew assumed it was suicide. Even though, just the day before, the woman had booked a hairdresser's appointment for the day she vanished! Or just recently' – Daniel had turned to the last page – 'the case of the Italian Adriano Moretti, who disappeared near Malta from the *Ultra Line 2*, after telling his friend in the disco he was popping to the loo.' Daniel crashed the file shut.

'I could go on like this for hours. There are entire websites dedicated to the phenomenon of missing passengers: internationalcruisevictims.org, cruisejunkie. com or cruisebruise.com, just to mention the three best-known ones. And these aren't conspiracy sites set up by nutters; they're serious contact points for relatives and *cruise victims*, as those people who believe themselves to be victims of a crime at sea call themselves.'

Julia noticed a thin film of sweat on Daniel's brow.

'Many of the sites are run by lawyers. No surprise there. The cruise industry is booming; it's a billion-dollar business. At this very moment there are three hundred and sixty liners sailing the oceans. This year alone, thirteen more will enter service. It's only natural that big US legal firms have specialised in taking out compensation suits against the owners ad nauseam. After the airline industry and tobacco industry, cruise companies are the next in the lawyers' firing line.'

'So it's all about money?' Julia asked.

'Of course. It's always about money. As soon as the police hear about Anouk, the *Sultan* will be seized and searched. All passengers will have to get off the ship and will demand their money back plus compensation. Every day we don't move costs us millions, and we're talking about weeks here! But that's peanuts compared to the group action we'll be served with later.'

Julia saw a bead of sweat drip from the end of his hair and run down the side of his head.

'I see,' she said, looking Daniel seriously in the eye. 'All these years your business has managed to pass off even the most bizarre missing-person cases as suicide. Which only works if none of them turns up again.'

Daniel nodded. 'Hundreds of cases. Each one will be reviewed. We won't survive. The entire industry will go down the pan.'

'And so now this girl's going to be sacrificed for profit?' Julia said, standing up.

'No, of course not.' Daniel sounded desperate. 'I'll do everything to prevent the worst.'

'The worst? What if you don't manage to find out what happened to Anouk before we reach New York?'

The captain looked up. He was stony-faced.

'Then they'll let the girl vanish again. But this time forever.'

13

Martin was standing outside the entrance to the ship's infirmary on deck 3. When he saw the name on the door he couldn't help thinking of another Elena who also had the title of doctor. The other Elena wasn't a medic on a ship, but a psychologist in Berlin Mitte, a marriage counsellor in Friedrichstrasse with whom Nadja had once booked an appointment, though they never turned up to it. Partly out of cowardice, and partly from the conviction that they'd get through without outside help.

How naïve.

Crises had often loomed in their relationship. No surprise there. Martin's job as an undercover investigator meant he'd spend weeks, sometimes even months, away from home at a time, and five years ago the big bust-up had occurred, which had made Martin realise that things couldn't continue as they were.

He'd come back unexpectedly a day early from a preparatory workshop. The classic scenario. It was eight in the morning, the apartment in Schmargendorf was empty; Nadja and Timmy were at school. The bed he sank into hadn't been made and it smelled of sweat. Of scent.

And of condom.

He found it on Nadja's side between the sheets. Empty, but unrolled.

She didn't deny it and he didn't blame her. During the long period they'd spent apart because of his work he'd had urges too, but he had drowned them with adrenaline. Nadia's only option for entertainment was an affair.

Martin had never found out who the guy was, nor did he ever want to know. Two weeks after his discovery of the condom they decided that his next operation would be his last. He'd even offered to quit his job straight away, but Nadja knew how much was at stake. He'd spent a quarter of a year cultivating a new identity as a drug addict and habitual offender. His arm had been dotted with needle marks, some of which were still visible today. The Polish authorities they were working with wanted to plant him in a prison for dangerous criminals in Warsaw, in the cell of a notorious neo-Nazi, the head of a band of traffickers. Martin was to win his confidence so as to obtain information relating to the people-trafficking ring he was running. He was convinced that the heroin he'd had to inject himself with in front of the Nazi was partially responsible for the blackouts he sometimes suffered in moments of extreme physical or emotional stress. At the time it was crucial that his cover wasn't blown.

If beforehand he'd known what would happen, he'd never have got involved with this supposedly final operation. Nadja and he had agreed that afterwards he should apply for a desk job. He'd given his promise and then treated her and Timmy to a three-week leg of a world cruise. This holiday was to distract her as much as possible from the thought that her husband was risking his life for one last time. And pretending to his son for one last time that he was going abroad to work as a tour guide.

Martin glanced again at the name plate that had set this chain of memories in motion, knocked on the door of the ship's infirmary and waited until it opened.

'My, my, it hasn't taken you long,' the ship's doctor smiled, offering her hand. Dr Elena Beck was in her mid thirties with a blond plait that came down to her shoulder blades. The only make-up she wore was a trace of bright-red lipstick and a touch of eyeshadow. Her skin was pretty much the same colour as her snow-white uniform; even in rainy weather it probably needed factor 50 cream. Her eyes offered an interesting counterpoint to her almost boringly symmetrical face. They shone like blue mosaic stones at the bottom of a swimming pool.

'Feeling sick already? We only left port two hours ago,' Dr Beck said, following on from the phone call they'd had five minutes ago. In his initial fury Martin had wanted to go straight to confront the captain, that fucking arsehole he partly blamed for the death of his family. But the headache that came over him in Gerlinde's cabin had forced him out into the fresh air, and when half an hour later he was finally able to think clearly again, he realised that an impetuous visit to the captain would only make him look foolish. Besides, the bridge was secured against unauthorised access.

After what Gerlinde had revealed, however, he couldn't just do nothing. And as he had no idea where to find the second eyewitness, the chambermaid Shahla Afridi, he'd arranged an appointment with the ship's doctor.

'But don't worry, Herr Schwartz, you're not the only one with an upset stomach.'

Dr Elena Beck invited him to sit on a swivel chair and opened a glass cupboard. She had to stand on tiptoes to reach a box in the top compartment. 'It's better you popped in now. It's not going to get any calmer out in the Atlantic. I'll give you an injection of something.'

She took a glass ampoule from the box and turned back to him.

'Thanks, but I've already done that myself,' Martin said.

It was as if he'd turned down the dimmer on Dr Beck's smile, which till now had been unchanged. It vanished slowly but completely from her face.

'You've *injected* something?'

'Yes, yesterday. HIV antibodies. Since then I've been on PEP.'

And from time to time I get razor blades shooting through my head.

'Why on earth did you do that?' Elena Beck asked.

She was nervy; her voice was jittering as much as her hand, which was holding the travel sickness medicine.

'To manipulate an HIV test. It's a long story,' he said, flapping his hand dismissively. 'Almost as long as that of Anouk Lamar.'

After the dimmer he'd now found the rapid-ice switch. Dr Beck's expression froze.

'Who are you?' she asked with a frown.

'The man who's telling you that you're going to pick up the phone and dial the number.'

'Which number?'

'The one they give you for when someone asks stupid questions.'

Dr Beck failed in her attempt to laugh. 'I don't know what you're talking about!' she said indignantly.

'About child abduction, for example. About covering up crimes, aiding and abetting, maybe even complicity. In any case I'm talking about you being struck off if it comes out that, in contravention of every ethical principle of your profession, you kept a young girl in custody against her will.'

It was obvious that each one of his words was like a slap in her face. Elena's pale cheeks grew redder by the second. By contrast, Martin became ever calmer in the comfortable patients' chair.

'Come on,' he said, crossing his legs. 'I've checked in using my real name. The captain knows me. The alarm bells must have been ringing ever since the booking system spat out my name yesterday evening.'

He pointed to a telephone on an impeccably tidy desk. 'Call him.'

The doctor fiddled nervously with her earlobe. Twiddled a pearl ear stud as if it were the volume control for her inner voice that ought to be telling her what to do now.

She sighed.

Without taking her eyes off Martin she removed a mobile from the belt pocket of her uniform.

She pressed a button on the keypad and held the phone to her ear. Martin could hear beeping. It was answered after three rings.

Dr Elena Beck said just two words: 'He's here.'

Then she handed over the phone.

14

'Welcome on board, Herr Schwartz!'

Martin stood. The man on the other end of the line had a firm, slightly hoarse voice. He spoke German with a barely detectable Slav accent. Martin guessed he must be in his mid to late fifties. The voice sounded familiar but no face appeared in his mind.

'Who is this?' Martin had been expecting the captain, but the coward probably didn't dare even speak to him over the phone.

'My name is Yegor Kalinin,' the man replied, to Martin's astonishment. 'How do you like my ship?'

'Your prison, you mean. Where is the girl?'

Yegor gave an amused chuckle. 'Aha, I see you've already had your chat with Gerlinde Dobkowitz.'

Martin paused, a pause that the ship owner used to let him know just how well informed he was about every step he took on board.

'You didn't really think you'd been summoned by an old bag for help, did you? Surely not. The truth is that *I* wanted to have you here.' His chuckling grew louder. 'Old

Dobkowitz thinks she's got one up on us by consulting you, but all she did was fall for one of my tricks.'

Martin nodded silently. He'd already considered this possibility. Although he hadn't changed his private number for years, this was only because there'd been no reason to. Sure, his lawyers knew it, but they'd never published it in any case notes. The billionaire must have excellent sources and deliberately given Gerlinde the file he'd scribbled the number down on.

'Why are you telling me all of this?' Martin asked. Turning his back to the doctor, he went over to the porthole. The sun was just setting and the horizon above the sea had a reddish shimmer.

'To win your trust.'

Martin laughed scornfully. 'By admitting to manipulating other people?'

'Yes, I'm an honest soul,' Yegor laughed. 'And, hand on heart, I had to use Gerlinde to get you to join us. If Bonhoeffer or I had called, you'd never have come on board.'

'Did you just say *join us*?'

'Yes. I wish to employ you.'

Now it was Martin's turn to laugh. 'As what?'

'As a therapist. Treat our Passenger 23.'

Martin tapped his head. 'I'm not a child psychologist.'

'But you did study psychology.'

'That was a long time ago.'

'Besides, as a result of your job you know how to deal with traumatised victims. And with people who hide away. Look after the girl. Find out where Anouk has spent the past couple of months.'

Martin pressed his hand against the cold glass of the porthole and shook his head. 'Why should I help you abduct a child?'

'Because you don't have any choice.'

'Are you threatening to do away with the girl if I go public with this?'

'Those are *your* words.'

He fancied he could hear a little dog barking in the background, but couldn't be sure.

'Bonhoeffer tells me you haven't been right in the head since your tragedy,' Yegor said. 'But you were *compos mentis* enough to solve the Anouk Lamar puzzle. And thus your own trauma too, perhaps. Am I not right in thinking you have a vested interest in this case?'

Martin thought of the teddy now in his duffle bag, and looked over at the doctor, who hadn't moved during the telephone call. She was still standing by the patients' chair, holding the ampoule, looking like someone out of place at her own party.

'I think I'm going to notify the authorities.' Martin said. The doctor gave the slightest of nods. A subconscious gesture of agreement.

'And tell them *what*?' Yegor's voice became deeper and he did a very passable imitation of Martin's baritone: '"Hello, I'm Martin Schwartz, the chap who once sued the Kalinin shipping company and its captain. Yes, I know nobody wanted to believe my claim that my family didn't jump to their deaths even though all the evidence pointed in that direction. Yes, the press wrote that I was blinded by my grief and in spite of the chloroform rag beside the bed I was set on finding someone to blame for the tragedy.

I lost all the cases and my credulity back then. But this time I've got real proof that something strange is afoot on this ship."' Yegor laughed as if he'd cracked a dirty joke.

'They will listen to me,' Martin retorted. 'This time there are too many witnesses.'

'Are we now talking about the crazy grandma who even in esoteric forums is regarded as batty? Oh, yes, and have fun with the FBI. They'll be rolling up here, you see, as soon as we report our Passenger 23. Anouk Lamar is a US citizen. They'll seize the ship and order a month-long search—'

'Which will cost you millions.'

'And you the truth, Martin. Do you really believe the FBI will make you the same offer that I am?'

'What offer?'

Martin had the feeling that his right ear was getting hotter; he put the phone to the other side of his head. 'I'll let you speak to the girl,' Yegor said. 'For as long and often as you like. The FBI, on the other hand, will immediately remove you from the case because they'll believe you're prejudiced. Only I can grant you unfettered access to all areas of this liner.'

'So you're expecting me to find out what happened to her without making the matter public?'

'Correct.'

Martin closed his eyes. Opened them again. Couldn't assemble a clear thought in his head.

'Where is Anouk?' he asked.

'Dr Beck will take you to her. First thing tomorrow morning.'

'I want to see her *now*.'

Yegor laughed. 'This is the problem with wishes. Only the wrong ones come true straight away. Have a good sleep first. Tomorrow is without a doubt going to be a tiring day.'

15

Querky: are you going through with it then?

Moonshadow: yes, thanks so much.

Querky: for what?

Moonshadow: for helping me! i wouldn't be able to manage it without you.

Lisa clapped shut her notebook and pushed it under the duvet, because she thought she'd heard a noise in her mother's cabin, but it was probably only the fixed furniture creaking as the ship moved. No knock at the connecting door.

Phew.

The last thing she wanted was for her mother to catch her with a computer. She'd handed over her mobile for the duration of the holiday, apparently willingly. Telephoning at sea was much too expensive and, in any case, she could surf the internet much better with the notebook she'd secretly smuggled on board. Luckily her mother hadn't noticed the little thing in her rucksack.

Like so much.

To be on the safe side she waited for a while before returning to her online chat.

She had to log in again, because the connection was automatically lost when you closed the screen, but that wasn't a problem. The Wi-Fi in the rooms was free and worked brilliantly while they were close to the coast. After dinner there didn't seem to be so many people online. Most were probably spending their first evening in the Aquatheatre, one of the bars where a figure skating show was being performed, or in the 4D cinema, or just promenading up and down the outer decks in the comparatively mild night air.

Lisa had sat through a very strenuous five-course dinner with her mother in a restaurant that made the dining room from the *Titanic* film look like a canteen for the homeless. At any one time six hundred guests could eat their meal on two levels connected by a large double staircase. A uniformed waiter was responsible for each table; on the face of the dandy who'd been assigned to them, Lisa had detected irritation at the fact that she, in her black pleated skirt and death's head T-shirt, hadn't altogether complied with the recommended smart-casual dress code.

So fucking what?

She'd rather he'd served her up a decent curry sausage rather than the underdone meat on a plum-something sauce, which she'd found as unpalatable as the worried questions her mother had asked: *'Are you alright, my love? Have you got problems? Do you want to talk about them?'*

At the end of the dinner, Lisa was so exhausted by her lies that she didn't need to feign tiredness to be allowed to go back to her room alone. She activated the most recently opened window in her browser.

Easyexit opened within seconds and she was back in the private chatroom which, as Querky had assured her, was encrypted several times over.

Moonshadow: sorry, back online now.

Querky: your mum?

Moonshadow: false alarm.

Querky: do you think she suspects anything?

Moonshadow: well, i know she's found the video.

She wished she could have blurted out the truth to her mother over dinner, when, after much beating around the bush, Julia had finally come out with it and asked apprehensively whether it was 'real'.

'Yes, mum, I'm the slut on the internet. But that's not the reason why I want to slit my wrists or throw myself under a train. Not because of the video.'

Lisa felt the anger rising in her once more.

Christ, the file had been doing the rounds on the internet for weeks. It was a miracle her mother hadn't discovered it earlier. Only because Schiwy had tipped her off.

What a huge shock it was all of a sudden, and yet she was the whore screwing her daughter's teacher. Jesus Christ, the stupid cow probably thought that shagging made them invisible. But you only had to wander past the wrong café at the wrong time on the wrong day and see the two of them ramming their tongues down each other's throat. *Puke.*

Querky: hey, are you still there?

She stared at the blinking cursor. In Easyexit chat you wrote in white letters on a black background, which was fitting for a suicide self-help forum, but it hurt your eyes after a while.

Moonshadow: when's the best time to do IT?

Querky: not straight away. first make her think that everything's okay with you.

Moonshadow: i think i managed that quite well today.

The ship's engines had barely roared into life before she was putting on an Oscar-winning performance, pretending she was really looking forward to the trip.

'This is so great, Mum.'

She'd even managed to squeeze out a tear. The encore had then been her show at dinner.

'Don't worry,' she'd told her mother. 'The video is a hoax, a fake. That's not me. All my friends know that. And no one in the school takes the scumbag who's posting all that shit about me seriously. We laugh about it, me and my mates.'

Yes, I know, Mum: 'My mates and I.'

'The reason why I'm hardly seeing my mates at the moment is my boyfriend. Yes. I've got one. My secret's out. Phew. I didn't want to tell you, but that's why I've been so weird recently. No, it's not what you think. We haven't done anything but a bit of cuddling.'

As she recalled this, something amusing occurred to her that she had to tell Querky right away.

Moonshadow: i told Mum we were a couple.

Querky: huh?

Moonshadow: when i told her i was going out with a boy she asked me his name. the only one that i could think of off the top of my head was your nickname.

Querky: she thinks your boyfriend's called Querky?

Lisa couldn't help smiling.

Moonshadow: i told her it was a nickname based on your surname, Querkus.

Querky: blimey! if only she knew... ☺

'He's older than me,' she'd said, continuing to spin her yarn. 'Seventeen. You're bound to meet him soon. But don't say anything to Dad, will you?'

Her mum had looked at her with the same relief on her face as her best friend had that time she finally got her long-overdue period after a school trip.

Her father would never have bought this crap. Lawyers were more suspicious by nature, she thought.

Lisa was torn from her thoughts by a humming noise,

but it was just the minibar, from which she took a cola. Like all soft drinks and food aboard the *Sultan*, it was free.

Back on her bed, she sat cross-legged again, took a sip from the tiny bottle and glanced briefly at the balcony door, which reflected the whole room. The ship trundled sideways as she typed into her notebook:

Moonshadow: i've read that drowning is gross. unbelievably painful. not like getting high as some people write.

Querky: you mustn't think about that. those sorts of thoughts will just hamper you.

Easier said than done. She thought about pain all the time. It began when her parents separated. Although her father was the first person who'd left her, unfortunately he hadn't been the only one. Curiously enough, emotional torment was far more intense than physical pain. On the contrary, whenever she cut herself, the pain was the only positive thing she felt.

Lisa was just about to ask Querky at what time she should go online tomorrow when the minibar hummed again. She stood up, confused.

The sound was too regular to be some sort of static noise. She was about to tell her chat partner she was going to be briefly offline to check something, but Querky got there first:

Querky: what's that humming the whole time?

Lisa slapped her hand over her mouth in shock.

She checked the icons on her screen. The microphone and webcam were switched off.

How can Querky hear that?

The noises got louder when she opened the minibar in the cupboard below the television.

Inside were a dozen bottles of soft drinks and beer, while the side compartment was filled with spirit miniatures and peanuts. Nothing that could make a humming sound. And yet something *was* buzzing, rhythmically.

Lisa opened the freezer compartment and found something.

Beside the ice cube tray was a light-blue envelope with the cruise line's logo. The bulging packet vibrated, making Lisa scream and leap back from the fridge in fright. To begin with she thought it was maggots crawling around inside the envelope, but that was impossible.

Not at minus eight degrees. And maggots don't hum at regular intervals!

It was a while before Lisa thought of the obvious thing to do: she took out the envelope to open it.

Sure enough.

The packet was padded and well insulated, which is why the mobile phone she found inside didn't feel especially cold.

'Hello?'

'Finally,' said a voice she'd imagined would be quite different.

'Querky?' Lisa asked, forcing herself to speak softly so her mother couldn't hear her in the adjoining cabin.

'Who else?'

'Bloody hell!' Lisa laughed, relieved. Her heart was

pounding as if she'd just raced a hundred metres. 'You really gave me a fright.'

'How so, sweetie? Didn't I tell you I'd be accompanying you on your big journey?'

Now Querky laughed too. 'I've got the screwdriver, the spray can and the list of security cameras for you. Listen, Lisa, I'll tell you where and how you'll find everything!'

16

Nautical time: 08.30
49°40' N, 07°30' W
Speed: 27 knots, Wind: 15 knots
Swell: 1.5–4 feet
Distance from Southampton: 219.6 nautical miles
Celtic Sea

On the steel door it said 'Crew Only', and the red paintwork was sufficient to warn unauthorised people that they were unwelcome here.

Dr Elena Beck swiped her key card through a reader, prompting a buzzing that sounded like an electric razor.

'Let's get one thing straight,' she said, pushing the door open with her shoulder, 'I don't think it's a particularly good idea to let a strange man see her...'

'Really?' Martin said. 'And I thought that fierce look was because you missed out on giving me an injection yesterday.'

The doctor was expressionless.

'But,' she said, continuing her train of thought, 'I'm very pleased that a psychologist is going to look after Anouk; someone who knows about violence and traumatised victims. That girl can do with all the help she can get.'

He followed her up a high doorstep and into a brightly lit, narrow corridor.

On deck A, just above the waterline, the service corridors had very little in common with the passenger area. You walked on linoleum instead of thick carpet, the walls were painted grey and you'd search in vain for framed pictures.

'Where's our coward, then?' Martin asked. He was tired and felt as if he hadn't slept for even an hour. After his shower yesterday he'd lain naked on a bed far too large for one person, and stared at the ceiling until the sun rose over the Atlantic again. Then he'd taken his first pill and picked up the phone to give Bonhoeffer hell and demand when he'd finally be able to see Anouk Lamar. Now it was shortly after half past eight nautical time (on the westward transatlantic route the clocks were put back by an hour every night); in total he'd had to wait three hours before Dr Beck came to fetch him from his cabin.

'Are you referring to the captain? Why he's not accompanying us?' She walked half a pace ahead of him, her blond plait bobbing from shoulder to shoulder, and the soles of her sneakers squeaking. Under her left arm was a clipboard and her officer's hat.

'He's got an officers' meeting in the planetarium and so asked me to fill in for him. He has a lot on his plate.'

Martin giggled. 'I can well imagine. A child abduction like this can keep you awake at night, can't it?'

She stopped and shook her head. 'Listen, I don't know what's gone on between you and the captain in the past, but I can say one thing for certain: Daniel Bonhoeffer is a level-headed man of integrity. All of us have nothing but the girl's best interests at heart, and this whole affair is just as unpleasant for him as it is for me.'

'Sure, sure.' Martin laughed disparagingly.

And chickens die of tooth decay.

They passed several doors on both sides of the corridor, some of which were open, allowing Martin a glimpse inside the crew cabins. Rudimentary cells with open cupboards and bunk beds like in a railway couchette car. Only narrower.

Before they'd descended into the cruise underworld, the doctor had told him that they would be passing the staff area of the first lower deck, reserved for the higher-ranking employees in the ship's hierarchy. Chambermaids, bartenders, waiters and other service personnel. Further below, decks B and C were home to the crew members who worked in the kitchens, laundry, desalination unit or machine room. People who would never come face to face with a paying guest.

Supposedly the staff area was more comfortable than the crew area, but even on deck A Martin felt as if he were walking along a prison cell block. Behind the closed doors he could hear both male and female laughter; someone yelled something in a language he didn't understand, and in the cabin they were just passing two men in boxer shorts were playing cards and listening to rap music.

When the half-naked men caught sight of the tall, slim doctor they stuck out their tongues and made panting noises. One of them grabbed the front of his pants.

'Hey, Doc, fancy examining what I've got in my hand?' he called out in English.

'If you can hold it in one hand I'm not interested,' she retorted, earning roars of laughter.

They turned into a slightly wider corridor, where a number of carts and serving trolleys were parked.

'This is Broadway,' she announced, pointing to an American road sign painted on the floor. 'All the thoroughfares on the lower decks are named after the streets of Manhattan.'

'That makes it easier to find your way around?'

'Pretty much. At the moment we're heading uptown towards Times Square, the entertainment hub for employees, where they play table tennis and gamble on fruit machines. If you get lost you just have to go back to Park Avenue – the one we just came down – and from there to Grand Central Station, which is where we entered this area.'

'Idiot-proof,' Martin said sarcastically. 'Even a child could find their way out after a couple of months here, eh?'

Elena Beck stopped again. Her expression had darkened, although evidently this was not due to him, but to the circumstances that had brought them down here. She looked around to see if anyone was listening, then said quietly, 'I feel the same way as you do: rather uneasy about the whole thing.'

'Oh, really? So why didn't you notify the police straight away?'

'Because that would have meant putting the girl's life in danger,' Elena said cryptically.

'How do you mean?'

'The captain's being bl—' she started, but then shook her head.

'Blackmailed?'

'Just forget it. I can't talk about it. Besides, you're from the police, aren't you?'

Yes, correct.

But here his ID was about as useful as the sheriff's badge he'd given Timmy for his fifth birthday.

'By the way, the captain asks you not to take any photos or videos,' the doctor said. 'You'd best keep your phone in your pocket.'

'I imagine you're not going to like hearing this,' Martin replied, 'but your secrecy is pretty pointless. Too many people already know about the girl's existence. Frau Dobkowitz may not be the most trustworthy source. But the chambermaid…'

'Shahla?' Dr Beck shook her head. 'She won't talk.'

'Why not?'

'That woman slogs away eighty hours a week for five hundred dollars a month, two thirds of which goes straight to her family in Karachi.'

'You're saying the cruise company has threatened to sack her?'

Elena shook her head again. 'Quite the opposite. They've tripled her salary on the condition that she brings Anouk food three times a day and cleans her room. She'll only be dismissed if she says anything to anyone, but with the prospect of fifteen hundred dollars for just one month's work I bet she'd sooner lie in an ironing press than talk.'

'What about you?' Martin said wearily. 'How are they putting you under pressure?'

The doctor raised her hand and wiggled her finger. The engagement ring was simple, but tasteful: white gold with a small inset diamond.

'Daniel and I are getting married in December.'

Well, well. She's in bed with the enemy.

'Congratulations,' Martin said sarcastically. In spite

of the circumstances that had brought them together, he actually liked the doctor. 'And so you're doing everything your future husband asks of you?'

'I'm doing everything I can to help him.'

'Including kidnapping?'

She opened her mouth, but then decided against responding to this comment, partly because a very young member of staff was walking past at that moment. The chambermaid, with her dyed mop of black hair, made room for them by darting behind her cleaning trolley, which she could only just peek above.

Martin wondered whether a stuffy liner such as the *Sultan* tolerated piercings, or whether this employee staring shamefully at the floor had to remove her nose stud before going up to the passenger decks.

After going on for a while in silence, he and Dr Beck finally stopped by a door. They'd taken lots of turnings and Martin had lost his sense of direction.

'Where are we now?' he asked.

In most of the corridors they'd bumped into people from a variety of countries in their work gear. But since they'd passed the staff canteen, where he'd mainly seen Asians at the buffet, they hadn't met a soul.

'There are three areas on a cruise ship,' Elena explained. 'One for the passengers, one for the staff and crew. And a third area, which nobody from either of these groups would ever enter voluntarily.'

She took her key card from the back pocket of her uniform trousers and pulled it through the reader by the lift door.

'We call this no-go area "Hell's Kitchen". It's where we put Anouk.'

17

Hell's Kitchen?

The doors opened, revealing a lift, on the other side of which was another door.

'Why does everyone avoid this area?'

'Superstition. This is the quarantine section.'

The doctor entered first and Martin followed her with mixed feelings.

'If we have someone ill on board with an infectious virus or a serious bacterial infection, they're relocated here to prevent an epidemic from breaking out. Which, after a fire, is the biggest nightmare on a passenger ship,' Dr Beck said, waiting for the electric aluminium doors to shut behind them.

'Looks new,' said Martin, who couldn't see any signs of wear on the stainless steel walls. Nor any buttons to set the lift in motion.

'It is. Hell's Kitchen hasn't ever been used. It would be extremely impractical in a real emergency, too. Although there's a goods lift you can transport beds in, the trip down here is asking too much of a seriously ill person. There's a persistent rumour that the cruise line is carrying out human experiments with insubordinate employees down here.' She laughed. 'Or on passengers who can't pay their bills. Sheer nonsense, of course, but the staff avoid Hell's Kitchen as a vegetarian does the meat counter. I've heard that cleaners offer each other money to avoid having to work down here.'

The lift doors opposite whooshed open and they got out again at the same level.

Martin was puzzled at first, then realised that it had been an airlock rather than a lift.

'In an emergency this area can be sealed off hermetically. It's got its own air and water systems as well as an independent electricity supply. And now the two of us have to put on protective suits.'

They crossed an anteroom with a rounded reception desk, where nobody was waiting for patients.

Beyond a further plexiglass door he suddenly found himself walking on the fluffy carpet he recognised from his suite. Overall, the small connecting room, with its two leather armchairs and wardrobe, looked like the cruise ship again. The door they were standing beside was also identical to those of the passenger cabins, except here the spyhole worked the other way around.

The doctor peered in. Apparently satisfied with what she'd seen, she invited Martin to try out his own card.

'Your key is programmed to give you access to all areas necessary for your work. You can see her any time you like, but I'd be very grateful if you'd let me know beforehand.'

'Is Anouk locked up?' he asked disapprovingly.

The doctor nodded seriously. 'For her own security. Until we know where she was and who might be after her, she shouldn't roam around the ship unchecked. There's a button behind her bed she can use to raise the alarm if she's in danger.'

She pointed upwards. Above the door was a red lever that reminded Martin of the emergency brakes in trains. 'In an emergency you can unlock the door that way, but it sets off an alarm on the bridge, so it's always better to bring your key.'

Martin slipped the plastic card from his jeans pocket, then hesitated. Before he entered he ought to have a better idea of what to expect behind the door.

'Is this your examination report?' he asked the doctor, indicating the clipboard beneath her arm.

Without saying anything she handed it to him. Martin scanned the report of her initial examination. Anouk Lamar. Female patient. Age: 11. Height: 1.48m. Weight: 35 kg.

In poor overall condition with signs of neglect. Patient doesn't react to offers of help or encouragement. Suspected mutism.

'Is she completely speechless?' Martin said, questioning the diagnosis.

Dr Beck nodded regretfully. 'Hasn't said a single word. All she does is moan, cry or grunt, but mostly that's in her sleep. She has terrible nightmares. Neurologically everything seems to be normal, as you'll see. Good reflexes, but...'

'But what?' Martin asked, then he saw it himself. The physical results in the bottom third of the report took his breath away: *superficial skin abrasions running vertically, right next to the labia majora (false passage).*

'Bruising on both inner thighs. Severe fissures at eight and eleven o'clock in the lithomy position?' Martin cited this part of the report in disbelief.

Elena nodded sadly. 'Obviously I've taken all the necessary swabs.'

Jesus Christ.

He closed his eyes.

According to this Anouk Lamar had been raped several times by her abductor, and bestially.

18

The same time, deck 5

Tiago Álvarez stepped out of the atrium cabin (as inner cabins on the *Sultan* with a view of the shopping mall were called) and greeted an elderly lady who was walking towards him from the spa area in a dressing gown. Delighted by the unexpected attention paid her by the young man, she gave him a beaming smile and coyly touched her candyfloss hair that had just been blow-dried.

Tiago didn't have to turn around to know that the woman was looking back at him. The Argentinian was well aware of the effect he had on women of all ages. They loved his dark skin, his black, curly locks, which hairspray could barely tame, and his dreamy eyes that also betrayed a hint of melancholy helplessness.

Happily humming to himself (he was always pleased when people liked him), he headed to the front of the ship, in the direction of the Atlantic Bar. In the last third of the corridor he stopped by the door of an outer cabin, shaking his head.

Of the twenty-three years he'd been on this earth, he'd spent the last six on cruise ships almost without a break. Much had changed since his maiden voyage on the *MS*

Puertos from Lisbon to Tenerife: the ships had become larger, the cabins more affordable and the food better. But the passengers had remained as stupid as ever.

How brainless must you be to use the 'Please tidy my room' sign? he thought, eyeing the green paper hanger dangling from the cabin doorknob.

Quite apart from the fact that it didn't summon the chambermaids any sooner, it was also the perfect invitation for thieves: *'Come on in; there's nobody at home!'*

He sighed at such stupidity and turned the sign around to the 'Please do not disturb' side. Then, having made sure no one was watching him, he put his key into the card slot and opened the door.

'Thanks, Stacy,' he whispered as he thought of the front office trainee who he'd done it with in the computer room at reception. She was tall, blond, loud, and not his type at all, but sex with the women who looked after the passengers was always the simplest way of facilitating his work. All staff at reception had a master key they could use for guests who'd mislaid their own or were interested in viewing a different category of cabin. While shagging, Tiago had swapped his key card with that of his ladyfriend. At some point the following morning Stacy had noticed that her universal key wasn't working any more. Assuming that the magnetic strip on her card was damaged, she'd issued herself with another one.

Child's play if you knew how to do it. And had the right Romeo qualities.

As Tiago checked out the cabin he'd entered, a smile of satisfaction appeared on his face. This was nothing like the pigsty he'd found in the previous room. The scumbag in the last atrium cabin – a pensioner from Switzerland travelling on his own, according to the travel documents in the desk drawer – had spread half his dinner in the bed and chucked his dirty underwear on the floor. Tiago hated this lack of respect. Didn't those bastards know the time pressure that a chambermaid was under? That they only earned a few cents per room?

All he found in this cabin, the third of his 'breakfast shift' today, were the inevitable traces of the night: crumpled sheets, a used water glass on the bedside table, jeans and underwear scrunched up on the sofa. But no gnawed chicken wings on the carpet, while even the bathroom looked like what you might expect from a civilised person. In the previous cabin, by contrast, the old fart had quite clearly got the flannel mixed up with toilet paper. Nor had he found it necessary to use the loo brush after doing his business. This impertinence had been the last straw that prompted Tiago's revenge. He really ought not to waste any time in his 'work', but the minute it had taken to remove the skid marks from the flannel with the pensioner's toothbrush was worth it.

Such a shame I won't be there when the old fart is slobbering all over the bristles tonight, Tiago thought in amusement as he opened the cupboard housing the built-in safe.

There were only a handful of hotel safe systems and Tiago knew them all. It usually took him a while to crack the general code, but here on the *Sultan* that wasn't necessary. Here you opened the safe with the cabin key. It couldn't get any better.

'What have we got here, then?' he asked himself as he examined the school ID card, which he'd found amongst cheap fashion jewellery, an iPod and some European cash. The young girl with her dyed hair and defiant stare suited the black jump boots and exclusively sombre clothes hanging here in the wardrobe. He read the name: *Lisa Stiller.*

If I had a fifteen-year-old daughter I wouldn't let her have a nose stud, Tiago thought. He was conservative in such matters. The body of a woman, especially that of a girl, was sacred to him. He even regarded pierced ears as abuse, to say nothing of tattoos and piercings elsewhere.

With the palm of his hand Tiago stroked the felt-lined bottom of the safe and came across a brand-new screwdriver and small spray can.

Black paint?

Surely Lisa wasn't planning on decorating the ship with graffiti?

He put the can back and counted the cash. One hundred and forty euros and sixty cents. Probably the sum of her pocket money. As she didn't have a purse she probably hadn't even counted it, but Tiago wouldn't take more than ten. Never more than ten per cent was his golden rule. And never personal objects which, in the worst-case scenario, could be traced back to their owners. When the sums were little the victims always imagined they'd mislaid the money themselves.

'You must have lost it, darling. Why would a thief leave your watch, all your jewellery and a large wad of money?'

It took a bit longer his way, but the Tiago method was foolproof. His passage in the inner cabin cost him $2,400 for the Cadiz–Oslo–New York legs, and so far he'd pocketed $2,200. By the time he changed ships in New York and set sail for Canada, he'd have a further $2,500. Not bad if your expenses were zero and you could live your life on a permanent holiday like a millionaire.

Tiago took two five-euro notes. As he was putting back the rest of the money he noticed an envelope leaning upright in the right-hand corner of the safe.

Another financial cushion? Perhaps a present from granny for the trip?

Overcome by curiosity he opened the padded envelope. At that moment an unexpected noise made him aware of an unforgivable error.

An error he'd made while entering the cabin and which he ought to have realised the moment he'd had the school ID in his hands, if not earlier. *How could I be so stupid?* Tiago thought before diving over the bed towards the balcony.

But he was too slow.

No teenager travels on a cruise ship alone!

The connecting door, which he hadn't checked, opened and he had no time to hide on the balcony to avoid being caught by the cleaning lady, who at that moment entered the cabin and who…

… was drunk?

Crouching on all fours behind the tall bed, Tiago watched what was happening with the help of the mirror set above the desk next to the television.

The way the chambermaid, with her white housecoat and archaic-looking bonnet, had staggered into the room, Tiago's initial thought was that she must have been drinking.

Then he saw the two men behind her, saw the fist of one of them hit her in the back, which is why the young woman lost her balance and as she fell hit her head on the door of the cupboard he'd opened.

19

Anouk's cabin reminded Martin of a delivery room in a modern hospital, in which anything that could possibly make patients think of medicine and illness was replaced by bright, everyday materials.

The floor was laminated, but the way it was embossed made it look just like real parquet. The walls were the hue of a well-stirred latte macchiato, and visitors were able to sit on a sand-coloured leather sofa instead of the ubiquitous hospital wooden chairs. Dimmed ceiling spots bathed the cabin in a soft, pastel light.

Within this setting, the height-adjustable hospital bed gave the impression it had been wheeled into a five-star hotel room by accident and looked completely out of place here, in spite of the power strip in the wall behind the bed with numerous sockets for medical devices, connections for oxygen, compressed air and telephone, as well as a red emergency button within the eleven-year-old patient's reach.

Anouk Lamar was sitting on the middle of the bed with her knees up to her chest, seemingly unaware that she was no longer alone. She was wearing a simple nightshirt, fastened at the back, and white cotton stockings. She hadn't changed position since Martin and Elena had entered the room. Her head was turned away from them, looking right to the external wall in which a porthole was framed by yellow curtains. The occasional wave sloshed up, creating that washing-machine effect typical of cabins just above the waterline.

Martin doubted that Anouk was staring at the drops on the glass, or anything else for that matter. He didn't have to look at her face to know that she was lost in her own thoughts and gazing right through everything in her line of vision, while scratching her right forearm with stoical regularity.

Her mere presence filled the room with an oppressive hopelessness, so weighty you could almost touch it. Sometimes Martin wished he had less experience, hadn't looked into so many empty faces to know first hand that there was no scalpel or chemotherapy in the entire world able to completely remove the cancer-like tumour that had established itself in this girl's soul after the hell she'd been through. In such cases psychologists and doctors were like engineers in Chernobyl or Fukushima. They could never get rid of the problem altogether, merely mitigate the consequences of the catastrophe.

'Hi, Anouk. I hope we're not disturbing you,' he greeted the eleven-year-old girl in her native English. 'My name is Dr Schwartz,' he introduced himself and noticed the doctor looking at him in astonishment. Bonhoeffer couldn't have shown her the case files or she'd have known that he had the title of doctor, although he set very little store by it. It was a rare exception for him to be using it today. He hoped that Anouk would find it easier to accept the presence of a second doctor rather than an investigator trained in psychology who wanted to root around in her past.

'We haven't come to examine you again,' he said. 'Don't worry.'

Anouk didn't react. No change in position, expression or gestures.

But her scratching got a little harder.

'She does that all the time,' Elena whispered.

'Let's talk out loud,' Martin said kindly. 'And in English.'

If he was right, Anouk was shutting herself off inside her own world, and you only reinforced this isolation process if, in the presence of a traumatised person, you behaved as if they weren't there. He knew this from other emotionally shattered people who he'd spent a very, very long time with.

He knew it from himself.

'I know you want to be alone at the moment and not talk to anybody.'

Especially not to a man.

'But I just wanted to check the equipment in this room.'

It was a crude attempt to suggest that she need have no fear of any probing questions. His experiences as an investigator had taught him never to pressurise traumatised witnesses. Victims of sex crimes, particularly children, were in a state of unbearable inner turmoil. On the one hand they wanted to be helped and see the perpetrator punished. But they also wanted the horrific event erased from their memory.

Martin looked at the ceiling, where a dark, flat screen hung from a swivel arm. He pointed up.

'Why's that not on?'

'The television?' Elena asked, confused. 'I, well... I somehow thought it was wrong.'

Martin nodded. An understandable error of judgement.

Normally you shouldn't leave a child alone for too long in front of the television. But this was anything other than a normal situation. Whenever he'd had to look after a child in witness or victim protection, which had happened a few times, the first thing he'd done in the safe house was to switch on the box, to take away the little one's fear.

He got the doctor to hand him the remote control and chose, from the extensive on-board menu, a children's channel with animated films.

'Do you like *Ice Age*?' he asked. No reply. Anouk remained as silent as the television that he'd muted.

Elena raised her eyebrows at Martin.

Later he'd explain to her that traumatised victims suffered complications for a shorter time if they were given the opportunity to take their mind off things as soon as possible after having been rescued. Studies showed that soldiers who were given Game Boys after horrendous missions were less likely to suffer from post-traumatic stress disorders than those who took part in psychotherapeutic discussions too quickly.

'In the few pictures taken of her by the on-board photographer she was often seen holding a sketch pad. So I left paper and pencils there,' Elena said. 'But it didn't go well.'

No wonder. It was far too early for gestalt therapy, even if the idea of letting Anouk draw the gruesome images out of her mind wasn't in itself a bad one.

'It's fine if you don't want to draw,' Martin said. 'You don't have to do anything here you don't want to.'

From her face, Elena blew a strand of hair that had come away from her plait. 'That's not what I meant,' she said, going to the bed and pushing the sleeve of Anouk's nightshirt up to the elbow. Indifferent to what was going on, the girl allowed her to do it. Martin could see a thin plaster above the left wrist.

'She tried to stab herself in the forearm with the pencil.'

Left forearm. So she's right-handed, Martin thought, making a mental note.

'Thank God I'd only just popped into the bathroom.' With her chin Elena indicated an almost invisible door in the wall beside the bed. 'To get some water for her tablets. I came back and saw Anouk harming herself.'

'Did you stab or scratch yourself?'

Once again he directed his question to the girl. Once again he got no response.

'Hard to say,' was Elena's attempt at an explanation. 'She was holding the pencil like a knife, it was more of a level movement.'

To cut out the pain?

Martin shook his head. Now wasn't the time for a diagnosis. The key thing now was to win Anouk's trust.

'I'm actually only here to test the button,' Martin said, pointing to the power strip behind her bed. 'This is a worry button. You can press it any time you feel worried or need help. Okay?'

She blinked, but Martin didn't take this as a sign of understanding. And yet it was absolutely vital that this initial phase of trust-building was successful. Anouk had to know that her situation had changed for the better and that she wasn't on her own here any longer, not at any time, not even when there was nobody else in her cabin.

'Shall we try it out?' Martin said.

Elena nodded to him when he put his hand on the red alarm button on the power strip behind Anouk's hospital bed.

'It doesn't matter whether you're frightened, in pain, feel sad or just want to talk to someone, you only have to press this and...'

Martin pushed the button, it made an audible click and almost immediately Elena's mobile rang, which was in a belt pouch tied around her black trousers.

Anouk flinched and pulled her legs up tighter to her bent-forwards torso.

'Don't worry, darling,' Elena said, stroking her hair tenderly. 'I told you about this before. The alarm activates my mobile. When it rings I'll come straight to you, any time day or night.'

'All you have to do it press the worry button above your bed,' Martin added. 'It works just as you saw.' Martin gave Elena a sign to go. He wouldn't be able to achieve any more at the moment.

'I'll be right back, sweetheart, okay?' She stroked Anouk's cheek softly then followed him out of the cabin.

'It's irresponsible,' Martin said once they'd closed the door behind them. He spoke in a hushed tone, even though he didn't think Anouk would be able to hear them out here in the anteroom. 'She's got serious injuries—'

'For which she's being given painkillers and ointments.'

'—and needs to get to a hospital as quickly as possible.'

'She *is* in a hospital,' Elena insisted. 'The *Sultan* is better equipped than many city hospitals.'

'Only without the appropriately trained personnel.'

The doctor voiced her protest. 'I lived in the Dominican Republic for three years and in the city hospital there treated more refugee children from Haiti who'd been raped than the head of the Hamburg women's clinic will see in a lifetime. And from what I've just witnessed, *Doctor* Schwartz, you seem to be very familiar with post-traumatic stress disorders. Listen, I'm not trying to defend what's happening here. But do you really think that round-the-clock treatment by the two of us is so bad for the child?'

'*Yes, it is,*' was on the tip of Martin's tongue, but he didn't manage to get the words out because all of a sudden Elena's mobile rang.

'Anouk,' she said, surprised.

The girl had pressed the worry button.

20

'There's no need to be afraid, we just want to ask you one little question,' said the man who'd knocked the chambermaid to the ground in Lisa's cabin. He spoke English with a harsh accent.

The young woman, whose bonnet was no longer perched on her black hair, blinked in fear after she'd picked herself up again. She was terribly thin; her arms, which she crossed protectively against her chest, were no thicker than a broom handle. From his vantage point, hidden behind the bed, Tiago could only see her profile and back in the mirror on the wall. She was stooped, her bony shoulders tensed. Her vertebrae poked through her top like pearls on a necklace.

Tiago didn't know the cleaning lady, or at least he hadn't noticed her before, but that wasn't a surprise given the army of people working aboard this ship.

Nor did he have any idea who the two men threatening her were.

Judging by the golden stripes on his uniform the guy doing the talking was the classic type of low-ranking officer you found on ships – a navigator or engineer – while the taller and more muscular of the two was wearing green trousers and a short-sleeved, grey polo shirt. He didn't have shoulder pads or stripes, which marked him out as a member of the crew, probably a workman who wouldn't attract attention if he came up to the passenger area for a while to carry out repairs.

Paradoxically, both of them looked like friendly chaps. Colleagues smiling in travel brochures with their smooth, tanned skin, freshly shaven faces and clean fingernails. The worker had a broad pout which softened his harsh features, whereas it was the officer's mischievously tousled blond hair that made him look like a Californian surfer rather than a thug.

It's easy to be fooled.

'I hear you've been spending quite a bit of time in Hell's Kitchen recently,' the officer said, gesturing with his finger to the worker, who put the chambermaid in an armlock.

'Is there anything down there I ought to know about?'

The hunched woman shook her head, frightened.

The officer bent his knees to bring him eye-to-eye with the chambermaid again.

'Really? So you're playing the innocent, are you, whore?' From close up he spat in her face.

'She's lying,' the taller man declared, pushing her arm further upwards, which elicited a howl of pain.

Like the officer, the worker spoke with a strong German, Swiss or Dutch accent. Tiago found it difficult to place the two men with geographical accuracy. In a similar way the chambermaid, with her dark, cinnamon-coloured skin, could be from Pakistan, India, Bangladesh or somewhere else.

'Are you taking the piss, Shahla?' the officer asked.

The young woman shook her head without wiping away the spittle running down her cheek.

'You're assigned to deck 7. This week you shouldn't be cleaning in the staff area at all.'

'Was changed. Not know why,' she stammered.

'The rumours suggest something different. The rumours suggest you're looking after a stowaway in Hell's Kitchen.'

She opened her eyes even wider. 'No!'

Something she ought not to have said. The officer's fist buried itself in her stomach.

The noises Shahla made sounded as if something far too big was trying to battle its way out from right inside her, while at the same time she tried to avoid any jerky movements which might put her shoulder out.

Dios mío, what am I doing? wondered Tiago, who was scarcely better equipped than the battered chambermaid to take on the two clearly experienced fighters.

He watched in horror as the officer reached for the water glass on the bedside table and smashed it on the edge. With a devilish smile he picked out a piece the size of a bottle top from the shards. Then he walked past Shahla and his accomplice into the bathroom, returning soon afterwards with a dressing gown belt.

'Open up!' he shouted at the chambermaid, who could do nothing but obey him, because the worker behind her increased the pressure on her shoulder joint further. The officer shoved the shard of glass in the mouth she'd opened to scream. Shahla's expression was contorted with terror, but she stayed as calm as she could with a half-dislocated shoulder.

Tears streamed down her cheeks and snot ran from her

nose. She whimpered when the puppy-eyed officer looped the belt around her head and tightened it into a gag in front of her mouth, thereby making it impossible to spit out the piece of glass. At a sign, the worker loosened the armlock.

'Okay, let's start from the beginning again, Shahla. You can say *Yes*. But you can't say *No*. But you mustn't lie either. Not unless you're keen on having a second breakfast.' The thug clenched his fist.

With a moan Shahla shook her head. Like Tiago, she'd understood what would happen if the madman punched her in the stomach again, triggering a swallowing reflex if she tried to breathe through her mouth in spite of the gag.

'You found a little white girl, didn't you?' the officer began his interrogation.

She nodded without hesitation.

'And the girl's still on board?'

Another nod.

'In Hell's Kitchen?'

The cleaning lady answered this question in the affirmative, and the next one too. 'And you're getting lots of money for looking after her?'

'Hmmmm!'

The man asking the questions laughed to his mate and switched to their mother tongue so that Shahla couldn't understand him. Unlike Tiago, who was a wizard at languages. Besides his native Spanish, he could read and write German, English, and French, while Dutch wasn't a problem either as he'd lived in Holland for three years as the son of a diplomat.

'Didn't I tell you this tart is sitting on a goldmine?' the officer said to his accomplice. 'They wouldn't be making such an effort otherwise. I see large amounts of cash here for us.'

The taller man gave an inane grin. 'Really? What's your plan?'

'We're going to let Pussy here take us to the girl and—'

Tiago would never discover the second part of the plan.

At a frantic signal from his chum, the worker let go of the chambermaid, whose eyes suddenly looked as if they were going to pop out of their sockets. She tore the gag from her mouth and staggered into the narrow gap between the television and the bed. Grabbed her throat. And opened her mouth. So wide that, in spite of his poor viewpoint from the floor, Tiago could see her tongue in the mirror. Stretched out.

Red.

Shining.

Without the shard of glass, which was now somewhere halfway between her throat and windpipe, *perhaps deeper*, and which Shahla was desperately trying to disgorge.

21

Martin opened the door, but let Elena enter Anouk's isolation cabin first.

'Everything okay, darling?' the doctor asked anxiously, but there seemed to be no cause for concern. Anouk had barely changed position.

She was still sitting cross-legged on the bed, but had stopped scratching. Although she was still refusing to look at Elena or Martin, her lips were moving very slightly.

'Are you trying to tell us something?' Martin asked, moving closer. And then the girl actually opened her mouth. She looked a little like a patient trying to form letters for the first time again after a stroke.

Martin and Elena remained as quiet as mice, just like the cartoon ice age mammoth on the muted television screen above their heads.

Cautiously, Martin approached the bed, but he couldn't understand what Anouk was trying to say.

Why did she press the worry button?

Deciding to take a gamble, he sat beside her on the bed, ready to move away again immediately if she took this as an unacceptable invasion of her privacy, but Anouk remained calm.

Her mouth opened again, and now it was quite clear. She was whispering something, trying to form a word, and to understand Martin leaned in so closely that he could smell the apple fragrance of her freshly washed hair and the ointment applied to treat her wounds.

He was secretly anticipating that what she was trying to tell him would have no significance, or if it did, then he wouldn't realise it to begin with. A made-up word, perhaps, something from baby language, to which traumatised children readily resorted. For example, they might say 'nana' for 'banana', or 'tato' for 'potato'.

But when he was so close that her breath was tickling his earlobe, he didn't have the slightest problem understanding the one and only word issuing from her mouth.

That can't be right. It's impossible, Martin thought, leaping up as if he'd been stung.

'What's wrong?' Elena said, horrified, as Martin slowly retreated from Anouk's bed.

'Nothing,' he lied.

He felt sick, but it had nothing to do with the rocking of the ship.

First the teddy. Now Anouk...

What on earth was happening here?

'What's wrong all of a sudden?' Elena asked. Now she was whispering again. '*What* did Anouk say to you?'

'Nothing,' Martin lied once more and told her that he needed a little break to get some fresh air on deck – which wasn't a lie.

The needle that had caused him so much pain in

Gerlinde's cabin yesterday now pierced his head again. And this time the bolts that flashed through his brain were even more agonising.

His eyes streaming tears of suffering, he hurried from the patient's room, Anouk's voice still echoing in his head.

The one word, the only word. As quiet as it was disturbing. 'Martin,' she'd whispered.

Even though he'd introduced himself to her by his surname only.

22

'She's swallowed it!' the worker shouted unnecessarily.

'Fuck! How did *that* happen?'

Maybe because you stuffed a fucking shard of glass in the chambermaid's mouth and she gagged on it?

Shahla had fallen to the ground and Tiago couldn't see her any more. He could only hear her. She sounded worse than a minute ago, when she'd been punched.

'What are we going to do now?' the taller man said anxiously. The officer ran a hand through his ruffled hair. 'I'll be fucked if I know,' he said. 'Let's chuck her out.'

The worker looked at the balcony. 'At this time of day? Are you out of your mind? What if someone sees us?'

The officer shrugged. He didn't seem particularly bothered by the fact that a woman at his feet was either suffocating or bleeding to death internally.

Or both, by the sound of it.

Finished. All over.

Tiago didn't know what he could do to put an end to the nightmare he'd become embroiled in, but nor could he hide on the floor like a coward any longer. He stood up, which Shahla, battling suffocation, didn't notice. Unlike the two thugs.

The one with the pout screamed like a girl watching a horror film, which might have looked funny from a safe distance, likewise the reaction of the officer. He couldn't close his mouth and stared at Tiago as if he were a ghost who'd just escaped from his bottle. 'Fuck... What...?'

Tiago went over to Shahla, who was huddled on the floor between the bed and the television set. Grabbing her under her armpits he lifted her up, to which she offered no resistance. Her vitality was starting to ebb away, but she hadn't yet been able to spit anything out of her mouth, save for foam.

'Take it easy,' Tiago ordered her in English, with an eye on the door and the two men who continued to stand there immobile with astonishment.

Tiago stepped behind Shahla, just as the thug had done a minute earlier, but he was trying to move the chambermaid into a position that could save her life.

If only you'd just bend forwards.

It took a while for Shahla to lower her torso, and this probably wasn't a voluntary movement, because her knees gave way too. Tiago had to muster all his strength to hold her up by wrapping his arms around her stomach like a belt and pulling his clasped hands into her diaphragm with a powerful jolt.

One.

From the corner of his eye he could see the two men watching him, but they weren't coming any closer.

Two.

Shahla's throat had stopped rattling and she seemed to be getting heavier.

Three.

He tried the Heimlich manoeuvre a fourth time, unsure whether he was doing it right. He pulled again, this time even more powerfully, and...

It worked!

Accompanied by a shower of vomit, the glass shot out of Shahla's mouth, flew half a metre through the room and landed right beside the worker's feet.

When Tiago let go of the chambermaid she collapsed to the floor again, wheezing, but at least she was breathing, and thus her condition had improved substantially.

The same could not be said of Tiago's situation. When the glass was freed, so were the two men from their paralysis.

They launched their attack without conferring. Without uttering a word. The men worked in sync like a well-honed team, which is what they probably were. While the worker leaped at him over Shahla, the officer dived headlong across the bed.

Tiago would not have been able to say who hit him first. Or which punch ensured that he yanked the television with him as he fell to the ground. *This is it*, was the thought that entered his head as he saw the fist hovering above his face. He was expecting to hear his teeth crunch and feel his jawbone shatter. But nothing of the sort happened. Instead, the fist vanished from his sight and he heard a woman's muffled voice call out from a distance, and in German, 'Lisa, are you there?'

He hurriedly pushed the television set away from his aching upper body and scrambled to his feet.

'Go!' he heard Shahla say. She was still unable to stand herself. Blood was running down her chin, her eyes were flooded with tears, but the skin on her face wasn't so blue any more.

She looked at the connecting door, which had closed again from the movement of the ship. The knob turned slowly.

'May I come in, Lisa?' the woman behind the door asked, knocking. Tiago had only a few seconds to copy the crew members and make himself scarce.

He leaped over Shahla's head to the door, which after the men's escape was about to close again, wrenched it open, dived into the corridor and didn't turn back to the voice coming from behind him. It was Lisa's mother, yelling after him, 'Stop! Stay where you are!'

He darted left down the short, empty section of the corridor, turned into the nearest stairwell and, without thinking about it, ran up six flights till he got to deck 11, where he dashed outside, bursting into a group of laughing holidaymakers who'd formed a semicircle for a group photo.

'Sorry,' he mumbled to the overweight man holding the camera, and looked around. It was just after half past nine, and most passengers were still busy with the breakfast buffets or looking on deck 15 for a place in the sun, which today was struggling to break through the cloud cover.

In front of him a steward was cleaning the planks; behind him the wall beneath the chimney was being repainted. No sign of the two madmen. Or of the mother. Yet his pulse refused to calm down.

What on earth did I get into there? he wondered.

Five minutes ago he'd still been a small-time crook, carving out an easy life for himself with a little charm and a few tricks. Now he was fleeing two madmen who shoved broken glass into their victims' mouths and had no scruples about watching them choke to death. Men who'd threatened to kill him because he'd witnessed an attempted blackmail he didn't understand, during the course of which he'd learned a secret that made no sense at all.

Tiago leaned against the rail and stared at the choppy sea deep below. Dark clouds were gathering, which at that moment seemed like a grim omen.

So what am I going to do now?

Feverishly he weighed up how he was going to hide on board from the two men for the next five days. He didn't even know who they were. Where they worked. And in which part of the ship they had their refuge, where they were deliberating how to get rid of him most easily.

For whatever reason.

Tiago was sure the officer would be able to work out his identity as soon as he took the time to trawl through the ship's computer. Every guest was noted on the passenger list, complete with photo, and the number of young, dark-haired Latinos under the age of thirty on this leg of the trip must be quite small. Feeling his trousers for his key card, unsure when he could dare return to his cabin, he came across an unexpected item in his back pocket.

The envelope.

From the safe. From Lisa Stiller.

In the rush Tiago had stuffed it into his pocket without noticing.

23

This time it had taken more than an hour, two aspirins and three ibuprofen before the attack was over.

Martin sensed that a residue of pain still lingered in his head, like a heap of smouldering embers just waiting to flare up again. The skin over his skull felt taut, as if he'd had sunburn, and his mouth was dry.

Bloody pills.

He was just crossing the Grand Lobby when he realised that it was his mobile that had been ringing so insistently the whole time. His standard ringtone was a guitar riff, which is why he hadn't responded to the futuristic plinking and bleeping coming from his trouser pocket. Here out in the Atlantic, hundreds of nautical miles from the coast of Europe, the mobile network was currently unavailable; someone was evidently trying to phone him via the internet.

He stopped beside the glass lifts at the edge of the circular lobby adorned with columns, and looked at his phone. *Indeed.* A Skype call.

The display showed the photo of Saddam Hussein and so it wasn't hard for Martin to identify the caller. He knew only one person who found the weekly changing photos of dictators in his contact profile funny.

He answered the call with the words, 'I can't at the moment.'

'I'm not interested in your irregular bowel movements,' Clemens Wagner replied with an audible grin. For an informer he took quite a lot of liberties, but the eccentric with his dyed, platinum-blond hair and flame tattoos on both forearms could allow himself these. When it came to getting background information there was scarcely anyone better than Diesel. A nickname the nutter owed to his pyromaniac tendencies.

'Found anything out for me yet?' Martin asked. Surprised, he looked up. The lifts were stuck between decks 5 and 7, so he opted for the stairs.

'No, I'm calling you because I miss your voice so much.'

Diesel's main job was as editor-in-chief of 101Punkt5, a private radio station in Berlin. Martin had got to know him through a colleague he was vaguely acquainted with. Her name was Ira Samin, an outstanding police psychologist, who'd saved a number of lives by negotiating after hostages were taken in a spectacular operation at Diesel's radio station. The editor-in-chief, as gutsy a man as he was crazy, had been a great help to her with his unorthodox methods, and after some hesitation, had accepted Martin's offer to earn a little extra cash as a private researcher.

Most people think that police investigations consist mainly of office work, and they're basically right. In times of scant resources and staff shortages, however, work is increasingly farmed out to private individuals. Diesel was put on a list of unofficial employees as a researcher, and just prior to his meeting with Dr Beck, Martin had emailed him with the confidential request to supply him with information about Anouk Lamar and her family.

'I haven't got much,' Diesel said. 'Cruise companies aren't exactly WikiLeaks informants. All I know so far is that Anouk is a single child. Highly intelligent, went to a school for gifted pupils. The result of her IQ test she took in year 5 was 135. She learns languages quicker than a computer; apparently she's fluent in five others apart from English. And she came second in a national memory championship. Intelligence is in her genes. When she was only seventeen, her mother developed a computer programme that allowed share prices to be predicted by observing fish schooling. Before her death Naomi Lamar worked as a professor of evolutionary biology at a private university.'

Martin approached the left side of a huge marble staircase which, together with its sister flight, rose from the lobby to a floor with luxury boutiques. A considerable number of passengers who passed through the foyer, or had sat down in one of its classy leather armchairs for an early drink, were holding a mobile phone or camera. With the golden handrail, the antique vases on the pillars and a tastefully illuminated fountain in the middle, the steps of the Grand Lobby were a popular subject for photographs.

'What do we know about the father?'

'Theodor Lamar? Civil engineer, built rollercoasters for amusement parks around the world. Died prematurely of cancer three years ago. You don't have to worry that he's hiding on your boat with a cleaver.'

'How do we know all this?'

Martin recalled an extraordinary case in which a man

with memory loss, who'd been declared dead years earlier, had been arrested at the scene of a murder.

'Because there was a forensic post-mortem examination,' Diesel said. 'Requested by the paternal grandfather, Justin Lamar. He was intending to sue the hospital because his son Theo had behaved strangely after the cancer operation.'

'Strangely?'

'He wasn't breathing any more.'

'Malpractice?'

'According to Grandpa Lamar, yes. But I wouldn't set too much store by his statement.'

'Why not?'

Diesel sighed. 'The grandfather's got a screw loose. Officially he lives in an old people's home, but it would be more accurate to describe it as a pensioners' loony bin. There are regular protests by local residents because for some unfathomable reason that straitlaced lot in their fancy neighbourhood don't want crazed coffin-dodgers sitting stark naked on the swings in their front gardens, which apparently happens all the time. Justin is less of an exhibitionist. His party trick is ringing the police.'

Martin had reached the top of the stairs and was checking out the display windows from the balustrade corridor.

Gucci, Cartier, Burberry, Louis Vuitton, Chanel.

The prices resulted in substantially fewer passengers on this level. Not even a dozen guests were wandering along the dark-red carpet. A family of three with a pram, two veiled women, a few staff members. He turned right to the corridor that led to the *Sultan*'s very own on-board planetarium. 'Anouk's grandfather rang the police?' he asked Diesel.

'On several occasions. The *Annapolis Sentinel*, a free local rag, ran a report on it. Shortly after Anouk and Naomi disappeared, Grandpa Justin called them to say they could abandon their search for his granddaughter. He'd chatted to her for half an hour on the phone, he claimed. She'd sounded jolly and was fine.'

'Yeah, right.'

Jolly.

Martin couldn't help think of the horrific injuries Anouk had sustained. Her dead eyes, the expression of her shredded soul. Even if the culprit had forced her to make the call (for whatever perverse reason) there's no way the girl could have sounded jolly, and certainly not for half an hour.

'Anouk's grandfather seems to be a very special person,' he said, thinking of Gerlinde. What a great pair the two of them would make.

'You can say that again. He's quoted in the article: *Naomi's not worth the bother. The sharks will rip the teeth out of that whore who fucked the cancer into my son's body.* Although *whore* and *fucked* are not spelled out in full – prudish Yanks.' Diesel clicked his tongue. 'But this is why I was calling you. Don't you find it strange that a man who hates his daughter-in-law that much should pay for the trip?'

'Was that in the paper too?' Martin asked, puzzled.

Justin Lamar paid for the cruise?

'No, it's what the grandfather claims in his online blog. No joke – he started it up aged eighty-two. The old man updates it every week with new crackpot observations. They range from UFO sightings, human experiments in his home and tips for canine hypnosis.'

Martin stopped in his tracks when he suddenly saw him there.

Bonhoeffer!

As Elena had said, the captain must be on the way to his officers' meeting, which was being held in the three-hundred-seater ocean planetarium.

'I'll call you back,' Martin said quietly. Daniel was walking around twenty metres ahead of him, accompanied by two colleagues in white uniforms.

'Fine, but not before ten, please. You know how I like getting up early. Just not in the morning.'

Martin was about to hang up when something occurred to him. 'Hang on a sec, seeing as you're on the line…'

'You want me to water your plants? Forget it!'

'Please find out how many missing-person cases there have been at sea over the last ten years where more than one person has vanished.' He asked him to look particularly at cases where children were involved. 'Not just on the *Sultan*, but all ships. And then check whether there are any overlaps between passenger and staff lists.'

Martin heard noises that reminded him of a pinball machine, but was not surprised. Diesel's office in the radio tower on Potsdamer Platz looked like an amusement arcade, with games of skill and gambling machines in every corner. Quite often Diesel would play them during important meetings or phone conversations.

'Anything else important you found out?' Martin asked.

'Oh, yes. I'm glad you asked. I almost forgot. Just one more thing.'

'What?'

'That you're a complete idiot. You shouldn't be on that

ship. After Nadja and Timmy's death the *Sultan* is the last place on earth you ought to be. And I'm a real arsewipe for having encouraged you to undertake your odyssey.'

'You're too hard on yourself,' Martin said, before putting his mobile away.

He walked faster and caught up with the captain who, as the last person behind three female officers, was just about to close the entrance to the planetarium.

Martin's footsteps were muffled by the carpet; Bonhoeffer didn't hear him coming. The captain suspected nothing as he kicked away the holder of the heavy entrance door. Martin grabbed him by the collar and pulled him back as the door closed slowly.

'Hey, what's—' a shocked Bonhoeffer asked.

He didn't get any further. The first blow to the stomach took the captain's breath away. The second broke his nose.

24

There was a crunching sound as if the captain's nasal septum had been put in a nutcracker. Streams of blood poured from Daniel Bonhoeffer's face.

He didn't appear to feel any pain at first; at least he wasn't screaming. But he collapsed to the ground with both elbows held protectively in front of his face.

Martin grabbed him by the collar and hauled him like a wet sack into the outer corridor that circled the planetarium, dragging him as far as the lavatories. The captain's attempts to dig his feet into the carpet were fruitless. Martin pulled him into the gents' and hurled him against a wall of bright tiles opposite the row of washbasins.

He checked the urinals and cubicles. All empty, as might be expected given that there wasn't an official function on and the officers were already in the planetarium for their meeting.

When he returned to Bonhoeffer he stood beside the captain and gave him a kick.

'What's going on here?' he yelled at him.

'I don't know what—' Bonhoeffer was holding his nose and mouth with his left hand. Without much success.

Dark blood dripped through his fingers and down his chin.

Martin slowly and menacingly clenched his fist.

'Hey, chill. Stay calm, please. I know you've got every reason to be pissed off, but please let me explain my part in all this,' Bonhoeffer pleaded, sounding as if he were suffering from a serious cold.

'*Your* part?' Martin bellowed. 'Anouk Lamar was raped.' He had to refrain from taking another swipe at the captain.

'I know, and it's horrific.'

Bonhoeffer looked at the smooth wall for something to help pull himself up. A stainless steel hair dryer was out of reach.

'Two mothers. Two children. They disappear. And both times the man in charge on the ship is you.'

'I can see how that might sound a bit suspicious.'

'Sound? It *is* suspicious. After all, you found Anouk again. *You!*'

'That's just a terrible coincidence.'

Daniel had made it to his feet and was staring at the mirror in horror. He looked like the sole survivor from a terrible accident.

'Coincidence?' Martin barked. For a split second he was back outside the Warsaw prison from which he'd been released five years ago. He felt just as angry, just as desperate. Just as empty.

Unwilling to risk the operation, the bastards in charge didn't tell him about what had happened on the *Sultan* – while he was struggling to survive in the Polish jail – until his undercover mission was over. When he left the prison,

Timmy and Nadja had already been missing for forty-three days.

'Like it was a complete *coincidence* that you didn't turn around after my family vanished?' he screamed into Bonhoeffer's face.

The captain briefly closed his eyes like a husband who doesn't know how to continue in a row with his wife.

'Turn around?' His voice was squeaking. 'Didn't you read the record of proceedings? The *Sultan* has a stopping distance of two kilometres. It takes an hour and a half to turn this thing around. There was a storm, the waves were several metres high and it was freezing outside. Without a life vest you couldn't survive in that part of the Atlantic for more than a few minutes. And your family had already been missing for hours.'

'So how do you know *when* they jumped? I thought the security videos of the hull were accidently recorded over. Did the same happen with Anouk? Did you tamper with all the evidence relating to her case too, to make it look like suicide?'

'No,' Bonhoeffer panted.

'Oh, yes, you did. Now, maybe you didn't personally abduct the girl and rape her – we'll see. But you can't deny you're a henchman. You'd do anything to keep your job. That includes hushing up a crime if necessary.' Martin spat on the ground in anger. 'Well, this time you've been unlucky. Now a Passenger 23 has suddenly turned up again, and this time you're not going to get out of it so easily.'

He pulled a heap of paper towels from a shell-shaped dispenser beside the basin and tossed them at the captain's face. 'Clean yourself up. You're going to be getting a visit soon.'

He turned to go.

'Visit? From whom?'

'The coastguards. They'd love to hear all about coincidences.'

'If you do *that*...'

'What?' Martin turned around. He looked significantly more enraged than the captain. 'Are you threatening me, like your boss tried to do yesterday? Are you also going to tell me that you'll have the girl disappear the moment I lift the lid on all of this?'

'Is that what Yegor said?' Bonhoeffer went to the washbasin and turned on the tap.

'A bluff,' Martin said.

In the mirror the captain looked Martin in the eye. 'No, it wasn't. There's far too much money at stake. The moment the mere flag of a police boat appears on our radar, Anouk will vanish into thin air a second time. Or do you imagine the owner of the fleet is just going to stand back and watch while you wreck a multi-million-dollar deal?'

'What kind of a deal?'

As Bonhoeffer's nose refused to stop bleeding, his attempts to wash his face were futile. He grabbed another paper towel and turned to Martin.

'Yegor Kalinin isn't aboard the ship for fun. He's planning to sell a large share of his fleet to Vincente Rojas, a large-scale investor from Chile. As we speak they're in the sauna finalising the details. Sixteen lawyers are standing by, eight shysters on either side. They've been clogging up the large conference room on deck 4 for weeks, but I've heard they're just twiddling their thumbs for a thousand dollars an hour, because all the documents are ready to be signed. Apparently they want to wait until we sail into New York, so they have the emblematic view of the Statue of Liberty as they sign the contracts.'

He threw the blood-soaked paper towel into a hole for rubbish in the basin unit and pulled out another one.

'Look, you've got to understand that I'm not a child abuser.' Bonhoeffer sounded more confident than desperate now, and secretly Martin had to agree with him. During the trial he'd made a comprehensive study of the captain's criminal profile. Nothing hinted at such tendencies.

'I want to find that bastard who abused Anouk too,' the captain said. 'But you're right: yes, I am a henchman. The ship owner's got me in his pocket. What can I do?'

'Stop behaving like a whore, for starters!' Martin shouted.

'You self-righteous arsehole!' Daniel screamed back. 'Off you go, then. Deck 13. The Admiral Suite, that's where you'll meet Yegor and Vincente. Why don't you go and clear things up? Tell the investor about our Passenger 23. But don't expect the girl still to be in Hell's Kitchen when you go down there with the Chilean.'

'And you'll make sure of that?'

Bonhoeffer opened his mouth, sniffed and now looked disappointed rather than angry.

'I swear I'd never do anything to Anouk. I'm afraid to say that Yegor has friends of a completely different calibre on board, employees he's saved from destitution by offering them a job. They'd hold a lighter to their own eyes if he ordered them to.'

They stared at each other until Bonhoeffer turned back

to the mirror. 'Please help me. We've got five days. In that time we can find out what happened to Anouk. And if we don't succeed, we can work out a plan for how to get her off the ship alive.'

Martin shook his head. 'Either you're nutty, or so desperate that you can't see the obvious solution. I'm going to go straight to Anouk, take a video of her as evidence and put it on the net.'

'Don't do that.'

'Why ever not? What's stopping me?'

'Because Yegor would have you exactly where he wants you.'

Martin frowned. 'I don't understand.'

'Why on earth do you think he got you on board? *I* want you to help me. *He* wants to frame you for it.'

'Me?'

The huge ship was pushed upwards by a wave, a sure sign that the *Sultan* was gathering speed on the open sea.

'Yes. You're the ideal scapegoat. A self-destructive investigator who hasn't got over the legally verified suicide of his wife and the death of his son, and who descends into a delusional search which finally drives him insane.'

'Me? A criminal?' Martin's incisor started throbbing.

'Yes. He'll claim the video you want to take is one of the trophies you've collected from your victims.'

'But that's utter madness. How am I supposed to have done anything to the girl? I wasn't even on board when she disappeared months ago.'

'How can anybody be sure?' Bonhoeffer asked. For the time being the bleeding had abated, if not stopped altogether, although it was hard to tell given the smears across his face.

SEBASTIAN FITZEK

'You're an undercover investigator, Schwartz. A master of disguise. It would be a doddle for you to travel under a fake name. Get a forged passport. Perhaps you're the killer Gerlinde Dobkowitz writes about in her book.'

'You're insane,' Martin said, but then thought he could hear Anouk's voice whispering his name again. *'Martin.'*

'No, I'm not,' Bonhoeffer answered back. 'But Yegor is. I may be the only one who's still capable of thinking clearly here. I know why you're really on board.'

As a target.

'When I realised how serious Yegor is about covering it all up, I knew I couldn't solve the problem without outside help. Then Gerlinde Dobkowitz showed me the teddy bear and the idea occurred to me. You're a psychologist and investigator, and since your loss it's been in your interest to keep yourself to yourself. I knew I'd be able to use this to convince Yegor to give me more time. Because no matter how much he wants that deal to be concluded, he's also very keen on catching the scumbag on his ship who sexually abused the girl. I swear that when he gave me the green light to contact you I had no idea he was planning to use you as a scapegoat in case everything went belly-up.'

'I don't believe a word you're saying.'

'I know. That's why you got a call from Gerlinde rather than me.'

That sentence sounds familiar.

The ground beneath Martin's feet trembled once more. Each time the ship rose, for some unfathomable reason the roaring of the air conditioning unit above their heads grew louder.

'What a fucking coward you are!' he said to Bonhoeffer.

'If you're telling the truth, what you've just revealed to me is that Yegor Kalinin is about to kill a young girl for reasons of profit and then pin the murder on me while you stand by without lifting a finger.'

The captain pulled another paper towel from the dispenser and held it beneath the tap. 'Once more: I want to stop all that from happening. But yes, if I can't then I'm not going to sacrifice myself for you, Herr Schwartz.'

He scrunched up the wet towel and threw it unused into the sink. 'You sued me. You ruined my reputation. I was suspended, almost lost my job – and much more besides. There's nothing I like about you. If this all goes tits-up then I'm not going to jail for you. And that would be the guaranteed outcome as soon as I turned against Yegor.'

Martin grabbed his shoulder and pulled the captain towards him. He forced Bonhoeffer to look him in the eye.

'What's he got on you?'

Bonhoeffer shook his hand away, then carefully touched the bridge of his nose with his thumb and forefinger. He looked as if he had to come to a decision. As if he were deliberating.

'A video,' he said eventually.

'What's on it?'

'The hull of the *Sultan*. It's the tape from the security camera that shows, amongst other things, the balcony cabin your wife was staying in. And which I was supposed to delete for Yegor.'

Martin felt the *Sultan* list sideways.

'What are you trying to say?'

Bonhoeffer nodded. 'I gave him the original and now my fingerprints are on the tape.'

Martin froze.

'Does it show...'

... the death of my family?

The words stuck in his throat.

The captain nodded. 'I'll prove that I don't want to work against you, but in cooperation,' he said. 'I've got a copy of the tape. You can watch it.'

25

A little puff of grey. The last image of his child, before he vanished forever. No colour, form or contours. Just a small, grey cloud, caught by a camera, its lens dotted with a number of raindrops partly amplifying, partly distorting the picture.

The first cloud that came away like a shadowy veil from the starboard side of the rear third of the ship must have been Timmy.

My son!

Martin was standing so close to the television that he was able to see the individual pixels of what was anyway a pale recording, and he got an inkling of what those people must have felt who saw their relatives leap to their deaths on September 11.

He recalled a heated discussion as they watched the burning towers – Nadja had said that she couldn't understand people who committed suicide because they were afraid of death. Was this the same woman who, years later, was supposed to have plummeted into the depths of the ocean, herself now a puff of grey?

It was as unimaginable as two aeroplanes flying into the World Trade Center one after another.

But that happened too…

'Do we have another view?' Martin asked. Bonhoeffer puckered his lips apologetically. They were in the living room of the captain's suite, the curtains closed and the lights dimmed. Half a minute ago Martin had asked him to stop the DVD at timecode 085622BZ, which was 20.56 and 22 seconds nautical time.

'Your family had cabin 8002, which is almost outside the range of the hull camera, right at the other end.'

The captain sounded chesty, a consequence of the bulging plaster across his nose, which restricted his breathing. Dr Beck had attended to him. Martin didn't know whether he'd admitted to his fiancée the true cause of his injuries or if he'd told her a white lie. He didn't much care either.

'It's a miracle you can see anything at all,' Bonhoeffer said, and he was right.

That first puff of grey had been illuminated for no more than a split second by the ship's lights. Before the body hit the water it had already disintegrated into the darkness.

My son disintegrated!

'Do you want to watch it to the end?' the captain asked, waving the remote control in his hand.

Yes. Absolutely. But before that, Martin wanted to know something else. He pointed at the timecode at the bottom of the screen, which was flickering in the freeze-frame.

'When did Nadja and Timmy last enter their cabin that day?'

Bonhoeffer sighed. 'Please don't lay into me again, but back then our access control data was routinely wiped at midnight. That's our system for recording the use of electronic key cards. Five years ago we were only allowed to store the data for twenty-four hours. Things are different today.'

'So you don't know how often they went in and out that day?'

'All we know is that they skipped dinner.'

'Okay.' As Martin opened his mouth it felt as if his heart were beating louder. 'Then please continue the video.'

To the end.

Bonhoeffer pressed a button on his remote control and the gloomy images resumed moving. The timecode at the bottom of the screen counted up in seconds until it happened again at 085732BZ: the second puff of grey fell.

Wait.

'Stop there!' Martin shouted frantically.

The words shot from his mouth before the realisation had quite dawned on him.

'The cloud,' he exclaimed, stepping closer to the screen and touching with a couple of fingers the outline of the shadow now hanging in the air about halfway down the ship. Gravity suspended by a simple press of a button on the remote control.

'What?' Bonhoeffer asked. From the lilt in the captain's voice, Martin could tell he knew exactly what he'd noticed. He'd seen it immediately. Any fool could see it at first glance. It was hardly surprising that this film must never be made public.

'It's too small.'

'Small?'

'Yes. The first cloud was larger.'

SEBASTIAN FITZEK

And that was impossible. Impossible if Nadja had first doped Timmy and thrown him overboard. Logically she could only have jumped after him. Which means the first shadow would have to be smaller than the second.

But it was the other way around!

Furious, he turned to the captain.

'I was right,' he said, pointing his finger at Bonhoeffer. 'It was all one big lie. Your cruise line…' he said, taking a step closer to the captain, whose eyes flickered, 'claimed it was suicide. You stigmatised her as a child murderer, just to…'

Yes, why in fact?

The obvious answer, which he could provide himself, drained Martin of any energy to continue his outburst.

Timmy and Nadja. Two grey clouds which had fallen overboard one shortly after another. There was no doubting this fact.

All that the sequence of their jumps proved was that someone else was responsible for their deaths.

Someone who'd stolen Nadja's suitcase, gathered Timmy's teddy as a trophy and passed it on to Anouk like a baton.

Someone who was probably still on the ship.

Someone who – if they'd left Anouk alive for so long – was probably still holding her mother prisoner too. He didn't know anything about this person's motives, nor who they were.

All he knew was that he'd find them.

He was dead certain about that.

26

Naomi

The computer had been there from the beginning.

Small, silver, angular. A laptop with a chunky battery and an American keyboard.

The glow of the screen was the first thing Naomi Lamar had seen when she awoke from her unconsciousness eight weeks ago.

'What's the worst thing you've ever done?' it said in smallish black letters on a white background. Naomi had read the question and collapsed inside the well, sobbing hysterically.

She'd named her prison *the well* because it had rounded walls that stank of mud, faeces, slime and filthy water. Not overpowering, but pervasive. The pong lingered in the rough metal walls like cigarette fumes in the wallpaper of a smoker's apartment.

She'd never escape from here without outside help.

She'd realised this from the second she'd first opened her eyes and glimpsed her surroundings.

Naomi looked at the bare walls, tatty and scratched, as

if legions of people before her had tried to get a hold with their fingernails, in a futile attempt to climb up.

For *up* seemed to be the only way out in a round room with no doors and a concrete floor with a fine crack. A gap not even big enough to stick your little finger into. An opportunity for a crowbar, if one had been to hand. Naomi was wearing nothing but tattered pyjamas. Fortunately it wasn't so cold in her dungeon; she suspected that some generators or other technical devices were warming her prison with their sticky, radiated heat. She slept on a mat that took up almost the entire room. Apart from this there was a plastic bag and a grey bucket, which was lowered every couple of days on a thin rope, smeared with Vaseline to prevent Naomi from getting any ideas about trying to climb it.

Oh, yes, she also had the computer.

At the start of her martyrdom – eight weeks ago, if the date on the screen was to be believed – she hadn't tied the bucket to the rope properly and her faeces came pouring out on top of her. Most of it had trickled away through the crack. But not all.

The bucket was also used to supply her with food: bottles of water, chocolate bars and microwave meals she had to eat cold.

Two months.

Without a shower. Without any music.

And without any light, save for the weak glow of the screen, which wasn't sufficient to tell where the plastic bucket disappeared to nor who it was – from whatever height – who lowered it to her. Besides the water, food and tissues, which she used as sanitary towels during her period, there would regularly be a new battery in the bucket. Naomi didn't use much energy.

The only software on the computer was a cheap word-processing programme with no saved documents. Obviously there was no internet connection. And naturally Naomi wasn't able to change the system preferences. Not even the brightness of the monitor, on which this single question flashed continually: '*What's the worst thing you've ever done?*'

For the first few days of her solitary confinement, sick with worry about Anouk, she had actually thought about her transgressions. About one which was serious enough to justify the horrific punishment she'd been suffering ever since she'd run out of her cabin that night in her pyjamas to look for her daughter. Anouk had left her a note at the foot of her bed.

I'm sorry, Mama.

There was nothing else on the piece of white paper, hastily scribbled without any explanation. No sign-off. Just: *I'm sorry, Mama*. In conjunction with the fact that it was half past two in the morning and Anouk was no longer sleeping beside her, there couldn't be a more distressing message for a mother.

Naomi wouldn't have discovered the note until the following morning if she hadn't been wrenched from her sleep by the turbulent sea. In the well, too, she clearly felt it when the waves were rough, which is why she knew she was still on the ship, rather than having been transferred to a container somewhere.

Naomi couldn't understand what was happening to her. How she'd got here. *Or why.*

After the note at the end of her bed, the last thing she remembered of her life was an open door in her corridor on deck 9, diagonally across from her own cabin. She'd thought she could hear Anouk crying. She'd knocked and called her daughter's name. Poked her head through the door.

After that... blackness.

From that point on her memory was as dim as the hole she now found herself in.

'What's the worst thing you've ever done?'

She had no intention of giving the spider an answer. In her imagination it wasn't a human being up there at the edge of the well, but a fat, hairy tarantula operating the bucket.

'Where's my daughter?' she'd typed into the computer, replying with her own question. Naomi had shut the laptop and put it inside the plastic bag (she'd soon learned why the bag was there – the bucket wasn't always cleaned) and tied it to the rope.

The answer came half an hour later:

'She's alive – safe and well.'

Naomi demanded proof. A picture, a voice message, anything. But the spider refused to grant that wish, upon which Naomi sent the notebook back up with the words: 'Fuck you'.

As punishment she had to go twenty-four hours without water. It was only when, crazy with thirst, she started drinking her own urine that a new bottle was lowered. Since then she'd never dared insult the spider again.

This was another way in which the bucket system worked brilliantly: to discipline her. Punish her.

The second, more gruesome punishment, as a

consequence of which she would probably perish, wasn't imposed until much later. Because of her first confession.

'What's the worst thing you've ever done?'

She hadn't answered the spider for seven weeks. With her intelligence – she did, after all, teach biology at an elite university – she'd compiled hypotheses, evaluated her options, analysed opportunities. Rather than blindly giving an answer.

Not me. No.

Naomi rocked her head forwards and back, and scratched her neck. Movements she was already making unconsciously.

Her hair was gradually falling out; it stuck to her fingers when she ran them over her head. She was pleased there wasn't a mirror in the well. It also spared her the sight of the worms that were crawling beneath her skin.

Fuck, I had to eat that rice.

Nine days ago. She would have starved otherwise.

For a whole week beforehand the bucket had come down with only empty bowls. Each time with the same command, written in felt-tip: *Answer the question!*

But she didn't want to. She couldn't.

'What will happen to me if I confess?' she'd dared ask the spider.

The answer came the following day with the computer, directly beneath her question.

'What will happen to me if I confess?'

'You'll be allowed to die.'

It was several hours before she'd stopped crying.

She was as convinced that the spider was lying to her about Anouk as she was about the truth of that statement.

'*You'll be allowed to die.*'

For a while she'd pondered whether there was any hope that she might escape the solitary confinement of this stinking prison, but then she'd resigned herself to her fate and made her confession to the computer, and thus the spider:

'*I killed my best friend.*'

27

Hell's Kitchen

One step forwards. Two steps back.

Working with Anouk was similar to his own life.

Her condition had improved slightly. And substantially worsened at the same time.

On the one hand it was a good sign that she recoiled in fear when he entered her room, as Martin could see that, for the time being at least, she was reacting to changes in her immediate environment.

A modicum of progress, possibly a result of the television, which was now showing Tom and Jerry haring around the screen.

On the other hand – and this was the bad news – she was in the process of slipping back into behaviour patterns of early childhood. She sat in almost exactly the same cross-legged position on the bed, sucking her right thumb noisily. And scratching herself with the other hand.

Martin could see that her fingernails had already dug deep furrows in her right forearm, and his heart sank. If she didn't stop this soon it would start bleeding… *and then she'd have to be strapped.*

He didn't want do think of the consequences this would have for her already badly damaged psyche, and he made a mental note to ask Dr Beck for gloves or mittens, even if Anouk were to take these off again the moment she was alone.

'I'm sorry to disturb you yet again,' Martin said, placing a brown paper bag at the end of her bed.

Anouk leaned back slightly; she was breathing faster. A sign that he must not get any closer. All the same, she didn't turn away from Martin or stare right through him. Her eyes were fixed on the bag.

As on his first visit he was now seized by an almost tangible feeling of melancholy, and he thought of all the nice things an eleven-year-old girl ought to be doing on a cruise ship.

Or a ten-year-old boy.

He was pricked by doubts about his faith, which in spite of everything he'd never abandoned altogether. He was convinced that there was more than just a long, dreamless sleep awaiting him after death. But he could only hope that he'd be spared a meeting with his maker. Otherwise he wouldn't be able to restrict himself to just a friendly chinwag with the being responsible for manning the ticket office of life, issuing innocent children with one-way fares to the torture chamber of sexually disturbed psychopaths.

'I've brought you something,' Martin said softly, taking the teddy from the bag. A faint sign of recognition flashed in Anouk's eyes. As if she were worried he might pack it away again, she hastily grabbed the filthy cuddly toy from his hands and buried her face in it.

Martin watched her in silence, noting the red blotches spreading across her neck and wondering whether he was doing the right thing.

It was possible that Yegor and Bonhoeffer were just bluffing and the girl wouldn't be in any danger at all if he notified the authorities and thus the whole world about this unbelievable case. But it was a huge risk. For there were indications that the captain was right and he already wore a stamp on his forehead that said 'scapegoat'. In all likelihood the truth was somewhere in between. The only thing for sure was that the moment he raised the alarm he wouldn't have any further opportunity to speak personally to the girl, or at least attempt to. And thus he was torn between the desire to do the right thing and reveal the cover-up, and the hope that through Anouk he might learn something about the fate of his own family.

Churned up by these unsettling thoughts, he'd decided to pay her a second visit, this time alone, without the doctor.

'I've got something else for you,' Martin said, taking from the bag a cardboard box wrapped in transparent film.

'It's a toy computer,' he explained, having removed a pink plastic device from its packaging. He'd picked it up in the ship's toyshop on deck 3.

The rectangular thing looked like a tablet from the technological Stone Age, manufactured clumsily and cheaply, but it didn't have any sharp edges and Anouk wouldn't be able to do herself much harm with the blunt stylus stuck to its side.

Martin turned it on, checked that the batteries were working, and put it beside Anouk on the bed.

Then he took a step back and slipped his hand into his jeans pocket. With a single press of a button he activated the record function of his smartphone.

'When I came to see you a couple of hours ago with Dr Beck you mentioned a name to me, Anouk. Can you remember what that was?'

The girl stopped sucking her thumb and, without letting go of the teddy, picked up the drawing computer. She placed it on her knee. Then she looked up.

'Do you have any idea where you are at the moment?' Martin asked. Anouk frowned in response. She looked tense, but not in pain. Like a schoolgirl given a difficult mental arithmetic problem she can't solve.

Martin decided to try some simpler questions.

'How old are you?'

His question was accompanied by a piercing beep, followed by six more and concluded with a final, drawn-out toot. The noise, muffled by several doors, seemed to be coming from the corridor leading to Hell's Kitchen. Suspecting that it was an internal alarm for staff, Martin ignored it.

Anouk looked as if she hadn't heard the noise at all.

Her lips were moving like Timmy's had when he had to learn something by heart. But they didn't form any words, not even a sound. Instead she lifted her nightshirt to scratch her tummy above the waistband of her tights.

Martin saw a number of circular burn scars, on either side of her belly button, which looked as if cigarettes had been stubbed out on her.

'My God, who did that to you?' he asked, unable to conceal the revulsion in his voice. He turned away so that

Anouk didn't relate the fury in his face to herself. When he'd composed himself again and was about to resume his questions, he couldn't speak.

That can't be true!

Anouk had put the teddy down beside her and written a single word on the drawing computer:

Martin

His name. In clear letters. Right across the touchscreen. Anouk still had the stylus in her hand.

She can't mean me, that's impossible.

Martin forced a smile and counted down from ten until his heart rate was sufficiently normal for him to ask calmly, 'But you know I'm not a bad man, don't you?'

I'd never hurt you.

It must be a silly coincidence, he thought.

He hoped.

Martin was a common name, in the US too. It wasn't unfeasible that the abuser might also coincidentally be called it.

Or called himself Martin. Or wore a shirt from the Caribbean island of St Martin...

Anything was possible.

But was it likely?

Anouk turned her head to the side. She looked around as if she were taking in her surroundings for the first time. Then she grabbed the stylus again and skilfully drew the outline of a large cruise ship. Martin peered through the portholes out at the water, which looked much darker than two hours ago. He had another stab at a direct question:

'Can you tell me the name of the person you've been with all this time?'

Anouk closed her eyes. Counted something on her fingers.

$$11 + 3$$

is what she wrote directly below her drawing of the ship. Martin couldn't make any sense of it.

'I'm sorry, but I don't understand,' he said.

He looked at his name, the drawing of the liner and the apparent sum.

Fourteen?

As the cabin numbers on the *Sultan* had four digits, this could only be a clue to a deck, if at all. Deck 14 was the pool with the waterslide, ice bar, driving range and jogging circuit.

'What do you mean eleven plus three?' he asked.

Her expression darkened. She seemed to be angry, as if his questioning was slowly getting on her nerves. Nonetheless she wrote again with the stylus:

My mama

'Your mama?' Martin asked, as if transfixed. 'Do you know if she's still alive?'

Anouk nodded sadly. A tear ran from her eye.

Martin could scarcely believe he'd obtained so much information from the girl in such a short time, even if he wasn't able to pin most of it down.

'I think we'd better have a little break,' he said. Anouk

looked exhausted. 'Is there anything I can bring you?' he asked.

The girl picked up the stylus one last time and wrote

Elena

beneath the drawing of the ship. Then she shoved her thumb back in her mouth and turned away from Martin, as if she wanted to make it absolutely clear that she had no more to tell him.

'I'll go and see if I can find her,' Martin said, and was just about to go looking for the ship's doctor when the alarm sounded again.

28

Naomi

'*I killed my best friend,*' Naomi Lamar had typed into the computer on the floor of her well-like prison.

Mel and I were ten years old and both of us were grounded because we'd been caught playing in the disused gravel pit yet again. We'd been forbidden to go there, you see. It was a weekday afternoon, our parents were at work and we both sneaked out even though we were grounded. We met – of course – at the gravel pit. It happened just before we had to leave to ensure we got back home before our parents. Mel wanted to slide down the northern slope on her plastic bag one last time. She was buried by a sand avalanche and disappeared. I screamed, called for help and dug with my bare hands, but couldn't find her. She'd literally been swallowed up by the earth. I slunk home and didn't dare tell my parents. Mel was found two days later and everyone assumed she'd slipped out of the house alone. I still think today that she died because of me and could have been saved if I'd raised the alarm. That's the worst thing I've ever done.

She'd written this nine days ago and sent the computer up in the bucket. The hunger cramps in her stomach were unbearable, but a few hours later no food came, only the laptop with the spider's answer:

'*That's NOT the worst thing you've ever done.*'

And right below it:

'*Every wrong answer will be punished.*'

Two hours later came the bowl with the rice and the label: *Spirometra mansoni*.

She'd had to eat it. She would have starved to death otherwise. At the time Naomi reckoned that instant death was the worse of the two.

But it wasn't.

To know that you were carrying a parasite – the nastiest sort of tapeworm – and were slowly being devoured from the inside, *that* was the worst thing that could happen to you.

Naomi was sure the spider knew this.

It wanted answers, a confession, and it would only get these if its victim's survival instinct was broken.

Till now the thought of her daughter had kept Naomi alive. But now the horror beneath her skin that was gradually making its way to behind her eyeball was eliminating all desire to live.

'*What's the worst thing you've ever done?*'

'I'm so sorry, Anouk,' Naomi whispered, taking hold of the computer. With fingers whose nails hadn't been cut for weeks she typed her second confession:

'*I committed adultery. In the most despicable way possible. I had sex for money.*'

She flipped shut the laptop, put it inside the bag and

placed it in the bucket. She tugged several times on the rope and, as she scratched herself again until she bled, waited for the spider to pull it up, satisfied with her answer.

So finally she could die.

29

By now Martin was virtually the only person on deck where – appropriately enough for October – it had turned quite chilly. Everyone else in his evacuation group had hurried to leave the assembly point by the diving station once the thick grey clouds, which had gathered soon after the end of their emergency drill, started emptying themselves – fine drizzle, but enough to soak all clothes through.

Martin wasn't bothered. He didn't have a hairstyle to worry about and was wearing clothes that needed washing anyway. In comparison to how he felt at the moment, a cold might even be an improvement.

He felt terrible, although this wasn't a consequence of his tiredness or the sea swell, which for true seadogs was probably no more than a bubble in a whirlpool. But Martin had reached the stage where he was going to ask the on-board pharmacy for Vomex.

As if responding to a telepathic command, Elena Beck joined him by the parapet. With a transparent rain cape over her head and uniform, she was wearing far more suitable clothing than him. In one hand she held a life jacket, in the other a black doctor's bag, which looked coarse in her slim hand.

'So here you are,' she said, her gaze fixed in the distance.

Anyone who expected to gain an impression of the vast dimensions of the ocean on a transatlantic passage certainly got their money's worth. Wherever you looked there was nothing but water. No land, no other boats. Just an endless, blue-black, choppy expanse. *If the surface of the moon were liquid it would look just like this*, Martin thought.

Some fancied they saw in the sea a symbol of the eternity and power of nature. All he saw in the waves was a damp grave.

'I've tried calling you, but your phone's off,' Elena said. Martin pulled out his mobile and when he looked at the display he remembered.

Of course! Because of the recording. He'd deliberately set his phone so the recording of his 'conversation' with Anouk wouldn't be interrupted by a call. But he hadn't been able to block out the international alarm for emergency drills at sea (seven short sounds and one long one).

Each passenger had to participate in this exercise no later than twenty-four hours after boarding, so that they knew how the life jackets worked and where the lifeboats were. If in a number of areas the captain didn't bother much about upholding maritime law, this was one regulation he stuck to rigidly. Martin switched his mobile off airplane mode and wiped the rain from his face. A disgruntled young couple, who must have been hoping for drier weather on their dream trip, pushed a double buggy with sleeping children past them. Elena waited until they were out of earshot before placing her doctor's bag on a metal table in the covered section of the area where the diving instructors held their introductory class before their students leaped into the pool with scuba tanks and masks.

'I've heard you had a lively discussion with my fiancé. I'm supposed to give you this.' Elena opened the bag and took out a disc without a cover.

'This is a CD-ROM with the passenger lists from the last five years,' she said, pre-empting his question. 'Plus a roll of on-board employees on all routes where a Passenger 23 was reported.'

'What am I supposed to do with these?'

'I asked Daniel the same question. He said he'd be surprised if you hadn't started your research some time ago. You'll find the *Sultan*'s floor and deck plans, all newspaper articles and press releases of every available missing-person case, as well as a cross-check with other liners.'

Martin's fingers were tingling as he took the CD-ROM.

'I'm supposed to tell you that the documents he's assembled over the past few months are proof of his goodwill. And...'

At that moment their mobiles started to ring. Both of them.

They exchanged baffled glances and reached for their trouser pockets at the same time.

'Shit!' the doctor said, abandoning Martin, who had no idea who the long number on his display belonged to.

'What's wrong?' he called after Elena, who stopped briefly by a swing door leading inside and turned around.

'Anouk,' she said. 'We've directed her alarm to your mobile too, Dr Schwartz.'

★ ★ ★

Five minutes later Martin stepped from the steel-cased airlock into Hell's Kitchen for the third time that day. As he crossed the entrance area of the quarantine station he watched Elena Beck slide her key card through the reader.

As he entered he was expecting another false alarm.

But then he wondered where all the blood had come from.

On Anouk's bed.

On her body.

Everywhere.

30

'Jesus Christ Almighty...'

Elena hurried to the bed, in front of which the girl was cowering on the floor, pressing her hand on her blood-soaked forearm. This had been bandaged before the emergency drill; now it lay on the floor like an unwound loo roll.

'What happened, sweetie? What happened?' the doctor cried, squatting beside the girl.

Elena was still partially in shock, but Martin had already identified the cause of the injury.

The blood was on the sheets, in Anouk's face, on her arms, fingers and nightshirt. Martin even found some spots on the polished stainless steel cupboard on the wall beneath the television, which suggested that the blood must have spurted from an artery in a high trajectory.

'Her artery's been gashed,' he said, then asked Elena where the disinfectant and fresh bandages were.

Judging by the colour in Anouk's face it wasn't as bad as it looked at first glance. Martin knew from experience that even small amounts of lost blood could create a godawful mess.

'Her artery?' Elena said in disbelief, pointing to the bathroom door. She told him a code, whose significance he only realised when he discovered the safe-like cabinet beneath the basin. The supplies were locked away for security.

Besides syringes, infusion needles, tubes, scissors and other items handy for committing suicide, Martin found the disinfectant spray and bandages he was looking for.

He brought them to Elena and watched her lift the child's chin. Anouk kept her eyes closed. A small white dot stuck to the fluff on her upper lip. Some cotton wool or a bit of tissue.

Martin busily removed the bedclothes and shook them out. Then he lifted the mattress, took off the hygienic cover, but he didn't find anything here either. *No razor blade, no knife, no pencil.*

'You were the last one in here with her,' Elena said reproachfully, after taking Anouk over to the leather sofa where she examined the girl's arm. The blood started flowing again when the girl stopped pressing her hand on it, like raindrops spattering from a fir branch, and so Elena immediately applied a tourniquet.

'Are you suggesting I egged her on when I was alone with her?' Martin asked in anger.

'No, of course not, but...' The corners of Elena's eyes were twitching nervously. 'Who was it, sweetheart?' She stroked Anouk's cheek. 'Who hurt you?'

No answer.

'I know who did it,' Martin whispered.

'What? Who?' Elena looked up at him.

'She did it herself.'

'I'm sorry? No! That's impossible. Why on earth would she do anything like that?'

There are many possible reasons: she wants to relieve pressure, let the pain out from her body, feel that she's alive…

'At any rate she wasn't trying to kill herself with these injuries,' he said. *Otherwise she wouldn't have tried to secure her arm. Or pressed the worry button.*

Everything suggested to him that although she'd deliberately cut herself, the depth of the wound wasn't intentional.

'How can it have happened?' Elena asked distraught. 'There aren't any sharp objects here she could have got hold of. I swear I gave the cabin a thorough search after the incident with the pencils.'

The pencils. Exactly!

Martin waited until Elena had finished tying the tourniquet, then asked, 'How many pieces of paper did you give her that day?'

She looked at him in horror.

'I don't know. I didn't count.'

Mistake.

Big mistake.

Elena saw the contrition in Martin's face and slapped her hand over her mouth.

'You mean…' She turned to Anouk. 'Darling, please tell me. Did you cut yourself with a piece of paper?'

Anouk didn't answer, but Martin was certain. When dealing with mentally disturbed patients you couldn't be careful enough. During his time as a student he'd come across a sixteen-year-old who'd run the edge of a piece of paper across both eyes.

'Did you keep one piece back?' he said, trying to get through to Anouk. With success. She opened her eyelids. Although Martin wasn't sure she recognised him, there could be no doubt about the fury radiating from her. She nodded and her eyes flashed angrily. Martin and Elena looked at each other meaningfully. 'You ate the paper afterwards, didn't you?'

That's why there was a speck of white on her upper lip. *Pulp!*

Anouk pressed her lips together mutely. She looked livid, probably because he'd got to the bottom of her secret so easily.

Martin fetched a wet towel from the bathroom to clean Anouk's face, something she only reluctantly permitted.

In the cupboard below the television were fresh bedclothes, which Martin put on while Elena sorted out a nightshirt for Anouk. Together they took the girl, who looked weak but not in a critical condition, back to her bed.

Martin caught sight of the drawing computer on her bedside table. The screen was dark but a yellow LED light was lit, signalling that it was in standby mode. As Anouk sunk back into bed, he picked up the device and activated the display.

'Wow!' he exclaimed. The drawing Anouk must have done during the emergency drill was unbelievably detailed and accurate. A masterpiece which left no doubt that she was a highly talented child, at least in art.

Because he didn't want to take the computer away from the girl, Martin fished his mobile from his pocket and photographed the screen. Then he left Anouk, who'd closed her eyes again and waited outside the cabin for Elena.

'Anouk drew *that*?' the doctor asked after she'd dressed the girl in a clean nightshirt and left the cabin too. 'All by herself?' She stared in disbelief at the picture on Martin's mobile, showing a hole yawning murkily in the ground – a well perhaps – at the bottom of which you could see water shimmering darkly. The drawing also showed a rope that extended down the shaft to the water.

'Is there anywhere here on the ship that looks roughly like this? A hole, a cavity or a bulkhead through which you can see the ocean?' he asked Elena.

The doctor knitted her brow and bent her head sideways to look at the picture from a different angle. 'Hmm,' she said indecisively. 'I've never seen anything like that. And, in general, cruise ships rarely have holes in their hulls when out at sea.'

Out at sea, Martin repeated in his head, and that gave him an idea.

Of course. When they're out at sea. But what about when they're not?

'Which deck is the anchor room on?' he asked excitedly.

'Anchor? You mean...'

A hole, beneath it water, a rope, *which could also be a chain.*

'Which deck?' he urged her. 'Please!'

Elena thought about it. 'There are several,' she said eventually. 'As far as I know there's one on deck 3. And another higher up, on deck 11, I think.'

11 + 3

The blood was pumping noticeably faster in Martin's veins. He glanced again at the image of the toy computer and said, 'Maybe it's just my imagination running wild. But it can't do any harm if we take a look around the anchor room.'

31

'Tiago Álvarez?'

Although it was no longer morning Yegor Kalinin was sitting on the sofa in his suite in dressing gown and leather slippers, tickling the neck of his Jack Russell terrier, Ikarus. Normally dogs and other pets were not permitted in the private rooms aboard the cruise liner, but the owner of the *Sultan* took no more heed of that than he did the smoking ban in the cabins. To the chagrin of his non-smoking wife, he'd had the smoke alarm deactivated in the bedroom.

'This chap here?'

On the tinted glass table in front of Yegor was a colour printout with the personal details of the passenger his third security officer had just provided a report on, including a photo, itinerary, cabin number and the status of his bill. To date the Argentinian hadn't made much effort to replenish the coffers of the cruise company. He had an inner cabin, never drank wine with his meals, didn't join any on-shore excursions, and hadn't bought a single souvenir in the shops on board.

'That's the bastard. I'm sure of it,' Veith Jesper said.

'And he was the one hiding behind the bed?'

'It's like I said. I saw him and then found his picture in the passenger files. There's no doubt about it.'

Yegor eyed the twenty-three-year-old man suspiciously. 'What were *you* doing in the cabin, anyway?' he asked Veith, even though he already knew the answer.

Yegor couldn't stand his nephew. He hadn't been able to abide the boy's cheesehead father, who his sister had insisted on marrying just because she'd let the loser get her up the duff while she was studying in Amsterdam.

At twenty-one, getting involved with a street musician might have been an enticing prospect. But twenty-three years later Irina had also understood that no money, no job and no condom weren't perhaps the best recipe for a promising future. It was only for his sister's sake that he'd given the useless brute who called him uncle a job on the *Sultan*. As far as he was concerned Veith could have wasted the rest of life as a trainer for adolescent street thugs in that Dutch shithole that called itself a martial arts school. His one achievement in life was that he didn't have a criminal record, but given his penchant for violence, drugs and easy girls, it could only be a matter of time before his accommodation was at the state's expense.

'I was dealing with the cleaner,' Veith said, unfazed. He looked as if he was just about to do a photoshoot for a surfing magazine, which only made Yegor even more irate.

The ship owner pursed his lips and briefly enjoyed fantasising about Ikarus biting into his nephew's I-have-them-all-on-the-first-date face. 'Please jog my memory,' he said. 'I thought you were employed to help the head of security. Not to torture chambermaids.'

Not a week passed on a ship without substantial friction, both between the passengers and amongst employees. Yegor had thought it wouldn't do any harm to have on board someone he could trust to deal with the rough stuff. But he'd also thought that Veith was as blond as he looked. A thug without a brain, easily manipulated.

How wrong you can be.

Since the Shahla incident he knew that his nephew was as shrewd as he was unpredictable. Fortunately the girl hadn't suffered any serious injury, even if she'd be coughing up blood for the next few days. And fortunately the passenger, after she'd established that nothing had been taken from her cabins, had believed the story about the jealous lover/ colleague they'd taken into custody.

'Let's cut the crap,' his nephew said in a tone that would have earned non-family members a visit to the jaw surgeon. 'I don't know what's going on here, Yegor. But you're hiding something massive – I'm not interested in what it is.'

'What do you want then?'

'My share.'

He grinned as if he'd just told a dirty joke. 'The girl in quarantine, exclusive treatment from our dear doctor, a bonus for the cleaner – keeping all this under wraps seems to be worth quite a lot to you.'

'Are you trying to blackmail me?' Yegor feigned surprise. In truth, anything else would have surprised him.

Veith raised his hand apologetically. 'Hey, I just want to make sure your deal with the Chilean doesn't go down the pan.'

Yegor smiled. In his daydream Ikarus was now working his way into his nephew's nether regions. Veith, who mistook the smile for an answer in the affirmative, bent forwards.

'It's not meant to be hush money; I want to earn it.'

Yegor, who'd come up with a plan some time ago, spent a while doing nothing but staring into his nephew's steel-blue eyes. For twenty seconds all that could be heard in the cabin was the roaring of the air conditioning unit, accompanied by the constant noises that a ship of that size produces as it ploughs its way across the sea. They were travelling at about twenty knots, and the swell had noticeably increased.

'Okay, here's the deal,' Yegor said finally, tapping on the photo on the passenger sheet in front of him. 'Find this Tiago and you'll get five thousand dollars in cash.'

Veith whistled like a builder who's just seen a girl in a miniskirt walk past. 'What's he done?'

'He raped a young girl.'

Veith's expression darkened.

Yegor would never understand why someone who shoved broken glass into the throat of a helpless young woman regarded himself as better than a paedophile, but luckily he'd never been in the situation where he'd had to engage with the pecking order amongst prisoners.

'The girl in Hell's Kitchen?'

'Yes, that one.'

'How old is she?'

'Eleven.'

'What was that fucker doing in the cabin?'

'The same as you,' Yegor fabricated. He didn't believe in the slightest that the South American wannabe Casanova had anything to do with Anouk's disappearance.

'Like you, he found out where Shahla was working and lay in wait to grill her. He wanted to know how close we were on his heels.'

The story that Yegor was spinning had holes the *Sultan* could sink into, but Veith didn't seem to spot them.

'What about the girl's parents? Where are they?' he asked.

Yegor flicked his hand. 'Friends of mine. They want to be kept out of it. Just go looking for that fucking bastard.'

'And if I find him?'

Good question. He'd hoped he wouldn't have to say it out loud.

Yegor lifted Ikarus from his lap, stood up from the sofa and shuffled over to a sideboard beneath the heavy crystal mirror in the entrance area. He opened the top drawer.

'Be creative!' he said. Then he checked the cylinder, turned a little lever on the underside of the barrel and handed Veith the revolver.

32

Throw me out when you need me. Bring me back in when you don't need me any more.

On his way to the prow of the *Sultan*, Martin couldn't help think of a riddle he'd read years ago in a book. He couldn't remember the title, only the answer: *anchor*.

He wished the puzzles served up to him by the most recent events on the ship were as easy to solve. But he feared that inspecting the anchor room would merely throw up more questions than answers.

He began by visiting deck 3, the ship's official anchor room and essentially its only one. Deck 11 merely housed a small spare anchor, its chains stored outside for aesthetic reasons, visible to everyone who came to the top viewing deck. There was no chance of keeping someone permanently hidden there unnoticed.

'Here we are!' Elena Beck said. After Martin had followed the ship's doctor down a narrow, windowless corridor, which took them along the hull behind the musical theatre, they'd reached the steel door marked 'ANCHOR ROOM' via a small entrance. Behind it they were met by Bonhoeffer and a deafening noise.

'Why's it taken so long?' Martin asked the captain, who for understandable reasons didn't want to shake his hand. With his fingertips he nervously checked that the plastic cap was sitting properly on his broken nose.

'Long?' Bonhoeffer looked at his watch.

It was just after 5 p.m. nautical time and it had taken almost two hours for him to get them access. Elena didn't have any explanation for this delay either.

'As you can see, we've got rather a lot of steam from the boiler at the moment,' Bonhoeffer shouted. As the prow narrowed, the walls formed an acute angle, like in an attic, and there were no closed windows, just open holes. Given how close they were to the sea here, and that *Sultan* had now reached its top speed, you had to shout at the top of your voice to be heard over the noise the ship made as it followed its course. Martin felt as if he were inside a steel kettle being bombarded from outside by a water cannon.

'Normally there's no access here when we're out at sea,' the captain said. He went on to explain to Martin that last year a drunken Canadian had managed to climb into the anchor room and let the chains down from the capstan. The anchor had damaged the propeller, gouged a hole in the ship and rendered it completely unsteerable. At the time the *Sultan* had just filled up with three and a half million euros worth of fuel. What would have happened had the anchor caused a leak in the fuel tank didn't bear thinking about.

Today the pisshead was in jail for dangerous infringement of ship security, and since then the doors to the anchor room could only be opened when the liner came in and out of port.

'I had to get my chief engineer to remove the electronic

security lock,' Bonhoeffer concluded. 'It couldn't be done any faster.'

Martin looked around. They'd entered the room on the port side. Turbine-like constructions, possibly generators, covered an area which would have easily accommodated twenty parking spaces. He saw a metal cage, which was used to store the mooring ropes, and several cupboards that looked like fuse boxes with warning stickers indicating high voltage.

And then, of course, there was the chain. Painted black and huge. Viewed up close it looked like something an enormous macho giant might wear across his chest. Martin could have easily slipped his forearm through the links. And he'd have needed a dozen arms to lift just one of them. 'Seventy tonnes,' Bonhoeffer said, knocking on the metal monster as if they were on a sightseeing tour.

The chain was coiled on a huge, pistachio-coloured metal reel – the chain winch, reminiscent of an outsized train wheel – and then ran down via a slightly smaller winch into a chimney-sized shaft, which at the moment was blocked by the anchor set firmly into the hull.

Anouk's drawing flashed through Martin's mind.

Through small gaps he could see the choppy water of the Atlantic.

'The anchor itself weighs ten tonnes,' the captain said, going further into the room.

As Elena and he followed Bonhoeffer, Martin realised that there were two anchors, one each for the port and starboard sides. The two large chain winches were separated in the middle by a podium, on which sat a box with a number of levers. Each large winch had a metal brake wheel which you had to rotate like a valve if you wanted to let the anchor down or stop it falling.

'What exactly are we looking for here?' the captain asked on the podium, with his back to the brake wheel for the port anchor. 'Surely not Anouk's hiding place?'

Martin allowed his gaze to wander around the anchor room.

He was surprised by how clean everything was, almost sterile. Given the prevailing smell in here, he would have expected rust and oil dotted on the floor, or at least signs of weathering from the aggressive salt water, which kept splashing up through the holes. But even in the non-public areas, cleanliness and tidiness were the order of the day. Everything looked as if it had been newly renovated. The walls were painted white, the floor laid with thick rubber mats to stop you from slipping even when it was wet.

Huge amounts of space.

But not a place you could survive for weeks. It was draughty, cold and damp. You'd get pneumonia within a week. In any case at least two sailors would enter this room to weigh anchor each time the ship came into port.

She can't have been here.

Elena seemed to share Martin's unspoken assessment. 'This is a dead end,' she shouted. She sounded shrill and several years younger when she had to raise her voice.

Martin nodded. They'd clearly got carried away. *Just idle speculation*, he thought, his irritation brewing. Treating a child's drawing as important evidence was just as foolish as seeing the face of the Virgin Mary in a slice of toast.

'Let's go.' As Martin bent down to tie the laces of his

boots, which had come undone, he found himself looking below the first step of the platform.

'Where's the chain?' he asked Bonhoeffer. The captain looked down at him blankly.

Martin pointed to the large metal reel to his left. 'I can only see the few metres that run from the huge wheel to the anchor shaft. Where's the rest?'

'Right where you're kneeling,' Bonhoeffer replied, getting down from the platform. He stamped his foot. 'Right under here.'

'Is there space down there?'

Bonhoeffer wiggled his outstretched hand, as if trying to imitate a rocking boat. 'Depends how much of the chain is hauled in. But there's always a bit of room. It's actually a favourite hiding place for stowaways. But they could only last a few days down there, not weeks.'

'Is there access to it?' Martin asked nonetheless. He rapped his knuckles on the metal plate he was squatting on.

'One deck lower. You can only get in from here if you unscrew the floor panels. Which happens once a year for maintenance,' said the captain, who was now kneeling beside him. With his blond, tousled hair and the protective cap on his injured nose he resembled Hannibal Lecter. All that was missing were the straitjacket and hand truck he was secured to.

'It's probably a waste of time...' Martin said.

'Maybe not,' Elena contradicted him. 'What have we got to lose now that we're here?'

'Just a moment,' the captain said, getting to his feet. He went over to a metal locker and opened it. Martin expected him to return with a toolbox, but when he came back he was holding a large torch. He kneeled beneath the platform again.

'Found something?' Martin asked, kneeling again too.

'Maybe. There. Can you see it?'

Bonhoeffer shone the torch directly below the platform to the spot where the anchor chain disappeared into the deck below the large metal reel.

'What is it?' Elena asked excitedly.

'Looks like a bag,' Martin said. The torchlight was reflected by a crinkled surface of brownish plastic.

33

Martin stood, walked around the winch and squatted down. Here he was at least a couple of metres closer to the bag-like object stuck to the last visible link of the anchor chain. Lying flat on the ground, he tried to squeeze himself on the cold floor beneath the metal reel.

Hopeless.

Either he was too broad or the gap too narrow. He felt like he had that time as a child when a marble rolled under the cupboard and, with his short arms, he hadn't been able to grab anything but fluff and dust.

'Shall I try?' he heard Elena ask behind him.

He looked up to her and nodded. 'Maybe you'll have more luck.' At any rate she was considerably more petite than he was.

The doctor took off her jacket and blouse, beneath which she wore a white, sleeveless man's shirt. Before lying on the ground she took off her jewellery, a chain with an oak-leaf pendant and a silver charm bracelet, which she wore on her right arm alongside her diving watch.

'Phew, couldn't get any tighter,' she said as she lay on her stomach. She turned her head sideways, pressing her ear to the ground. 'Nor any louder.' She inched forwards to the target that Bonhoeffer's torch was illuminating from the side.

'A little bit to the right,' Martin guided her, as from her position Elena couldn't see a thing.

Finally her fingers were touching the chain. 'Really does feel like a plastic bag,' the doctor said, picking at it with her thumb and forefinger. 'But I can't work it loose.'

'Stuck fast,' Bonhoeffer declared. Martin, too, now saw the adhesive strip with which the bag was affixed to the link of the chain. A good tug would be enough to remove it, but Elena needed to crawl further under the platform.

'I'm getting a cramp,' she moaned.

Martin tried to encourage her. 'You'll do it. Just a few centimetres more. That's it, excellent...'

Now the doctor was able to get her whole fist around the bag.

A large wave slapped against the ship, which sounded as if a twenty-metre carpet were being beaten against the hull. The *Sultan* listed sideways, sending the chain moving a few centimetres as well.

'This thing can't go down on its own, can it?' Elena asked with warranted concern. If the lock was disengaged she'd be yanked along with the chain. 'I don't want to end up as anchor grease.'

Bonhoeffer shouted something about her not having to worry, but Elena had already detached the plastic bag and was scrabbling backwards beneath the platform. When she emerged again, the side of her face that had been in contact with the floor had an oily, black trace.

'It feels slippery,' the doctor said, standing up.

With her arm outstretched she held the bag as far away from her body as possible, as if she were putting something revolting in the dustbin. 'Like there's jelly in it.'

She walked past the anchor winch and over to a green crate where she lay the bag on a hard plastic lid.

'That may be evidence,' Martin said. 'We ought to open it in a sealed container.'

Under an extractor. With safety goggles.

Elena wasn't listening to him. She might be a good doctor, but she had no idea of the basics of crime scene work. With nimble fingers she tore off the adhesive strip which the bag was tied with before Martin could intervene. Fortunately his fear proved unfounded; there was no combustion. And yet Elena recoiled as if a splinter had flown into her face.

'Good God!' she panted, turning away with a hand over her mouth.

Martin could understand her reaction, as well as that of the captain, who stared in disgust at the bag and its contents, which now poured out unimpeded over the lid of the crate. Maggots. Hundreds of them wreathed and coiled as if plugged in to the mains.

'That's fucking disgusting!' Bonhoeffer cursed, stamping on the first of them that had already fallen off the edge to the floor. He grabbed his work mobile and asked someone at the other end to send a cleaner.

Martin moved a little closer and opened the bag to get a better look inside.

Well, well.

The maggots were not the only contents.

With the tips of his fingers he pulled out a laminated, rectangular piece of paper and wiped the insects off it.

'A postcard?' the captain asked.

Part of one at least.

It was part of an advertising postcard that was distributed for free in every cabin. It was just a torn-off edge, but big enough to see that the image on the front was an aerial picture of the *Sultan*.

Martin turned the card over.

THAT'S WHAT HAPPENS WHEN YOU GO STICKING YOUR
NOSE IN EVERYWHERE...

He read out the message that had been scrawled in block capitals. It was in English and written with a black biro that was starting to run out of ink.

'*What* happens?' Bonhoeffer asked. 'What does the bastard mean by that?'

'Oh, fuck,' Martin said as if paralysed by shock. He'd turned around to ask Elena's opinion. The answer to Bonhoeffer's question was literally written on her face.

'Jesus Christ, Elena, what's wrong with you?' the captain screamed. He too had turned to his fiancée and noticed her disfigurement. The doctor's face had completely swollen: cheeks, brow, lips. It looked as if her face were about to burst. You couldn't make out her eyes any more, only the tips of her lashes stuck out of the swollen bulges.

THAT'S WHAT HAPPENS WHEN YOU GO STICKING YOUR
NOSE IN EVERYWHERE...

The entire sight of her was ghastly, but worst of all were

the swellings on the right-hand side of her face, where she'd come into contact with the grease.

'Elena, darling, say something, please!' Bonhoeffer cried, beside himself with worry. But Martin realised that the doctor, who was grabbing her throat and choking, was no longer capable. After her eyes, lips and cheeks, now her windpipe seemed to be swelling too.

34

00.24 nautical time
50°27'N, 16°50'W
Speed: 21.5 knots, Wind: 18 knots
Swell: 10–15 feet
Distance from Southampton: 592 nautical miles

Martin Schwartz failed to notice the danger that approached him from behind. With his eyes closed, he was standing against the railings on the aft-port section of deck 17, the highest freely accessible outside area of the ship, allowing the powerful wind to blast his face. He could taste the salty air, but it seemed to be saturated with soporifics rather than oxygen.

With every breath he felt weaker and wearier, which may have also been down to the toothache that was still simmering on a medium flame in his upper jaw, while those PEP pills must also be discomforting him still. At least he hadn't suffered any headaches for a while now.

He took a deep breath. Tasted the salt in the air.

Did you stand here too, Nadja, and contemplate death?

Martin bent over the railings and peered seventy-five metres down.

It was a moonless night. The seething crests of the waves were lit up solely by the ship's outside headlights. He tried to imagine how it must feel to slam against the surface of the sea down below.

You can't have wanted that death, Nadja. Nobody can want that.

Martin listened to the archaic swishing of the waves, the untamed wilderness separated from the luxuries of the Western world only by a few plates of metal.

And from rapists, traitors and murderers.

He lifted his head, felt the hypnotic effect of staring into black nothingness, all of a sudden able to understand that suction described by melancholic individuals when they felt drawn to the depths of the ocean.

The ocean, magnet for depressives.

But you weren't depressive, Nadja.

He stood on the lowest strut of the railings, with one foot at first, then with both, trying to put himself in his wife's shoes for her final seconds.

She'd been afraid of the darkness. The night when she apparently jumped must have been very murky. The clouds were low; it was foggy. They might not have even been able to see the water.

Martin's thoughts turned to Timmy. As a young boy he'd pointed at the water and said, 'Ouch!' whenever they'd seen a lake, the seaside, or even a swimming pool. He'd barely been able to stand when Nadja explained to him how dangerous the water could be for a child. 'Water is very big ouch!' she'd told him time and time again, and even though every parent guide advised against using baby language wherever possible, this had worked. Timmy never lost respect for the wet element and he'd been the best swimmer in his class. How likely was it that a mother who loved children so much that she'd become a primary school teacher, would throw her own son on a foggy night into that very same 'ouch' she'd warned him about all his life?

'Right, I've done it. Here I am again,' Diesel announced, having first wanted to finish a round of his online game. 'I just had to shoot down a helicopter first.'

For a moment Martin had completely forgotten that he'd rung him. Because of the wind he was wearing an earphone and could speak hands free. The Skype connection was astonishingly clear, given that he was in the middle of the Atlantic.

'Is the doctor going to pull through?' Diesel asked. Martin had sent him a short email with the outline of recent events, together with the passenger and crew lists that Bonhoeffer had provided him with.

'I hope so,' he said.

During the summer the platform he was now standing on functioned as a naturist area. In autumn this was the loneliest place out of doors, especially at night when the temperatures dropped to single digits. This is why Martin had chosen deck 17 for his night-time excursion. He'd wanted to be alone and ponder possible connections: the death of his family, the call from Gerlinde Dobkowitz, the raped girl, the new cuts on Anouk's arm and the attack on Elena that could have just as easily got him.

When he realised his thoughts were going around in circles and he needed someone to help him, he'd called Diesel.

'We won't know more precisely for twenty-four hours,'

Martin said. 'It's not clear what triggered those damn swellings on her face. The ship's laboratory doesn't have the equipment to analyse what was in that grease on the floor of the anchor deck.'

'So who looks after the doctor if the doctor's unwell?' Diesel asked. There was a hissing in the background. Diesel had warned Martin at the beginning of their conversation that he was about to warm a plate of ravioli on his Bunsen burner. The editor-in-chief didn't think much of microwaves.

'Jacques Gérard, her assistant,' Martin said. 'We've got to bring him into the loop. Dr Beck is currently in the room next door to Anouk on the quarantine station.'

Of course there were beds free in the official ship's clinic, even some with a swing function that balanced out every wave movement, but just as in a casualty department these beds were only separated by curtains. No other passengers were in-patients yet on the *Sultan*; should that change the captain wanted to avoid at all costs a stranger getting a glimpse of the ship's doctor in this state. And so Martin had carried the crumpled body of Dr Beck from the anchor deck to Hell's Kitchen, where a weedy Frenchman with tortoiseshell glasses and a drooping mouth had immediately given Elena a huge injection of cortisone. At the very least this had removed the danger of suffocation. Now, seven hours later, the ship's doctor still looked as if she'd been in a nasty street fight, but she was stable, if unresponsive.

'Luckily your killer doesn't seem to be an expert on poison doses,' Diesel said.

Or maybe he was.

Martin doubted that the culprit had intended to kill the doctor or anyone else.

More likely he wanted to give them a demonstration of what he was capable of if they didn't put an end to their investigation.

'Whether it was a failure or planned that way, the attack tells us quite a lot about your adversary,' Diesel said after Martin had shared his thoughts with him.

'Such as?'

'First, the man who raped the girl is still onboard the ship.'

Martin shrugged. 'Which means he could be a crew member or a passenger.'

'More likely crew, I'd say, because – secondly – he's got access to the sealed-off areas.'

'Locks, especially electronic ones, are easy for any amateur hacker to break,' Martin disagreed.

'Possibly. But the key question is: who knew that you were going to visit the anchor room?'

'The captain, me...' Martin thought about it. 'And the technical manager who had to disable the lock.'

And maybe two hundred other people, depending on who Bonhoeffer's been jabbering to.

'What sort of techie is he?'

'No idea.'

'Then you ought to give him a good talking to, same with Gérard Depardieu.'

'Jacques Gérard?'

'That's the fellow. I can't imagine the assistant won't get suspicious about where his boss has been all day. Check all men who could potentially be Anouk's rapist; work out whether they're intelligent and arrogant. After all – *thirdly* – the man in question was able to predict your movements and – *fourthly* – he obviously likes playing games with his victims.'

Which means your analysis can go straight in the bin, Martin thought.

Manipulative criminals were usually of above-average intelligence and, through the art of transformation, able to give their victims and the police the runaround. You could stand face to face with them and they'd be able to disguise their real personality with virtuosity. Depressives would wear permanent grins on their faces, while sadists acted tame. Besides, anyone who kept his victims hidden for weeks and tortured them was quite clearly a psychopath who couldn't be identified by normal methods. And certainly not by amateur attempts at profiling.

'And if I were you, I'd feel free to ask whoever it is you put your finger on about their mother.'

'Why?' Martin asked, slightly confused.

'I'm not sure what it means; it's just a feeling I get in my stomach. Do you know that? Sometimes it starts bubbling and you think you're going crap your pants, but it turns out just to be wind.'

Rather than giving Martin any time to digest his revolting comparison, Diesel went straight on. 'Right then, like you asked I've been researching other double cases of people missing at sea – where it's not depressives travelling on their own with money, health or marriage problems, who in all likelihood jumped overboard of their own accord.'

'And?' Martin asked. 'What did you find out?'

'First of all, besides Timmy and Anouk, there aren't other instances anywhere in the world where children have disappeared on a cruise ship. Not even a teenager who's taken the golden plunge in the past ten years. When I think of all those balcony rails I mucked about on plastered when I was sixteen, I find that astonishing.'

It sounded as if Diesel was seeing how many ravioli he could stuff into his mouth at once, as the words that followed became ever more incomprehensible. 'What's more, no more than two people have vanished at any one time.'

Which makes the repetition of these cases on the Sultan *even more suspicious.*

'But three times, on different liners, one parent of a family has disappeared. And what's striking here is that each time it's the woman who's never been seen again. I'll send you an email with the name and routes.'

'Wait a minute.' Martin ran his hand across his shaved head, on which a wafer-thin fuzz had grown in the last few days. 'Does that mean there's a serial offender targeting women?'

'No idea. That's something you've got to find out. I don't have time to play Miss Marple for you. Now I've got to follow another trail.'

'What trail?'

'The fragrant trail of my girlfriend who's just got back from work.'

'Love to Ira,' Martin said before severing the Skype connection.

He was wondering whether to pay a final visit to Anouk and Elena before retiring to his cabin when he heard a crack behind him and at the same time felt a painful stab in his side.

Martin was about to grab his hip, astonished that such a large insect could have stung him so far from the coast, and through a leather jacket too, when he found himself on the ground, unable to do anything but watch his feet hammering convulsively against the planks of the deck. Meanwhile it felt as if molten lava were being channelled into his body through the puncture site. Thinking he was burning internally, Martin wanted to scream, but this was rendered impossible by the darkness that suddenly surrounded his head. An elastic darkness that tasted of plastic, which flapped into his mouth when he tried to breathe in air.

Now Martin felt something beneath his arms wrenching him back to his feet. The attacker must have immobilised him with a taser, before shoving a bag over his head. Nothing else could be responsible for the situation he was in.

Martin felt his head crash against something hard, he heard himself retch, thought of Anouk and her toy computer, on which he would have now written 'HELP', in capitals and double underlined. Paradoxically the taste of spaghetti carbonara, Timmy's favourite meal, was on his tongue and the smell of burned plastic in his nose; his eyes were streaming and he was thrashing around like a madman, but unfortunately without any control, and feebly.

All of a sudden something pressed against his stomach that felt like a rod.

The first wave of pain from the electrical charge subsided, which is why Martin realised his feet were losing contact with the ground.

The pressure of the rod against his stomach became more intense when he staggered forwards.

He heard someone cough and thought it was himself to begin with, but that was impossible.

I've got my mouth full of bag.

His arms began to tingle, as if they'd been in the freezer and were now gradually thawing. As Martin tried to tear the plastic from his head his hands hit the object pressing into his stomach, and at that very moment he understood what was happening to him.

The parapet! he yelled inside his head. All his mouth could do was force out an agonised grunt.

I'm hanging over the parapet!

On his stomach, bent forwards, as he could tell from the slowly increasing pressure in his head.

Paddling backwards with his arms, Martin was able to grab the handrail and brake his forwards movement. His fingers clawed into the wood. He got a splinter beneath his thumbnail and thought he was hanging upside down, the rod now pressing against his thigh.

'Ouch,' he heard his wife's voice, mingling with Timmy's, although it had been so long since he last heard his son that he barely remembered it.

'Water is very big ouch!'

He felt his own weight pulling him down, pressing against his wrists. Felt another stab, this time in the back. Felt his elbows double up.

His fingers come away.

He felt himself fall.

35

Julia touched her forehead and felt sweat. The television's LED clock glowed red in the room: 00.35. She hadn't slept for even an hour. The nightmare she'd just woken from, in which she'd seen her daughter, in sexy attire and half naked, get into a car with a strange man, had seemed far longer than that.

She wondered what had torn her from her sleep. She thought she'd heard a noise, a gusting wind at first, then a bang like a door slamming shut, but that could have been in her dream.

In all likelihood it was her full bladder stopping her from staying in bed.

She blindly felt for the switch of the night light. A dim, blueish glow helped her orient herself in the cabin.

She got up. Cold air poured in through the balcony door, which she always left open a crack at night. Having just been wrapped in a thick duvet and Egyptian cotton, now she was freezing and she wished she'd chosen flannel pyjamas to wear at night rather than a silk top with spaghetti straps.

She trudged to the bathroom as if in a daze, while the swell of the sea confused her sleepy sense of balance even further. The creak, groan and squeal of every single furniture joint, familiar by now, echoed the state she was in. She felt battered. Her mouth was dry, her head aching. She had to go to the loo and needed a sip of water, preferably flavoured with aspirin.

The soft carpet beneath her feet suddenly felt different. Julia turned on the desk lamp, bent down and spotted an envelope that had been pushed beneath the connecting door.

On the front it said 'For Mama' in Lisa's unmistakeable squiggly handwriting. At once Julia was wide awake. A horrible, familiar feeling took her breath away.

A few years ago Julia had heard muffled shouting while standing at a supermarket checkout in Schweizer Viertel. At first she thought a mother was calling for her child in the carpark, but then the shouting became more hysterical. All of a sudden two customers and a member of staff started running to the exit. As Julia exchanged a worried look with the cashier, she saw in the woman's eyes the same morbid schizophrenia she was feeling herself: torn between the desire to satisfy her own curiosity and the fear of bearing witness to something so terrible that she wished she'd never been there. The contradiction that had troubled her back then now visited her again. Only with a thousand times greater intensity.

She *had* to open the envelope. She *absolutely* wanted to find out what was in it, even though she was almost certain that a letter a daughter secretly leaves for her mother at night couldn't be good news. Just like the wailing screams of a mother in a busy car park, where suddenly no cars were moving.

She was trembling as she tore it open, cutting herself on

the sharp writing paper as she pulled it out. She opened up the page folded in the middle and read Lisa's message, which she ought not to have received for many hours, not until nine o'clock, when her alarm would ring for them to have breakfast together. The letter consisted of a single sentence, itself only three words long.

I'm sorry, Mama.

This was all Julia needed to feel sheer terror for her daughter, to which nothing else in the world could compare.

36

'Don't you want to talk about it?'

Sticking his bottom lip out defiantly and drawing his chin more tightly to his chest, Timmy shook his head.

'Aren't you having fun at school any more?'

His son shrugged.

Timmy was sitting at his little desk and scratching his knee beneath it.

'Look, I don't care about the five you got in Maths,' Martin told his son.

This was just a symptom. One of many that had manifested themselves recently, such as Timmy's unbelievable need for sleep. These days Nadja was barely able to get him out of bed in the morning, and he'd already had three lates in the register. Then he'd stopped playing tennis. Just like that. Martin and Nadja were not the sort of parents to force their child to do something, but the decision to give up from one day to the next had taken them by surprise. They thought he'd been happy and was desperate for the next season to start when he had a good chance of being selected to play for Berlin. If Timmy hadn't been ten years old, Martin would have assumed that his

*odd behaviour was down to girl trouble. But there had to
be another reason.*

'Have you got problems at school?'

*Timmy looked up. Martin saw with horror how tired his
son was. Almost as tired as he was.*

*'No. Everything's okay. No one's making me eat doners,
if that's what you mean.'*

*At Timmy's school, a 'doner' was a handful of leaves
and mud that the strongest in the class gathered up to
shove into the mouths of the weakest. Just because they
could.*

*'It's because of you. Because you're away so often, and
with Mama...' Timmy's voice cracked. Martin could see
how desperately hard he was trying not to cry in front of
his father.*

*'Hey, come here.' He went over to him, kneeled beside the
desk and put his arms around his son.*

*He could feel how much weight Timmy had lost since the
gaps between their marital arguments had become so short
they were now sustained fire.*

*'When Mama and Papa row it's got nothing to do with
you. I hope you know that.'*

Timmy nodded and sniffed.

*'It's all my fault, big man. I'm away far too often. But I
swear that's going to stop. I've just got one more job to do,
then I'm going to resign and find a job I can do from home.
How does that sound?'*

*His son freed himself from their embrace. His face was
writ with scepticism. It was evident that he didn't believe
the good news.*

'And then you'll be with me all the time?'

'Yes. I promise. I'll come back soon and then we'll be together forever.'

Martin gave Timmy a kiss on his forehead and tousled his hair.

Then he got up, went to the door and took his duffle bag that he'd already packed.

He opened the door to Timmy's room and turned around again, as something had occurred to him.

'I'm afraid I've lied to you, sweetie.'

Timmy, who hadn't moved, nodded.

His tears had vanished. With a stony face he said, 'I know, Papa. We'll never see each other again.'

Timmy swallowed. 'I'm going to die. Just like you, now.'

'Me?'

'Yes. You know. Water is ouch. And you're falling into the...'

Water.

Hard.

Black.

The pain of impact wrenched Martin from his memory-filled unconsciousness. The sensation – as if a giant were tearing his spinal column from his back – shot upwards from his coccyx to his brain. At the same time, the deeper he sank, the greater the pressure in his ears.

Martin gasped for air, but not even water would flood into his lungs. His head was still stuck inside the bag. At least his arms were no longer like lead and he could free himself from it.

Disoriented, he thrashed about with his arms and legs.

His boots hung like weights on his feet. His clothes would become a coffin if he didn't get rid of them.

There was no hope in making it back to the surface with them on.

But do I want to make it back?

While his body was instinctively being guided by a survival programme, in his head Martin was already regretting having survived the fall.

You're falling, he heard the dream voice of his son say, and thought of another Tim. *Tim Sears*, one of the few people to have survived a jump from a cruise ship. But he'd plunged twenty metres into the warm Gulf of Mexico after a booze-up. In the ice-cold Atlantic there's no way Sears would have survived seventeen hours before being rescued.

Although... it wasn't that cold. The electric shock that the killer had shot through Martin's body must have reset the synapses in his nerve centre.

He couldn't feel the thousands of pins sticking into his face. The water was cold, but not icy.

A warm current?

Martin thrashed around more frantically. Wore himself out.

Air, I need...

Air. Cold. Wet.

Suddenly the pressure in his ears was gone.

Martin's head pushed through the surface of the water. He screamed for oxygen. And anticipated the worst: to be fully conscious on the choppy ocean in the middle of a black nothingness. Unable to see any lights. Neither those of the *Sultan*, which would have sailed on without anyone raising the alarm, nor those of the stars in the cloudy sky above him.

What he didn't anticipate was the arm he knocked against. And the laughter he heard.

Then Martin was moved by a force he couldn't explain. He felt a jolt and the water beneath his back turned hard.

And as the laughter rose in volume and a woman with a British accent and shrill voice said, 'He must be as pissed as a fart,' Martin stared up at the dark, hooded figure by the railings. Up to the faceless individual on the naturist deck who'd immobilised him with a taser and shoved a bag over his head, before dragging him over to the front end of the deck and hauling him over the railings, sending him five metres down into the *Sultan*'s outdoor pool.

37

The connecting door wouldn't open. Lisa had bolted it from her side and she wasn't responding. Neither to the hammering of Julia's fists on the door, nor to her shrill, angst-ridden calls.

'Lisa, darling. Open up!'

Key, where is the sodding key?

Her own was in a small, mouse-grey wall cabinet by the door. But where was the spare key card for Lisa's cabin? Until yesterday it had been on the sideboard right next to the telephone. Now the small paper wallet with the cruise line's logo, which had held the card, was gone.

How is that possible?

Julia tossed some prospectuses and magazines from the table, lifted her handbag and a blotting pad. Nothing.

Oh, God, dear God...

Suppressing the urge to run screaming into the corridor and throw herself against Lisa's door, she picked up the phone. The hectic beeping in her ear made it even more difficult to concentrate.

Room Service

Housekeeping

Laundry

Spa...

Ten direct-dial buttons. None of them was labelled PANIC.

1310... 1310...

She'd just been about to call reception when she remembered Daniel's direct number.

After four rings he answered with a sleepy 'Hello?'

'She... she's...' Julia's voice cracked. Only now did he realise that she was crying.

'Lisa? What's happened?' The captain's voice already sounded much more awake.

'I think she... she's... going to...'

She didn't have to say any more. Daniel promised he'd be with her in a couple of minutes and hung up.

A couple of minutes?

A long time if you were having your fingernails extracted. And even longer if you were worried your own flesh and blood was about to kill herself.

Now. This very moment.

Julia couldn't wait. She yanked open the balcony door.

She was hit by damp, cold wind. She knocked her bare foot on a lounger, heard the rushing of the ocean which to her ears sounded like the roar of a wild animal throwing open its mouth to devour anything coming within range of its fangs.

'Lisa?' she screamed against the raging sea.

The balconies were separated by hard, white plastic screens. Julia leaned far over the railings to peer past the screen onto Lisa's side on the right.

Light!

The ceiling lights were on and, because the curtains behind the balcony door weren't drawn they lit up part of Lisa's balcony too.

That means she must still be in the cabin, Julia thought with relief. Until the pendulum of fear that had swung away from her for a split second came crashing back with a vengeance. To save energy, the electric circuit was broken when you took the key card from the wall cabinet as you left the room. Normally a lit-up cabin was evidence that the passenger was in. Unless they hadn't taken their key card.

Or they'd chosen another way out.

When Julia bent further forwards, she felt as if she were being struck by a wave.

Too far to have a safe grip.

The wind spat into her face. Drizzle fell in beads from her eyebrows. Rain and tears. All she could see was a blur. She blinked, she howled. Screamed.

And then she caught sight of them! The boots! *Lisa's boots.* They were lying on the floor between the bed and the TV chest, half covered by a bedspread, beneath which the rest of Lisa's body appeared to be lying.

Julia's brain switched to a primaeval instinctive mode. She was a mother. Her harassed daughter had written a farewell letter. Stolen her key card for the cabin. Locked herself in. Failed to respond to her knocking. And was lying motionless on the ground.

She didn't need to ignore the thought that Daniel would

be there any second now, as it didn't even cross her mind. *One hand on the screen, the other on the railing. One foot on the bottom rung. The other on the second...*

She climbed automatically.

She didn't realise she was risking her life until she was standing on the balcony rail and, with both hands firmly gripping the edge of the partition screen, tried to lift a foot so as to put it down on Lisa's side. And... slipped.

Her bare foot was still numb from having knocked into the lounger. She didn't feel any pain, but nor did she feel that her wet sole had lost its grip.

Suddenly the entire weight of her body pulled on her arms. She didn't have a chance. The screen needed a joint, a grip or something else to hang onto. But now hands followed feet and slipped too.

And her body fell.

Julia screamed, but the water below her roared back more loudly. The predator sensed blood when it saw Julia hanging onto the railing, right between the cabins.

In falling she'd managed to hold onto the highest rail. But it was wooden, too wide for her slim hands, and too wet to hold on for long. And Julia was too exhausted, too weak and too heavy.

Don't look down. Don't look down! she commanded herself, as if that could change anything. As if she could make the sea disappear simply by closing her eyes.

The wind wrested her like a flag. Julia closed her eyes and felt her fingers slowly slide from the round rail.

I'm sorry.

Were those the final words? Her daughter's final words in this life?

One last time she screamed the name of her daughter and heard her own as an echo.

'Julia?'

Someone was calling from a distance, but it wasn't her daughter. Lisa's voice wasn't so deep. And her grip not so firm.

'I've got you!' cried the man, whose face suddenly hovered above hers. And pulled her back up at the last moment, back onto the ship.

Back into the nightmare.

38

Tiago was lying on his bed, sweating. In his new cabin the air conditioning wasn't working, in itself a good reason why number 4337 was empty. The fact that water dripped from the shower with the velocity of honey and that the bedroom stank of cat's pee definitively made the cabin uninhabitable.

If he'd had the choice he'd have looked around for a better bolthole, but the computer at reception, which Stacy had allowed him a brief glimpse of, hadn't shown a suitable alternative. A total of 2,892 passengers. The *Sultan*'s cabins were totally booked out apart from this one renovation case where he'd been hiding for twenty hours.

What a shitty trip!

Tiago sat in bed, his back leaning against the padding of the cabin wall, using the remote control to surf the channels of the television which he'd set at whisper volume. The light was dimmed, the door joints covered with towels so that no one passing would notice the cabin was being used.

What a nightmare.

He hadn't even stolen enough to cover the fare and he was buggered if he was going to spend the rest of the passage in this sweatbox.

Tiago's stomach grumbled. He'd long since finished the pack of nuts from the minibar, but his hunger wasn't so great that he'd dared leave the room.

Outside. To the thugs, who must know who he was by now and were just lying in wait for him to show his face again.

'Were you listening in on us?'

He'd barely slept and spent most of the time in his new abode mulling over the mess he was in. He kept imagining he could hear the voice of the officer:

'You're dead.'

As dead as channel 5 of the on-board television programme, which he had alighted on, and which showed images from a selection of outside cameras. From the bridge looking forwards and to the stern. At this time they were all black. The only variety was provided by a banner running along the bottom of the screen, letting Tiago know that they were sailing at 19.4 knots with moderate swell and heading westwards.

How did I get into this mess?

This much was certain: he'd been witness to a violent episode of blackmail. Apparently a young girl was on board, a stowaway perhaps, and the cleaning lady knew of this secret which, according to the officer, was worth a lot of money. So much money that it was worth feeding chambermaids with broken glass.

Or am I just paranoid?

Quite possibly the two madmen were no longer interested in him. The more time that passed without someone who'd been witness to a violent attack showing their face, the safer they might feel.

Might. Perhaps. Possibly.

The most uncertain words in the world.

Tiago would never have made it so far if they'd been part of his lexicon. Here, in this windowless cat loo, he was safer than anywhere else on the ship. Cabin 4337 wasn't on any cleaning plan. Nobody knew that he was here.

Hopefully.

He thought about getting another drink from the minibar and stood up. The few supplies that clearly had been forgotten in the small fridge would not last for long. There were two juices left, past their best-before date, a diet cola and then spirits.

Tiago left the minibar door open and brought his small travel case into its light. An old-fashioned box with a brown snakeskin design that he'd inherited from his father. It dated from a time when suitcases with extendable handles and wheels were derided as women's gear.

Real men carry their load, was his father's view. A view that he'd passed on to him together with the suitcase. Tiago opened it. The side compartment was full of drinks. Before switching cabins he took the wise precaution of emptying the minibar in the old one. To avoid anyone noticing his disappearance and possibly reporting him missing he'd have to return to it occasionally – at least once a day – to rumple the bedclothes, chuck a few towels in the shower and leave the usual tip on the pillow.

But the question was: *when?*

Now, in the middle of the night, when the corridors were empty? Or perhaps in a few hours, around nine, during peak breakfast time, when he'd be protected by the bustle and when someone could come to his assistance in case of an attack?

At a loss, he stared at a can of tonic water as if this might be able to make the decision for him. Then his gaze fell on the envelope which he'd taken by mistake from Lisa Stiller's cabin. It was lying on top of his clothes.

Tiago picked it up.

Until now he'd held himself back. He might be a thief, but he wasn't a voyeur. He didn't stick his nose into other people's private business for fun, and as the envelope didn't have any money in it (a quick glance had established that) he wasn't interested in the contents of the letter.

On the other hand...

Might it be an important document? The envelope, after all, looked classy and highly official. What if Lisa needed the letter? If it was a doctor's certificate, for example, detailing the dosage of essential medicines?

Tiago couldn't help smiling at himself. It was more likely that the envelope contained a lottery ticket with a guaranteed win in the next draw. He searched for an excuse to satisfy his curiosity, which reminded him of one of his father's sayings: *When a woman strokes a head, sometimes she just wants to know its secrets.*

Tiago stroked the seal of the envelope, unable to resist any longer.

He pulled out the two-page letter. A whiff of lavender tickled his nostrils as he unfolded the first page.

Probably a letter to her first boyfriend, he thought, amazed by the almost artistic-looking handwriting.

The 'P' bulging out at the top, the 'l' with an elegant

sweep, leading into a razor-sharp 'a', which like the 'n' almost had living features.

The letters were beautiful. Unlike the words they formed. And the dreadful text they comprised.

'Plan,' Tiago read, and after the first sentence his eyes flew from line to line, jumped from paragraph to paragraph. When he'd reached the horrendous conclusion and glanced at the second page which listed the position of all the security cameras onboard the *Sultan*, he knew he mustn't stay one second longer in this cabin.

39

Julia was teetering. She hadn't even allowed herself ten seconds. Coughing, panting and shivering with tiredness, she'd pulled herself up on Daniel Bonhoeffer's arm. Now she had to hold onto the frame of the sliding door so as not to collapse again. Her saviour was standing beside her, his hands outstretched in case he had to intervene again.

'Where is she?' Julia rasped. She'd screamed herself hoarse and gripped the rail so tightly that her fingers were still white. Her legs were shaking; she could feel large bruises forming on her kneecaps. In the struggle she must have bloodied her legs on the ship's side as well as biting open her lips. She could taste blood.

'Where. Is. My. Daughter!'

She pointed at the empty bed.

The boots lay at her feet. There had just been pillows under the bedspread on the floor.

No body. No Lisa.

'Where?' she screamed at Daniel, but the captain merely shrugged.

'We came as quickly as possible.'

He pointed to a suntanned officer in the cabin door with wildly unkempt, blond hair, although every strand appeared to have its defined place.

'That's Veith Jesper, one of our security officers,' he introduced the man.

'I've searched everything,' the pretty boy said self-importantly. As if looking for a teenager in a thirteen-square-metre cabin demanded the training of an FBI profiler.

Veith had steel-blue eyes surrounded by light lashes that were bushier than Daniel's hairline. He looked at least ten kilos lighter than the captain and yet stronger.

'She's not here in the cabin,' he said, stating the obvious. The bathroom door was open, the connecting door was still bolted and she'd already checked beneath the bed.

'Did you bump into her?' Julia asked.

Maybe all this is just a dirty trick. Did Lisa flee when she heard me coming?

'No.' Daniel and Veith shook their heads in sync.

'And that would be hardly likely,' Veith Jesper said, pointing ruthlessly at the door.

In spite of the panic that had grown on Julia like a second head, she realised what the security officer was getting at.

The chain.

It was dangling from the doorframe. Broken. Torn out.

Daniel must have broken it when they stormed into the cabin.

Because Lisa put the chain on from the inside!

Just as she'd bolted the connecting door from her side.

'*No!*'

Julia pressed both hands over her mouth and bit her fingers. She turned back to the balcony.

There were two doors you could leave the cabin by.

And Lisa hadn't used either of them.

40

Anyone entering their home with a reasonable expectation of finding themselves alone will be scared to death if they suddenly hear a voice from the darkness. Even if that voice says calmly, 'Please don't be afraid.'

Whipping around, Martin instinctively reached for a heavy lamp on the cupboard in the foyer of his suite, firmly expecting to be attacked again. But it was just Gerlinde Dobkowitz, approaching him with a broad smile. She was wearing a long-sleeved, flowery dress with a green silk scarf that hung down to the spokes of the wheelchair she was sitting in.

'How on earth did you get in here?' Martin asked, half in astonishment, half in anger. He put the lamp back in its place. Gerlinde moved closer. The grey tyres of her wheelchair drew deep furrows in the carpet.

'*She* let me in.'

Gerlinde pointed behind her to a thin, black-haired woman who got up shyly from the chair where she'd been sitting with her knees tightly together.

She was wearing the old-fashioned chambermaid's uniform – black skirt, white apron and silly bonnet

– which was the norm for cleaners on the *Sultan*. Unlike Gerlinde, she appeared to feel completely out of place. She stood in the light of an arc lamp, swallowing with difficulty and grabbing her neck. Her eyes were fixed on the floor and she made no move to come closer or say anything. Martin guessed she was in her later twenties. She had Indian features and looked unusually pale with her natural cinnamon-coloured skin.

'That's Shahla,' Gerlinde said. 'I waited for you all day to arrange a meeting, but you haven't thought it necessary to pop in to see me for even a minute.' Gerlinde pursed her lips. She sounded like an offended grandmother scolding her grandchild for not coming to visit often enough. 'You didn't even call!'

'It's almost one in the morning,' he said.

'My official patrol time.'

'And so you thought you'd just break into my cabin?'

Martin took off his soaking wet leather jacket, which took some effort. All the vertebrae in his back, which had taken the impact of the water, seemed to be displaced. He'd be as stiff as a plank in the morning.

'I thought I'd let you in on the latest developments. Shahla was attacked.'

Welcome to the club.

'They tried to find out from her something about the girl, which means that the culprit is still...' Gerlinde hesitated and adjusted her monstrous glasses that had slipped too far down her nose. 'Hmm, am I mistaken or did the shock make you wet yourself?'

She pointed at the damp patch on the carpet between Martin's boots.

'I've been swimming,' Martin replied tersely, which seemed to be an adequate answer for the crazy cruise passenger as she didn't quiz him further about his dripping clothing. 'Okay, Frau Dobkowitz, Shahla...' he said, nodding to the nervous chambermaid. 'It's been a hard day for all of us, and I'd like to be on my own now.'

To get out of these clothes. To take a hot shower. And a bathful of ibuprofen.

He'd squandered the last of his energy shaking off the helping hand of the young British woman who'd pulled him from the pool and, amidst the laughter of the group who thought he was smashed, hobbling back to the naturist deck, where the man who'd heaved him over the railings had long since vanished.

But Martin had recovered his mobile phone. It must have dropped from his hand as he fell. The display was a little cracked, but it was still working. As he'd bent down painfully to pick it up, he saw that the Skype programme was still open. In the box for sending text messages, the attacker had left him this:

Timmy is dead. Next time you will be too.

First Elena and now him. Both of them had received their warnings. Of course it didn't worry Martin one bit, but if he didn't get at least an hour's sleep now, soon he'd no longer be able to find his own shoelace, let alone the person who evidently knew the background to his family's disappearance.

'Let's continue tomorrow morning,' he told Gerlinde, but she wasn't listening.

'Tell him what happened,' she prompted Shahla.

Shahla cleared her throat, but didn't say anything. She was clearly terrified.

'Heavens, I imagine she's completely messed up,' Gerlinde groused. Then, turning to the cleaning lady, she said, 'You were almost killed, my child, and that was just shortly after you'd seen Anouk Lamar come back from the dead in the middle of the night. For goodness' sake, Shahla, it cannot be a coincidence. If you don't want to talk to me, then talk to this man here.' She pointed at Martin. 'Tell him who it was. He's from the police; he can help you.'

Shahla stoically shook her head, her lips firmly pressed together.

Martin knew that the chambermaid was nowhere near ready to discuss the incident, especially not with a stranger. As he was not in a state at that moment to conduct a sensitive interrogation, he said. 'Why don't we speak again when we've all had some rest?'

'Fine,' Gerlinde said, which sounded like *What bloody sissies!* 'Well, then, I beg you to at least have a look at the torch, so that my journey here hasn't been a complete waste of time.'

'What torch?'

'This one here.' Gerlinde removed it from a drinks holder set into the armrest of her wheelchair. 'As you can see from the almost-empty batteries it must have been in permanent use.' She switched on the little torch and demonstrated its weak, barely visible beam.

'I would have told you about this much earlier if you hadn't dashed out of my cabin like a Dervish, just because I mentioned the name Bonhoeffer.'

Martin gave her a wary look.

'The teddy wasn't the only thing that Anouk threw in the bin.'

'Okay, fine. So she also had a torch on her when she was found?'

Besides the teddy.

Gerlinde nodded. 'So you're not as dense as you always seem.'

'Oh, yes, I am. What's it supposed to mean?'

'That there's finally some proof for my Bermuda Deck theory.'

Martin recalled the term, underlined twice, on the board in Gerlinde's study.

'What the hell is the Bermuda Deck?' he made the mistake of asking. He'd offered the old lady a perfect opportunity, which she promptly made use of.

'I'll tell you in a sec. But first a question of my own: Why is the girl being hidden?'

'If the ship is seized it'll cost them millions,' Martin said, gesturing to the door. 'Please, Frau Dobkowitz…'

'And jeopardise the deal with the Chilean investor, correct. But sooner or later the FBI's going to come rushing on board, isn't it?'

'Not if the girl vanishes again.'

'Yes, she will. Of course she'll vanish again. But not until they've got a cover-up they can present the authorities with.'

'I've heard the captain say something similar,' Martin muttered, but unfortunately not softly enough to prevent Gerlinde from hearing.

'Bonhoeffer?' Gerlinde crowed irately. 'Don't believe a word he says. He's deep in it too. Let me tell you what I think. No one's intending to kill the girl. The poor child just has to disappear as quickly as possible back to where she came from and in a way that doesn't induce the authorities to comb every nook and cranny of this boat looking for her.'

'How's that going to happen then?' Martin asked, now curious after all.

'By giving the police the wrong culprit and the wrong hiding place, to divert them from the right culprits and hiding place.'

'Why should the cruise line go to such an effort?'

Martin took off his boots in the hope that this would be a clear signal. If it didn't work he'd have to push the old woman out himself.

'Because the *Sultan*'s real business is not transporting passengers, but what happens on the Bermuda Deck. Look.'

From underneath her she pulled out a transparent sleeve with a pile of typewritten pages. 'This is precisely the topic of the book I've been working on for years with Gregor.'

Moistening her thumb, she leafed through the papers and pulled out one sheet, which she handed to Martin.

'Read the last paragraph.'

Barefooted and his shirt unbuttoned, he took the paper from her hand. Suspecting that any protest now would ultimately cost him more time, he read out loud:

'*As always, Gerlinde was astounded by the size of the member stretching out before her, but now was not the time to abandon herself to the pleasures promised by—*' He looked up, flabbergasted. With her hand she made a stroppy gesture for him to carry on. '*... his magnificent sceptre. Not before she knew whether the man who'd given her the most wonderful orgasms in her seventy-three years was really* *staying in cabin 8056, or whether he was actually working on a secret between-deck, not detailed on any floor plan, where at regular intervals passengers vanished for ever, which is why it was also—'*

'... called the Bermuda Deck,' Gerlinde said, completing Martin's reading with exaggerated menace. 'It's a novel with autobiographical elements. I've made the main character a little younger.'

But clearly no less insane.

'Come on, then, ask me.'

'What?'

'What happens on the deck.'

'To be honest, I just want to—'

'Human trafficking,' she answered herself. 'I'm not sure whether the passengers disappear unwillingly or whether they might even pay for it.'

'Pay?'

Martin laughed and went to the bathroom when she made no move to comply with his request to leave his cabin with Shahla.

'Don't roll your eyes at me, young man,' he heard her say through the closed bathroom door. 'Criminals, tax-avoiders, refugees. There are enough rich people willing to buy themselves a new life. As a detective, you know that better than anyone. And there's nowhere in the world easier to vanish into thin air than on a ship like this.'

'Are you finished?' asked Martin, who by now had completely undressed and dried himself.

Evidently not, for she kept talking through the door. 'The clients pay one or two million. Officially their disappearance is declared as suicide, which is why there are so many cases where people say, "Voluntary death? That's impossible." And the doubters are right, because unofficially the supposed victims are hiding—'

'… on the Bermuda Deck.'

'It's perfectly feasible. Perhaps it might be a state witness programme with a plastic surgeon who gives the passengers a new appearance.'

Martin shook his head and put on a dressing gown. 'How does your theory work with Anouk?'

'It's quite simple. Her mother forced her onto the programme, but the poor little thing doesn't want a new life. What she'd experienced on the Bermuda Deck must have been so dramatic that she fled. This is the truth and it's so explosive that they're even torturing witnesses to find out how much the poor chambermaid has seen.'

Martin stepped out of the bathroom. 'Okay, Frau Dobkowitz. That's enough now.'

He could see that Shahla wanted to leave, but Gerlinde blocked her way with the wheelchair.

'Just one final question and then we *will* go. Have you ever searched the internet for plans of the lower decks in the bowels of a cruise ship?'

'No.'

'There's no point. Because you won't find any. Everything below deck 3 is secret. There aren't any publicly available drawings.'

Gerlinde turned to the chambermaid. 'Shahla, tell him what the captain said to you about the girl.'

The young woman responded to the old lady like a schoolgirl might to her teacher at the start of the twentieth century.

'He said thought she was ghost,' she replied.

'But why?'

'Because suddenly there. In front of him. But no door anywhere. Then she runs away.'

'You see!' Gerlinde gave Martin a meaningful look. 'All of a sudden Anouk appears from nowhere, standing in the middle of an empty corridor – apart from me – without there being any door nearby.'

'And she was holding a torch,' he said sarcastically.

'A torch with weak batteries, correct. Because she'd spent so long looking for the secret exit.'

Martin tapped his head and then grabbed the grips of her wheelchair. 'So you're saying the cruise line would rather hand over a psychopathic serial killer to the authorities and somewhere a cabin is being prepared, which they'll later present as a dungeon, rather than run the risk of this Bermuda Deck being discovered during a search of the ship?'

'You've understood!' Gerlinde praised him, as Martin pushed her wheelchair through the room. 'Anouk should never have re-emerged. She's putting the entire multi-million-dollar business model in danger. That's the only reason the authorities haven't been informed.'

'With respect, that's a complete load of nonsense.'

'Really?' She twisted her head back while at the same time keeping her eyes on the door. 'So how do you explain...'

She stopped mid-sentence and her mouth stayed open.

'What?' Martin asked, turning around. Shahla was standing two steps behind him with her head cocked to one side, as if she were listening closely.

'What's up with the two of you all of a sudden?' he asked, but now he noticed too.

The ship. The noises.

The ever-present sonorous vibrating of the generators had gone quiet.

The *Sultan* wasn't moving any more.

41

Too late.

From a distance Tiago could see the opened cabin door, through which bright light shone into the corridor like car headlamps. He knew he hadn't arrived in time to be able to avert the catastrophe.

If only I'd opened the envelope earlier!

Holding Lisa's letter, he'd slowly approached the cabin which only yesterday he'd searched for cash. Now there was an unusual level of activity here for this time of night. Although he couldn't see or hear the people inside, their bodies cast flickering shadows in the corridor whenever they got in the way of the light streaming out of the cabin.

He stopped and wondered whether there was any point in turning himself in. Tiago knew why the door was open. What the people in there were looking for. It was in the letter, which now he put back in his pocket.

He realised that he couldn't hear engine noises any more. The ship was swaying but he felt no vibrations. Just as Tiago was touching the handrail against the wall with the tips of his fingers, *he* stepped out of the cabin.

Shit.

Tiago turned around, but not quickly enough, unfortunately. The security officer had recognised him.

'Hey!' he heard the man call out, the same man who'd tortured the chambermaid with the shard of glass, and even this *Hey!* sounded as if glass shards wouldn't suffice as a starter in the menu he had in mind for Tiago.

Tiago made the mistake of turning around. They were alone in the corridor. He and the officer, who launched into a sprint without any discernible transition.

Fucking shit.

Tiago ran back the way he'd come. The thud, thud, thud in his ear of heavy shoes on thick carpet was accompanied by the rushing of his own blood – the soundtrack of his growing fear.

He banged a shoulder against the swing door to the stairwell and pushed the lift button, but when none opened he dived down the stairs without thinking. For if he had he'd have realised that he was heading towards the ship's basement, where the surfer type knew his way around.

He ran down a wide corridor. A brass sign told him where he was.

Deck 3. Where now? Where?

The shops were closed, the atrium empty, the theatre closed. He stopped, looked around.

The casino. This is the casino. It's open round the...

Crash!

He heard the crunching of his own bones as he fell to the floor, as if hit by a demolition ball.

Tiago tried to breathe, but something was lying on his face. Something was lying on his entire body.

He felt a kick between his legs and a roller of pain

ground up his spinal cord from his stomach. Something was tugging at him, his head was hitting against it somewhere (or was it something hitting his head?) but no force in the world would have been capable of removing his hands, which he pressed against his crotch without being able to relieve even a hint of the pain that was bringing his balls to bursting point.

He became aware that his lips were touching a metal bar, a carpet trim, perhaps, but he kept his eyes closed simply because there was no single muscle in his body that wasn't contracting, not even the one controlling his eyelids. Tiago was suffering a full-body cramp. 'Got you,' the officer said. A door closed near by.

Tiago turned on his side. Saliva was seeping from his mouth. He looked around. Tried to form an image of where the officer had dragged him. The roller was still parked on his balls, juddering back and forth so as not to let the flame of pain cool down.

Tiago saw chair legs, a mattress and a door. He smelled the mucus and bogies pouring from his nose. He had to close his eyes again because he didn't want to watch himself vomiting.

But before he could throw up the peanuts that he'd most recently eaten, his jaws were forced apart and he tasted a strange metallic tang in his mouth, which wasn't blood. He'd had so many nosebleeds as a child that he was easily able to tell the difference.

He opened his eyes again. Saw the hate-filled face of the officer above his. And felt the barrel of the revolver between his lips being edged more deeply down his throat.

'Hmmmmmm,' Tiago groaned, which was supposed to

signify something like, 'Please wait. I've got something you have to take a look at.' The weapon in his mouth made it impossible to formulate a clear word.

The weapon and the pain.

Tiago feverishly sought a way out, an opportunity to get free, repel the attack, but there was no TV showdown in this killer's script.

No delay. No conversation in which he could explain his real motive, allowing his saviour to ride to the rescue in time. No respite in which the victim could free himself with cunning.

Finished. All over.

Tiago no longer had an opportunity to show this crazed officer Lisa's letter and explain to the man why it was so bloody important that the girl's mother read it. Or the captain.

The killer didn't laugh, didn't play the superior savouring his omnipotence, didn't even make him beg. He yanked the barrel from his mouth, aimed at Tiago's forehead from no further than twenty centimetres and hissed, 'You fucking paedo.'

Then he shot.

42

'Why on earth have we stopped?'

Martin confronted the captain just as he was about to leave his cabin to go up to the bridge.

After he'd finally managed to get rid of his unwelcome visitors (Shahla was visibly pleased to be able to leave, whereas Gerlinde had only wheeled out of his suite under protest) he'd briefly lain on his bed, but quickly realised that he wouldn't get any peace while the ship wasn't moving forwards.

Because the generators had been switched off, the stabilisers weren't working either. Each wave that slapped against the ship's side sounded twice as loud, and the rolling and pitching of the liner were more pronounced than ever.

'Maintenance,' Bonhoeffer said, his hand already on the handle of the door that concealed the narrow private staircase to the bridge.

Martin didn't believe a word. 'Maintenance? In the middle of the night?'

Before leaving his cabin he'd thrown on a few clothes he'd bought yesterday in the on-board shop. As he hadn't intended to stay on the *Sultan*, he'd boarded only with a change of socks and pants. Now he was wearing a grey, old-style polo shirt with the cruise line's emblem and a pair of black jeans that he had to turn up as they were much too long. But he hadn't bought himself another pair of shoes, which is why he was now standing beside the captain barefoot. It was only thanks to his quick reactions that he'd avoided being soaked through again. On the way to see Bonhoeffer he'd almost crashed into a drunk passenger staggering out of the ship's disco on deck 11, carrying a neon drink that glowed in the dark.

'I've really got my hands full at the moment,' Bonhoeffer said in an attempt to get rid of him. 'I have to...' The captain let his hand slide off the doorknob and made a weary gesture mid-sentence as if all efforts would be in vain. 'What the hell, I've got to make an announcement anyhow; you might as well hear it from me first.'

'Another Passenger 23?' Martin speculated.

Bonhoeffer nodded. The deep bags beneath his eyes looked as if they'd been made up. He pinched the bridge of his nose, which now was only covered with a thick plaster. 'Lisa Stiller, fifteen years old, from Berlin. We're showing her picture on the on-board television, just in case someone's seen her. She's a victim of cyberbullying and she left a farewell note.'

'When?' Martin turned his arm to look at the watch on his wrist, and even that movement pulled painfully on his shoulder muscles. On the other hand, his toothache and headache had both gone for the time being.

'When did she probably go overboard? Mother and daughter had dinner till 21.44, then the two of them retired to their cabins. According to the computer log Lisa last used her key card at 21.59.'

Leaving a window of three hours at most.

In that time the *Sultan* would have done a good fifty nautical miles.

'What do the security cameras say?'

'Nothing.'

Bonhoeffer raised both hands like a boxer trying to fend off a blow to the head. 'No, it's not the same as with your family,' he whispered, even though there was nobody in the vicinity. 'We have a recording of the girl spraying a camera lens with black paint. That was at 21.52. She must have known the precise location of the camera covering her balcony.'

Bonhoeffer spoke with an animation that went beyond the normal degree of professional sympathy. The captain wanted to turn away again, but Martin held him back.

'What's happening now?' he asked.

'We've stopped the ship and we're searching the sea from the bridge with floodlights and telescopes. At the same time ten of my men are combing all the public areas and we're soon going to start with the announcements. I don't hold out much hope.' He told Martin that both the door to the corridor and the partition door between Lisa's and her mother's cabin had been bolted from the inside, unlike the balcony door that had stood wide open.

'Mother and daughter were travelling without the father?'

The captain nodded.

A parent travelling alone, a child vanishing.

A pattern was gradually emerging, although Martin

couldn't tell what picture it was forming. Either he was standing too far away from the screen with the answer, or too close to it.

'Where's the mother now?' he asked Bonhoeffer.

'Julia Stiller's...' The captain looked as if he'd just had a flash of inspiration. 'Good idea,' he said excitedly and fished a key card from the breast pocket of his shirt. He nodded at the door.

'She's waiting in my cabin. Talk to her. She could use a psychologist.'

43

All of a sudden this man was in the room. Tall, shaven head, with a large nose and a face that looked as exhausted as she felt. Julia had just popped to the bathroom to splash a handful of water in her face and she'd screamed at the mirror. When she returned to the sitting room in these ridiculous disposable slippers, which housekeeping always put beside your bed, and a white dressing gown that Daniel had helped her into, the stranger was waiting for her.

'Who are you?' Her heart beat faster, and the pressure of the tears welling behind her eyes grew greater. She automatically assumed the worst. That this man with the sad look was a messenger bringing her the news she wouldn't be able to cope with.

'My name is Martin Schwartz,' he said in German with a slight Berlin accent. In normal circumstances she would have asked him which district he came from and whether they might be neighbours.

'Do you work here? Are you looking for my child? What news have you got? You are looking for Lisa, aren't you? Can you help me?'

She heard herself babble, without commas or full stops,

probably because she wanted to prevent Martin Schwartz from speaking and telling her that they'd found something.

A video of her jumping, an item of clothing in the ocean.

She wiped her nose on the sleeve of her dressing gown and noticed that the exhausted-looking man was wearing neither shoes nor socks. Curiously the sight of this came as some relief; they certainly wouldn't send a bare-footed messenger to announce that her daughter was no longer alive.

Or would they?

'Who are you?' she asked again, anxiously.

'Someone who knows exactly how you're feeling right now.'

He passed her a tissue.

'I doubt that,' she said feebly, with an introverted voice. Fresh tears filled her eyes and she turned to the terrace door, not because she was embarrassed of crying in front of a stranger, but because she couldn't stand that damn sympathy in his eyes any more. In the reflection of the dark glass she saw his lips move.

'You feel as if every single one of your thoughts has been dipped in syrup and candied with tiny pieces of broken glass,' she heard him say. 'And the more intensely you think of your child, the more these thoughts scour the open wound in your heart. At the same time there are at least two voices screaming inside your head. One is demanding to know why you weren't there when your daughter needed help, why you failed to see the signs. The other is asking reproachfully what right you think you have to sit around here while the thing that gives your life meaning has vanished into thin air. But this cacophony inside your head together with my voice and everything around you – it sounds muffled and hazy as if you're listening to it from behind a closed door. And as the worry for your daughter weighs more heavily, as heavy as all the weights in this world put together, plus an extra two thousand kilograms, a ring is circling your vital organs, throttling your lungs, squashing your stomach, thwarting your heart; and all you feel is that you'll never be able to laugh, dance, *live* again, no, you're certain that it will never be good again, and that everything which once mattered, such as a sunrise after a party, the last sentence of a good book, the smell of freshly mown grass just before a summer storm, that none of this will have the slightest meaning any more, which is why you're already thinking what might be the best way to switch off the broken-glass thoughts and the tinnitus voices in your head should this suspicion ever become terrible certainty. Am I right? Does that in any way reflect your emotional state, Frau Stiller?'

She turned around, captivated by his monologue. And by the truth of his words.

'How...?'

Seeing his tear-stained face, she didn't need to formulate her question.

'You've lost someone too,' she stated.

'Five years ago,' he said bluntly, which she could have slapped him for, as he'd just spelled out that the unbearable situation she was in could last for *years*!

I couldn't even bear it for a day, she thought, and the next thought that entered her mind was that Martin Schwartz hadn't been able to bear it either. He was standing before her, talking, breathing, weeping, but no longer living.

She closed her eyes and sobbed. In a film this would

have been the moment when she cried on the shoulder of the stranger. In real life it was the moment when the slightest contact would have made her thrash around like a rabid dog.

'If only we hadn't got on this ship,' she groaned.

If only I'd taken Tom's call five minutes earlier.

'It's the perfect place for a suicide. Daniel said that himself.'

'Daniel? Do you know the captain personally?' Martin looked at her sceptically.

'Yes, he's Lisa's godfather. He invited her.'

'Who did I invite?'

They both turned to the door, which must have opened silently. Daniel took a raincoat from the wardrobe in the corridor.

'You invited Lisa. On this trip.'

The captain shook his head in confusion. 'What gives you that idea?'

Julia stared at him as if he were an alien. 'Just stop this now – you gave her the bloody trip as a birthday present.'

'No, Julia. You're mistaken.'

'I'm *mistaken*? What's got into you, Daniel? We telephoned on her birthday. I even thanked you.'

In her turmoil she could feel the blood rushing to her cheeks. Daniel was still shaking his head, but he looked thoughtful.

'For the upgrade, I thought, yes. I moved you up from an inner cabin to two balcony cabins when I saw the booking. But that wasn't made by me; it was done normally, over the internet. In fact I recall being surprised you hadn't got in touch earlier.'

'Does that mean…'

She bit her lower lip.

'That Lisa lied to you,' Bonhoeffer said.

'Worse,' Martin chipped in from the side. He first looked Daniel in the eye, then at her, before saying. 'It means your daughter planned all this long ago.'

44

One parent. One child. A third person who pays for the cruise, but isn't on board themselves.

Just like Naomi and Anouk Lamar.

Just like Nadja and Timmy.

The parallels were becoming increasingly clear.

And even if Martin wasn't able to make sense of the clues, he knew that it couldn't be a coincidence.

'But... where... where, I mean... a trip like this is expensive, where did Lisa get the money from?' the bewildered mother said, to no one in particular.

'Was the booking made by credit card, debit card or transfer?' Martin asked.

'I'll have to look,' Bonhoeffer said, hurriedly checking his watch. Apparently he was expected back at any moment.

'Lisa doesn't have a credit card,' Julia said, before slapping both hands over her mouth.

'Oh, Christ, the video!' she gasped.

'Which video?' Martin asked.

The captain put his raincoat down on a chest of drawers and came into the sitting room, shaking his head.

'That's nonsense, Julia, and you know it.' He tried to put his arm around her, but she moved away.

'I don't know anything any more.' she screamed at him. 'Would I recognise my daughter if she were here with me now and not somewhere...' Her voice cracked.

'What video are we talking about?' Martin tried again.

'It supposedly shows her daughter prostituting herself,' Bonhoeffer explained. Then, turning to Julia, he added, 'It's a nasty fake, like everything on isharerumours. Lisa's the victim of cyberbullying, not a whore selling her body to pay for a cruise.'

There was a crackling in the ceiling and Martin heard a whisper that grew louder when the captain turned a knob on the cabin wall.

'... *we request you to switch to channel 5. Lisa Stiller was last seen yesterday at dinner in the Georgica Room. We apologise for disturbing you in the middle of the night, but we hope that with your help...*'

Bonhoeffer turned down the volume of the cabin speaker again. Having found the remote control on the glass coffee table, Martin switched on the plasma-screen television. Channel 5 was showing a close-up of a portrait taken for a biometric passport. Because you weren't allowed to smile for these photos, the young, sleep-deprived girl with her chalk-white skin and jet-black hair looked rather grumpy. At the sight of her, Julia Stiller burst into tears. And Martin's heart did a double beat.

'I know that girl,' he said, his gaze fixed on the screen. 'I saw her yesterday.'

45

'What?' Bonhoeffer and the girl's mother asked as if one person.

'You know Lisa?'

Martin nodded to Julia. 'Yes, I've seen her. Here on the ship.'

'Where?'

'Down below.'

'What do you mean *below*?' Julia shouted.

Below. Deck A. The staff area.

Martin slapped his head. A dull pain was throbbing beneath his right temple once more.

Lisa Stiller had got out of his way in the corridor yesterday morning, when Elena took him to see Anouk for the first time.

'I'm such an idiot. I ought to have twigged immediately.' *No chambermaid would be allowed to wear a piercing on this conservative ship. She didn't belong down there.*

What the hell was she looking for? And how had she gained entry to that area in the first place?

The pain spread across his forehead to the bridge of

his nose. His eyes watered as he tried to figure out how everything fitted together.

Timmy's the second one to jump, but without his teddy, because Anouk's got that and she knows my name, and she's in Hell's Kitchen, where I bump into Lisa, whose trip had been paid for by someone else...

He thought of Anouk's grandfather, of his blog (*The sharks will rip out the teeth of that whore who fucked the cancer into my son's body*) and as the pain cut like a welding burner across the back of his head to the neck, he thought of the torch, of how Anouk liked to draw, how she scratched herself. Elena's face that had blown up into a balloon alternated with the drunk man from the disco and his neon drink... and for a second he had it.

The answer.

The solution.

All of a sudden everything was clear, but then there was a crack in both ears and this time it wasn't the speaker in the ceiling, but the overflow valve in his head that had shut itself off on its own.

And while the fraught voices around Martin got quieter and quieter, the sun set in his mind's eye and the world turned black.

46

Naomi

I committed adultery. In the most despicable way possible. I had sex for money.

It began with a misunderstanding during my student days. At the time I was still called Naomi McMillan. I was working as an assistant at a trade fair stand in San Francisco marketing automobile accessories to earn a bit of money in the holidays. Us girls were accommodated in a hotel on site, and on the last day of the fair we were in high spirits as we partied at the bar. I got to know a young, good-looking rep from Chicago. We laughed, drank, one thing led to another and the following morning I woke up in his room. He'd already gone on his way, but not without leaving something for me: two hundred dollars in cash.

The man had assumed I was a prostitute.

I remember staring at that money on the bedside table for a solid hour. I was shaking, but not with anger at the guy whose surname I never knew and whose first name

*is irrelevant. No, I was shaking in disbelief at myself.
For instead of feeling thoroughly ashamed or thinking
I was cheap, deep down I found myself getting excited
at the idea of having surrendered myself to a stranger
for money. And what was even worse, I was minded to
repeat it.*

*When the next university vacation came around I
returned to the trade fair hotel. In skimpy clothes and
sexy make-up. I sat at the bar. My husband never found
out how I financed my studies.*

My expensive handbags.

The trips to Europe.

*I know that what I did isn't just bad, it's sick too.
Because although I reached the point where I had more
money than I could spend, I didn't stop even after we
got married.*

The spider had taken its time to comment on her
confession. More than ten hours, according to the clock on
the notebook.

In the meantime, while she had waited for the bucket,
squatting on the cold floor of the well, Naomi had almost
gone mad.

Her arms, which until a few days ago she'd feared were
infected with tapeworm, were no longer itching, nor her
throat, beneath the skin of which the parasite had wriggled
so vigorously, especially at night, when she kept being
woken up.

Although the burning and throbbing had gone, she did
feel a strong pressure behind her left eye and it was perfectly
plain what that meant.

How do you scratch behind your eyeball?

Naomi wished she had stronger fingernails that didn't keep breaking. Ideally as long and pointed as a knife, then she'd be able to put an end to all this at once.

Without the horrific question-and-answer game.

While she'd been waiting for the answer the engines had stopped. Abruptly. Just like that. Were they in a port? But if so, why was she being rocked from side to side?

After a very, very long time the gap above her head finally opened and from the darkness the bucket with the notebook was lowered down to her. Together with the punishment, for the spider clearly wasn't satisfied with her answer.

'*Sex for money? A really dirty secret, Professor.*' These were the words typed directly below her last entry. '*But not what I wanted to hear.*' And then: '*Think about it again. I know you can. What's the worst thing you've ever done?*'

While Naomi read the comment about her confession a small dot moved on the screen. Then another. And another.

With a scream she recoiled from the computer, but the dots had already started to spread out over her arm and wouldn't readily be removed from her skin, filthy clothes or hair.

Cimex lectularius.

'Who are you?' she howled in disgust, while trying in desperation to hit and shake the bedbugs away, even though as a biologist she knew how ridiculous that was. The bloodsuckers could survive forty days without food and in the most intense cold. The well would have to be heated to fifty-five degrees for three days. Even after that you couldn't be certain that one of the critters wouldn't survive on her body.

Screaming, she started scratching herself again.

'*Why are you doing this to me?*' she typed into the notebook and sent the bucket up again. '*WHO ARE YOU???*'

This time the answer came back with surprising rapidity. Just a few minutes later Naomi was able to open the notebook again. In the bluish, fluorescent light of the screen she read:

The truth is, you've no right to ask me questions. But as my answer will put you on the right track and bring all of this to a swifter conclusion, I won't be so petty. You won't find out my name. But if I were a character from a fairy tale, my story would begin like this: 'Once upon a time there was a beautiful little bundle of joy. Although he had no brothers or sisters, he did have a mother who loved him more than anything else in the world. And a strict father who always gave him funny looks when they were alone together.' Well, are you bored yet? Don't worry, there is a point to my story, which I bet you haven't been expecting...

47

Martin woke with a persistent ringing in his ears, which sounded as if a telephone had come off the hook nearby. To begin with he didn't know where he was. The bed he was lying on, the smell of his pillow, the entire room was unfamiliar, even though he could barely make out anything of his surroundings. It was dark. The little light there was in the room was seeping through the narrow slit where the two curtains met.

As he sat up the first memories washed back into his consciousness, bringing with them a touch of queasiness.

Timmy. Anouk. The *Sultan.*

Rolling onto his side he felt blindly for the bedside light, but then waited for a while before switching it on for fear that the light might burn his retina.

With each movement he made, not only did his head feel as if his brain had the consistency of a fried egg, but his entire body was jammed in a corset of pain. And yet he seemed to recall that it had been even worse yesterday, when he

… was talking to that woman. The mother, yes.

Slowly everything came back to him.

The attack on the naturist deck, his fall into the pool, Gerlinde's Bermuda Deck theory, Julia, her daughter Lisa, the victim of cyberbullying who'd apparently thrown herself overboard because of a sex video... him fainting.

His boss had warned him. Christ, they'd all advised him against injecting antibodies.

Or coming aboard this ship.

Martin plucked up courage to turn on the light. The flash that shook through him wasn't as unpleasant as he'd feared.

As he felt for his mobile he asked himself two questions. First, how had he got into his suite? And second, how could the cordless telephone be sitting properly in the charger, inactive and with a dark display, when he could hear the dialling tone loud and clear?

He stuck fingers into both his ears and the sound didn't get any quieter.

Great. This is what it must feel like when you begin the day as an alcoholic.

Pounding skull, phantom noises, gaps in the memory and a bladder as full as a train after a local derby.

He grabbed the telephone, stood up and shuffled to the bathroom. It felt like it took him ten minutes to get there, and indeed he had to sit down on the bed once for a rest, otherwise he'd have collapsed halfway.

He left the bathroom light off as he wanted to spare himself the sight of his face in the mirror. He also found the loo in the dark.

He lifted the lid, pulled down his boxer shorts (*who undressed me?*), and dialled Diesel's mobile number as he sat down. It took an age for him to answer.

'Hello?'

'It's me.'

'Do I know you? I mean, you could easily be Martin Schwartz if you didn't sound so fucking awful.'

'What's the time?'

'You're calling me because you want to know the time? Jesus, you *must* be bored.' Diesel laughed and said, 'At the next stroke it will be two-oh-eight p.m. precisely.' Then he burped.

Two p.m.! Taking into account the time difference it was now noon on the Atlantic. He'd slept for at least ten hours.

'But I'm glad you've rung. Have you checked your emails?'

'No.'

'You ought to. I've been through the staff and passenger lists your buddy Bonhoeffer gave you.'

Martin started to relieve himself while Diesel went on talking.

'We've got almost six hundred matches for guests and employees who were on board both the day that Nadja and Timmy vanished, as well as five years later when Anouk and her mother were officially declared missing.'

'How many of those are potential rapists?'

'For a start, 338 employees. From the carpenter and the cook to the captain, all of them are on there. That's assuming the list is complete. And here we have the biggest problem.'

'Are you saying that Bonhoeffer didn't give me the complete documents?' he asked.

'I'm saying he *can't* have given you any complete documents. To save money most cruise lines engage foreign low-wage firms as subcontractors. And for tax reasons these subcontractors sometimes invent names or omit them, or even put down too many to get extra money. It's a hopeless mess.'

Martin thought hard. This meant the staff and passenger lists were a dead end. 'What about passengers?' he asked all the same. 'Do we have any repeat guests?'

'Yes, of course. People who go on cruises are repeat offenders. Although the selection here is smaller. If you filter the eighty-seven passengers who were on board both five years ago and two months ago, removing all lone women travellers and pensioners on their last legs, you're left with thirteen men as possible rapists. And now, hold on tight.'

Diesel paused.

'What?'

'One of them is called Peter Pax.'

My cover name?

'That's impossible,' Martin rasped.

'Well, what do you want me to say, buddy?' Martin could practically hear Diesel shrug.

'If you'd got your seahorse badge while at primary school, I'd advise you now to swim back home. I think someone's trying to pin something on you.'

Yes, and I know who it is.

Martin took hold of the loo paper. 'His name begins with Yegor and ends with Kalinin.'

'The ship owner?'

'The captain might be in on it too, but I'm not so sure, he's such a weed. Can you find out what cabin this Pax is supposed to have been in?'

Unlike with normal hotels, where it was all down to the benevolence of the receptionist whether you got a sticky cell next to the underground car park or a light-filled sanctuary, when booking cruises you could usually choose your own cabin number.

'Yes, I've got it somewhere. Hang on a mo, I'll check.'

Martin stood up and flushed.

'Oh, no, please. Please don't tell me that while talking to me you've been doing what it sounds like,' Diesel begged in disgust.

Martin didn't respond to this, but asked him to check another person.

'Who?'

'Lisa Stiller, fifteen years old, from Berlin. Her mother's called Julia and both are on the current passenger list. Please find out who paid for the cruise and where it was booked. And have a look for a video on' – he had to rack his brains until he remembered the name of the portal that Bonhoeffer had told him about yesterday – 'on isharerumours or something similar. It's tagged with the name Lisa Stiller.'

'What's the point of that?'

'Lisa's fifteen years old and has been missing since yesterday. This video is supposedly the reason for her suicide.'

Diesel sighed. 'Another child? Bloody hell, what's going on?'

'It's all connected. For example, I saw Lisa yesterday when I was on the way to Anouk on' – Martin paused – 'on the lower deck where actually she shouldn't...' he muttered, stopping mid-sentence.

What is that?

'Hello? Hey there? Have you jumped too now?' he heard Diesel call out.

'Shut up for a moment.'

The dialling tone inside his head had quietened down, but now there was another noise vexing him. A whole bundle of noises! They must have been there the whole time; it's just that he'd only become aware of them now.

Placing his hand on the basin, Martin could feel the vibrations. He teetered out of the bathroom, oriented himself by the slit of light in the curtains, went over to it and then opened the curtains as well as the door to his terrace. Cold, clear air poured into the cabin.

What he saw corresponded with the creaking, scraping, droning, vibrating and humming he heard around him.

And with the rocking of the ship.

'We're moving,' he said, looking in disbelief at the foam-crested mountains of waves before him. The misty grey horizon had shunted so close to the ship that you could stretch your arm out to it.

'Obviously you're moving. I mean, it is a *cruise*, isn't it?' Diesel said, who couldn't know that the captain had stopped the *Sultan* yesterday night for a man-overboard manoeuvre. But now the engines were running again, which could mean one of two things. Either they'd found Lisa. Or given up altogether.

'Found you!' Diesel exclaimed, and for a fraction of a second Martin thought he was actually talking about the girl, but of course he meant Peter Pax's cabin number. 'He had the same one on both trips,' he said. 'Perhaps you ought to pay 2186 a visit.'

48

Nautical time: 12.33
50°27' N, 17°59' W
Speed: 23.4 knots, *wind:* 30 knots
Sea swell: 10 feet
Distance from Southampton: 630 nautical miles

'Number 2186?'

The captain was massaging the back of his neck. The plaster on his nose was smaller and the rings around his eyes darker. If exhaustion could be traded on the stock market, Bonhoeffer would be one of the wealthiest men on the planet. His eyes had shrunk to the size of a five-cent coin and they didn't seem to be helping much in the search for the right key card.

'2186,' Martin confirmed, surprised that they were looking for a cabin with this number on deck 3. They were outside a greyish-ginger door with no number in a side corridor that branched off from the entrance to the atrium. Bonhoeffer was now making his third attempt to slide a key card through the reader. He was holding a selection, the size of bank cards in a variety of colours, all of which had a hole in the upper right-hand corner and were threaded on a fine metal chain.

'Don't you have something like a skeleton key?' Martin asked.

'Not for the nest.'

'The nest?'

'As you can see, this isn't a passenger cabin any more,' Bonhoeffer said, his eyes on the missing number on the door. If you stood up close you could see the residue of glue with which it had originally been stuck.

'So what is it?' Martin asked.

'A relic. Something like the *Sultan*'s appendix. After all, this lady is eight years old now and no longer the youngest in the industry. When she was launched, the expectation was that the demand for inner cabins would rise, but that was a mistake. Most people want a suite, or at least a cabin with a balcony. At a pinch they'll take something overlooking the atrium. And nobody wants to be just above the waterline. That's why six years ago we converted the ten lowest inner cabins on deck 3 into storerooms and offices.'

'And a *nest*?' Martin asked. Bonhoeffer nodded.

'The number's an in-joke, a play on numbers. When 2 become *1* and want a private *d8*, they can come here to have *6*.'

He couldn't help yawning and didn't bother to put his hand in front of his mouth.

'It's forbidden for employees to have sex in their own cabins, and it's not very practical either because most have to share with a colleague. But the crew have needs, especially on trips around the world. Of course the nest doesn't exist officially, but we turn a blind eye when during their months at sea employees use this as a refuge for their tête-à-têtes, so long as they're discreet about it.'

Bonhoeffer yawned again, a bigger one this time.

'You ought to lie down. Or will your bad conscience prevent you from sleeping?' Martin asked sarcastically.

Bonhoeffer had told him over the phone what had happened in the night. After his seizure-like collapse, the captain got Elena's assistant doctor to bring him back to his room, where he'd slept right through an eight-hour search operation that, 'as expected', to use Bonhoeffer's words, had failed to bring any results.

When, following the security call, the coastal station began to coordinate measures and a Royal Navy ship from the British fleet, on manoeuvres in the area, had arrived, there was no longer any reason for the *Sultan* to hang around in the middle of the ocean. *Or to incur the wrath of the almost three thousand passengers still alive, who could saddle the owners with compensation demands for unreasonable delay.*

Julia Stiller had suffered a nervous breakdown when the main engine started into life again and had been catapulted into a dreamless sleep by a sedative, from which she would awaken at some point in the captain's cabin. Hundreds of nautical miles from her daughter. She'd actually wanted to change onto the navy vessel, but had been refused entry as an 'unauthorised person'.

'I don't have a bad conscience,' the captain protested. 'We paused the journey to—'

'For eight hours?' Martin interrupted him. 'Are you saying a child's life isn't worth any more than that?' He laughed cynically.

Bonhoeffer took a deep breath, then exhaled noisily through puckered lips. It sounded like air escaping from a shrivelled balloon. Furious, he said, 'A farewell letter, cyberbullying as a motive, no traces of violence or any other crime in the cabin, and even though no one could survive out there for an hour without a life vest the search goes on till the following morning. What do you expect?'

'That for once you succeed in arriving at the destination with all your passengers.'

'I could just as easily say you ought to have taken better care of your family. Have you ever googled suicide? There are forums where half the world exchanges ideas on the most effective ways of topping yourself. And do you know what's right up there? Exactly. Cruises. Those twenty-three passengers per year who take a leap into the blue shelf. If every depressive with internet access decides to do train drivers a favour and book a cruise rather than throw themselves on the track, then don't fucking well blame me!'

Now worked up, he slashed one of the cards at random through the slot and happened to get the right one. There was a click and a green light flashed.

'I'm not responsible for this insanity,' he barked, pushing on the handle. The door sprang open and they were immediately met by an unpleasant metallic smell.

'Nor for this either?' Martin asked. He pointed at the floor of the cabin.

They both stared speechlessly at the man at their feet, who'd been shot in the head.

49

They bolted the door behind them and Martin ordered the captain not to move or touch a thing.

The body was sitting on the floor, with legs outstretched and back leaning up against an unmade single bed. The head was bent at the neck and the lifeless eyes were staring up at the dusty cabin ceiling. In the overhead light the pillow beneath his head had a wet shimmer.

Judging by the amount of blood the exit wound must be far larger than the small hole in the forehead above the right eye.

'Who is that?' said Martin, who'd now switched to crime scene mode. Experience had taught him that first impressions were the most important ones. So he scanned the surroundings, paying particular attention to anything out of the ordinary.

Such as an inverted cross on a wall, a shattered mirror below a cupboard or an apartment so tidy that it reveals the criminal's intention to be as inconspicuous as possible.

The oddities weren't always apparent; often, clues to the circumstances surrounding the crime, motives, victims and suspects were located subtly. Like the piece of metal on the carpet by the fitted cupboard in this cabin.

Martin bent down to the hairclip. It was small, colourful and cheap. The sort of thing you might see on a doll.

Or a young girl.

'Good God, that's…' Behind him Bonhoeffer was staring at the corpse, his eyes as wide as saucers. Clearly the shock at what they'd found was preventing him from uttering the dead man's name.

'Who?' Martin asked harshly. Bonhoeffer swallowed.

'His name is Veith Jesper,' he said, pointing at the man in the blood-soaked uniform. 'One of my security officers.'

50

'Will you ever interrupt my work with a piece of good news, Bonnie?'

Yegor briefly put his phone down, threw Ikarus off the bed and got up. In truth he hadn't been working, but enjoying a snooze after some disappointing sex with his wife. But he'd rather run up and down the promenade deck naked with a flag sicking out of his arse than let his captain in on the fact that he took the occasional siesta.

'Shot in the head?' he asked, the mobile back to his ear.

Sleepily, his wife turned over in the bed and farted. Bloody hell, that was even more disgusting than the mess his captain was describing.

On his way to the bathroom, Yegor wondered whether there was any way of sweeping the matter under the carpet, but realised it was doubtful. So he said, 'Leave everything as it is.' While only half listening to Bonhoeffer he breathed into his hand and pulled a face.

Half an hour's siesta and I've got breath like an Albanian sewage works.

'Of course we're going to continue,' he interrupted the captain's nervous torrent of words.

Are there only idiots working for me?

'We're almost halfway; what point would there be in turning around now? Don't touch anything in that room, and notify the authorities.'

Yegor flipped open the loo seat and undid the button fly on his pyjamas. 'And muster all those PR luvvies on my payroll. The losers can finally work for their money. I don't want to read reports like "Horror cruise on the *Sultan* – one dead and one missing" or anything similar.'

Although it would be almost impossible to avoid the headlines, of course. And that was partly his fault, as Yegor knew.

It took a while for the first drops to come. In the past his urethra had burned when he'd been with the wrong sort of women. The feeling he had now reminded him that his check-up was long overdue.

Getting old is a whore, Yegor thought, peering through the open bathroom door into the semi-darkness of the bedroom. His wife's feet were sticking out from under the duvet. Even from this distance he could see her crushed stiletto toes. Revolting.

Wait. What did this bird-brain of a captain just suggest?

'Stop? Again?' In his anger the ship owner found it difficult to avoid peeing on the floor. Ikarus, startled by his master's outburst, padded into the bathroom with his ears pricked up.

'Our Chilean moneybags might have put *one* suicide down to bad luck. He's a superstitious Catholic. The worst sort of person. If another body turns up, the jerk will see it as a bad omen and put his chequebook away quicker than you can say "prison". I don't mind how you do it, just draw the fucking thing out until the contract's been signed!'

Yegor hung up, had a shake and flushed. From the bedroom he could hear his wife's drowsy voice, but he couldn't care less what she was saying.

He was annoyed with himself. He'd intended to stay calm. People who shouted didn't have a grip on themselves or their lives. But since they'd left Hamburg, *no, since the approach into Oslo,* when that tongue-tied Anouk suddenly reappeared from nowhere, he'd had one shit-filled profiterole after another hurled at him.

Not bothering to wash his hands, Yegor made his way back to bed. He had to get past Ikarus, who gave him a look of irritation. He bent down to his dog and tickled the terrier's neck.

'Yes, I know. It's Daddy's own fault. But do you know what, Ikarus? I just can't bear being blackmailed.' The dog put its head to one side as if it understood every word. Yegor smiled and poked his wet nose.

'Veith was a waste of space,' he whispered so his wife, now awake, couldn't hear him. 'I must have given him my special revolver.' *The one that shoots backwards if you turn the lever.* Which is precisely what he'd done before handing the weapon to that violence-hungry fool. It was a present from a comrade. Custom made. A joke amongst old friends from the Foreign Legion. Not traceable back to him.

'Do you understand, Ikarus?' The dog panted and Yegor took that as a *yes.*

Yegor turned off the bathroom light – the only one that had been on – and got back into bed. His wife wanted to stroke his arm, but he pushed her hand away.

What a shame that Veith isn't a Jap, he thought. *They commit hara-kiri for all manner of crap. Code of honour and so on.*

They might have been able to make it appear as if the security officer couldn't deal with the shame of having failed to find that suicide brat.

But who'd believe that of a clog-wearer?

Yegor yawned. There was nothing worse than being wrenched from the middle your siesta. He was dog tired. For a while he pondered whether it had been a mistake to let Veith eliminate himself. But the man himself was to blame. What kind of crusade did he have against that... *Tiamo... Tigo...?*

Yegor couldn't recall the name. And ultimately he didn't care. As his eyes gradually closed, he merely wondered where that Argentinian Lothario was now, after probably – almost certainly – staring death in the face not long ago.

51

Daniel hung up, taken aback by the ship owner's reaction. Kalinin had sounded really tired at first, as if he'd just been woken from sleep, even though it was still broad daylight outside. Then Yegor didn't seem surprised in the slightest, as if he'd been waiting for the news that one of his officers had been shot dead. It was only during his angry outburst at the end of their conversation that he'd sounded normal again.

'Who knows about this love nest here?' Schwartz asked, shaking a locked fitted cupboard beside the bed by the handle. The presence of a corpse and the accompanying stench seemed to bother the investigator far less than it did the captain.

Daniel looked at the bolted cabin door. He just wanted to get away from this stinking, windowless hole as quickly as possible.

'Almost two thousand people,' he replied. 'All the employees plus a handful of passengers who engage in a little holiday flirt with a member of staff.'

And don't want to play out their adventure in their own cabin because there's usually a cuckolded partner waiting for them there.

'And do you have an idea of who uses this nest.' There was a crack and Martin had the metal handle in his hand.

Bonhoeffer massaged his stiff neck. 'No. As I said, this room doesn't exist officially. Which means you can't reserve the nest either. There's no visitor rota or anything like that.'

'But someone must have coordinated the allocation and handover of the key?'

'Yes, and I'll give you three guesses who the management suspect.' Without looking at it, Bonhoeffer pointed to the corpse at their feet. The ship pitched heavily and he felt terribly sick. His stomach contracted like a bagpipe, squeezing its acidic contents back up his gullet.

He suggested they continue their conversation elsewhere, but the detective was using the metal handle as a lever to force open the cupboard.

There was a crack and the plywood door was left hanging from one hinge. Soon afterwards it had been ripped off altogether.

So much for Yegor's order to leave everything as it was.

'Well, well, what do we have here?' Schwartz muttered as he took a little plastic case from the cupboard.

It was slightly larger than a piece of hand luggage, with lots of stickers on the front and back, some badly effaced. Most of them were flags, symbols or maps of places this case had probably journeyed to. The colour of the case (pink) and the palm-sized sticker of a boyband on one of the side pockets suggested that its owner was young and female.

'Wouldn't you rather we looked at this in my cabin?' Daniel said, barely able to hold back whatever it was trying to find its way out of his stomach. But Schwartz ignored him. With rapid hand movements he opened the zip and flapped the lid to one side.

'Anouk,' he said. Daniel wasn't sure whether this was a hunch or a certainty. He saw typical girls' clothes, tidily packed, filling every centimetre of the case. Skirts, underwear, tights and – right on top of the pile – a drawing pad and pencil case.

But that's absurd, he thought.

'Anouk can't have been hiding here the whole time.'

Schwartz shook his bald head. 'I can't imagine it either. Unless the staff haven't used this love nest for a couple of months.'

My arse.

It was only three weeks ago that Daniel's first officer had been bragging about how he'd had it off with a cook here. He himself had never had any truck with the nest, but he'd certainly have got wind of the uproar there'd have been if cabin 2186 had been out of action for any length of time.

'What's that?' Daniel asked, pointing at the back of the case lid. He might have been mistaken, but in the inside netting wasn't that a…

'A torch,' Schwartz said, pulling it out.

So it was.

The thing was narrow, with a light-blue shiny metallic casing. And it looked exactly the same as the one they'd found on Anouk.

Schwartz turned the switch at the end of the handle and the weak beam on this torch was hard to see with the naked eye too.

'A dim light with empty batteries?' Daniel asked. His bafflement at least mitigated the feeling of sickness. And the confusion only grew when Schwartz found another torch, wrapped up in a sock, in a side compartment. This one didn't work any better either.

What does that mean?

An abducted girl, two broken torches?

Daniel couldn't make any sense of the discovery. Unlike Schwartz. All of a sudden he grabbed the pencil case and rummaged inside. When he seemed to have found what he was looking for, Schwartz slapped his forehead like someone who's overlooked something obvious. Then he turned the switch of the torch again, and yet again, and each time he gave a soft sigh, even though Daniel couldn't notice the slightest difference.

No bright light.

Nothing that might give him a flash of inspiration.

'What have you found?' he asked the detective.

Schwartz clenched the torch handle tightly, now holding it like a baton just before the transfer to the next runner.

'I know what's going on,' he said flatly. The detective strode past Bonhoeffer, climbed over the body and yanked open the cabin door.

52

Naomi

... IF I could, I'd tuern back the clock, or at least apologies for what I did. But I don[t think I'lll ever get the ppportunity, wikll I?

She'd blindly written the last lines, riddled with typos, looking at the screen as if through a wall of water, the letters blurring in the fog of tears, with clammy fingers that tried to overtake each other as she typed, faster and faster, because Naomi Lamar would have bitten a chunk of flesh from her body out of disgust at herself, if she'd had even a second while she was writing to consider *what* she'd done. What she'd just confessed to the spider. Which was: *the worst thing*.

She hadn't *remembered* it again, because that would have meant having to forget it first. Deep down she'd always known what the spider wanted to hear. She just hadn't been capable of writing it down. *Thinking* about it was bad enough. But thoughts could be suppressed, by pain, hunger or cold, for example. Things she'd had in spades over the last few weeks.

To know it was written down, even the process itself of writing it, was something else entirely.

To see the wickedness in black on white, her own shame before her very eyes, was much worse than merely thinking about it, and the spider knew this.

That's the reason, that's the only reason I've had to type into this wretched computer here at the bottom of the well.

Without correcting her spelling (which, for some reason she couldn't even explain to herself, Naomi had done previously when typing the invalid confessions – it was probably just force of habit; she'd always stressed to Anouk the importance of good spelling) she'd tugged on the rope. She was desperate to tie it around her neck rather than on the bucket the notebook was placed in. Although with her on the end of the rope she doubted it would be yanked up.

Ever since the computer had vanished upwards into the darkness above her head, she'd started scratching again.

Her arms, neck, skull.

Naomi was sure she'd given the spider what it wanted.

Hunger, thirst, the tapeworm, the bedbugs; there was a point to all those punishments, she understood that now.

She had no idea how the spider had got to the bottom of her secret. On a cruise ship of all places.

But if you looked at it in the cold light of day, there was a point to everything now.

It's just that I'll never get to look at anything in the cold light of day again.

Naomi felt a menacing thought brewing inside her and started to hum. She knew she'd be allowed to die soon.

Not because I'm partly guilty for the death of my best friend.

She opened her mouth.

Not because I had sex for money.

Her bright, brittle humming turned into a throaty sound, grew...

With unknown men. Lots of men.

... into a scream, which got louder and louder until, multiplied by the echoes deep down inside the well, finally managed to...

But because three years ago I...

drown out in her head...

I started to...

... the thoughts of the worst thing she'd ever done.

... because I...

A scream so loud and stifling that for a while all she felt was the desire to see her lovely little girl just one more time before, finally and hopefully, her life came to a rapid end.

53

Anouk. Torch. Pencils. Drawing.

Single-word thoughts made a racket in Martin's head, knocking him violently from the inside against the bell of his skull and producing a muffled, droning sound, which like discordant film music accompanied those images that were currently playing in his mind's eye. Images in which he recalled his meetings with Anouk: the girl in her nightshirt, sitting silently and stoically on the bed, her arms a whetstone for her fingernails.

Martin thought about how Gerlinde had told him of the torch and remembered on his way to the captain barging into the disco-goer with his luminous drink. All of a sudden, seemingly unconnected scraps of thoughts were piecing together.

For this – as Martin assumed – final descent to Hell's Kitchen, Bonhoeffer had let him go alone, although to begin with he'd raced after him and even blocked his way by the entrance to the staff deck.

'What have you discovered?' he'd asked.

Martin was just about to explain his suspicions to Bonhoeffer when the captain's mobile rang.

Julia Stiller, the mother of the missing girl, had woken up in his cabin and was demanding to see Bonhoeffer. To be precise, she was *screaming* at him.

'YOU FUCKING BASTARD! WHERE ARE YOU? HOW CAN YOU DO THIS TO ME?'

Martin had been able to hear every word, even though Bonhoeffer had pressed the phone tightly to his ear.

The captain had promised to return as quickly as possible once he'd seen to Julia, but right now Martin was standing alone outside Anouk's room. His fingers were sweating as he swiped the key card. He entered without knocking.

And stood in an empty cabin.

For a moment he was unable to formulate a clear thought. He gazed hypnotically at the abandoned bed, as if Anouk would materialise before his eyes if he stared long enough at the crumpled sheet.

*How can that be? Anouk doesn't have a key. She can't get **out** of here!*

Martin's bewilderment lasted little more than a second, before he was freed from his paralysis by the noise of the loo flushing. The bathroom door on his right opened and Anouk shuffled out. She was wearing a fresh nightshirt and must have taken off her tights. Her feet were bare. When she saw Martin, she retreated to the bathroom in fright.

'Stop,' Martin called, jamming his foot in the door just before Anouk could slam it in his face. 'Don't be scared; I'm not going to hurt you.'

He yanked the door open again. Anouk ducked, wrapped both arms around her head and stepped backwards until she knocked against the toilet. She sat on it.

'You do remember who I am, don't you?'

He put the key card into the breast pocket of his polo shirt and waited until Anouk's breathing started to calm down. It took her a while to understand that he wasn't going to touch her. When she felt brave enough to lower her elbows and look him straight in the eye he gave her a smile. Or at least he tried to pull the corners of his mouth into the appropriate position. Since he'd entered Hell's Kitchen, his headaches had returned. A dull pressure behind the eyes that would soon turn into a tugging.

'Watch me, I'm just going to stand here,' he said, raising both hands. 'May I ask a favour if I promise not to move and not come too close?'

No nod. No twitch of the eyebrows. No reaction. Anouk remained silent. And yet, in spite of the sick pallor in her face and terrified body language, Martin thought he could see signs of mental recovery in the girl.

Her gaze was no longer lifeless, but expectant, furtive. She didn't let him out of her sight for a second, unlike yesterday when she'd spent most of the time looking straight through him. And there was further evidence that she'd managed to climb a few rungs of the ladder out of her emotional cellar: she was neither scratching nor sucking her thumb, even though she was in a high state of agitation.

Seeing the plasters with animal figures that held the white gauze bandages in position, Martin guessed that Elena's assistant had changed the girl's dressings.

'Don't worry, we don't have to talk,' he said in a reassuring tone.

If he was right he'd soon find out everything he wanted to know from her, without the traumatised girl having to open her mouth even once.

'I only came to give you something I bet you've been missing for quite a while.'

He showed her the torch.

The effect was striking. Anouk reacted in a split second. She leaped up from the loo seat and grabbed Martin's hand. She was about to snatch the torch from him, but he was too quick and pulled it away just in time.

'You have to tell me the truth first,' he demanded. He felt a lump in his throat, for his words stirred a memory of Timmy and how he used to blackmail him.

'Can I go to tennis, Papa?'

'You have to tidy your room first.'

Often Timmy had rebelled, throwing himself on the floor, crying and defiantly ignoring the 'tidying for playing' deal.

Anouk was obstinate too. She wanted the torch. But she wasn't yet ready to trust him.

She stared at him grimly with a deep frown.

'Okay, I'm going to tell you what happened,' Martin said. 'I think you know where your mother is. You even drew the place for us, on your toy computer, although we didn't understand your clue and we don't know where this shaft is. But you know the way. You marked it with the UV pens that I found in your pencil case. Unfortunately, these marks can't be seen with normal light...'

When he made the mistake of briefly glancing up at the overhead light, he was suddenly struck by a flash. The adverts claim that there are thirty-seven types of headache that can be treated with non-prescription medicines. Clearly this wasn't one of them. It felt as if someone were sticking very thin, red-hot needles from the inside of his head through his eyes to the other side of the pupils. Martin even thought he could feel the points of the emerging needles, bloodily tearing the insides of his lids whenever he blinked.

Leaning against the door, watched mistrustfully by Anouk, who was standing as if rooted to the basin, he waited until the pain had subsided to a tolerable level. Then he turned off the light.

The darkness was a relief. His headache faded to a pale shadow of itself. The attack died away as quickly as it had come.

He briefly allowed his eyes to get used to the almost complete darkness. Then he turned on the torch. And the beam that was barely visible in normal light suddenly filled the entire room, making the white bathroom tiles fluoresce, as well as Anouk's nightshirt, teeth and fingernails.

Pens. Drawing. Torch.

'I knew it,' Martin said to himself. There was no hint of triumph in his voice when his theory proved correct. Anouk's eyes shone spookily in the black light. She looked like a ghost without lips from a horror story.

The torch he was aiming at the girl wasn't weak, but a UV lamp shining light at a frequency barely visible to the naked eye. He'd once used a similar model on an operation.

But where did Anouk get these torches from?

A question he had to postpone, for now there were more important things to clear up. 'It showed you the way to your mother, didn't it?'

When Anouk failed to react, he asked insistently, 'Where was she taken to?'

Anouk's response pulled the carpet from under his feet again. For, just as at their first meeting, she whispered his name again.

'Martin.'

'I don't understand what you're trying to tell me,' he wanted to reply, wondering why he couldn't hear his own voice even though his lips were moving.

Then he wondered why he wasn't fainting.

The pain behind his eyes had returned, this time with a run-up and twice the momentum.

Martin sank to the floor and felt it getting worse. Anouk had stepped over him and turned the overhead light on again. He felt as if a ghost had swapped the bathroom light for a blowtorch. Its blazing light was attempting to bore into his eyes. Unlike last night in the captain's suite, however, he didn't feel as if he was losing consciousness. But he could barely move his extremities.

He felt Anouk, who was suddenly kneeling above him, open his fingers. He could do nothing to stop her taking the torch from his hand. 'What are you doing?' he mumbled.

'Yes,' she said, which was probably related to the fact that she'd discovered the key in his breast pocket.

Which she could open the airlock with. Which she could get out of here with.

'Hey, wait please. Wouldn't it be better if I came with you?'

Wherever you want to go.

With the greatest effort of will, Martin managed to shift onto his side. He saw her bare feet toddle out of the bathroom. Heard her say 'Yes' again, loudly and clearly, which made no sense as there were no signs she was going to wait for him.

'Where are you going?' he wanted to call out, but he could muster barely more than a whisper.

Anouk turned briefly towards him. Saw her lips say, 'To the blue shelf,' and heard the words too, which came to him with a slight delay, as if the distance between them had already reached a range where sound took noticeably longer than light.

To the blue shelf?

Martin hauled himself to his knees, supported himself on the balls of his hands and crawled behind Anouk on all fours.

He'd heard that term somewhere before.

But where? *Where?*

Unable to crawl out of the bathroom any quicker than in slow motion, he watched helplessly as Anouk opened the cabin door and left without turning back to him.

54

Naomi

The familiar creaking. Was she hearing it for the last time?

The noise that heralded the opening of the gap sounded to her like an overture, a fitting introduction to her farewell song.

Naomi Lamar stood up and, on wobbly legs, watched the bucket swinging down towards her.

She was so nervous that she could feel her bladder, even though she'd just been in the *circle*. There wasn't a corner in the well, but she'd found a spot where she reckoned the urine ran most rapidly into the crack in the floor.

Naomi put her head back and wiped from her brow a bedbug that had crawled out of her hair. Her body wasn't twitching any more. It was just burning, she'd scratched herself so sore. Neck, arms, chest, her hairy legs.

But deliverance is coming from above.

The bucket hovered half a metre above her head. There was an astonishing jolt and she was terrified that the computer might fall out. Naomi stretched her arms up (to the spider), but nothing happened except for the fact that now she could reach the bucket.

She clutched it, held it tight, as tightly as she'd hold Anouk if she could just see her once more in her life.

When it was at waist height, she sank to the ground together with the bucket. And cried.

She recalled the day when the exam results had been posted at university and she hadn't wanted to go to the foyer, hadn't wanted to queue up with all the other students whose dreams were boosted or shattered with a single glance. And yet she hadn't been able to wait in her room for a minute. Curiosity had got the better of fear and so she'd taken the quickest route to the noticeboard, just as now her curiosity wouldn't allow her any hesitation in taking the computer from the bucket and flipping it open.

Naomi managed to keep her eyes closed for one, maybe two seconds. She couldn't hold out any longer.

She began reading the spider's message. The last message she would ever receive from it, after Naomi had admitted indisputably the worst things she'd ever done to anyone in her life:

Well done, Mrs Lamar. That's exactly what I wanted to hear. Finally you've told the truth. If there's anything else you'd like to say before you die, you may now type it into the computer. Once you've sent it back up to me, I shall allow you to die.

55

As Martin staggered into the entrance area of Hell's Kitchen he tried to cling onto the counter, pulling down a plastic pot with artificial hydrangeas.

Anouk had long since vanished.

When he'd finally made it back to his feet and out of the sickbay, all he'd seen was her back, a strip of bare skin where the hospital gown wasn't properly tied. Then the electric doors had closed and Martin was helpless to stop the girl from leaving the quarantine area.

To hunt for the black-light markings in the ship's bowels. Barefoot. Holding the UV torch.

His eyes filled with tears, Martin stared at the steel doors of the airlock, completely at a loss as to how he was going to open them again, that was assuming he could manage the indomitable three metres between him and the exit.

Fucking side effects.

Something – the pills, his tooth operation, his fall into the pool, his sheer exhaustion, probably a mixture of all these – had turned his head into a pressure vessel.

Every step triggered a moderate tremor, which is why it was better to think carefully about where he should go now.

Towards the exit would be a pure waste of energy. Anouk had his key and without it he wouldn't get out of here.

I'm sick. Exhausted. And locked in.

Martin felt for his phone, but it was no longer in his trouser pocket. He couldn't recall Anouk having taken this as well while he was lying on the bathroom floor; it probably slipped out as he fell.

As he turned around his brain sloshed in the other direction. He could taste bile and smell his own sweat.

Martin wanted to lie on the floor and sleep. But if he was determined to get out of here he didn't have any choice. He closed his eyes and felt his way back along the reception counter to the sickbay. The less he was distracted by his external senses, the greater the chance he might avoid being sick. And in fact he made better progress blind. Until he got to the cabin area there was nothing he could knock against, and he just had to keep going straight. All the while he was careful to breathe deeply to supply his brain with oxygen.

When he reached the end of the counter he waited for a moment until he was able to localise the pain in the back of his head. A good sign. So long as the pain was restricted to certain areas rather than being ubiquitous, he could focus on it and – hopefully – overcome it.

When he dared open his eyes he saw the door to Anouk's room, which thankfully was still ajar.

Pondering what he should do if he didn't find his mobile, Martin realised to his relief that he didn't need it. All he had to do was press the worry button, which was connected to his mobile and... *Elena's!*

Thinking of the doctor made him pause.

Why hadn't it dawned on him straight away? He wasn't

alone down here. After the attack on Dr Beck, the ship's doctor had also been transferred to Hell's Kitchen!

Martin turned right.

Daniel had told him that her cabin was diagonally opposite Anouk's. On this side of the corridor there was only one door it could be, and this was locked.

Martin screwed up his eyes tightly. The fireball beneath the left-hand side of his forehead had grown to the size of a fist, which was squashing his brain as if it were a sponge. Better than the demolition ball from earlier on. He hammered on the door. Shook the handle. Called Elena's name. Nothing happened.

Martin massaged his neck, pressing his thumb directly onto the extension of his cervical spine, in the hope that it might increase the pain level at first before reducing it. As he did this he cocked his head to one side, looked up and, above the door saw the red lever Elena had shown him on his first visit to Hell's Kitchen.

'In an emergency you can unlock the door that way...'

Without hesitating, Martin pulled the lever. He heard a hydraulic hissing, then the door opened slightly inwards.

'Elena?'

He entered the dimly lit cabin, which was furnished exactly like Anouk's. The same blend of hotel and luxury sanatorium. The air smelled of a mixture of bad breath and room spray.

The doctor was lying on her side, head facing the door, eyes closed. In the glow of the bedside light the consequences of the attack were still unmistakeable. Swollen eyes, puffy cheeks, a bloated neck. But her breathing was regular and she didn't appear to be in pain. He also took it as a good sign that she didn't have any tubes in her arms or a mask on her face.

He went over to her bed and stroked her bare upper arm. When she failed to react he tried to shake her awake.

She grunted, smacked her lips softly and made a sluggish movement to knock his hand away, but he just held it there more tightly. 'Elena, you've got to help me.'

Drunk with sleep, she opened her eyes and didn't seem to recognise him at first. Only gradually did her eyes become clear.

'Whash...' she asked in a daze.

He bent down to her. 'I need your key! Where is it?'

She pulled a face as if having bitten into something sour. A faint quiver around the corners of her mouth was the sign of a suppressed yawn.

'Why, you've got... you... must... have...?'

Martin didn't want to lose a second. He was locked in here, Anouk running around the ship on her own, and even if all probability dictated the opposite, his gut feeling told him that her mother was alive. And in great danger.

'*The key!*' he yelled, grabbing her by the shoulders.

Terrified, Elena looked to the chair on the left, over which a dressing gown and her uniform were hanging. Martin understood without the need for any words.

He limped to the chair, feeling first in her trousers, but then found it in the breast pocket of her blouse.

'Where are you going?' he heard Elena's hoarse voice say when he was at the door.

He turned around. 'Do you have any idea what the blue shelf is?'

The doctor's eyes opened wide.

'The blue shelf?' she asked, her elbows digging into the mattress to push her up.

'Yes.'

Elena threw off the duvet, beneath which she'd been lying in just panties and a T-shirt. Her eyes flashed with distress.

'Why didn't I think of that immediately!' She tried to stand up, but needed a second attempt because she fell back on the bed at the first.

'What's going on?' he asked when she was finally on her feet.

'We've got no time to lose,' she said, grabbing the dressing gown. 'Quick. I'll... I'll take you there.'

56

'The blue shelf?'

Daniel Bonhoeffer was closing the connecting door to his bedroom, where he'd just been checking on Julia, when his mobile rang. The sedative was no longer working. When she wasn't screaming at him, she was prowling up and down the room like a tiger and punching the fitted cupboards.

'Yes, it's between decks B and C, amidships beside the control rooms. But what the hell do you want there?'

In your state?

Elena didn't answer him. Either she'd hung up or the connection had been lost. Daniel couldn't understand either.

His fiancée was sick. She ought to be in bed rather than taking a stroll to the lower decks that housed the monster she was going to visit with Martin Schwartz.

The blue shelf.

A rather cynical description of a machine dating from a time when environmental protection was the expensive hobby of eccentric do-gooders and rubbish was still disposed of on the high seas. The *Sultan* was one of the first large luxury liners to have its own on-board water treatment and waste incineration plant. But the ship hadn't been launched with it. In the first three years of the *Sultan*'s career, when not even all European ports were skilled at recycling and separating waster, rubbish for which there were no or only overpriced delivery points was officially dumped in the sea.

The rubbish was first squashed in a shaft-like, circular press and then thrust into the sea as lumps weighing several tonnes.

Into the blue shelf.

The machine which used to dump the rubbish and which owed its name to its polluting activity, was located in the place he'd just described to Elena: the blue shelf.

Wait, of course...

Daniel pressed a speed-dial button on his desk telephone, but before he was connected to the MCR, the machine control room, a livid Julia stormed out of the bedroom behind him.

'Hey, Julia, wait...' He hung up again to stop his friend from leaving, but she was already at the door.

'Don't touch me!' she hissed angrily when he tried to grab her arm. She was wearing the white dressing gown he'd put her in yesterday. Her hair stuck to her temples like seaweed. Overnight her face seemed to have got narrower, while her body didn't fill the towelling dressing gown, as if she'd been shrunk by fear, worry and despair.

'Julia, please. Stay here. Where do you think you're going?'

'Away,' she said. 'Away from the man who wouldn't help me save my daughter's life.'

'Julia, I understand...'

'No. You don't understand. You don't have any children. You've never had any. You'll never understand me,' she hurled at him before throwing open the door and disappearing into the corridor.

Daniel, upset by her bitter, hostile accusations, didn't react and let her go.

As if in a daze he returned to his desk where the phone was ringing. He slowly picked up the receiver.

'It's Rangun here from the MCR. Did you just try to call us, Captain?'

He nodded. Tried to concentrate. 'Yes. I just wanted to find out whether the blue shelf is still connected.'

Officially the dumping machine had been out of service for five years. But unofficially it had never been disconnected from the electricity supply in case the waste incinerator conked out again and there was a refuse problem on a lengthy passage. At any rate nine tonnes of solid rubbish were produced on the *Sultan* every day, in addition to 28,000 litres of sludge. Every single day!

'Theoretically, captain, yes,' the technical officer replied.

Daniel knew the man. With his falsetto voice, on the phone he sounded like a woman. In the ship's choir he sang a bright soprano at the Christmas festivities, although no one made fun of him because what Rangun's voice lacked in masculinity was more than made up for by his trained body.

'Theoretically? What does that mean?'

'As was recommended, we didn't disconnect the rubbish press from the electricity supply, but it hasn't been service in a long time. I'm not sure it's still fit for purpose.'

Daniel suspected that the engineer might be surprised at the topic of their conversation, but his lower rank prevented him from asking direct questions, and Daniel had no intention of sharing his hunch with the man: that there couldn't be a better place for hiding someone for months on end.

Or for getting rid of them!

The blue shelf had a floor which, at the push of a button, opened up in the middle and retracted into the walls until the shaft was no more than a bottomless tube through which the press could push the squashed refuse straight into the water. 'Can you switch it off?' he asked Rangun.

'Not from here. It's not wired up to the new control system. But it's possible to cut the circuit over there. Do you want me to take a look?'

'No, wait. I'll come to you.'

Another witness; that was all they needed!

Daniel hung up, grabbed his captain's hat from the desk, hurried to the exit, opened the door...

... and found himself staring into the barrel of a revolver.

57

Naomi

Naomi's farewell note had taken some time to write, even though in the end it consisted of only one sentence. Astonishingly, she'd felt strangely relaxed since closing the computer and putting it back in the bucket.

Despite the imminence of her death and even though she had no idea how it would happen, she no longer felt afraid.

This must be what Catholics understand by the purifying power of confession.

Deep down inside her, in the shadowy world of her consciousness, she'd always sensed that her life would come to a terrible end. It *must* do, if an entity existed that ensured justice was done.

And it did.

It sat at the other end of the rope and had made her confess the unutterable. Drag what had been suppressed into the light of day.

Write it down.

My confession.

Naomi would have liked to have seen it, the spider

deciding her destiny. She'd loved to have known what the person looked like who'd managed to unmask her.

Now she knew how the spider had discovered her most intimate secrets. And why it wanted her to die. Ever since she'd given a thorough answer to the question 'Who are you?' Naomi had known the spider's past and thus its motive.

She understood why she had to be punished and this understanding gave her an inner peace. She wasn't scratching any more, her breathing was regular and her eyes were barely twitching, like someone whose body was being shaken by a vibration.

It's happening, she thought, without knowing what the spider had planned for her end.

She heard a scraping sound, like that of two millstones grinding together, then she saw the crack in the middle of the well open. Slowly, but steadily.

More curious than fearful, she got up from her sitting position and watched what was happening to the ground beneath her feet.

It's moving!

The two halves of the circle were vanishing into the sides of the shaft, like a sliding door into a wall.

She noted with interest that the gap was now a foot wide, and that she could hear the churning water bubbling beneath her. If the floor plates kept moving at this speed it would be less than two minutes before she'd completely lost the ground beneath her feet.

And plunged two and a half metres into the Atlantic.

Naomi smiled at the prospect.

58

If anyone had been watching the two of them propping each other up as they moved forwards, clasped to one another like drowning souls, they'd have thought Martin and Elena were drunk. But on the way to deck C they didn't bump into anybody, due to the fact that Elena had taken them down a hidden route. Most employees had no business being in the *Sultan*'s basement, certainly not in this area which housed the cargo hold. Here they stored all the spare parts that weren't needed on a crossing. To get there you took the cargo lift rather than the metal emergency stairs.

'A short cut,' Elena had mumbled, but then lost her bearings at the bottom of the steps when they got to a tubular room lined with pipes, where you had to duck to avoid hitting your head.

Martin felt as if he'd been transported inside a submarine of the sort he'd seen in films. The pipes had vents that could be opened with bilious-green wheel valves. There was a cupboard that seemed to consist of several fuse boxes with numerous instruments whose needles were barely moving.

Elena responded to his question as to which direction they should take by calling the captain on her phone and asking him the way. Martin was amazed that Bonhoeffer was able to understand his fiancée given that she was still mumbling, but after a brief exchange he appeared to have put her on the right track because she pointed to the left and let him go first.

The route brought them to a white bulkhead which required considerable strength to open. Martin needed both hands to shift the wheel and push open the metal door that was as thick as that of a large safe.

The room beyond was wider and darker. It smelled of dust and diesel. Dirt littered the floor and spiders' webs hung from the instruments inside the cupboard, which looked older than the ones they'd just passed.

'Where are we?' he asked Elena, who was leaning exhausted against one of the dusty boxes.

'No idea. An old control room. Over there...' she said, gesturing to another door on the far side, too weak to finish the sentence.

Martin went in the direction she'd indicated.

He stepped on thoughtlessly discarded screws, tissues, paper and other rubbish that hadn't been disposed of for ages, and at the end of the room came to another bulkhead, which was even more difficult to open than the previous one.

Beyond it he discovered a cathedral.

Or at least that was his first impression when he crossed the threshold into a room the height of a house, lit merely by a strip of halogen lamps on either wall.

At the far end – in the altar area, so to speak – was a shimmering oval copper tube, not unlike a brewing copper. Two thirds of its shell bulged into the room, while the rear third was integrated into the *Sultan*'s outer hull. A sort of fire ladder ran up the vessel and vanished into the darkness five metres above Martin's head.

'Here it is!' he called out, to let the doctor know that he'd found the blue shelf. As they'd descended into the depths of the ship's hull she'd explained to him where the term came from and why the waste disposal plant was no longer in use.

He looked back, but couldn't see Elena in the entrance, nor did she answer him.

She was probably just catching her breath. He'd go and check on her in a minute, but before then he wanted to take a closer look at the blue shelf and its surroundings.

He climbed several steps to a platform that ran along the perimeter of the vessel, and looked around. Anouk was nowhere to be seen. He called her name, but there was no reply.

Martin peered up.

The rubbish, he guessed, would probably be pushed into the shaft by a device at the top, a deck and a half higher up.

The shaft! The water in the well!

In his mind he saw Anouk's detailed drawing.

Given how curved the ship's hull was here, at least a third of the bottom of the tube must be over the raging Atlantic. As soon as the shaft was full, all you had to do was open the floor and the waste would tumble into the sea.

From his vantage point at the bottom of the blue shelf he couldn't figure out what equipment would be needed to accomplish this. He was wandering around the vessel, wondering whether to climb the ladder, when he discovered a door. It was head-high, presumably a staff entrance for cleaning or servicing inside.

Martin put his hand on the door which was secured by a lever that reminded him of the closing mechanism of an aeroplane door. He was rattling it when he suddenly felt an intense quaking beneath his feet, accompanied by a bloodcurdling crunching sound.

I thought the blue shelf wasn't in service.

The vessel appeared to have come to life and it felt as if something inside was moving.

Martin was even more startled by a movement behind him.

'Elena?'

He'd assumed the shadow on the vessel and the draught on his neck was from the doctor, finally catching up after overcoming her exhaustion; but he hadn't reckoned on this thin, faceless figure standing in the gloom, its head wrapped in a hoodie. He recognised who it was even though they'd met only once. The person was holding a bucket.

Martin was about to call out their name when the figure leaped forwards and hit him on the side of the head with an object that looked like a laptop but felt like a brick when the edge thundered against his temple.

59

Unlike the headaches that had recently assaulted him like a raiding party, the pain from this blow was of a different quality. In the first instance it felt unbearable, but then, after Martin had collapsed to the floor, it subsided considerably more quickly.

Quickly enough, at least, for him to realise that the attacker was on top of him and ready to strike again, this time with a taser. Instinctively Martin jerked his knee up between the killer's legs, but this merely made the assailant writhe rather than bend double. At least they dropped the taser, which meant that both of them were now scrabbling for the weapon on the bare metal floor.

With the powerful blow to the side of his head still affecting his reaction speed, Martin lost the contest. Although the taser had fallen closer to him, it was now back in the killer's hand. The other hand was gripping Martin by the throat with a force he would not have believed possible; the arteries in his neck were being squeezed.

Blue flashes flickered before Martin's eyes.

The attacker had already activated the taser, now just a few centimetres from his head, ready to shoot ten thousand volts through his muscles. Martin felt the damp breath of his opponent in his face and wondered how on earth this thin, delicate person could possibly be responsible for all those crimes that had been committed on the *Sultan*. *Abduction, rape, murder.* He thrashed out again to shake off the killer, but found himself hitting thin air.

Where? Where are you?

The hooded attacker was no longer above him, but must have moved to the side to ram the taser into his flank, like before on the naturist deck. As a warning.

Timmy is dead. Next time you will be too.

But the time for warnings had passed.

Instinctively Martin pressed both hands to his body and kicked in the direction where he suspected the killer to be. Then he heard a horrific scream, followed by the noise of crunching bones.

Martin, who again had failed to hit his attacker, pushed himself up on his elbows and now could at least see some clearer outlines with one eye.

The killer on the ground.

Elena beside the killer.

With a laptop in her hand and her body trembling, she stood beside a motionless figure at the bottom of the platform. The head lay in a red puddle slowly growing bigger beneath the hood.

'I... I...'

Elena was gasping, unable to believe what she'd done.

'I aimed for the head... and...' As Elena wiped the tears from her eyes with the sleeve of her dressing gown, she dropped the notebook. It hit the floor with a clunk. She pointed at the head lying at an unnatural angle. The attacker's neck had been broken in the fall from the steps.

Martin crawled on all fours to the body and removed the hood from the head.

'No!' Elena screamed. Her horror at the sight of the corpse intensified once more, causing her to pass out and collapse next to the body. Martin, who managed to cushion the fall by thrusting his arm beneath her head, felt for her pulse.

It was fast, but regular.

Unlike Shahla's.

Martin turned to the corpse. Stared into her wide-open, utterly expressionless eyes.

Even if it made no sense – for this culprit couldn't possibly have raped Anouk – right in front of him, in her own blood, lay the chambermaid who had purportedly found the girl, but in all likelihood had abducted and kept her hidden for weeks.

And, if Martin wasn't mistaken, below here was also where Anouk's mother was being held prisoner.

In the blue shelf.

Where the floor had been vibrating for the ninety seconds or so that their struggle had lasted. As if it was moving.

As if the hatch was opening.

Martin stood up and teetered to the door in the vessel.

It took a further ten seconds for him to finally open it.

60

Now the floor beneath her feet was no larger than a narrow ledge, no wider than a bookshelf. The rest had already disappeared into the wall. And if Martin hadn't opened the door to the cleaners' entrance the blue shelf wouldn't have had a floor at all any more. He had activated an emergency stopping mechanism which had halted the opening of the dumping chute.

At the last second.

One centimetre more and Naomi Lamar wouldn't have been able to hold on any longer.

One third of her feet were protruding over the edge. She looked like a swimmer waiting for the starting gun before plunging into the water below. Martin was sure that the next time the *Sultan* pitched, Anouk's mother would disappear into the ocean.

'Naomi,' Martin yelled, but she was as paralysed with shock as her daughter had been earlier. She didn't react. Perhaps she hadn't even heard him; the Atlantic was roaring so noisily beneath her.

From below, spray slapped her scratched face. This filthy

woman, her skin covered in weals, was dripping all over. Martin, too, was soaked by the showers of water.

'Come.' He was holding on to the edge of the vessel door, leaning perilously forwards into the shaft. He held out his free right arm as far as he could into the refuse compactor. With a little courage, surely Naomi would be able to grab his hand. But Anouk's mother gave Martin an impression of world-weariness and looked anything but courageous. As if she didn't *want* him to help her. At any rate she wasn't showing the slightest inclination to move towards him. She stood there as if screwed to the floor, staring into the foam bubbling at her feet.

'Anouk's alive!' he shouted, and the mention of her daughter's name did seem to have an effect.

Naomi moved her head. Raised it. Turned her chin to the side, in his direction. Looked at him. And opened her lips.

'I'm sorry,' she said, or something similar.

Her voice was far too weak to compete with the raging of the sea.

'Noooooo!' Martin screamed, because it appeared as if Naomi were about to take a step forwards. To death. If she jumped now she'd inevitably be sliced to pieces by the ship's propeller.

'Your abductor is dead!' he yelled.

Naomi paused one last time. Opened her lips as if for a final farewell, but then something in her expression changed. The corners of her mouth wrinkled. To begin with it looked as if she were crying. But then as if she were trying to laugh. Finally it seemed like she was doing both at once.

Martin noticed that she was no longer staring at him, but at a point above his shoulder.

He glanced behind. The reason for the change in her emotions was standing right behind him.

Anouk.

She'd finally found the way there.

At the last second.

Holding the torch, she slowly came closer.

Her face was wearing an expression he'd not seen in the girl before. Hardly surprising, as she was smiling.

He heard a cry of joy, which came not only from the girl but Naomi too.

Martin turned back towards the mother, now bellowing her daughter's name. So loudly that even the Atlantic couldn't swallow it up.

Naomi was laughing too. Raucously, a huge belly laugh. A big mistake. For the joyful trembling and quivering that had seized her entire body made Naomi stumble.

Once more she looked like someone on the edge of a pool, but this time she gave the appearance of a non-swimmer thrashing her arms about in a desperate attempt to avoid the inevitable.

Plunging into the sea.

'Come to me,' Martin yelled, this time in German as the tension of the situation had overtaken him. It was more by luck than design that Naomi grabbed hold of his hand as she lurched forwards.

Martin felt a jolt that darted from his shoulder to his jaw, which he clenched as tightly as possible while trying not to let either of his hands slip. Not the one Naomi was dangling from, her feet centimetres from the seething surface of the

water. And certainly not the one stopping him from falling
to his own death. Luckily Anouk's mother weighed barely
more than a little girl. The lack of food that had almost
killed her might now prove to be her salvation if...

... I don't let go of her.

Naomi was light, morbidly emaciated, but her hand was
damp. Wet. Slippery.

Martin felt as if he were holding onto a soapy leash. The
more he squashed her hand, the faster it seemed to slither
from his. And this made him furious.

I haven't gone through all this shit...

With a mighty jerk that he felt all the way down to his
lumbar column...

... only to fail...

... he pulled the mother towards him...

... just before the end.

... over the edge of the blue shelf. Onto the floor of the
platform. Beside the vessel. To safety.

Made it!

Martin lay on the ground, totally shattered. He tried
breathing in and out at the same time, which unavoidably
produced a coughing fit. But he felt good.

He looked at Naomi, whose joy at being reunited with
her daughter gave her more strength than him, for she
managed to get to her feet and stretch out her arms.

To her daughter, who staggered towards Naomi, no less
wobbly on her feet.

Martin closed his eyes in satisfaction.

Although it wasn't his son who he'd saved, not even a
child, he'd managed to avert the death of a mother, reunite
a family – and provide Anouk with a smile.

And thus, on this shaking floor beside the blue shelf, which reeked of cold rubbish and sea salt, he felt happy for the first time in a long while, very happy.

Albeit only briefly.

Just until the smile she'd greeted her mother with vanished from Anouk's face, and she struck Naomi in the chest. Rapidly executed, not a particularly hard blow, not even for an eleven-year-old, but strong enough for Naomi Lamar to lose her balance and fall backwards into the blue shelf, towards the water.

61

Time was ticking away and Bonhoeffer was getting fed up. On this trip he'd been beaten to a pulp by a paranoid detective, his dear goddaughter had killed herself, for which the ex-wife of his best friend held him responsible, and in the ship's morgue his security officer, a gunshot to his head, lay in one of the refrigerated cabinets that were now compulsory on board due to the large volume of pensioners the cruise line carried. Evidently the chain of crazy incidents hadn't yet been broken.

'Can't you point your weapon somewhere else?' he barked at the man calling himself Tiago Álvarez, who'd forced Daniel back into his cabin with a revolver and made him sit at his desk, while the dark-haired Latino prowled around the suite like a caged tiger, his gun permanently aimed at the captain's chest.

'Okay, I've been sitting here now for' – Bonhoeffer said, checking his watch – 'at least twenty minutes and you haven't yet told me what you're hoping to gain from this hold-up.'

Not that Tiago hadn't had a huge amount to say. He'd spouted forth like a waterfall, revealing himself to be as perplexed as he was frightened. Now Bonhoeffer knew that 'purely by accident' – whatever that meant – he'd been party to a quarrel between an officer and a chambermaid, since when he'd been on the run from that officer, who at the end of his account turned out to be Veith Jesper.

'Are you now going to kill me like you did him?' he asked Tiago.

'I didn't kill that man,' the dark-haired Argentinian protested, making every effort to remain composed. 'It was *he* who shoved the gun in *my* mouth.'

'But decided against it at the last moment and instead shot a bullet through his own head?' Bonhoeffer laughed. This was clearly a madman before him. Anouk's kidnapper, perhaps?

He wondered whether the revolver in the man's hands actually worked. The section behind the barrel looked as if it had burst somehow, while the trigger seemed to be missing too.

'Did you abduct the girl?' he asked Tiago straight out. Maybe Veith had caught him in the act. In such circumstances there was every reason to get him out of the way. *But what the devil does he want from me then?*

Even if you couldn't tell a criminal's deeds just by appearance, Bonhoeffer doubted very much that he had a perverted rapist before him. On the other hand, the man had managed to smuggle a weapon through security and presumably killed the officer with it, for whatever reason.

'I haven't laid a finger on anyone,' Tiago protested. '*I* was the one about to be killed. I'm the one who needs protection.'

Bonhoeffer smiled and said, 'Perhaps you ought to

repeat what you've just said, but without brandishing that revolver.'

The phone rang in his pocket, but before the captain could take the call Tiago ordered him to put it on the table.

'Listen here, I'm needed on the bridge,' Bonhoeffer lied. 'You don't have much time left to tell me your demands. They'll soon notice I'm missing.'

'I don't have any demands. Who do you think I am?'

A *fucking awful combination*, Bonhoeffer thought. *Mad and armed.*

Veith must have discovered Tiago's hiding place, cabin 2186, the love nest where he'd held Anouk prisoner. Yes, that made sense – after all, the girl had been found near there.

'Where's the mother?' Bonhoeffer said, venturing a direct confrontation with the man.

'The mother?' Tiago asked. He sounded bewildered, but that might just be acting.

'Anouk's mother. Is she in the blue shelf? If so, your hideaway's been busted. My people are on their way there as we speak.'

'What the hell are you babbling on about?' Tiago asked. 'I don't know any Anouk. Only a Lisa.'

'Lisa?' Now Bonhoeffer was lost for words. 'How…?'

'Here,' Tiago said, pulling an enveloped from his back pocket. With one hand he shook out two pieces of paper.

'What's that?' Bonhoeffer asked.

'A plan,' Tiago said. 'I've been meaning to hand it over for ages.' He passed Bonhoeffer the first of the two pages.

The captain smoothed out the paper on the table and started to read.

Plan:

Step 1: Put security camera out of order.

According to Querky's list Nr 23/C. Access via outside steps on deck 5.

Step 2: Put farewell note in Mama's cabin.

Step 3: Lock cabin door and connecting door.

Bonhoeffer looked up. 'Where did you get this?'

Tiago couldn't cope with the captain's stare. Clearly he found it too uncomfortable to answer, and when he finally did, Bonhoeffer finally knew why the Argentinian had been umming and erring for so long. He was a thief. A common crook specialising in the plundering of passengers' safes. A description that fitted the troubled and distraught young man far better than that of a murderer and rapist.

'So it's only by accident that you came into possession of this... this...' Bonhoeffer searched for the right words and then used Tiago's. 'This *plan*.'

Tiago nodded. He looked genuinely contrite. 'You don't know how much I've been blaming myself. If only I'd plucked up courage to tell someone earlier. But this killer, this officer...' Tiago shook his head. 'I was in fear of my life. I still am. Till now I've had no idea what I got into. Don't know how it all hangs together. Who can assure me, for example, that it wasn't you who set this Veith on me?'

'Do you know what?' Bonhoeffer said, standing up from

the desk. He couldn't care less about the revolver any more. 'You can go fuck yourself! I don't give a shit about you or Veith. Lisa Stiller was my goddaughter. I loved her. Her suicide is worse than any bullet you could stick in me.'

Tiago, who'd just been about to grab his revolver with two hands, froze.

'Lisa killed herself?' he asked, confused.

Bonhoeffer was at a total loss. 'Is this supposed to be a joke?' he asked, shaking the piece of paper in his hand. 'You read the bloody plan yourself!'

'Yes, I did.' Tiago passed him the second sheet. 'But it doesn't talk about *Lisa's* death!'

62

Anouk was back in her own world. She'd put one foot in front of the other as if mechanically, apparently feeling neither Martin's arm supporting her nor Elena's hand leading her. Out of the cathedral, through the control rooms, back up the steps to Hell's Kitchen, where she now lay back in her bed, self-absorbed, but her eyes open, staring at the ceiling. Stoical, with a dispassionate expression, refusing to answer any of the questions that he and Elena had put to her in turn.

'But why?'

'Why did you do that?'

'Why did you kill your mother?'

Because since losing consciousness Elena had barely been able to stand, Martin accompanied her back to her sickroom, where they now sat face to face across a small dining table.

Martin did indeed find his mobile again in the bathroom. Now it lay before them on the shining matt Resopal top, beside the open laptop which Elena had used to save his life. Blood still stuck to one side, in the spot where it had struck Shahla's head.

As far as Martin was concerned it was okay that they hadn't managed to reach the captain till now. The news they had to pass on was devastating. And seeing as Shahla was dead and Naomi couldn't possibly have survived her fall, there was nothing they could do until their arrival at New York except take Anouk into safekeeping again and try to question her. The first they'd already done. The second was likely to be fruitless.

Moreover, he and Elena needed time to resolve all the questions that had been plaguing them ever since they'd discovered who was behind Anouk's abduction and her mother's torture.

To begin with they hadn't been able to make head or tail of it. Their minds couldn't progress beyond the question of how Anouk could have been raped by a woman.

All they had to aid their quest for the truth was the weapon that had killed the culprit.

The laptop.

Martin had opened it without any great expectations, merely curious as to why Shahla had been carrying it in a bucket when she attacked him. He'd assumed that the computer would be damaged by the blow to her head and by having been dropped. But the laptop was still in perfect working order. When he flipped up the lid Martin came across the exchange between torturer and victim. At first glance it appeared as if Shahla had been conducting a sort of perverted voyeuristic conversation with Naomi.

'She wanted Anouk's mother to confess to the worst thing she'd ever done in her life.'

'Why?' Elena croaked. She sounded as if she'd been screaming her heart out at a rock concert, although she wasn't mumbling any more. Once again the shock had strange consequences. The fact that she was responsible for someone's death, even if that individual had probably been a psychopath, had loosened her tongue but irritated her vocal chords.

'Because Naomi was only allowed to die if Shahla was satisfied with the confession.'

Martin, who'd already skimmed the beginning of the text, gave Elena a brief summary of what Anouk's mother had admitted to the chambermaid.

'Good God. Is there any sort of hint as to *why* Shahla did that?'

'Yes, there is.'

He tapped his finger on the screen.

'Naomi asked Shahla who she was, and to begin with the answer was slightly cryptic, in the style of a fairy tale, making a few points that Naomi would barely be able to compute. Then Shahla became more concrete. Here.'

Martin read out the relevant passage:

I was eleven when I was abused for the first time. My father was away on business; he was the managing director of a Pakistani electronics firm that would later be sold to Microsoft. But when I was a child my dad spent more time on aeroplanes than at home with us.

I had everything a child could wish for. A house in an area with security guards, our evergreen garden shut off from the hardship of normal people that we only ever saw when the chauffeur bypassed the traffic jams on the way to our private school. Then we would peer through the tinted windows of our limousine at the ordinary houses where people lived who'd never be able to afford the mobiles and computers that my dad made.

My life as a young teenager consisted of ballet, golf and English lessons. And sex.

Or 'cuddling', as my mum called it.

'Her *mother*?' Elena interrupted him in disbelief. She was so unsettled she bit her bottom lip.

'Yes,' Martin confirmed. 'Apparently it wasn't the father who abused Shahla.'

Most people would find that unimaginable. But as a detective Martin knew that the sexual abuse of children by their mothers, although a taboo subject, wasn't completely uncommon. According to estimates, ten per cent of all sexual abusers were women. Children's organisations spoke of much higher unreported figures, as only very few victims ever took action against their mothers and, if they did find the courage to do so, would come up against the same disbelief shown by Elena:

'Shahla was raped by her mother? How's that possible?'

'She describes it a little later. Here...'

Martin scrolled down three paragraphs.

Mummy knew what she was doing and what she demanded of me was wrong. Whenever my father was away for a period of time she came to 'comfort' me, as she called it. I didn't think anything of it to begin with. I even liked it. The way she stroked and caressed me felt nice. But later her hands started to wander, her fingers touched me in places I found embarrassing. She said it was okay. And that she would kiss me down there. It would help me grow up, she said. A perfectly normal occurrence between a mother and her child. But then she got pushier. When she forced me to put on the condom...

'Wait. A condom?' Elena asked, now even more incredulous. Her voice was squeaking with tension.

Martin, who'd already read the next couple of sentences, was able to explain the apparent contradiction.

'In this exchange of messages, Shahla describes her own experiences of abuse to extract a confession from Anouk's mother,' he told Elena. 'And now she reveals another bombshell.' He grabbed his throat, which had just started to constrict. 'We've already heard that it was the mother rather than father who jumped into bed with her. Now Shahla tells Naomi' – he cleared his throat – 'that she was born a boy.'

63

Julia Stiller opened the door to her cabin. The room seemed alien. No, she felt *alien* inside it. She didn't belong in this environment. Not in the cabin, nor on the ship. Not even in her own body.

She opened the cupboard and with the tips of her fingers touched the sleeves of her neatly arranged clothes that she'd never wear again. Like the travel bag on the suitcase rack. Her inseparable companion on every journey, she'd never hold it again.

When she disembarked from the *Sultan* she'd leave it behind, like everything else that had once had meaning in her life: her keys, ID cards, photos, money, love of her life, hope, future.

Lisa.

Julia went into the bathroom and smelled the bottle of expensive perfume she'd bought specially for his trip. Its fragrance now made her sick.

She sprayed it on, as nausea was easier to bear than impotence and grief.

As she looked in the mirror, she saw for some reason

the image of her sick three-year-old daughter, when Julia had been obliged to swap shifts with a colleague because she couldn't send Lisa to kindergarten. Lisa had a temperature of forty degrees, a 'snotty nose' and a hacking cough. With a brittle voice that sounded as hoarse as that of the wicked witch Ursula, who Julia always had to imitate when she was reading. At the time Lisa had lain in bed and asked her, 'Do I have to die now, Mama?'

Julia had laughed and wiped away the sweaty hair from her brow. 'No, my darling. People don't die that quickly. You're going to live a long, long time.'

Another twelve years.

Julia pressed both her hands firmly on her forehead, eyes and cheeks. So firmly that she saw stars.

For a while she remained motionless in that position, before filling a glass with water from the tap. She brought it to her lips, but then didn't see the point any more so tipped it down the plughole.

One of many pointless actions that would follow on from each other in her life from now. Useless activities such as thinking, feeling, breathing.

I have to call Max.

It was the first time she'd thought of her ex-husband, *since Lisa...*

She left the bathroom.

Someone had made the bed. A small bar of chocolate lay on her pillow. One on each side. *Two bars too many.*

Julia looked for the note Lisa had left for her – *'I'm sorry, Mama'* – but it wasn't on the cupboard any more. She'd probably given it to Daniel; she couldn't remember.

She shook the connecting door, but it was still locked on Lisa's side.

Perhaps it's better that way.

If she'd had a key she'd have entered Lisa's cabin and gone through her things.

What difference would that have made?

Julia pushed open the balcony door. Fresh wind blew through her hair.

Given where they were in the Atlantic, the sea was astonishingly calm, the water almost still in contrast to this afternoon. The biggest waves were being made by the ship itself.

The evening air had a soft tang of salt and diesel. Laughter washed down from the upper balconies. In the distance she could hear pop music mingling with the swishing of the sea. The ship's programme had announced a karaoke afternoon.

'Why?' Julia thought, shaking the railing she'd climbed over the night before. '*Why did you have to hold onto me, Daniel?*'

She leaned over the railings and looked down. The sea no longer looked menacing, but enticing. She heard a whispering in the gentle whooshing of the waves. It sounded like her name. Enticing.

People don't die that quickly!

'Lisa?' she wanted to shout out, but her voice failed.

Why didn't I insist?

Why didn't I force Daniel to stop the ship and turn around so we could go overboard?

I knew about the video, didn't I?

Full of fury and self-hatred, she kicked the screen between

the balconies. Hammered on it with her first. And kicked again. Once. Twice.

On the third occasion her foot went right through the plastic wall.

Without destroying it.

It felt as if she were kicking into thin air. Julia had gone at it with such momentum that she almost slipped and fell, only staying on her feet because she was holding onto the railing.

What the devil...?

She stared at the door that her foot had kicked in the screen. It looked like the cat flap in a back door, except that large dog could have got through this. *Or a human being.*

Julia's pulse started to race. She bent down and looked through the flap onto Lisa's balcony. The hairs on her forearms stood on end. She felt electrified by an intuition.

The door was fastened shut. Normally you'd need a tool to open it, to make maintenance easier or speed up transporting things between cabins. But the lock seemed to have been unfastened.

By Lisa perhaps?

Julia took off her dressing gown and, dressed only in panties and a bra, slipped through the flap in the screen. She scraped a knee and shin, but she was no more aware of this than she was of the chilly wind that could now assail the entire surface of her body.

Is this what you did too, my love?

She tried to peer through the glass into her daughter's cabin, but the doors were locked and the curtains closed. With both hands she shielded her head from external lights, but still couldn't see anything.

Did you lock the connecting door from your side, Lisa? And put the chain on afterwards?

She turned back to the flap.

Did you creep through there to vanish through my cabin?

Julia felt her heart beating faster. Had it been the breath of wind when the balcony door was opened, or the sound of a door snapping shut that had woken her from her sleep?

The door by which you left my cabin, darling?

Julia knew she was about to fall into the worst state of grief possible, in which relatives try their best to deny the truth and cling to any theory, however absurd, that offers hope. But what else could she do?

She struck her fist against the glass, kicked the sliding door with her bare foot, rammed it with her knee, yelled Lisa's name… and got the fright of her life, when the curtains opened.

To reveal her daughter's face.

64

'Shahla was a man?' Elena was growing more confused by the minute. She looked at Martin as if he'd grown a second nose.

Martin answered her in Shahla's words that he read from the screen of the notebook:

When I refused the put the condom over my penis, she shouted at me that I was a loser. Useless. She said she didn't love me, that she'd always wanted a girl rather than a smelly boy. She slapped me in the face and let me go away in tears, only to repeat the game the following day. At some point I gave in, put on the condom, and in time slept with her. All the while a single thought dominated my head: *I wish I were a girl. I wish I were a girl.*

During the sex, during my rape (it took me years to understand what she'd done to me) my personality split. My mind flew off into a girl's body and stayed there, long after my mother had let me be. I no longer wanted to be the defiled boy, but the girl my mother had always wished for and who would have been spared all that if only I'd been born in the right body.

324

Four days after my eighteenth birthday my father sold his firm and not long afterwards he and my mother died when their private jet crashed.

The first thing I did with the fortune they left me was to have a sex change, which no responsible surgeon ought to have been allowed to carry out. But I bribed the examining psychiatrist, who certified me to be of perfectly sound mind. As you might imagine, the changes to my body didn't relieve my emotional suffering. Without a penis, with shattered and reconstructed cheekbones, a more feminine nose and small breasts, I felt dirtier than I ever had in my mother's arms.

In an online suicide forum, where I was researching suitable methods of suicide, I met by chance a thirteen-year-old girl who'd had similar experiences to me and whose suffering was still ongoing. Her mother forced her to masturbate in front of her.

She wrote that she was about to go on a cruise where she was planning to take her life. It was through this girl that I realised our mistake.

Why should we victims kill ourselves while the real criminals went on living?

That was ten years ago.

I signed up as a chambermaid on the ship where the girl was planning to leap to her death and made sure she survived the crossing. Unlike her mother. My first in a short series of victims.

Elena laid her hand comfortingly on Martin's forearm and asked him to speak more slowly. Without knowing it he'd sped up with every line.

To begin with I was satisfied with numbing my victims and throwing them overboard. But over the years I learned to perfect my system. With a keen intelligence and above-average financial means I purchased the suicide forum called Easyexit that had put me on the right path, albeit by chance. Today it has offshoots all over the world; the website has local listings in thirty-two countries. It's unbelievable how many people can't bear to live on this planet any more. Millions of them.

And amongst them I find my traps. I proceed with great caution. When I learn that a child has been abused by their parents (it doesn't matter whether it's a boy or a girl) I use a chain of travel agents called Querky Travel – owned by me – to book passage for the child and parents, who of course know nothing of their 'luck'. So I disguise the trip as a lottery win. This works in only a few instances – most are mistrustful when someone wants to give them something – which is why my success quota has remained very low.

Once, however, in the case of a German family, I was helped by chance.

Martin paused. Scrolled up, then down again, but couldn't find any clue as to what to make of these words.

'Why have you stopped?' Elena asked. 'Is there anything about your wife and son?'

'No, unfortunately,' Martin whispered.

Or perhaps thank God.

He cleared his throat and went on reading:

By now the rumour seems to have circulated on Easyexit that there's a travel agency which organises the final passage for people who get what they deserve. I imagine this is why Justin Lamar contacted me. Am I right in thinking your father-in-law doesn't seem to like you very much? He covered the costs of your trip. And offered a special commission if, rather than reeling off the normal programme, I made you suffer for your sins. Which is perfectly possible here on the *Sultan*, where the blue shelf provides the ideal space for it.

Let's get a couple of things straight, Naomi.

I never put tapeworms into your food. And what you took to be bedbugs were harmless mites. I wasn't intending to poison your body physically, but mentally. Just as my mother did to me. She didn't hit me or insert any objects into me. But all the same she infected me with a virus that ate me from the inside out. Just as Anouk, to whom I've been a mother over these last few weeks, will continue to be devoured on the inside by what you did to her. And what you're going to confess now.

He looked up from the screen. Elena stared at him agog. 'Anouk was...'

Now the circle is closing. Now there's a point to all this madness.

Nodding energetically, Martin skipped to the end of the document. To Naomi's confession.

65

Julia's biggest fear was that she'd lost her mind. Or, even worse, that she was only dreaming that Lisa had opened the balcony door and was now standing before her. If she were suddenly to awake in Daniel's cabin, still sedated by the drugs he'd forced on her, and if her daughter were to vanish into thin air for a second time, the pain she'd feel on waking would finally be unbearable. She was absolutely certain of that.

At her mother's funeral the pastor had said that parents do not die until their children stop thinking of them. He forgot to mention the reverse situation where parents die inside when nothing remains but the thought of their children.

And yet Lisa seemed anything but an illusion. And if she were, then the Fata Morgana ordering her to come into the cabin and sit in the armchair beside the bed was astonishingly realistic.

'There you are. Finally. I've been waiting for you all day.'

Wearing a black lace-up dress, Lisa was standing a short distance away in front of the television, in exactly the spot where the chambermaid had been cowering as she bled from her mouth. The sight had been substantially less frightening than the one of her daughter now. Lisa looked as if she'd made herself up in the dark on choppy seas. Eyeliner that had run and mascara applied too thickly disfigured her pale face. In her hand she held a long screwdriver.

Julia looked at her daughter as if she were a ghost, which essentially she was, and uttered just a single word:

'Why?'

Why are you still alive?

Why did you do that to me?

An abortive smile formed on Lisa's lips.

'You don't know?' Her voice was cold. Pitiless. It matched her expression. 'You destroyed it,' she said.

'What, darling. What did I destroy?'

Lisa yelled at her, 'He belonged to me. I had him first.'

He? Who was she talking about?

'I... I'm sorry, I don't know what...'

Her daughter interrupted Julia's helpless stammering and screamed, 'With us it was love. But you... you just wanted to *fuck* Tom!'

'Tom?'

At that moment Julia performed a cliché. Her jaw dropped. And she felt incapable of closing it again.

'Don't look like that! He was my first.' With a vulgar gesture Lisa grabbed her crotch. 'He took my virginity, Mama. We were to be together forever. But then you came along.'

'Tom?'

Tom Schiwy?

'Wasn't it enough taking my father away? Did you have to steal the love of my life from me too?'

'Your liaison teacher… *the man I had an affair with*, Tom Schiwy…?'

… abused you?

Lisa took a step closer. In the mirror Julia could see that her combat boots weren't done up. The laces were flapping loose.

'Loved. Oh, yes. We were going to get married. He told me I was much more mature than all the others.'

'But darling, sweetheart…' Julia was about to get out of the armchair, but Lisa threatened her with the screwdriver and made her sit back down.

'Don't try telling me it wasn't your fault. I saw the way you spruced yourself up for him. You went to the parent consultation dolled up like a cheap tart to throw yourself at him. You'd have loved to go to school just in your underwear, wouldn't you?' She gave Julia a scornful stare, pointing first at her panties and then at her bra. 'Christ, do you actually know how unhappy I was?'

Lisa blew a strand of hair from her face.

'Didn't you notice I wasn't able to eat any more? That I was only wearing black clothes? And skiving off school with my new friends? No, you didn't. You only had eyes and ears for your Tom.'

You're wrong. Oh, God, darling. You're wrong.

'Listen to me, Lisa,' Julia instructed her. 'I understand your anger. But what your teacher did with you…'

'Don't you go fucking justifying yourself,' Lisa interrupted her. 'Querky said you'd try to talk your way out of it.'

Querky?

'Wait a sec, I thought that was your boyfriend?'

This time Lisa managed an honest smile. Derogatory and derisive. 'Querky's a she. Yes, you know what, dearest

Mother? I didn't know either. I met her on the internet. In a suicide forum.'

'Jesus Christ, Lisa...'

'Shit, I wanted to kill myself when Tom dumped me for you.'

Tears flooded into Julia's eyes at this admission. 'I'm really sorry, I didn't know...'

'But Querky opened my eyes.' Lisa stabbed the screwdriver in Julia's direction. 'It wasn't me who had to be punished, but you.'

'And that's why you staged your own suicide?'

To scare the living daylights out of me?

'You needed to experience what I had to go through. What it means to lose the thing you love most in life.' Lisa gave a self-satisfied grin. 'That was part one of my plan. Me and Querky worked it out together. Man, that woman is so cool. She works here on the ship. She hung a chambermaid's uniform in my cupboard and programmed my key so I could go anywhere on the ship, even down to the crew deck where I hid last night.'

That's why Martin Schwartz saw her down there, Julia remembered. It must have been while Lisa was preparing all this nonsense and looking for somewhere to bunk down.

'Querky really thought of everything. She even paid for the trip so we could entice you on board.'

Jesus Christ!

In spite of Lisa's threats, Julia couldn't hold out in her seat any longer. She stood up and took a step towards her daughter who was now wielding the screwdriver like a dagger.

'What are you planning?' she asked, looking Lisa directly in the eye. Her daughter held her gaze effortlessly.

'You'll see, Mama.' She gave a crooked smile. 'You'll see.'

66

Naomi's last confession consisted of just four sentences:

The worst thing I've ever done in my life is to force my daughter to have sex with men.

Martin heard Elena gasp. He continued reading:

There's no excuse for what I did. Not even the fact that, when it began I was taking hard drugs which were ruining my already unstable psyche. Nor that I stopped it when one of the groups of men I gave her to were so violent that she's likely to have permanent physical damage. I deserve to die.

'Jesus Christ, that's how Anouk got her injuries!' Elena croaked after he'd uttered the final sentence.

Martin nodded. They'd thought the rapist was still on board. But Anouk had been abused before their departure – and at her mother's instigation! The wounds hadn't been inflicted on the ship, but back at home.

'Now it's all beginning to make sense,' Martin whispered.

He looked Elena in the eye. Anger flared in her face. She too had understood why Anouk had hit her mother.

No, not her mother. *Her rapist!*

Although she hadn't written it explicitly, everything suggested that Shahla had wanted to free Anouk from her mother rather than abduct her. They would probably find a den in the lower deck, not far from the blue shelf, a place where Anouk had been more or less able to move around freely during the last couple of months. He still didn't understand what Anouk and Shahla were doing that night when the captain saw them in the corridor near the 'nest', where Gerlinde had taken the photograph. But now it was perfectly clear why Anouk had refused to speak a word the whole time, even though she knew exactly who'd taken her away and where her mother was. Why she needed the UV light, so that she could find her way to Naomi without the chambermaid by means of invisible marks. To torture her, observe her, or just to take pleasure in her suffering. *Or to kill her,* as she had done in the end.

'We have to let Daniel know,' Elena said, grabbing Martin's mobile on the table.

It started to vibrate.

67

Martin took the call by pressing the touch screen of his smartphone and the picture of Stalin vanished from the screen.

'Diesel?' he asked.

'Call me Edward Snowden if you like.'

Martin's finger was already hovering over the icon to disconnect the conversation.

'Listen, I can't talk now. All hell has been let loose here and...'

'I've hacked Lisa's Facebook profile,' Diesel interrupted him impassively.

Martin didn't waste time asking how he'd done that. He knew that the editor-in-chief could count not just tattoo artists and pyromaniacs amongst his friends, but numerous technology freaks as well, who provided him with the newest versions of cracked computer games.

'And?'

'Well, I stumbled on an interesting exchange with a chap called Tom Schiwy.'

'Who's that?' Martin asked. He'd put it on loudspeaker so Elena could hear.

'Her liaison teacher. She obviously had a relationship with him.'

The doctor frowned, but the disfigured half of her face remained unmoved.

'Isn't this Lisa still only fifteen?' Martin asked.

'Precisely. But there's more! This teacher had something going with the mother too.'

Martin and Elena exchanged glances of amazement.

'With Julia Stiller?' Martin asked.

'How many other mothers has she got?' Diesel must have been chewing gum because his words were accompanied by disagreeable lip-smacking noises. 'And now, here's the hammer blow. Are you belted up?'

'What?'

'The video you wanted me to search for on isharerumours. com...'

'Is it genuine?' Martin stared at the phone, as if he could press the answer out of him just with his eyes.

'Yes, looks like it. And I'll give you three guesses who the bloke is.'

Martin paused. He hardly dared voice his suspicions. 'This Schiwy guy?'

Diesel did an impression of a trumpet fanfare and dropped another bomb straight away. 'Bingo! Lisa's hopelessly in love with that arsehole. In her eyes her mother is a cheap whore who's nicked her Prince Charming. To win back that shit she offered to behave like a strumpet too, if that's what he wanted. And the cunt went for it at once. Acted out a perverse role play with the girl in which she had to play the child prostitute strolling down Frobenstrasse and jump into his car.'

'But how did the video get onto the internet?' Martin asked.

'Hold onto yourself, this is where it gets extraordinary: Lisa uploaded it herself. Yes, no joke. I found that from her email traffic too. When Tom refused to get back with her, despite the child prostitute game, her knee-jerk reaction was to upload it and threaten to blow his cover. But that cut no ice with the arsehole, because he wasn't identifiable on the video. When the nasty comments appeared, Lisa changed her strategy and tried to blackmail the bastard with her suicide. Just before they got on board she sent Tom a final email in which she threatened to leap into the sea if he didn't come back to her. This apparently put the wind up Schiwy. He sent an email to Julia, forwarding the video, probably to warn her. He didn't want to be responsible for her death. But, if you ask me, that doesn't make it any better.'

Diesel lowered his voice as if he weren't alone in his office and said shiftily, 'If you know someone who doesn't have a problem with touching male genitalia, perhaps you should send them round to Schiwy's with an electric screwdriver. Just saying.'

Martin watched Elena pull the mobile closer to her on the table.

'And you're one hundred per cent certain?' she asked.

'Who's there with you?' Diesel asked. 'Sounds like a dragon whose voice is breaking.'

'I'm Elena Beck, the doctor treating Anouk Lamar.' Elena spoke as clearly as she could. 'Listen, it's absolutely vital that you answer my question. How reliable is all this stuff about Lisa's teacher?'

'As reliable as using a rubber johnny and the pill together, darling.'

The doctor leaped up from the table. All exhaustion seemed to be blown away.

'We've got to go,' she said frantically, waving her hand. Martin stood too.

'Where?'

'To see Julia Stiller. We have to find her.'

He shook his head. 'What's the point? To tell her that Lisa isn't just dead, she was also forced to have sex with her teacher before she died?'

Elena looked at him as if he were dim. 'Think about it, Martin. A daughter is abused before she goes missing. What does that remind you of?'

Shahla!

And that she'd always gone for the mothers.

Julia!

Martin ended the call without saying goodbye to Diesel. As he hurried behind Elena he tried to reach Bonhoeffer again.

68

Lisa was sweating.

A fresh breeze was blowing in from the open balcony door, but her daughter looked as if she were standing in a spotlight. Her body was reacting to the flame of insanity simmering deep inside her. A fine trickle of sweat ran down her cheek and collected above the collar of her T-shirt.

'I've tried to get Tom back,' she told her mother. 'I've called him, emailed him, bombarded him via Facebook and WhatsApp. I turned up to one of his consultation hours after he dumped me overnight. I even got him back into bed once.'

Lisa's wistful smile at the end unsettled Julia as much as what she'd said.

'Are you talking about the time when I... *had a relationship with Tom?*'

Her daughter's smile gave way to a stony face. 'But it didn't mean anything to Tom any more. He said the sex was better with me, but he could only imagine having a relationship with you.'

Jesus Christ! Julia closed her eyes for a while.

Lisa's faked suicide. Her resurrection. The hatred in her voice.

She wasn't sure how much more she was capable of taking. Julia looked at her daughter's hand gripping the screwdriver tightly, observed the reflection of the slowly setting sun on the silver metal and asked Lisa softly, 'What are you going to do now, darling?'

'Get Tom back.'

Lisa virtually spat these words at her bare feet. If it hadn't occurred to her earlier, now Julia was having doubts about who she was talking to.

The girl before her, with that haunted look and those quivering lips, was no longer her daughter. In all senses of the word Lisa was *disconnected*.

Julia had once read that, besides grief, lovesickness could inflict the worst emotional wounds. Evidently including those that didn't heal on their own.

'Lisa, if someone's to blame for your heartache, it's Tom. He should never...'

'Blah, blah, blah... Don't talk crap. So now you want to pin it on him, do you?'

Julia just wanted to shout 'Yes!' and – had that fucker been here – grab him by the balls and throw him overboard. But as Tom Schiwy was as far away as a clear thought was from Lisa's mind, she just shook her head. 'No, it's not just his fault,' she said to placate her.

She was no psychologist, but she knew that something inside her daughter had broken that could not be stuck back together with logic.

'So you admit that you deserved my plan?' Lisa asked triumphantly.

'What plan?'

'The one I worked out with Querky.' A dark cloud veiled

Lisa's expression. It looked as if she'd just been visited by a nasty thought.

'Did you steal the envelope from the safe?' she asked with menace.

'What?' Julia didn't understand anything. Her daughter might just as well have been whistling. 'What are you talking about?'

Lisa flicked her hand dismissively, as if what she'd said wasn't important any more. 'I told Querky that you forced me to go on the game,' she laughed grubbily.

Boom!

Another hand grenade of madness lobbed in her direction by her daughter. And her aim was getting better.

'What? For Christ's sake, why?' Julia asked.

'Because she wouldn't have helped me otherwise. She only looks after children who've been raped and abused. So I fibbed to Querky. To prove I was being forced to have sex with strange men against my will I sent her the video.'

Julia blinked. In the split second that her eyes were closed, scraps of memories flashed in her mind, in which she saw the back of her daughter's head in the lap of a groaning man who now had a name: *Tom!*

'The video in which I did him the favour of playing you.'

'Me?'

'A whore.'

In her mind's eye Julia saw Lisa take the money.

Okay. Stop. Enough. It couldn't go on like this.

She took a step towards Lisa. Now there were only a couple of arm lengths between Julia and her daughter. 'Look at me, Lisa. I know I've made mistakes. I wasn't there for you when your father left us. I didn't look after you enough when you hit puberty. And, yes, I had a relationship with your teacher. But I ended it.'

'You're lying.' Lisa gave her the finger.

'No, it's the truth, darling. Without me knowing what was going on between the two of you...'

'Is. What *is* going on between the two of us!'

'Fine, fine, fine!' Julia raised both hands to calm her down. 'Without knowing what is going on between the two of you I noticed that Tom...'

'Don't you dare speak his name again!'

'... wasn't the right man for me.'

'Ha!' Lisa sneered at her. The sweat was now dripping from her eyebrows too. 'So you think you're better, do you? Was he just a disposable item for you?'

Julia closed her eyes. This wasn't getting anywhere. She might as well have begged the sea to stop swooshing. She turned angry. Not at Lisa, who was manifestly no longer in control of her senses and in urgent need of professional help. But at Tom, who'd abused his position of authority as a teacher, destroyed the sensitive heart of an adolescent teenager and also deceived her. Her unbridled anger surfaced so quickly that she could no longer control what she was saying. 'Okay, fine. I'm the guilty one!' she barked at Lisa. 'I pinched Tom off you. I deserved being given the biggest fright of my life. But none of that is going to bring that filthy bastard back, who only used you...'

'Aaaaaaaaaaaaaa...'

Emitting a sound reminiscent of a war cry, Lisa leaped forwards with the screwdriver, as if out of her mind.

And stabbed.

69

'Please, I beg you. There might still be time.'

Bonhoeffer put his hands together as if Tiago were a god he was beseeching to hear his prayers.

'If what Lisa wrote is true then the girl is still on the ship. At this very moment she might well be carrying out the last part of her plan.'

Tiago, who hadn't given in for the past twenty minutes, scratched his thick mop of hair and shook his head in resignation. 'I've almost bought it once. My gut feeling tells me that if I let you go now it'll definitely be game over.'

In fury the captain slammed his palm on his desk, where he was still being forced to sit. 'But what the hell do you plan to do with me then? Keep me prisoner here until we arrive in New York?'

'No.' Tiago stared at Bonhoeffer as if he'd just had an idea. 'Call the US coastguard. The border police or the FBI. I don't care. I want to speak to them and outline my position.'

Bonhoeffer looked at him dumbfounded. 'That's your demand? Did you just think of this now?'

Tiago nodded. He looked conscience-stricken. 'I'm scared. I can't think straight when I'm scared.'

Bonhoeffer sighed. His mouth was dry. He'd talked so much that he could smell his bad breath. 'Okay, fine. Here's the deal, Tiago. You let me make two phone calls. With the first one I'll stop the ship. With the second I'll try to get hold of Julia Stiller. As soon as that's done the two of us will notify the authorities together and then you'll finally hand over that bloody weapon of yours. How does that sound?'

'Lousy,' Tiago said, pointing at Bonhoeffer's phone. 'But I hesitated too long once before.'

Bonhoeffer nodded and started dialling.

'Just pray to God you haven't done it a second time.'

70

Martin virtually broke through the door. He'd left Elena behind on his dash out of Hell's Kitchen, and had raced through the staff area and up the six flights of stairs from deck A to the fifth passenger floor of this ocean giant.

He'd barged into women, leaped over children, knocked a tray carrying room service from a waiter's hand and compelled him to hand over his skeleton key. And still he came too late.

Or that's what he thought when he saw Lisa lunge with a screwdriver at her mother, who for some reason was naked, or at best very scantily clad. But then Lisa tripped, catching the laces of her combat boots around a leg of the bed. This gave Julia time to retreat to the balcony that her daughter was also steaming towards.

'Hey, Lisa,' Martin shouted with the last of his breath. Lisa hadn't heard the door crash open, but she responded to her name. She slowly turned around to him.

The telephone on the bedside table was ringing; nobody paid it any attention.

'Who are you?' Lisa said, keeping one eye on her mother. The wind was blowing her hair forwards like a hood.

Noting her glassy look Martin understood the situation at a glance. Lisa Stiller was in a sort of alpha mode, a state in which she would only react to the most powerful external stimuli. The voice of reason had been switched off, as had her ability to distinguish between right and wrong.

She was probably suffering from a dissociative disorder. If Diesel was right and the teacher had sexually exploited and abused the girl, this negative experience would have touched her sensitive emotional nexus like a burning match and set the whole thing alight.

She seemed to be blaming her mother for the mental torture she must have been suffering. Over weeks, months perhaps, she'd built Julia up as a bogeyman figure. Martin knew that he wouldn't be able to deter her quickly from her actions with sound argument. And certainly not with the truth. So he lied to her and said, 'I'm a friend of Querky's.'

Bingo!

He'd remembered the name Shahla had used when contacting potential clients on Easyexit. Elena's suspicion proved well founded. There was a connection between Lisa and Shahla too. And by pretending to be Querky's accomplice he'd gained Lisa's attention. But also that of her mother, who stared at him wide-eyed and was just about to open her mouth when she read – correctly – from the brief glance he shot at her that this was not the time to butt in.

'Querky doesn't have any friends,' Lisa said, somewhat bewildered.

'Oh, yes, she does. I'm her assistant.'

'You're lying.'

'No I'm not. She sent me here to tell you to stop.'

'Bullshit.'

'No, honest. The plan has been put on hold.'

'Oh, really? So why didn't she come to tell me herself?'

'Because she…' Martin's first instinct was to tell the truth. *Because she's dead.* But that might provoke the worst reaction possible. Searching for the appropriate response he began, 'Because at the moment she's…'

'Here. Here I am.'

Martin swivelled around in shock. Elena was standing in the cabin doorway, as out of breath as he was.

'You?' Martin heard Lisa say behind him. He turned back to the girl. 'You're Querky?'

'Yes,' Elena said. 'We met on Easyexit.'

'You, you sound completely different.'

'Because I had an accident,' Elena said, pointing to her disfigured face. 'It's going to take a while before I get my old voice back.' She pushed past Martin. 'I've got a message for you from Tom.'

'From my boyfriend?' Lisa's face lit up.

'He says he wants to get back together with you.'

'Really?'

'Yes. On the condition that you don't hurt your mother.'

Mistrust flickered in Lisa's eyes. Elena had overdone it.

'You're not Querky.'

'Hey, Lisa, think about it. How else would I know about Tom and the video if you hadn't emailed it to me?'

'No, you're lying. I bet you don't know my nickname.'

'Your…' Elena's voice started to wobble. She swallowed. It wasn't only Martin who saw the visible signs of her uncertainty.

'Tell me the nickname I'm registered on Easyexit with.'

'You are…' Elena turned to Martin in desperation. 'Your

nickname is...' Red patches spread on the undamaged side of her face.

'Forget it,' Lisa said scornfully. 'You're not Querky. And Tom doesn't want to have anything to do with me any more. You haven't got any message from him.'

Her hand gripped the screwdriver more tightly.

'Drop it!' Martin said, now just a couple of paces away.

She looked at him, incensed. 'You don't reckon I stand a a chance against you, do you?'

'If you try to attack your mother...' Martin shook his head.

One minute earlier she could have hurt Julia badly, so badly perhaps that she'd have been able to throw her mother overboard.

But now the most she could do was give her mother a scratch before Martin snatched the screwdriver from her hand.

'Well, the plan has failed then,' Lisa said with a shrug.

She turned to her sobbing mother.

'I hope you're happy with Tom,' she said, tossing the tool overboard.

Then she leaned against the railings and, together with the parapet she'd loosened with the screwdriver in the hours she'd waited for her mother, she fell into the depths like a guillotine.

71

Two weeks later
Internal Investigations
Berlin

The fan on the air conditioning unit, which was currently switched to heating mode, rattled as if a leaf had got caught up in it. Given that the interrogation room was in a soundproofed basement at least two kilometres from the nearest tree, this would have been rather surprising. It was much more likely that the humming box was on its last legs.

Martin was expecting a loud bang at any moment, to announce that the ancient thing below the ceiling had finally gone out of service.

Over the last few hours while he'd been attached to the lie detector, the unit had provided the room with warm air to some extent, but it stank of burned rubber.

'Shall we take a break?' his interviewer said, leaning back in her swivel chair. She'd been introduced to him as Dr Elizabeth Klein. Apparently she'd worked for years at the Federal Intelligence Service, where she'd developed a reputation as an interrogation expert, specialising in psychopathic serial killers. At first glance, however, she looked more like the spiritual course leader of an esoteric self-help group. All items of her clothing shimmered in every tone of orange imaginable, from the cardigan she'd knitted herself to the voluminous culottes.

'No,' Martin replied, removing the patches from his arm and chest. 'We're not going to take a break. We're going to finish here.'

Against expectation Dr Klein nodded. 'So you've got nothing more to tell us?'

'Apart from the fact that anyone who contradicts my version of events can kiss my arse?' Martin put a finger to the corner of his mouth and pretended to think. 'No.' He shook his head.

Dr Klein gazed at one of the many bangles on her right arm, twiddled it and nodded. When she looked back up at him there was a wise expression in her eyes.

No sympathy, please. I can't cope with sympathy now.

Martin cleared his throat and asked whether he might get up. Dr Klein sighed. 'Alright. Of course, we're a long way off concluding this internal investigation. You must know how long it takes when an officer is caught up in a homicide.'

She gave him the hint of a smile.

'But I can tell you now that for the most part your statements concur with the information we've received from the captain, the doctor, this' – she leafed through a slim file in front of her – 'this Tiago Álvarez character and Gerlinde Dobkowitz.'

'Fantastic.' Martin rubbed his cold hands. 'Was I able to convince the technology too?'

He pointed first at the camera in the ceiling, then at the

laptop between them, on which the lie detector had recorded his vital signs during his statement.

The interrogator wiggled her hand from side to side.

'According to the polygraph you seem to be telling the truth. Apart from…'

Martin raised his eyebrows. 'Apart from what?'

She gave him a long stare. Then she took a tissue from one of the many pockets in an item of clothing – now Martin couldn't be sure whether it was a pair of culottes or wraparound dress.

She blew her nose, stood up, went over to the security camera and pulled out a cable that ran directly from the wall into the device.

'Let's talk privately, Herr Schwartz.'

She looked down at him like a vulture targeting its prey. Martin eyed her sceptically as she returned to the desk.

'The machine didn't show any striking fluctuations,' she said. 'In any event, where you pieced together from hearsay all those things you weren't personally witness to, polygraphic assessment isn't much use. But at one point…' She turned the laptop to face him. 'Here you start to sweat and your heart rate shoots up. Even without the camera, I also detected various microexpressions that signalled to me you weren't telling the truth.' She showed him a section of graph where the waves looked like the ECG of someone on the verge of cardiac arrest.

'What was I saying then?' Martin asked, even though he had a very good idea.

'You were basically telling Dr Beck that you hadn't seen anything in Shahla Afridi's notes referring to your son's fate.'

Martin nodded.

'That was a lie, wasn't it?'

He swallowed deeply, but didn't say anything.

'Herr Schwartz, it won't change my assessment one bit. As far as I can see, you've not done anything wrong except take absence without leave. I'm only interested privately in what you found out about Timmy and Nadja.'

Oh, really? Are you? Why? For a bit of sensationalism, perhaps?

Looking into her good-natured eyes he knew he was being unfair on her.

'The video that Bonhoeffer showed you. Where you see them jumping from the ship,' she insisted. 'You know now why the larger shape went first, followed by the smaller one, don't you?'

Martin gave a terse nod. He'd learned the truth three days following Shahla's death, after the *Sultan* had berthed in New York and the FBI had taken up the investigation. By that point Daniel's men had already located the secret place near the blue shelf where the chambermaid had hidden Anouk for the last few weeks, and which had also been Lisa's hiding spot during the night she faked her suicide. In the bare, container-like room, which had been used to store recyclable metal and other raw materials before the waste dumping facility was decommissioned, they'd found a mattress, a banana crate that had served as a bedside table and a metal shelf unit screwed into the wall with books, children's games, puzzles, cuddly toys and even an iPad full of films, e-books and computer games.

Besides the multimedia content, FBI technicians discovered in the browser a link to a cloud server where

Shahla had stored personal documents. After they'd managed to crack the code, they came across a diary entry relating to the day when Timmy and Nadja died. In a break during questioning, the chief FBI investigator had left Martin alone with an extract from the diary.

Just like this internal investigation by Dr Klein, the FBI also came to the conclusion that although Schwartz was an important witness, he wasn't a suspect and so should be allowed to return to Germany along with Julia and Lisa Stiller, on condition that he make himself available for further questioning. Letting him see the diary entry was probably a favour from the FBI investigator, seeing as Martin wasn't only a colleague, he'd also proved highly cooperative throughout questioning.

For five whole minutes Martin had read over and over again the few lines Shahla had written, so often that they clung to his memory like leeches, and he could still recite them verbatim in his mind:

I often wonder whether it was chance or destiny that helped me with this German family. During dinner I was about to do the turn-down when I caught the mother in her cabin, indecently assaulting her son. She was lying naked on top of him, and wasn't able to wriggle off quickly enough.

That was five years ago. Her name was Nadja Schwartz.

When Martin read this for the first time he had to laugh. A paradoxical reaction of his mind, which really ought to have made him scream. He recalled sensing that he was getting a bad nosebleed, but his nose remained dry. Instead he heard a loud, high-pitched buzzing, which didn't signal a headache this time, but split into two voices. One of them, a deep, calm and pleasant voice, whispered confidentially in his ear that he shouldn't believe what he was reading. That Shahla was a liar. The other one emitted a shrill, hoarse yell and uttered a single word: *condom!*

It took Martin back to the day five years ago, before the cruise, before his last mission, when he'd come home early from the meeting. He'd never found out who his wife's lover was, the man who'd left the condom in his bed.

Unrolled, but unused.

But now, when he thought of how he'd met Nadja, everything took on a different meaning. In casualty with the black eye that her boyfriend had given her. Not out of jealousy, as she'd claimed. But because she actually had got too close to the man's son.

Martin couldn't help thinking back to his last conversation with Timmy too: *'Don't you want to talk about it?'*

The last conversation between father and son, which essentially wasn't about the five in Maths, nor the unusual increase in his need for sleep and why he'd suddenly stopped wanting to play tennis.

The signs of abuse.

What had been Timmy's answer back then?

'It's because of you. Because you're away so often, and with Mama...'

... with Mama, who saw in her young son a substitute partner? Just as Shahla's mother had done?

The deep voice whispered that he was wrong, but it became ever softer.

And after Martin had thrown up for the third time, the hoarse voice didn't have to bellow so loudly to convince him that there was no reason why Shahla, who could never have anticipated that her diary would fall into *his* hands, should have lied when writing it. Particularly as these lines shed light on the mystery as to why Nadja had fallen overboard first.

And then Timmy!

Shahla had written:

When I saw the mother with her son I flipped out. In a blind fury I grabbed the nearest object, a heavy desk lamp, and hit the woman over the head. She lost consciousness immediately; perhaps she was dead. Her son ran into the bathroom and locked himself in. What was I to do? It was a messy situation. If I hadn't lost it, I'd have been able to deliver the punishment much more cleanly on another occasion. But now I was forced to dispose of the mother's body at once. Luckily the weather was bad that night and there was a large sea swell. Besides, it wouldn't be in the cruise line's interest to try to prove an act of violence by video analysis. Suicide is better for a shipping company's image than having a serial killer on board, which is why I didn't hesitate for long before throwing Mrs Schwartz overboard. Unfortunately her son had by now left the bathroom and was watching me. When he saw his mother fall over the railings he ran to the balcony, right past me, climbed the parapet... and leaped after her.

First the large shadow.

Then the small one.

Here in the interrogation room, Martin had great difficulty not bursting out into a crying fit, similar to the one he'd had when he read the diary extract and understood for the first time the full implication of Shahla's account.

Timmy loved his mother. In spite of everything.

Just as the battered wife stops the police from arresting the husband who beats her, Timmy's love for his mother and fear of losing her was much greater and stronger than his fear of further abuse.

Tears shot into Martin's eyes, which did not go unnoticed by Dr Klein.

'Don't you want to talk about it?' she asked.

Talk about what? he thought.

That there are mothers who abuse their children? And children who love their parents in spite of everything?

Until death.

'Let me guess,' the interrogator said. 'The truth you now know is so horrendous that you don't care about your own life.'

'I felt like that before.'

'Was that the reason?'

'The reason for what?'

'That you jumped in after Lisa?'

Martin closed his eyes.

He briefly felt the impact again, twenty metres down, as a result of which he'd broken his foot. Elena had splinted it with an elastic bandage, which was why he was now limping.

He'd felt as if he'd jumped into a saucepan, except that the foaming water lapping above his head had burned like thousands of pins. Pins of ice, which sucked all strength from his body almost the very moment that the Atlantic had him in its claws.

'I haven't given it a thought,' Martin said, and if he'd still been wired up to the lie detector this would have registered that he was telling the truth. He'd just jumped, a reflex, without making any conscious decision.

Lisa had come off worse. When she hit the water she broke her hip and dislocated her left shoulder. Thank goodness, because she was screaming blue murder when her head popped back up above the surface of the water. The stillness of the sea and the lucky coincidence that the captain had already stopped the ship beforehand, had made it possible to save her.

'I expect you'll be given an award,' Dr Klein said.

'A medal, I hope. I can at least use that as a coaster,' Martin muttered. 'I didn't do anything.'

In his mind he could taste the salt water which he'd swallowed by the litre and later vomited.

'You pushed the detached railings over to Lisa so she could keep herself alive until the rescue crew got to you.'

Dr Klein reached for Martin's hand and squeezed it. He was unsure whether he found this gesture unpleasant or whether it should make him unhappy.

'I don't know that Lisa Stiller's so thrilled about it,' he said, pulling his fingers back.

If Martin was correctly informed, both Anouk and Lisa were currently in psychiatric institutions; one in Manhattan, the other on the outskirts of Berlin, where Julia Stiller was also taking professional help to process the horrific experience. Martin hoped they wouldn't too quickly expose the children to the world of doctors with their questions and pills, but not everyone shared his preference for televisions and Game Boys when the aim was to liberate traumatised and mentally ill patients from their world of shadows and illusion.

'Can I go now?' he asked, standing up.

Dr Klein nodded. She took a mobile phone from a trouser pocket.

'Of course. Shall we call you a car?'

Martin forced an innocuous smile and politely declined.

What address would he give to the taxi driver? His life was now void of destinations.

72

Four weeks later

The needle of the speedometer seemed to be nailed down at one hundred and forty kilometres per hour. You might have thought that Kramer had switched on the cruise control, but Martin knew that the head of the operations regarded such aids as 'pensioners' accessories'. He bet that in the 1980s Kramer would have sneered at power steering and automatic transmission too, and if the man had ever been on a demonstration, then it would have been to protest against the compulsory wearing of seatbelts.

'How about a coffee?' Martin asked when the sign for Michendorf service station appeared. They were driving in the vehicle he'd last sat in outside the Pryga villa in Westend, and where he'd pulled out one of his own teeth. In fact a visit to the dentist was long overdue; the sweet lady from casualty had even left him a concerned message on his answerphone telling him he mustn't forget to have the interim denture replaced. But he had time. He could cope with the throbbing in his jaw and could sleep well with three ibuprofen, occasionally even four hours at a time. The painkillers also helped with his headache. In addition, the attacks he'd had on the ship had become less frequent ever since he'd prematurely ditched the PEP pills.

'No coffee. We're late,' Kramer decided, even though there were three hours till their meeting at the motorway car park just outside of Jena.

Martin yawned and turned his wrist outwards so he could see his arteries. And the tattoo. A rose with eighteen tiny thorns. A Russian prison tattoo. The sign that you'd reached the age of maturity in jail. He'd had it inked ten days ago for this operation. Their goal was to infiltrate a Croatian biker gang that was seeking to take over the Berlin bouncer business. The people who controlled the doors to clubs and discos also controlled the flow of drugs. A lucrative business that was bitterly contested. In the coming weeks the Croatian gang was planning on eliminating a few bouncers and Martin was going to offer his services as a contract killer.

'Doesn't the tattoo look too new?' Kramer asked, returning his gaze to the almost-empty road after a glance at the rose.

'I'll say I had it freshened up in celebration of this day,' Martin replied. He yawned again. Yesterday hadn't been a four-hour night. More like four minutes.

They passed the service station and thus the chance of a coffee. Martin shut his eyes and leaned his head against the vibrating window.

'Hey! Walivakelive ulivup yolivoulivu ilividilivioliVot!' he suddenly heard Kramer say beside him. Turning to him, he saw his boss giggling into his double chin. Martin, who couldn't make head or tail of this nonsense, asked Kramer if he was having a stroke. 'If so, you'd better let me drive.'

'Rubbish, I'm fine. That's how my daughter talks at the

moment.' The head of operations was wearing the smile of a proud father. '*Helivellolivo*, for example, means *hello*.'

He indicated to overtake a white rust bucket that was hogging the middle lane.

'It's called Livish,' he explained as if Martin might be interested in the silly secret language that Kramer's daughter had concocted.

'Lottie's practised it with her friend throughout the entire autumn holiday and now she's driving her teachers potty too. The principle is very simple. Shall I tell you how it works?'

Martin shook his head, but this didn't spare him Kramer's explanation.

'You put *liv* after every vowel, then repeat the vowel afterwards. *Walivakelive ulivup yolivouliu ilividiliviolivot* means *wake up you idiot*.' Kramer slapped the steering wheel, as if he'd just told the joke of the year.

'I understand,' Martin said, before adding 'alivarseliveholivolelive'. Kramer stopped laughing and looked straight ahead sulkily.

Martin's mobile rang. Although the number wasn't one of his contacts, it seemed familiar, so he took the call.

'Martin?' Gerlinde Dobkowitz began the conversation with reproach in her voice. 'What sort of a way to behave is that? I mean, I can understand that you didn't propose to me, even though I'm still quite a catch, but to skip offboard without so much as a goodbye, and then not even a call afterwards to say you're back on dry land, well, that's pretty steep!'

He was going to tell her that he was deliberately avoiding contact with anyone who reminded him of the *Sultan*, and thus of Timmy but, as ever, she didn't let him get a word in edgeways.

'Anyway, I was just giving you a bell to say that I've finished my novel. You know, *Cruise Killer*.'

'Lovely title,' Martin said, seeking a polite way to end the conversation.

'Isn't it just?' she agreed perkily. 'Although I thought *The Bermuda Deck* was even better.' But it appears that my second theory about the secret deck and experiments on people hasn't proved correct, although I haven't altogether given up the hunt for a secret way in. Anyway, a female serial killer in the ship's basement isn't to be sneezed at, is it?'

'You had a nose for it, Frau Dobkowitz, but—'

'I'll send you a copy if you like. Or I'll give it to you in person. I'm coming to Berlin next month.'

'You're leaving the ship?' This was a surprise to Martin.

'Of course, what do you think? As soon as my bestseller came out, they'd have kicked me off the boat anyway as a traitor. Besides, I've had enough of being here now. My need for death and violence has been sated. If I don't watch out I might vanish too in all the excitement. At seventy-eight plus five you've got to take things a bit more easily.'

'Seventy-eight plus five?' Martin asked, blinking nervously. He froze. Gerlinde giggled to herself.

'At my age you don't just count the years, but the months too. And even the days, if possible, when the final checkout is looming. I mean, I wouldn't say the worms are already licking their lips when I wheel myself across the meadow, but—'

Martin muttered a goodbye and hung up before Gerlinde could finish her sentence.

'Hey, what's wrong?' Kramer asked, peering at him from the corner of his eye. 'Is everything alright?'

No, it's not.

Martin could sense that his mouth was hanging open, but there were more important things to do than close it again.

Gerlinde's comment about her age had unsettled him. The black van was holding its lane, but in his head a thought had derailed, which he desperately wanted to grab hold of again. *Needed* to grab hold of.

What had Diesel said about Anouk?

'The result of her IQ test she took in year 5 was 135... And she came second in a national memory championship.'

Seventy-eight plus five.

Helivellolivo!

'Stop!' he screamed at Kramer, who'd just moved into the slow lane. 'Let me out!'

'Here?'

'Right now!' Martin opened the sliding door on the passenger side. An icy wind flew inside. He heard Kramer curse, but the van slowed down, veered right and finally came to a halt on the hard shoulder.

'You're wrecking the operation,' Kramer yelled after him, as Martin had already jumped out. 'If you bugger off again without permission, that will be that, you psycho.'

Martin briefly glanced back and nodded.

He ran over to the other side of the motorway to find someone who'd get him back to Berlin as quickly as possible...

78+5

... so he could search through the memory on his phone in peace, where somewhere the truth was hiding...

73

It took him four hours to get home. Thirty minutes for the transcript of the session with Anouk that he'd recorded on his smartphone on the *Sultan*. And two hours after that he sensed that he was on the verge of cracking the riddle.

Martin sat in his poorly ventilated period apartment at a wobbly kitchen table, from which he'd first had to elbow a pile of unpaid bills, reminders and advertising flyers onto the floor to give him enough room for his work.

In front of him were his mobile phone and two sheets of A4 paper. On one sheet he'd jotted down the questions he'd asked Anouk on his second visit to Hell's Kitchen. On the other were the girl's answers, at least so far as he could recall them, for Anouk hadn't said them out loud, but written them on her toy computer, which was now in possession of the FBI, like Shahla's notebook and her iPad.

On the left-hand piece of paper, the one with the questions, Martin had noted the following:

1. *When I came to see you a couple of hours ago with Dr Beck you mentioned a name to me, Anouk. Can you remember what that was?*

2. *Do you have any idea where you are at the moment?*
3. *How old are you?*

Martin picked up his mobile and rewound again to the relevant point. During the recording itself he'd felt that there was something not quite right about Anouk's behaviour, even taking into consideration her trauma. At the time her answers seemed to follow an opaque logic. It was as if he'd been listening to an unfamiliar foreign or secret language.

Like *Livish*.

Martin listened to his third question again.

'*How old are you?*'

On the recording he heard the signal for the emergency drill, which he'd ignored. Then it clearly took a while for him to formulate his fourth question.

'*My God, who did that to you?*'

Martin remembered discovering the round burn scars from cigarettes on Anouk's tummy. Now he knew that these had been inflicted on her before the trip by the men Naomi had left her alone with. But back then he'd assumed they were the work of a rapist who was still on board.

According to his notes, question 4 was the first that Anouk had answered, by writing his name on the screen of her toy computer:

Martin

He picked up the sheet of questions again.

4. *My God, who did that to you?*

5. But you know I'm not a bad man, don't you?

Martin couldn't hear it on the recording of course, but he saw Anouk before him screwing up her eyes in concentration and counting on her fingers. And then writing something which first he'd taken to be a mathematical sum and then a clue relating to the anchor deck: 11+3.

'Seventy-eight plus five,' he heard Gerlinde say. This is what had put him on the right track.

'How old are you?'

Below this he jotted down Anouk's third answer in pencil:

11 + 3

Stunned, he pushed himself back from the kitchen table and stood up so frantically that his chair tipped over backwards. *That's it. That's the solution. The pattern.*

Martin knew that he was on the verge of unlocking a secret he'd thought far too little about until now. All the madness he'd experienced on the *Sultan* hadn't given him time to get to the bottom of things. And once he was back on land the grief devouring him on the inside had prevented him from seeing the basics.

The truth!

The cloth with the chloroform.

If Shahla's account was true, how had it got into their cabin?

If the chambermaid had only caught them 'by chance', why would she have had chloroform on her?

All of a sudden Martin saw a hole in the entire story – the

discrepancies which, in his loathing of himself and his fate, he hadn't called into question.

Picking up his mobile he dialled the number of the New York clinic where Anouk was being kept. Elena, who'd accompanied the girl to Manhattan, had called him from there. He just had to press recall to get the main office. He introduced himself as Dr Schwartz in the hope of being connected quicker as a potential colleague, but it took a good quarter of an hour before he got the doctor in charge, Dr Silva, on the line.

'Anouk is not who we think she is,' he explained to the elderly gentleman who sounded as if he had a cold.

'What are you saying?' Silva asked.

Martin was pacing in circles around his kitchen, far too agitated to keep still.

'She's not traumatised, at least not to the extent that it appears.'

'Not traumatised?' Silva was incensed. 'First the girl was raped and then abducted.'

Martin paused briefly, to order his thoughts and avoid sounding like one of the befuddled patients his colleague treated.

'Have you ever worked with highly intelligent children, doctor?' he asked Silva. 'You know what happens when they're not stretched. Children who are that bright start displaying behavioural problems. A few go silent, others stop eating and sink into depression, and others become loud, aggressive and even violent sometimes. To other people or themselves.'

'I'm still listening,' Dr Silva said when Martin paused.

'What I'm trying to say is that I believe Anouk suffered

from understimulation stress for months. Of course she was badly traumatised by the serious abuse. But that wasn't what stopped her from talking or made her scratch her skin.'

'So what was it?' Silva asked.

'To put it crudely, Anouk got bored.'

'What?'

'Being locked up on a ship, first in a windowless dungeon, then on an isolation ward, without any opportunity for normal development. Even mentally healthy people would find it hard to cope with that. So how must a hyperactive, highly intelligent child feel? Scratching herself was an expression of her lack of stimulation.'

'What other evidence do you have?'

'The code,' Martin replied. 'Anouk couldn't tolerate sitting still any more or continue to obey Shahla's instruction not to talk to anyone. That's why she made up a game and communicated to me in a secret language. A highly intelligent game. Anouk's code is difficult to decrypt. You have to be a memory champion like her to master it.

'How does this secret language work?' Silva sounded faintly irritated. Martin could understand that. He'd have reacted just as sceptically if a supposed colleague had rung out of the blue from abroad to give him a lecture.

'Have you also noticed that Anouk never answers the first three questions? Not in any conversation?' he asked.

A pause. When Silva spoke again he sounded dumbfounded. 'I'm afraid it's not my place to discuss the findings of our treatments with outsiders,' he said in a manner which left Martin in no doubt that he'd hit the bullseye.

Excitedly, he outlined his theory to the psychiatrist. 'This is Anouk's system. She delays her answers by three, which *basically means...*'

'*That she doesn't answer the first one until she's been asked the fourth.*'

'*And then answers the second when she's asked the fifth and so on. You have to adjust the answers by three positions.*' Martin *looked triumphantly, first at the paper with the questions, then at the sheet of answers. Everything made much more sense if you put Anouk's first answer beneath the first question, her second answer beneath the second question, and so on. The results were as follows:*

Question 1: When I came to see you a couple of hours ago with Dr Beck you mentioned a name to me, Anouk. Can you remember what that was?

Answer: Martin

Question 2: Do you have any idea where you are at the moment?

Answer: Anouk draws a ship.

Question 3: How old are you?

Answer: 11+3.

Question 4: My God, who did that to you?

Answer: My mama.

Question 5: But you know I'm not a bad man, don't you?

Answer: ??? (Probably nods in agreement.)

Everything was so clear, so logical. And effortlessly easy when you knew the system. And yet, when on the phone to Silva, Martin had arrived at the sixth question, he felt as if he'd overlooked something fundamental again.

'This is quite remarkable information, Dr Schwartz,' he heard the psychiatrist say. A couple of other sentences followed, but Martin wasn't really listening.

He picked up his pencil and stuck the end with the rubber into his mouth.

He'd asked nine questions in that therapy session. Anouk had answered five with her system. The sixth had remained open.

'Can you tell me the name of the person you've been with all this time?'

Martin sat back down at the kitchen table and wrote No. 6 on the answer sheet. A tingling sensation ran down his back from the neck to the coccyx. 'Would you agree with me?' he heard Silva say. He said yes, even though he had no idea what the question had been.

Question 6.

When he first recalled their session he'd assumed that Anouk hadn't written anything after 'My mama'. But now he wasn't so sure.

Martin shut his eyes and once more turned his thoughts back to that loathsome ship. He was in Hell's Kitchen again.

Asking the exhausted-looking Anouk, *'Is there anything I can bring you?'*

He recalled the alarm for the ship's exercise drill. Seven short tones and one long one.

Anouk picking up the toy computer one last time.

'Can you tell me the name of the person you've been with all this time?'

And the name she'd written on the screen before turning away and sticking her thumb in her mouth.

It's not possible.

The truth struck like a stab of a knife which didn't kill him, but made him bleed slowly.

'Hello, Dr Schwartz? Are you still there?' Dr Silva said several thousands of kilometres away, but Martin had stopped listening some time ago.

He'd left the phone on the kitchen table to pack his stuff. Another trip awaited him. He had to hurry. He'd already wasted too much time.

74

Thirty-five hours later
Dominican Republic

The two-storey, clay-coloured finca was just a stone's throw from the Casa de Campos polo fields, in a cul-de-sac lined with hollies, with a brown shingle roof that jutted out over the entrance like a peaked cap and was supported by two white columns.

It was barely different from any of the other well-maintained holiday homes here that belonged almost exclusively to foreigners, although it was significantly smaller than the villas of the high-profile people who had secured the best spots five minutes from La Romana, directly on the beach or around the golf course.

It was two o'clock in the afternoon, the hottest part of the day. Not a cloud in the sky to prevent the sun from driving the muggy air on the ground up to thirty-six degrees.

Martin got out of the small, air-conditioned car that he'd rented at the airport in the morning and started to sweat. He was wearing khaki shorts, a white linen shirt and dark sunglasses. With his white, pasty skin, he looked like a typical tourist on the first week of his holiday. He protected his head, now covered in stubble again, with an old-style baseball cap.

Looking around, he pulled the shirt from his chest. He'd barely been out of the car for twenty seconds and it was already sticking to his body like a rubber glove.

At this time of day there wasn't anyone in their right mind who'd voluntarily leave their air-conditioned house.

Nobody watched him as he hobbled across the freshly mown lawn (the long-distance flight had caused his foot to swell up again) to get to the rear of the finca, where he saw the obligatory swimming pool, pine needles swimming on its surface.

The garden bordered on an unfinished new development, and so there was nobody here either who could see Martin check the back door for hidden cables and cameras, and jimmy open the lock with a penknife after ensuring that he wouldn't set off any alarm.

Martin thought it would have taken longer to locate the address, but after just an hour he'd found a taxi driver at the port who'd recognised the photo. And who, in return for two hundred US dollars, had told him where this person regularly went whenever the ship docked in La Romana.

He closed the back door and walked across the sandstone tiles into the large sitting room.

Inside the finca it was only slightly cooler than outside, a sure sign that a European lived here who had misgivings about leaving the air conditioning on during the days and weeks when they were absent.

The décor inside was typically American. An open-plan kitchen, a U-shaped sofa arrangement in front of the family altar on the wall: the gigantic plasma screen directly above a mock fireplace.

Martin switched on the air conditioning, took a beer out of the fridge, removed from his trouser pocket the pistol he'd bought in La Romana, placed it on the coffee table and sat on the sofa. Only now did he remove his cap and sunglasses.

He didn't know how long his wait would be, but he was prepared for a long one. His duffle bag was in the hire car. This time he'd brought along a few more changes of clothes than for his excursion on the *Sultan*. Martin would spend the winter here if necessary.

That it wouldn't be necessary became clear the moment he picked up a truncheon-sized remote control from the coffee table: the television switched on by itself.

The colour of the screen changed from black to turquoise. In the centre the Skype symbol appeared, beneath which it said: *Incoming Call.*

So it wasn't an alarm system visible from the outside. The house must be secured by webcams that registered any movement inside the house and called the owner as soon as anything unusual occurred.

Fine by me.

Martin pressed a round button marked OK.

He heard an electronic sound reminiscent of the plop of water in a cave of stalactites, and a computer icon of two hands shaking signalled that the connection had been made.

'That took a long time,' he heard a voice say. The matching face didn't appear on the screen, but Martin was pretty sure that the TV camera was transmitting his picture. 'I was expecting you earlier.'

Martin put the remote control beside his beer, shrugged and said, 'How can I put it poetically? Time is the life jacket of truth; it always brings it to the surface. Isn't that right, *Querky*? Or would you rather I call you Elena?'

75

He heard a chuckle.

In his mind Martin could see the doctor's hand playing with the oak-leaf pendant on her necklace.

Oak – in Latin *quercus.*

'I'd say rather that time gives baddies the opportunity to retreat to safety.'

Martin shook his head. 'You're not safe from me anywhere, Elena. As you can see, I'll find you wherever you are.' The ship's doctor giggled. 'Oh, please. That really wasn't hard, seeing as I practically gave you my address.'

Martin nodded. Her revelations about her past life when they were in the corridor of Hell's Kitchen had been a mistake.

'*I lived in the Dominican Republic for three years and in the city hospital there treated more refugee children from Haiti who'd been raped than the head of the Hamburg women's clinic will have seen in a lifetime...*'

'Anyone who's been on holiday here knows how lax the immigration controls used to be. Especially if you were stepping off a ship. I shouldn't have let on to you that I'd been living on an island where until a few years ago you could do almost anything with bribes, so long as you knew the right people. The easiest thing of all was to get a house in a different name.'

The slatted blower of the air conditioning unit changed the direction of the airflow at regular intervals. At the moment it was blowing straight into his face.

'I didn't come here to discuss your conjuring tricks,' Martin said.

'I know. You want to kill me because I killed your family.'

'Precisely.'

'But it's not going to come to that, Martin.'

'I might not have got you here. But, believe me, I'll hunt you around the world. I'll find you and bring you to justice, if it's the last thing I do.'

'You'd be making a mistake.'

'I don't think so. Anouk herself told me that you abducted her.'

Can you tell me the name of the person you've been with all this time?

'I analysed her secret language. She wrote your name down when I asked about the culprit.'

Martin heard Elena clap her hands.

'Bravo. But you're wrong about one fundamental thing. I didn't abduct Anouk. She came with me willingly. I looked after her.'

'While torturing and killing her mother.'

'No, that was Shahla.'

'Don't talk crap. Shahla was just your pawn. You're behind all the killings that you blamed on her.'

Unnerved, Elena blew air from her pursed lips, making

her sound like a snorting horse. 'For a detective you're rather slow on the uptake. Shahla was anything but innocent.'

'I don't believe a word you're saying,' Martin objected. 'The notes on the computer, the conversation with Naomi, you cobbled that all together.'

'Partly, yes. But I only wrote down the truth.'

The cold waft from the air conditioning unit wandered across Martin's face again, making him shiver. Outside, by the front entrance, he thought he could hear a scratching. *Or footsteps?* Martin stood up from the sofa and grabbed his gun.

'Shahla really was a boy who'd been abused by his mother,' Elena said. 'I was never raped, I'm not a crazed, deluded victim who lets people suffer. My interests are quite different.'

'What are they?'

Martin went to the door and peered through the spyhole. Nothing.

'Money. I earn my living as a contract killer. Ships are my workplace. There's nowhere else I can kill more quickly and safely, or dispose of the bodies more easily. And the cruise line even actively helps me cover up the crimes. It couldn't be better. I work on twelve different giants of the seas. Sometimes as an employee, sometimes as a passenger. Recently I've been spending more time on the *Sultan* because I really did fall in love with Daniel. But I'm afraid that's over now too, as I'm sure you can imagine.'

Martin felt as if his senses were playing tricks on him, as if he were still taking the PEP pills. His mouth was dry. The scratching sounds now seemed to be coming from the back door he'd entered the house by.

'Do you find your clients on the internet?' he asked Elena as he moved over to the garden door.

'Yes,' she said. Her voice became softer, but as clear as a bell, as if she were in the neighbouring room. 'Here I was actually fibbing. The firm disguised as a travel agency belongs to me, not Shahla. It's a brilliant system, even if I'll probably have to make some modifications now, but so far my clients have simply booked a passage for those they wish to get out of the way, and I've taken care of the target once they're on board.'

Martin was surprised to hear her so talkative. He sensed she was trying to play for time, but why? What was she up to?

'With Naomi Lamar I was paid by Anouk's grandfather, who'd got to the truth of the mother's atrocities.'

'And who booked you in for a two-month ordeal?' Martin pressed her. He had to speak louder for Elena to understand him, though she didn't seem bothered that he'd strayed from her field of view for a while. He gazed into the garden through a window by the door. A mangy dog was padding languidly around the pool. Had it been scratching at the door?

'The grandfather wanted Naomi, before she died, to experience physically what the daughter had gone through. But that's not my thing. Shahla took care of that. I don't enjoy torture. As I said, for me it's all about money.'

'So who paid for you to kill my wife?' Martin asked, on his way back to the television.

'Nobody,' Elena said. 'It happened just as you read it. By chance Shahla caught Nadja indecently assaulting your son. The sight of it tore open the wounds her own mother had inflicted on her. She flipped out when she saw what your wife was doing to Timmy.'

In the background Martin could hear a gentle hubbub. Elena was phoning from a public place. She was probably sitting in an anonymous internet café.

'You know I'm telling the truth, Martin. You must have detected the signs of abuse in your son, didn't you?'

There was nothing Martin could do. Tears came to his eyes.

'There you go,' Elena said, proving that she was able to see him. 'Back then Shahla was employed to clean the ship's clinic. Over time we became friends. I learned of her terrible past. Nadja's death was an overreaction, an accident if you like. And when it happened, when she'd struck Nadja dead, she stormed into my office and asked for help. She didn't know what to do.'

'So the two of you threw my wife overboard together and placed the cloth with chloroform in their cabin?'

'Precisely,' Elena said. 'From that point on Shahla owed me a favour, which I called in for Naomi's punishment. I knew the pleasure it would give her to exact revenge.'

'Anouk was with you the whole time?'

'With Shahla,' Elena replied. 'She set up a den for her near the blue shelf, where she was supposed to stay till we got to Oslo.'

Martin had never seen it, and yet the fluorescent markings shone in his mind, which Anouk had followed with her UV lamp in the darkness of the lower deck whenever she wanted contact with Shahla, Elena or perhaps even her mother.

'Her grandfather has friends in Norway. Anouk was going to stay with them.'

379

There was whistling on the line, but Elena's voice was still easy to understand. 'We were planning to get her off the ship and Shahla took her to the nest where she was meant to spend the last night.' Elena sounded contrite. 'Unfortunately Anouk played stubborn that day. She was thoroughly bored, nervous, overwrought. She didn't want to be locked up any longer and managed to run away from Shahla, armed with her favourite teddy and a torch, which she was going to use to pay her mother one final visit.'

'But she ran straight into the captain!' Martin shook his head. Bonhoeffer had actually been telling the truth from the start. After Anouk had run away from the nest, the chambermaid had to quickly grab a pile of towels to give her an excuse for being around at that time, should she meet someone while searching for the girl. That's why to Gerlinde it had looked like a coincidence that the chambermaid had bumped into Anouk, when in actual fact she had been on the run from Shahla.

Martin was no longer able to suppress his anger. Hurrying back to the coffee table he grabbed the beer and hurled it at the television.

For a while he thought the connection had been lost, but then he heard Elena say calmly, 'You're directing your anger at the wrong person.'

Martin was almost lost for words. 'Are you trying to tell me that Nadja and Timmy's deaths are not your fault, but Shahla's?'

'I find it pointless to discuss questions of blame in my profession. But if you're into poetic justice then you ought to thank me. After all, I killed Shahla.'

'Because you wanted to give yourself the perfect alibi.

A killer, caught in the act and no longer able to blow the whistle on her accomplice. No, you're not going to get away with shifting your guilt onto others. Or was it Shahla who gave Anouk the teddy to make me come aboard? Or told her to say my name during that first session to rattle me.'

He kicked the coffee table so hard that the gun fell to the floor.

'The teddy was Shahla's idea,' Elena admitted blithely. 'She kept it as a souvenir of Timmy and in truth only gave it to Anouk so she had something to play with. There was no ulterior motive there. But it did give Daniel the idea of contacting you. I was against it. I knew the reputation you had as a detective and didn't want you getting in my way. That's why I showed you the report about the rape wounds as I knew from that point your search would be focused on a man.'

'And just to be on the safe side you injured yourself too?' Martin picked up the pistol.

'I'm allergic to groundnut oil and so I smeared some on my cheek when I was crawling around on the floor in the anchor room,' Elena confessed. 'I didn't want to be around you any longer; I just wanted to look after Anouk unimpeded. Which I was able to do when I was practically lying next to her in Hell's Kitchen.'

Her voice became firmer.

'But let me say this again: I'm not mad. Killing is my job. Not my calling.'

Looking at the weapon in his hand, Martin twiddled it and watched his distorted reflection change in the chrome barrel.

'You wanted to use Lisa to kill her mother.'

'Yes, that was wrong.'

If she weren't such a damn good actress, Martin might have imagined he detected genuine remorse in Elena's voice.

'Lisa is Daniel's goddaughter. She wrote an email to him saying that she had man trouble. Daniel forwarded it to me, thinking that as a woman I'd be better placed to help a girl with this problem. He didn't know what the "man trouble" actually consisted of.'

Elena's sounded breathy. She cleared her throat.

'And Lisa didn't know who I was when I invited her to the Easyexit chatroom. But she very quickly opened up her heart to me. In retrospect I ought to have known that she was lying. Her stories became increasingly far-fetched. To begin with, she made only vague mention of abuse, then she told me she was having sex with an older man, and finally that her mother was forcing her to. I began to doubt her, but when she sent me the video I believed her again and so I booked a passage for her and her mother to clear the matter up.'

So that was the reason, Martin thought.

That's why she was so flustered when Diesel rang and said how the video had been staged.

'I didn't twig that Lisa was lying to me. I knew nothing of how obsessed and unhappy she was. If Julia Stiller had forced her daughter to have sex with that Tom she would have deserved to die.'

Martin laughed sarcastically. 'And after Naomi you were in practice.'

'I corrected my mistake in time.'

'We almost died!'

Martin recalled the scene in Lisa's cabin. By the irony

of destiny, Elena had told the truth when she said she was Querky. She could have passed Lisa's test and said her chatroom nickname. The only reason Elena had hesitated was that it would have blown her cover.

'And you don't think you're mad, Elena?' Martin asked. 'You're absolutely potty!'

The petrol mower had now sprung into life on the front lawn of the neighbouring house. Martin wondered whether it was drowning out other sounds. Sounds that might reveal Elena's true intentions.

'Where are you?' he asked her.

As expected, Elena didn't respond to this, instead asking a question of her own: 'Are you still in contact with Lisa's mother?'

'What? Yes, why?' Martin had spoken to Julia Stiller once. She'd just been visiting her daughter on the closed ward of the psychiatric unit and wanted to thank him again for having saved her daughter's life. It must have been the tenth time she'd done so. He might well be the only person she could talk to about the sluggish progress in Lisa's treatment.

'Tell Julia I'll make amends for my mistake,' Elena said. She sounded as if she were about to hang up.

'Make amends for your mistake? Are you out of your mind? You're a murderer. You can't make amends for what you've done.'

Martin aimed his pistol at the television, imagining she was standing before him.

'You'll see,' Elena retorted.

'I'll see *you*,' Martin said, sounding dead calm. 'And then I'll kill you.'

He could virtually see her shake her well-coiffed hair.

'No you won't,' she said.

He frowned angrily. 'You know what I'm capable of when I set my mind to something,' he threatened.

'Yes. I don't doubt that. But you won't hurt a hair on my head when you stand face to face with me, nor will you tell a soul about our conversation today.'

He laughed out loud. 'What makes you so sure?'

Martin gave another start. The lawnmower had fallen silent. But now he heard the scratching noises at the door again, and this time it definitely wasn't a dog. Someone was fiddling with the lock. He looked around. As it was an open-plan house there was nowhere on the ground floor to hide, particularly not if Elena was watching him via camera. But he didn't think it was her trying to get inside the finca, and if it was, then she knew he was armed. He pointed the gun at the door, but then had a better idea.

With a couple of rapid strides he made it to the stairs and ran to the upper floor, his pistol at the ready if anyone was lying in wait for him up there.

His mobile rang in his pocket.

Unknown caller.

He answered as he entered the first room at the top of the stairs and shut the door.

'You won't kill me,' he heard Elena say, continuing their conversation while Martin looked around in astonishment at the untidy room. The bed wasn't made and dirty socks littered the floor. The walls were sprayed with gaudy, but amazingly talented graffiti images, and a laptop with a sticker of a heavy metal band sat on a glass table supported by two beer barrels.

'How can you be so sure?' he heard himself ask.

Footsteps echoed in the sitting room below.

Martin grabbed hold of a tennis racket that had been leaning against an open wardrobe. The footsteps were coming up the stairs.

'Because you won't shoot the woman who's been a mother to your son,' Elena said, and then Martin heard a second voice in the hall beyond the door. The voice of a young man, around fifteen years old.

'Mama? Are you in there?' he asked. 'I thought you weren't coming back for a fortnight.'

The door opened and two men who resembled each other like father and son, stood opposite each other, paralysed with shock.

76

Elena hung up.

She'd prepared Timmy for this moment. Two weeks ago, when she'd visited him soon after their stop in New York, he'd asked her yet again about his father (he never enquired about his mother) and she showed him the photo that the Polish newspapers had published shortly after his arrest.

Shahla had caught Nadja.

He'd never left the bathroom.

That was the lie she'd dished up to Martin to make him abandon the search for his son. In vain. She'd suspected that he'd get to the bottom of the truth at some point.

After Shahla had battered the mother with the desk lamp and locked Timmy in the bathroom, Elena had helped her to wrap the corpse in a sheet and throw it overboard. The security cameras showed two victims. Unfortunately it was noticeable that the suitcase was smaller than the mother's body. They ought to have disposed of the suitcase first and then the corpse. A massive error, but luckily the cruise line had played the role of silent accomplice and made the recordings disappear to hush the matter up.

Elena immediately started to look after the boy. Timmy,

386

scared out of his wits and deeply troubled, didn't have any idea how to get in touch with his father.

Her research found out that his father was in prison in Warsaw as a dangerous criminal with links to the mafia.

The perverted mother dead; the father a murderer. The relatives might not be any better. Under no circumstances were they going to send the traumatised boy back to such a wretched family. At this point Elena had no idea that Martin was working as an undercover investigator; she only found out years later when Daniel told her of the case that Schwartz had tried to bring against him. So at the time she decided to take Timmy into her care. She hid him for a while on the ship, took him to her house in Casa de Campo and put him in a boarding school there. Several times a year she visited him in the Dominican Republic, for as long and as often as she could.

Later, when she found out who Timmy's father really was, it briefly occurred to her to bring the two of them together, but she abandoned the idea. Martin was a detective. One of the best. The danger was too great that he'd stick to her heels and hunt her down. Which he must be considering now. From today she was on the run; she'd done all she could to postpone this moment for as long as possible.

During the years that she'd kept Timmy hidden from his father, he'd grown into a fine young man who enjoyed life in the Caribbean and now played tennis so well that he'd got to the final of the Caribbean junior championship.

Two weeks ago Elena had told him who his father really was and that he was sure to come looking for him. So Timmy was forewarned. All the same, she didn't want to imagine the shock he must be feeling now.

With a sigh Elena put the mobile back in her Louis

Vuitton handbag, opened a compact mirror, applied another layer of lipstick and pulled the décolleté of her little black number a little lower. Then she got up from the lounge chair by the windows.

The swell in Ari Atoll was pleasantly calm, the MS *Aquarion* lay like a plank on the Indian Ocean and she had no trouble making it to the on-board bar in her ten-centimetre heels.

'Gin and tonic, please,' she said to the barman of the small but elegant cruise ship which had room for just under a thousand passengers. One of them, a man with unbelievably deep eyes, who was holding a beer, gave her a smile that did not fail to do the trick.

'Please allow me,' said the good-looking German, who she hadn't let out of her sight since they'd left Sri Lanka.

'That's very kind of you, Herr...'

'Schiwy,' the man told her his name, which of course Elena already knew. 'But please call me Tom.'

She smiled and said the name she'd used to check in for this trip.

'Tell Julia I'll make amends for my mistake!'

'So, what brings you on board?'

'Whew.' He pretended to wipe sweat from his brow. 'It's a long story.'

'We've got a long journey ahead of us,' Elena said, with an even friendlier smile and brushing, as if by accident, Tom's hand on the bar with the tip of her finger.

'Okay, well, if you want to hear the short version: I'm running away.'

'From love, perhaps?'

He nodded smugly. 'If you like, yes. Can you imagine a

situation where both a mother and daughter fall in love with you at the same time?'

Elena winked coquettishly. 'With you, Tom, yes.'

He made a dismissive gesture. 'Yes, yes, I know it sounds funny, but believe me, it's absolute hell. Two jealous creatures, who are also related. One wanted literally to kill herself for love, and she'd have done it too, if I hadn't warned her mother in time.' He gave a lecherous grin. Evidently he thought that this frivolous story would enhance his attractiveness.

'And so you booked this trip to flee from those wild women?' Elena asked innocently.

'No, no, this was just a slice of luck in the midst of adversity. I won the trip in a silly online card game. I mean, I often get mail telling me I'm the hundred thousandth visitor to some website or other, but this time it was actually true. The tickets were delivered to me directly.' He was grinning from ear to ear. 'They arrived right on cue.'

'Just like you, Tom.' Elena took his hand and squeezed it gently. 'So, lucky at cards, are you?'

'And in love... Well, I just have fun,' he grinned back.

'Sounds good,' Elena said, getting down from her bar stool.

'How about...?' She nodded in the direction of the lifts. 'I know my way around here fairly well. Do you fancy a tour behind the scenes of the ship?'

Tom Schiwy finished his beer in one gulp and handed the barman his room card to put the drinks on his bill, before hurrying after the elegant blond.

In excited anticipation of the evening and everything it would entail.

About this book and thanks

Before my final surprise on page 401 (which of course you can jump to straight away if you're not interested in my ramblings about how *Passenger 23* came about) I'd like to honour tradition and first of all thank you for choosing my book from amongst the hundred thousand new ones that appear each year. Now you've finished reading it, I expect you've got completely the wrong idea of me.

Whether you believe me or not, I like cruises. Yes, I really do! As a small child I even once toyed with the idea of becoming a captain, but very quickly ditched this at the tender age of eleven when crossing the English Channel with my mother; the two of us had a competition as to who could feed the most fish by the end. Whenever I'm aboard a ship these days I always wear a scopolamine plaster behind my ear – a sure sign of a sissy on the high seas – but I'll happily put up with the indulgent smiles of sea dogs so long as I control the destination of the food I eat rather than the other way around.

Although I enjoy being on water, *Passenger 23* isn't an expression of my – admittedly sometimes strange – sense of humour. For me it's no contradiction to like cruise ships while making one the setting for gruesome crimes. I mean, I like Berlin too and have no scruples about populating my home town with people who collect eyes and crush souls.

When I say that I like cruises I'm not talking about prescribed fun on the sun deck or the highly regimented excursions, the advertising of which is strongly reminiscent of those political leaflets that promise outlandish miracles. It might not read 'More pay for less work' but you could well see something like 'Idyllic Robinson Crusoe experience' to describe the visit to a bonsai-sized cave with eight hundred like-minded people!

I simply like the idea of pitching and tossing into foreign countries together with your hotel room, without having to endlessly pack and unpack suitcases. I also love the sea (I've been told by an astrologist that this is typical for an October Libra baby) but on a beach holiday I'm generally too lazy to move from the sun lounger, enter the water, dry myself off, then reapply the sun cream (as you never know if sun cream really is waterproof just because it says so on the bottle) and all that stress for three mere swimming strokes, because swimming isn't my thing... whatever, I'm digressing. What I wanted to say was that for people like me who simply enjoy looking at the ocean, long days at sea are ideal.

Passenger 23 is a novel. This should mean that I've been lying to you. None of it happened. But, as I've said elsewhere, every good lie has a kernel of truth. And in this respect, *Passenger 23* has more kernels than a watermelon. For example, the basic principle that a couple of dozen people vanish without trace from cruise ships every year is as true as the claim in the book by Captain Daniel Bonhoeffer that, in the US, large law firms have now specialised in representing the relatives of *cruise victims*. In fact, I'm sorry to say that all the mysterious missing-person cases Bonhoeffer outlines in chapter twelve are real. I've just changed the names of those concerned and of the ships.

In 2011 and 2012 a new sombre record was set: fifty-five people disappeared. If I'd based the novel on these two years alone, I'd have had to call it *Passenger 27.5*.

I hit upon the idea for this book back in 2008, when I read in *Park Avenue* (a magazine that has since vanished into the ocean of the periodical market) an article about the phenomenon of passengers that go missing from cruise ships.

The reason it took me until March 2013 to finally get going on the first draft is plain and simple: the flash of inspiration didn't come until much later – that's to say the idea that rather than putting a missing person at the heart of my story, I should feature a passenger who resurfaces and whose reappearance alone disproves the suicide theory that cruise lines often advance as a knee-jerk reaction. For it's also true that the booming cruise industry has no interest in including in those glossy brochures the warning that every passenger with a half-decent brain can figure out for themselves: when several thousand people come together in a small space, conflict is bound to occur. And of the millions of people who now opt for this sort of holiday, you can be sure that not every single one of them is nice.

Crimes on the seas are by no means isolated cases and the websites quoted in the book, which act as forums for victims, relatives and lawyers, do actually exist. The incidents they document have reached such proportions that the International Cruise Victims Association (IVC) is calling for 'sea marshals' which, unlike air marshals on aeroplanes, don't yet exist. These floating hotel forts are small towns without a police station. If there are any security personnel, these are financially dependent on the cruise line, which means in an emergency it's unlikely that their own staff will be subject to scrutiny.

In all honesty, however, it must be stated – and here the facts in the book are equally true – that even a sea marshal would be able to do little when a person goes missing. The several-kilometre stopping distance of a cruise ship alone precludes a rescue operation with much hope of success, especially if the potential victim has not been seen for several hours. And, as has been adequately described, the ship itself is far too big to permit a thorough and rapid search.

Moreover, no uniform global regulations exist for such cases. As Martin Schwartz notes critically in the novel, the moment passengers board a ship they are stepping onto foreign soil, while Kendall Carver from ICV points out that they're at the mercy of the authorities of the country where the ship is registered. For this reason, in 2010 the USA passed a law giving the FBI and the US Coast Guard wide-ranging powers, according to which officers from these bodies can launch investigations even on ships registered in foreign countries. But only following the disappearance of an American citizen.

Researching the subject was very simple so long as it related to the areas above the waterline. Deck and cabin plans, video documentation of the bridge, TV reports – all of these are only a mouse click away. It's more difficult getting information on crew accommodation, the anchor room and the kitchen, but during a research trip I was permitted to go on a tour (before those responsible knew what my book was ultimately about). It is almost impossible (for security reasons) to access complete plans of the lower deck including machinery and cargo rooms, or the waste incineration unit.

I come now to the official acknowledgements, beginning with a warm thank you to Captain Volker Bernhard, now retired, for his expert advice. He took the trouble to read the novel in advance and gave me valuable insights into those areas that would usually remain off limits to an ordinary cruise passenger like me.

All the mistakes that are still in this book are on my sailor's head and, as usual, are rebuffed with the standard excuse of creative people: 'It's artistic licence!'

I'd happily take a cruise with the following people from Droemer Knaur Verlag and hope that none of them go missing, for without their sterling work *Passenger 23* would not be in your hands now: Hans-Peter Übleis, Christian Tesch, Theresa Schenkel, Monika Neudeck, Sibylle Dietzel, Carsten Sommerfeldt, Iris Haas, Hanna Pfaffenwimmer. As always, let me make a very special mention of my wonderful editors, Carolin Graehl and Regine Weisbrod, whose intelligent questions and comments have again ensured that – to keep the imagery going – my story didn't list or hit a reef halfway along its journey. Since 2006 the following man and his Zero agency have ensured that my books don't appear naked on the shelves. And since 2006 I've consistently forgotten him in acknowledgements, but hey, that's a bloody difficult name you chose, dear Helmut Henkensiefken. Many thanks for the cover!

Many people regard the author as the captain, but on my ship it's Manuela Raschke who wears the cap. This superwoman organises my entire professional existence, and even some of my private life now, too – recently she's been cutting my children's hair! Thanks, Manu, and oh, before I forget, the recycling is now being collected on Thursdays ;).

Writing is a lonely process, but fortunately work around the book is not, and I'm delighted that over the years something akin to a 'family business' has emerged, which means I enjoy the privilege of being able to work only with good friends and relatives. Or at least the following people are very good at pretending they like me: Barbara Herrmann, Achim Behrend, Sally Raschke, Ela and Micha, Petra Rode, Patrick Hocke and Mark Ryan Balthasar.

I would like to thank Sabrina Rabow again for her outstanding PR work and for always dabbing a bit of her powder on my face at photo calls, despite my protests. Although I can't bear the stuff, I have to admit that without it the only use for my photos would be as 'before' images in Botox adverts.

Googling can change one's life. Mine, for example. In 2001 I typed 'literary agent' into the search box and the algorithm spat out the name of the best in the world: Roman Hocke. Thanks are due to him and the rest of the fabulous team at AVA International: Claudia von Hornstein, Claudia Bachmann, Gudrun Strutzenberger and Markus Michalek.

I'd also like to thank the man without whom I'd never have managed fifty readings in a week and would have either turned up late to all my other appointments, or not at all: Christian Meyer from C&M Sicherheit.

Thanks to all the booksellers, librarians, bookbinders and organisers of readings and literary festivals. All of you are keeping alive the most important medium in the world and allowing us authors to follow our dreams.

Shortly before the completion of *Passenger 23*, I heard the sad news that one of my friends, to whom I owe a great debt of gratitude, is no longer with us. I know, of course, that the good ones always die young, but so young? Wherever you are now, Peter Hetzel, here's a grateful hug from me. We all miss you!

Like Peter, the following friends have supported me from the beginning: Karl 'Kalle' Raschke (thanks for all the inspiration your 'everyday' experiences provide me with), Gerlinde Jänicke (thanks for your first name!), Arno Müller, Thomas Koschwitz, Jochen Trus, Stephan Schmitter, Michael Treutler and Simon Jäger.

Thanks also to Michael Tsokos. It's always good to know an expert in forensic medicine, especially one who answers his mobile after midnight when you've got a question about the precise wording of traces of torture in a medical file.

I received dental advice from the wonderful Dr Ulrike Heintzenberg. (Yes, yes, I'll get to the prophylaxis soon.)

Most people think it's a joke when I say that I actually

write family stories rather than psychological thrillers, but it's the truth. Everything, good as well as evil, has its origins in the family, and I'm extraordinarily fortunate to have a fantastic community around me, first and foremost my father Freimut, as well as Clemens and Sabine, who also helped with medical advice for this book.

If you're currently toying with the idea of taking a cruise, or even if you're on a ship at this very moment, I sincerely hope that I haven't spoiled your enjoyment with this novel. I'm anything but a missionary as an author. My aim is to entertain rather than convert, despite the accurate figures in the book relating to the waste generation and energy consumption of giant ships.

In writing this thriller I may well have screwed things up for myself with the established cruise lines forever. After *Passenger 23* my being invited to an author reading on a cruise is about as likely as a *Titanic* film evening in the on-board cinema. But you never know. On a transatlantic crossing that I took with my mother in 2005, the announcement was made a day before our arrival in New York that the ship was now exactly where the *Titanic* had sunk. Passengers rushed out on deck. Not in panic, but – no joke – to take photos of the water!

Life writes the most bizarre stories and you the nicest readers' letters.

If interested you can contact me, as ever, via www. sebastianfitzek.de, www.facebook.de/sebastianfitzek.de or by email: fitzek@sebastianfitzek.de.

Occasionally it can take me a while to reply; sometimes

I'm submerged. But generally this is just because I'm writing...

Many thanks and goodbye

Sebastian Fitzek

Berlin, on a stressful day for registry offices

(7/7/2014)

P.S. Oh, yes, for all of you who were wondering what happened to the doctor in the prologue... I've got some more for you...

Epilogue

Sultan of the Seas
Six weeks later

'Shall we get rid of her?'

Yegor's question was a serious one, but the surgeon merely offered a weary smile. They'd been observing Gerlinde for about twenty minutes via a security camera covering the portside corridor on deck 3, not far from the spot where Anouk had been picked up. This must have been the tenth time that the old lady – why had she chosen today of all days to be up and about at the crack of dawn? – had felt the joint in the cabin wall with her bony fingers, right where the wallpaper wasn't completely flush.

'It's five o'clock in the morning – hasn't the old bat got better things to do?' Yegor said, while beside him Konradin Franz bent over the monitor and breathed into the ship owner's neck a mixture of gin and peppermint. The fifty-six-year-old surgeon, who liked to be called *doctor*, even though he'd never completed a PhD, wiped his sweaty brow with the back of his hand. 'If she doesn't bugger off soon I'll have her on my operating table too,' he said, even though it was clear that he'd never be in a fit state for any surgery today, not even if he started drinking.

'When is Tayo's scheduled checkout?' Yegor asked, even though he knew the answer. The 'client,' as the surgeon called all the patients he operated on aboard the *Sultan*, was to be disembarked in Barbados using the usual procedure. At six a.m. – an hour's time – as soon as the ship had come into port. Wrapped in sheets, in a dirty laundry container from the infirmary, marked with the following warning in four languages: *Contaminated, risk of infection*.

This, together with the bribes paid to staff at the port authority, would ensure that it wouldn't occur to anybody to peek inside the container on wheels, in which the world-class athlete would struggle to find enough room. The other clients before him had been substantially smaller and less muscly, and hadn't caused any transport problems.

Tayo, on the other hand, hadn't beaten the 400m record on three occasions for nothing. He ran the distance in under 43.20 seconds, not fast enough, unfortunately, to escape from the Nigerian gambling mafia, to whom he'd promised to fix races in the summer Olympics. Tayo had agreed to falter just before the finishing line; a tiny stumble, but a decisive one. In the heat of the race, however, he'd forgotten all about it, with the result that the clan had lost a lot of money on the wrong horse. Money they now wanted back from Tayo. There was photographic proof that they weren't squeamish about collecting debts. They'd removed the eye of a drug dealer with a corkscrew for misappropriating twelve dollars. Tayo wouldn't get off so lightly; he owed them twelve million.

After selling all his cars, his house and closing his bank

accounts (Tayo had earned very well, not least through
sponsorship agreements) he had enough money to pay back
the mafia a good third of what they'd lost. Or to abscond
with four million dollars.

Opting for the latter, Tayo had checked in on the *Sultan*.

'It's time we started calling him by his new name,' the
surgeon said. Yegor nodded, albeit reluctantly. Of all the
suggestions on the list, why did their client have to plump
for the name *Sandy*?

Sandy? Yegor didn't even know whether men in the US
were called Sandy. But what business of his was this man's
life? Or to put it more precisely: what did he care about his
new life?

His work was over. He'd got Martin Schwartz on board
and ensured that the crisis was averted. What happened to
the girl didn't concern him. Yegor had never been interested
in solving the case and, in all honesty, he'd never expected
that damaged detective to actually bring anything valuable
to light. Schwartz was supposed to act as a scapegoat.
Either he or Bonhoeffer, that clueless idiot who still hadn't
fathomed what was really going on aboard his ship. The
captain continued to believe that it was all about salvaging
a deal with a Chilean investor, but Yegor had never intended
to sell his ship. Vincente Rojas and his useless lawyers were
only on board the *Sultan* to fuel the rumours on the stock
market of a takeover and send the share price soaring.

'It's infuriating.' The doctor's ranting snatched Yegor
from his thoughts. The surgeon was bashing the table,
causing the monitor to wobble.

'Oh, shut up!' Yegor ordered, even though Gerlinde
couldn't possibly hear them. Although she was only ten

metres away, the rooms of the in-between deck were completely soundproofed.

In principle, however, he could understand Konradin's outburst. It was desperate.

Having spared no effort, they'd managed to stop their business being exposed at the last minute, but now this old bag was creating problems for them again. Was she going to prevent their client from being unloaded?

When Anouk Lamar unexpectedly reappeared some months ago, Yegor really did believe they were scuppered. A missing Passenger 23 wasn't a problem. It was a regular occurrence, and so nobody searched a cruise ship in its entirety. But a Passenger 23 who came back from the dead? That was something else altogether. As soon as news of the girl had become public, all hell would have been let loose and their business would have been finished. Worst-case scenario. The FBI would have seized the ship and forensically searched it with an army of agents. Which mustn't happen under any circumstances. Suicide? Fine! A serial killer on board? So what! Somehow the PR department would be able to iron all that out. But if a search of the ship uncovered the place where the cruise line actually earned its millions – the in-between deck – they'd spend the rest of their lives in prison. Him, the surgeon and everyone else who made a mint from the private witness and victim protection programme. A programme used by the rich and desperate of this world who wanted to vanish from the face of the earth forever, mostly for illegal reasons. Whether to escape imprisonment, taxation or – as in Tayo's case – the Nigerian gambling mafia. Where better could you do this than on a luxury liner of these dimensions? A police-free zone, with countless opportunities to hide. A world in itself where entire families could easily be prepared for the new life they were literally heading for.

The in-between deck wasn't actually a real deck. It consisted of lots of intricate and winding spaces distributed across several levels, cleverly designed so that the recesses weren't apparent from the outside to those who didn't know.

Yegor and Konradin were sitting beside the transport airlock, a secret door through which the container with Sandy was going to be wheeled. Just as soon as old Dobkowitz, only a few steps away on the other side of the wall, finally vanished.

'By the way, how is our patient on his big day?' Yegor mumbled without taking his eyes off the monitor. Gerlinde was just manoeuvring her wheelchair a metre backwards, as if a little distance would afford her a better view of things.

'Excellent. He's healing well. As so often with clients with well-trained bodies,' Konradin replied.

Tayo's treatment had lasted over a year. A fake crash of a private jet above the Gulf of Guinea, embarkation in Praia, months of psychological training, concocting stories, then the surgical interventions. He'd booked the full programme, costing him almost two million dollars, half of his savings. But this was money well spent. Because he hadn't been given the usual cosmetic alterations. Tayo was an international superstar, and his pursuers had a global network. They'd needed to make drastic changes to his external appearance to prevent him from being immediately recognised in his new home. In the end the surgeon hadn't only persuaded him to have chin, lip and nose alterations, he'd even talked Tayo into having his leg amputated. After much deliberation, this military measure would surely save Sandy's new life. There was one irrevocable truth in their business: for people to become invisible, they had to break permanently with their old habits. A gambler must never be seen in a casino again, a musician must never pick up a guitar and a sportsman never run again. When they took on Tayo's case they knew that he would present a particular problem. A man feted by the press as 'Mr Ultrasonic' would not be able to keep away from the tartan tracks of his new home in the Caribbean for long. Like a junkie with drugs, Tayo was addicted to sport. His running style was unmistakeable. Even if he were to put a stone in his shoe to slow him down, people would start talking after a few training sessions. And the whispering about the unknown thunderbolt doing his laps in the arena at night would soon reach the wrong ears.

To be absolutely certain that Tayo wouldn't be discovered and agonisingly tortured to death, there was only one possible course of action: they had to ensure that he never ran again. Because he wasn't *able to* any more.

Endless discussions ensued and Tayo kept having second thoughts right up to the operation. In the end the constant dithering had made the surgeon so mad that the tipsy hothead had gone up to deck 8½ straight afterwards where, on a dark and stormy night, from a place not monitored by the cameras, he'd tossed the amputated leg overboard. An inexcusable breach, which ought to have cost him his job, although '*Plastic surgeon in private victim protection programme on secret in-between deck of cruise ship*' was not exactly a job that applicants were queuing up for. Yegor even put up with Konradin's increasingly evident alcohol abuse. Besides, the surgeon hadn't committed any other similar indiscretions. He himself had got a massive shock on his jaunt up to deck 8½ when he'd almost been spotted disposing of the leg in the Indian Ocean. By none other than Anouk Lamar, who'd taken herself there to do some drawing.

That night Konradin had returned the girl to her mother. When she vanished just a few days later, he told Yegor how he'd sensed Anouk's reluctance to go and that he'd felt sure she'd rather have stayed out on deck alone, despite the inclement weather and darkness. Back at the time, when they'd all assumed it was a case of extended suicide, Konradin thought that Anouk had anticipated her mother's plans to kill them both. But now they knew the real reason why she didn't want to be taken back to her mother that night.

'How is it actually possible that this grannie out there is on our case?' the surgeon asked.

Yegor groaned. 'She isn't. She just happened upon it by chance. That's why she isn't looking in the right place, but nearby.'

Where she'd bumped into Anouk.

The whole thing with this old woman was sheer lunacy!

Martin's investigations had provided the FBI with a culprit and crime scene, even Anouk's hiding place, which is why in the end the ship hadn't been gone over with a fine-toothed comb. The FBI agents' questions had been answered.

But not Gerlinde's.

'I thought the old bag was due to disembark some time ago,' Konradin said.

'No, she's got another fortnight. Mallorca. As soon as we're back in Europe.'

'Fucking brilliant!' The surgeon looked at his watch. 'We won't get the container out the back.'

Yegor nodded. There was an inconvenient stairway exit, which the surgeon had used to throw the leg over the handrail. But they couldn't get Tayo off board that way.

'We'll have to wait till we've anchored. At some point the old nutcase out there is going to have to strike sail. We can...' Konradin broke off mid-sentence and laughed. 'Look! She's buggering off.'

Indeed she was. Gerlinde had given up. Her wheelchair was moving away from their field of view.

Yegor followed her for a while with the adjustable camera and gave a grunt of satisfaction when she vanished into an open lift.

'Let's get going,' he said. 'Is Ta... er... Sandy good to go?'

The surgeon nodded. Then he went to fetch the client so that Yegor could say goodbye. A bit of fun that the ship owner never passed up on. Yegor loved the before–after comparison and feeling the power of setting someone out in a new life that he'd helped shape.

He opened the sparkling wine that he'd chilled for the occasion and filled three glasses. One for him. One for the surgeon. And the last one for the tall black man who had to duck to avoid banging his head on the cabin ceiling as he hobbled into the airlock on crutches.

At the same time Gerlinde looked at herself in the lift mirror with disappointment and decided to give up her search for the Bermuda Deck for good. Today she'd even kept going till sunrise, longer than usual. And what had she achieved?

Nothing but a goddamned headache.

She decided to spend her final days on the *Sultan* doing nothing but relaxing.

'Bloody Bermuda Deck. I got carried away,' she admitted to herself, then grumbled a while longer until the lift doors opened again. As she wheeled herself out she was surprised by the unexpected change.

It took Gerlinde a while to understand that it was the colour of the carpet which was confusing her. On her deck, deck 12, it was quite a bit darker. And thicker.

I'm on the wrong floor, was her first thought. Then she realised what had happened. The lift must be broken. At any rate it hadn't gone anywhere. She was still on the same level where she'd entered the lift.

'Nothing's working today,' she groused, wheeling herself out of the lift to try the next-door one.

While she waited she looked at herself again, this time in the brass panelling that had been polished to a mirror finish. Its reflection made everything look a little friendlier. Her eyes didn't appear so tired; she looked slimmer, her hair not so flat. Everything was nicer, prettier, softer and more harmonious.

Apart from the door.

The door behind her and slightly to the side, which opened in the wall as if by magic. Just as Gerlinde turned around to take a look, a head-high laundry container was being wheeled out from it...

About the author

SEBASTIAN FITZEK is one of Europe's most successful authors of psychological thrillers. His books have sold 12 million copies, been translated into more than thirty-six languages and are the basis for international cinema and theatre adaptations. Sebastian Fitzek was the first German author to be awarded the European Prize for Criminal Literature. He lives with his family in Berlin.

About the translator

JAMIE BULLOCH is the translator of almost forty works from German, including novels by Timur Vermes, Martin Suter and Robert Menasse. His translation of Birgit Vanderbecke's *The Mussel Feast* won the 2014 Schlegel-Tieck Prize. He is also the author of *Karl Renner: Austria*.